SCAMMED

SCAMMED

KRISTEN SIMMONS

TOR TEEN

A TOM DOHERTY ASSOCIATES BOOK
NEW YORK

SCAMMED

Copyright © 2020 by Kristen Simmons

A Tor Teen Book
Published by Tom Doherty Associates
120 Broadway
New York, NY 10271

www.tor-forge.com

Tor® is a registered trademark of Macmillan Publishing Group, LLC.

Library of Congress Cataloging-in-Publication Data

Names: Simmons, Kristen, author.
Title: Scammed / Kristen Simmons.
Description: First edition. | New York : Tor Teen, a Tom Doherty Associates Book, 2020. | Series: Vale Hall ; 2
Identifiers: LCCN 2019045325 (print) | LCCN 2019045326 (ebook) | ISBN 9781250175830 (hardcover) | ISBN 9781250176349 (ebook)
Subjects: CYAC: Swindlers and swindling—Fiction. | Secrets—Fiction. | Political corruption—Fiction. | Boarding schools—Fiction. | Schools—Fiction.
Classification: LCC PZ7.S591825 Sc 2020 (print) | LCC PZ7.S591825 (ebook) | DDC [Fic]—dc23
LC record available at https://lccn.loc.gov/2019045325
LC ebook record available at https://lccn.loc.gov/2019045326

Our books may be purchased in bulk for promotional, educational, or business use. Please contact your local bookseller or the Macmillan Corporate and Premium Sales Department at 1-800-221-7945, extension 5442, or by email at MacmillanSpecialMarkets@macmillan.com.

First Edition: February 2020

Printed in the United States of America

0 9 8 7 6 5 4 3 2 1

For anyone who's found a family worth fighting for.
This one's for you.

SCAMMED

CHAPTER 1

My grip tightens around the leather-padded wheel. My calf flexes as I press my foot down on the brake. Carefully, I check my mirrors and the windows for any sign someone might be watching.

In the passenger seat, Caleb Matsuki tightens the belt across his chest. His black hair is sticking out on the side from where he keeps scrubbing a hand through it, and the dark plastic rims of his glasses only frame the concern in his deep brown eyes.

"Five minutes," he says.

Anxiety wraps hot tendrils around my lungs.

It's not enough time.

I eye the last parking spot at the end of the row. We need to get the black SUV back there before anyone notices it's gone. It's not far, less than the length of a city block, but our path is impeded by a dozen cars sliding in and out of spots, and pedestrians carrying shopping bags.

Five minutes.

I ease off the brake, but the SUV lurches forward, and with a squeak, I slam my foot down again. Caleb rocks forward for the seventh—eighth?—time, and braces a locked arm against the dashboard.

"Sorry."

"It's okay." He ratchets the seat belt strap tighter across his waist. "I actually love whiplash. It's right up there with bamboo shoots under my fingernails and people who eat tarantulas on nature survival shows."

I bite my lip. "You see him?"

Caleb squints out the passenger window, through the autumn-kissed trees, toward the corner of the brick-and-mortar strip mall. On the opposite side of the building, Hugh Moore is in a coffee shop, removing the foam from his latte, or doing whatever stiff private school security guards do for fun, while our classmate Henry finishes his SAT at the testing site next door.

"No." Caleb checks his phone. "He said he'd call when Henry was done."

After we finished our tests, Moore gave us free rein of the shops, as long as we agreed to check in. He also gave me the keys to the SUV so I could stash my sweatshirt inside.

That was probably a mistake.

"Take your foot off the brake," Caleb says. "Slowly this time."

I check the side mirrors, hyperaware of the cars scattered around the lot. If I hit one of them, Moore won't be pleased.

Then again, it's not like he doesn't have a whole garage of shiny sedans and SUVs to choose from.

I settle into my seat. My days of scamming for pennies are over. Devon Park is in my rearview; I'm high-class now. If I want a car, I'll have my pick of them.

I just need to learn to drive first.

Gently this time, I ease off the brake, and the car rolls forward at a non-life-threatening speed.

"See? Pro," I tell Caleb, grinning. "This driving thing is cake, like I—"

A car pulls out of the parking spot five spaces away and I slam on the brakes, sending Caleb hands first into the dashboard again.

"That was close," I say under my breath.

"If forty feet away is close, then yes."

"What are all these people doing out in the middle of the day? Don't they have jobs?" I blow out a tense breath. "Who taught you to drive anyway?" The second the words are out, I regret them. Caleb's mother takes the bus, and his dad's laid out in a hospital bed in White Bank, his spine held together by pins and the gracious monetary donations of our school's director.

"The one and only Dr. David Odin," he says, all emotion hidden behind his careful con-artist mask.

I cock a brow his direction. "Aren't you special."

Caleb gives a one-shouldered shrug.

Vale Hall's director doesn't generally spend a lot of one-on-one time mentoring his students, even ones who've been enrolled as long as Caleb, in anything but lying. It's career building and financial aid all wrapped up in a pretty package—we con his marks into spilling their deepest, darkest secrets, and in exchange Dr. O gives us free room and board, and a nice little scholarship to the university of our choice.

And, in Caleb's case, medical care for his father.

Which all goes away the second we screw up.

Caleb points ahead to the bend in the lane. "Circle around the blue truck and go back to where we started."

I mean to, but just as I'm taking my foot off the brake, a car from behind zips past on my left, close enough that it would take off my arm if I reached out the window. The driver shouts something I can't make out, and though I only catch a glimpse of his sunglasses and raised middle finger, the familiarity is enough to cram my lungs up my throat.

Grayson Sterling.

On a gasp, I'm sucked into a memory I don't fully own, one I've constructed lying in bed on sleepless nights.

The senator's son, hunched over the wheel, chasing Susan Griffin's car down Route 17.

I was just trying to get her to slow down. She wouldn't pull over, so I tried to get in front of her.

I didn't see the turn until it was too late.

The day he drove me to the crash site may have been three months ago, but I still remember every detail. The sweat staining the collar of his shirt. The way he kept taking his hand off the steering wheel while he told the story. He'd just wanted to talk to her, he said. He wanted to convince her to end the affair with his father.

He never meant to drive her off the road.

Still, I can hear him yelling through the window for her to pull over, his voice sharp as shattered glass and louder than the growl of his engine. I can see how he would've sliced his hand through the air to get her attention. How, frightened, she would have sped around the turn to get away.

I can picture her swerving off the road, losing control, the gravel potholes jostling her around the seat before she crashes head-on into a tree and snaps her neck.

"Brynn?"

Jumping in my seat, I blink at Caleb's face, warped in concern. My gaze drops to his hand, resting on my thigh. Another searing breath, and the clutch of that vision is ripped away.

We're not on Route 17. I'm not with Grayson. Susan is gone.

Those things are in the past, and I need to forget them.

Heat floods my collar.

"You all right?"

The edge in Caleb's voice grinds what's left of my composure, and I squeeze the wheel so he doesn't see my hands shake.

"Yeah."

"That guy almost took off your mirror." I follow Caleb's gaze to the edge of the parking lot and the beat-up black sedan pulling out onto the main street. It's nothing like Grayson would drive.

Now that I think about it, that guy didn't even look like the hard-edged boy Dr. O assigned me to con last summer.

"I'm fine. It's not a big deal." But these are lies. I'm not fine. I can't stop thinking about Grayson, and haven't been able to sleep since he took me to the crash site. But I can't tell Caleb this, because if I do, the rest of it might slip out—the truth, that no one knows but Grayson and me.

That I'm the reason he's missing.

If I hadn't told him to run that day, his father would've punished him for leaking the truth they'd worked so hard to cover up. Dr. O may have offered to help Grayson, but he would have taken that back once he realized who really ran his sister off the road that night.

Best-case scenario, Grayson would have been charged with vehicular manslaughter. Worst case, his father would have made him disappear to save his own political career. I set Grayson free to save him, and in doing so, I banished him from his own life. Now I have no idea where he is, or if he's even alive.

And I don't even know why I feel guilty, because he's the one who drove someone off the road.

Caleb gives my thigh a gentle squeeze. If he only knew that the weight of his palm was keeping me tethered to this seat.

I want to tell him everything about what happened that day, but I can't. It's not that I don't trust him, but if Dr. O ever finds out I let Grayson go, I'll be out of Vale Hall and back on the south side.

And I am *never* going back.

I shift my focus back to the turn at the end of the lot, moving my foot slowly from the brake to the gas pedal. We jump forward five feet, and Caleb laughs weakly.

"How'd you do on the test anyway?" I ask, trying to diffuse the tension in my chest. To come back to this car, with him, where it's safe.

He looks back at the corner of the building, his lips pulling in a straight line. "Okay, I guess."

I was nervous, although admittedly Shrew—or Mrs. Shrewsbury, as she's technically called—was just having me take the test as a baseline. It's Caleb's second time, and his score was pretty high the first round. Still, Shrew wants him to get into a prestigious college for premed, which means every point matters.

"Just okay?"

I glance again at his ink-stained fingers, reminded of the buildings he sketches when no one else is looking. A good score shouldn't hurt if he goes out for architecture, either.

"Could have used Sam on the math section."

Our fellow students have special abilities. Sam can score a perfect sixteen hundred on the SATs. We know this, because before Vale Hall, he made a nice little income taking it for other people.

Of course, it landed him in jail, but you can't win them all.

Our original parking spot comes into view, only instead of it being empty like before, there's a man standing between the white brackets wearing a black button-down shirt, slacks, and a look that spells certain doom.

I slam on the brakes.

A boy in dark jeans and a plaid shirt appears behind Hugh Moore, waving frantically and pointing toward the security guard as if we don't already see him. Henry looks a lot cheerier than last night, when he was surrounded by wads of scratch paper and balled up chip bags, screaming at everyone to use their "inside voices" so he could memorize a few more word associations.

Caleb checks his phone. "So much for the warning call."

A second later the driver's door is ripped open, and Moore is standing in the gap, one open hand extended toward me.

"Keys," he says between his teeth. I put the car in park and place them in his hand, now unable to remember why I thought this was a good idea.

"So . . ." I start, but Caleb interrupts.

"My fault, officer." He leans across the seat, every part the cocky con I've seen on the job. "I told her she needs to get her license before we graduate."

That's actually what I told him when I jumped into the driver's seat. By the look on Moore's face, he's guessed as much.

"Next time you decide to commit grand theft auto, take someone else's car." He juts a thumb toward the backseat, mad, but not get-us-expelled mad.

Caleb and I navigate to the back, keeping a good three feet between us. He crosses his arms and lowers his chin to his chest, the picture of repentance.

"Sorry," I whisper.

His gaze meets mine, and I catch the smirk he's hiding. It cues a lightness in my chest, a fluttering behind my ribs. Somehow, being in trouble feels pretty on-brand for Caleb and me.

Moore clears his throat in the front seat, and I fix my stare out the window.

"Did you have enough alone time?" whispers Henry, strawberry-blond hair cutting over one eye as he turns in the front seat. "I can go back and redo reading comprehension if you need a few more minutes."

"Stop talking," warns Moore.

"Yes, sir." Henry salutes.

Half an hour later, we're turning down the private driveway, beneath the black iron gate marked by twin ravens. The tree branches overhead weave together, creating streaks of shadow that splash through the windshield, and soon a stone fountain appears, spraying water in high, arcing streams.

Behind it rests the kind of mansion only movie stars should live in, and the sight of the stone walls, reaching up toward the castle-like spires, brings on the memory of my first time here, when I didn't think this dream would be possible.

Vale Hall.

Inside those walls, I have my own bedroom, my own clothes and laptop and books. I have friends to laugh with, who have my back when I need them, and a kitchen where I can eat whatever I want, whenever I want. No matter how complicated our jobs are for Dr. O, this has become my home.

Moore lets us out in the circular drive, and Caleb and I hurry out of the car before he decides he doesn't actually forgive us after all. Henry chases us up the stone steps, and through the door into the foyer, and when he cuts in front of us like some kid sprinting to an ice cream truck, we all crack up.

But the laughter dies in our throats as Henry crashes into the person leaving Dr. O's office and repels off, nearly knocking us over.

My stomach sinks like a stone.

There before us, in jeans and a tattered gray hoodie, stands Grayson Sterling.

CHAPTER 2

Whenever I think of Grayson now, he's wearing a navy suit. It was the last thing I saw him in, formal wear for his father's fund-raiser at the Rosalind Hotel. Even when I imagine Grayson chasing Susan Griffin down the road, or hiding in motel rooms, eating greasy fast food, he's dressed like a prince. His hair is neatly gelled. His gaze is sharp and desperate. And he's wearing that damn suit.

But this.

This version of him, in dirty jeans and scuffed dress shoes, his hair growing just over his ears and his gaze darting between us like a scared rabbit, I don't know.

His eyes find mine, and the smallest sound of relief slips from his mouth. All at once it feels like there's too much blood in my veins, like I might burst if he looks at me another second.

I can't speak.

Grayson Sterling is here. In Vale Hall.

In my *home*.

"Sarah?" His eyes widen. He steps closer, then rocks back when Caleb and Henry close in on both sides. "Brynn, I mean. Right?"

"Right." My voice is a whisper. Sarah was what I called myself before he found out I was conning him for information about Susan's death.

Panic skims the edge of my control. There are rules about

outsiders coming into the school. None of our assignments are allowed to know where we live. The fact that mine is here could mean my expulsion. Could mean we're all at risk of exposure.

I told Grayson I was a con. I told him my *name*. I let him go after he confessed he'd run our director's sister into a tree.

If he's let any of that slip, my time at Vale Hall is over.

Before I can ask what he's doing here, Min Belk, Vale Hall's other security guard, comes through Dr. O's office door. His thick brows furrow in our direction, and he tightens his blunt ponytail with jerky hands.

The ground grows unsteady beneath my feet. Grayson's already told Dr. O. Security is here to escort me off the property.

But Belk only motions Grayson toward the stairs. "Let's get you settled."

I balk.

"Hold on." Caleb's brain must be working faster than mine. He steps in front of Grayson, ink-stained fingers hovering inches away from my assignment's chest. "What's going on?"

"Is that you, Caleb?" Dr. O's voice comes from inside the office. "I need to see you in my office, please."

Caleb twitches, but doesn't move.

"All of you." Belk tilts his head toward the open door.

Grayson's stare is burning a hole through me. His hands, down at his sides, open the slightest bit as if to ask, *what do I do?*

I have no idea.

"Go." Belk tilts his head toward the open door.

Henry squeezes my wrist and then heads into the office. I follow on numb feet, uncertain what awaits me inside. The last time I was here, Dr. O informed me that our classmate, Geri, had planted drugs on me on his orders, knowing that I would later use them to get my mom's good-for-nothing boyfriend and members of the Wolves of Hellsgate motorcycle club arrested.

I've avoided this room since then.

My pulse quickens as Dr. O comes into view. He's seated behind his antique desk, framed by the oil paintings and his degrees on the wall behind him. With one hand he motions us forward, not taking his eyes off the laptop as he finishes typing.

The tap of the keys scratch at my nerves until I feel like I might scream. *What is Grayson doing here? What did he tell you? What are you going to do with me?*

I can't lose this.

And neither can Caleb or Henry. It occurs to me only then that they're here because they're going to be punished with me, which cannot happen.

It is one thing to expel me, but another entirely to cut off the care Caleb's father depends on to live.

Caleb stands close on my right side. His pinky finger hooks around mine and squeezes, and soon I'm squeezing back hard enough to bruise. He edges closer, hiding our clasped hands from the director, and when his shoulder rises with a steadying breath, I follow suit.

But I don't chance looking at him, not here before Dr. O. This man controls our fates, and I will not forget the power he wields over us.

"Is this real life?" Henry blurts out. "Because I had a dream just like this once, only I'm pretty sure I was a lot taller—"

"All done," says Dr. O, rising from his chair like a king greeting his subjects. His red sweater is offset by a crisp, white collar and black slacks, all tailored to fit him perfectly. The smudges beneath his eyes, present ever since I told him about his sister, are more prominent today. If I had to guess, I'd say that was probably because of Grayson's presence.

"How were the SATs?" Dr. O asks, as if he didn't just face the boy responsible for his sister's death. As if he can't send me packing, can't make me disappear, with little more than the snap of his fingers.

"Okay?" Henry looks over to Caleb and me for help.

"What is Grayson Sterling doing here?" I have to force the words out of the straw that has become my throat. Caleb's grip on my hand is unfaltering, and I hold it like a lifeline.

Dr. O's chin lifts slightly.

"We're going to have a visitor for a few weeks while some things get sorted out. The other students have been informed, but as we didn't have much time to prepare for his arrival, I wasn't able to give you fair warning before your tests."

"He's going to stay here?" My voice doesn't sound like my own. It's too low, too unsteady. If Grayson's staying here, that can only mean that I'm out.

"He is." Dr. O's focus reduces me to the size of a mouse. "And while he's here, it's imperative that we make him feel welcome and safe. His life has been a bit chaotic recently."

Because of me. Because I told him to run.

"I don't understand," says Caleb. "We've never had a mark come to Vale Hall before."

"Does he know what we do?" asks Henry. "Is he a new student?"

"No." Dr. O raises a hand. "Nor is he to be part of any conversation regarding your work here. We are an elite boarding school, nothing more. As of today, Vocational Development is on hold, and any discussion regarding your assignments is strictly off-limits. With the exception of Brynn."

The pressure in my lungs increases. "What do you mean?"

"You're to resume your work with him," Dr. O says. "He knows you. Make him comfortable. Make him understand that we're on his side while I deal with his father."

What is this, a resort? What does that even mean, *deal with his father*? I can't believe what I'm hearing. Dr. O just invited Grayson Sterling to live under his roof, and we're supposed to pretend like everything's fine?

I squeeze Caleb's fingers harder. "How is that supposed to work?"

Grayson was a mark. He knows I conned him. I can't fool him twice—not now that he knows the game.

Lines tighten around Dr. O's eyes, then relax. "Gentlemen, you're excused. I need to speak to Brynn alone, please."

Caleb releases my hand, stepping forward. "Sir, I don't think it's safe for him to be here given how things went the last time they were together."

Caleb may have tried to pull that smooth conning voice with Moore when we were caught in the car, but he doesn't now. He is one hundred percent Caleb, and fully vigilant.

"Let me and my staff worry about safety concerns," says Dr. O.

"He could've killed her," argues Caleb.

Sweat dews on my hairline as I remember those final moments coming around the turn on Route 17 when I thought Grayson meant to crash us, the way he had Susan.

Dr. O circles his desk, passing Caleb to stand before me. "Do you think Grayson means to harm you?"

Caleb opens his mouth to interrupt, but is stopped by Dr. O's flat hand. Henry is watching me, but I can't break from Dr. O's pointed gaze. How can he ask me this? I doubt Susan Griffin thought he meant to harm her before that day, either.

"No," I manage. "I don't think so."

"That's not very reassuring," says Henry.

"Grayson will be watched." Dr. O inhales. Exhales through his teeth. It's the first hint of discomfort he's shown since we came into this office, and I find it mildly reassuring. "Until he's gone, I expect you to treat this like any other assignment. Protect our secrets."

A tense silence fills the room.

"Yes, sir," says Henry finally.

Dr. O motions toward the door. When Caleb doesn't move, Henry reaches around me to grab Caleb's sleeve.

"Yes, sir," Caleb concedes in a hard voice.

He passes me a look that says *find me later,* then I'm alone in the office with Dr. O.

A change falls over me, a fusing of my muscles, the crystallization of my nerves. With my friends close, danger is able to seep into my pores, reminding me that however competent I may be, there is much to lose.

But without them, when it's only Dr. O and the job, I am reduced to my old self. I am Brynn Hilder of Devon Park, and my skin is my shield.

"He knows who you are," says Dr. O as soon as the door closes. "He thinks you're a con artist."

Because I told him I was, after my ex-boyfriend Marcus outed me.

I stand tall.

"It was the only way to win his trust."

"Trust isn't won, Brynn," Dr. O says carefully. "It's earned. Painstakingly. Through deliberate efforts to prove yourself."

I swallow.

"You risked everything by giving him that information."

In the blink of an eye, I see Caleb. Henry. My friends Charlotte and Sam, upstairs right now, with no idea how I've jeopardized their safety. If the police become aware of this program, we could all go to jail. Every student here who's conned their way into someone's life stands to lose the scholarships and dreams they were once promised.

I know the costs.

"You risk more by bringing him here," I say quietly.

Dr. O is quiet. He runs a hand over his face. Sits on the edge of his desk.

"You can't kick me out," I say. "I'm the only one he trusts."

"I know that." His spine bows. "Brynn, I don't want to kick you out."

My shoulders fall an inch. This version of Dr. O is familiar; it's what drew me to him in the first place. Beneath this mantle of privilege, he's trying to do the right thing.

But even when he yields, he holds power.

"I can't turn Grayson away," he says. "He's on his own because of me."

This is true—if he hadn't sent me to con Grayson's secrets out of him, Grayson might still be at home with his father.

Living in fear.

But Grayson was already walking the line before Dr. O pushed him over it. Matthew Sterling had been violent with Grayson before—who knows what he would have done if his son had made the cover-up of Susan's death public.

"How did he find me?" I ask.

"He didn't." Dr. O sighs, crossing his arms over his chest as he leans against the desk. "I've been looking for him since he left you on the road that day."

"You have?" This shouldn't surprise me; I told Dr. O what Grayson had done. Of course Dr. O would attempt to find the person behind his sister's death.

Ice settles in the pit of my stomach. Dr. O tracked down Grayson but didn't turn him over to the police. He brought him to Vale Hall—to our home—likely without informing his mother or anyone else that he'd been found.

As far as they know, he could still be missing.

"What are you going to do with him?" I ask.

The director's gaze lifts, his blue eyes bloodshot and tired.

"I'm asking him to testify about what happened to my sister."

My fear takes on a sharp, jagged edge. "His dad will kill him."

Grayson isn't a 4-H project. You don't name and befriend the pig you send to slaughter.

"We'll trade his confession for protection, so we can put the right man behind bars."

The *right* man. Not Grayson, but his father, Matthew.

Dr. O's still going after the senator, even though he has the guy who committed the actual crime in his house. It doesn't line up. Either Dr. O has bigger plans for Grayson that he's not telling me, or he has a serious vendetta against the senator.

An image of Grayson's father fills my mind, his smooth jaw tilted with his trademark smile, his clothes neatly pressed. Senator Matthew Sterling may look like an angel, but he's a snake. In the three months Grayson's been missing, he hasn't even made a public announcement of his son's disappearance. There's been no missing person report, no manhunt. A senator's runaway son should have made national news, but not even our local celebrity gossip site, *Pop Store*, has picked up the story.

The Sterlings are keeping this quiet, but they must be looking for Grayson. He has too big of a secret to be cut loose.

"You're going to use the phone," I realize. "This is what you've been waiting for."

For three months, Dr. O has had the proof that someone was with his sister the night she died—a cell phone Grayson took from Susan's car before the police arrived at the scene—but he's sat on it, waiting for Grayson's confession.

"It's not enough. This isn't the first time Sterling's covered his own tracks. We must be careful. *Diligent.*" Dr. O shoves off his desk, pacing to the oil painting on the wall beside the fireplace. A woman in a white dress sits in a chair, looking over her shoulder.

Susan painted it herself, Dr. O told me once. From a picture he'd taken on her birthday.

"Grayson may have been behind the wheel that night, but his father is the one at fault. He lied. He bullied his son into hiding the truth, then threatened him when he tried to do the right thing and go to the police. All Matthew Sterling cares about is power, and it doesn't matter who he steamrolls in order to keep it."

Dr. O's voice goes low and gravelly as he pounds a fist against his thigh. "I *will* stop him. He *will* be held accountable . . ."

He drifts off, staring at the portrait. His grief is a well, big enough to drown this whole room. It pulls at me, makes me want to help him.

This is dangerous ground. There is a fine line between working for Dr. O, and getting used.

"What do you mean this isn't the first time?" I ask, retracing his words.

Dr. O continues to stare up at his sister. "There was another before Susan. An intern named Jimmy Balder who was working on the senator's staff. He went missing last year."

"How come I didn't hear about this?" It should have come up in the news. At the very least, I would have dug something up in all the research I did on the Sterlings.

"Susan mentioned him once, right before she died." His shoulders heave in a tight sigh. "I didn't know what she was talking about at the time. She just said he was causing problems in the campaign." He shakes his head. "There's nothing online. I'm afraid he's already been wiped out of the system, like so many other of Matthew Sterling's roadblocks."

My jaw tightens. The senator isn't the only one who can make people disappear. Dr. O has that power, too—when Caleb's ex-girlfriend, Margot, broke the rules, any record of her association with Vale Hall became nonexistent.

Dr. O taps his knuckles against his thigh. "I need someone connected to the Sterling campaign to tell me what happened to Jimmy Balder. Someone who knows what this family is capable of and can conduct themselves with a certain . . . discretion."

He moves closer, like a tidal wave of anger and grief. I have the sudden sensation that my legs are being swept out from beneath me, sucked into the undertow.

"The Sterlings own a private club in Uptown where the campaign staff conducts most of their business—The Loft. It's in the same building as the senator's office." He stops, and his brows pinch together. "Mr. Moore's already submitted your application for the hostess position. I hadn't anticipated finding Grayson before discussing it with you."

A tingling starts at the base of my neck, spreading through my shoulders. I knew another job would come—that's the price for enrollment here at Vale Hall—but playing politics with my old mark's dad isn't exactly what I expected.

"You want me to spy on their meetings?"

Dr. O's eyes lift, a hopeful light gleaming in their depths. "All you need to do is ask around. Make friends. Get people talking. See what you can find out about Jimmy Balder. The senator is rarely there, and when he is, we'll make sure you aren't." He holds my gaze, and I can't help the swell of pride that comes with his confidence. "And when you're home, I want you to see what Grayson knows about it."

A grim feeling crawls up my spine. The director is normally reserved, methodical about his assignments, but because of Susan this is personal. And personal can mean messy.

It doesn't matter. If Dr. O's taking this chance to send me in, it's got to be worth the risk.

"I understand," I say.

His smile is tight, lips pulled over teeth.

"Mr. Moore will give you the details. He's preparing your alias now."

Would have been nice of Moore to give me a heads-up this was coming, but of course that isn't how it works. His loyalty is to Dr. O, just like all of ours.

"This must be handled quietly," the director says. "I don't want you speaking to anyone about this job. Not Grayson, not the other students here."

"Why?"

"It's imperative we secure Grayson's trust. If you tell your friends, and they accidentally let it slip when he's around, how do you think he'll react? He believes we're here to help him. That we are a traditional, elite boarding school. If his only friend takes an internship with the man he fears, that destroys any chance at rapport."

Dr. O is right, but I don't like the idea of lying to my friends.

"As does any relationship you might be engaged in. Grayson does seem . . . *fond* of you."

At Dr. O's knowing look, my hands fist at my sides. What I have with Caleb is my business and no one else's. But as with every order Dr. O delivers, there's a whisper of threat.

If I refuse him, I lose Vale Hall. This roof over my head. This food in my belly. The safety of my friends.

My head falls forward. He's right. Grayson is singularly focused, and he doesn't like to share. Intimacy is often formed in times of stress—we learned that one week in conning class. When the mark feels alone, and scared, they're more likely to fall for any gesture of kindness.

If I'm going to keep Grayson's trust, I'll have to put whatever Caleb and I have on hold. He'll understand. He'd do the same thing in my position.

It's not like it's forever.

"What am I supposed to tell people when I leave?" I ask.

Dr. O gives a small shrug. "Tell Grayson you're visiting family. Tell your friends I've asked you to investigate a potential student. You're creative, I'm sure you'll think of something."

I glance to the stone tablet to my right, near the door. Etched in it are three words: *Vincit Omnia Veritas.* Truth conquers all.

Caleb and I promised we wouldn't lie to each other, and the thought of betraying Charlotte or Sam or Henry drives twin spikes of anger and desperation straight through me.

These are some of the first real friends I've ever made. I don't want to lose them.

"They'll understand," Dr. O says, reading my unguarded expression. "It's the nature of your positions here." His smile is laden with sympathy. "Send Caleb in when you leave. There are a few things we need to discuss as well."

"Yes, sir," I mutter on my way out.

CHAPTER 3

Caleb is waiting for me at the top of the spiral staircase, at the mouth of the girls' wing. Pinched lines have formed between his brows, and the carpet is a wash of his pacing footprints. As I come into view, he rushes toward me.

"What's going on?"

"Grayson's staying until Dr. O can put his dad in jail." I glance over his shoulder. The hallway appears empty, but anyone could be listening. We're going to have to be careful about what we say in the open from now on.

"How long will that be?" The hitch in Caleb's tone triggers an automatic hush from me. I grab his hand, pulling him into an alcove beside the supply closet. The thump of the bass from Paz's radio will muffle our conversation here.

"He can't stay here," Caleb growls. "He killed someone. He could've hurt you."

I dig my thumbs into my temples. "It was an accident." There are so many factors at play Caleb doesn't understand—that no one could have, unless they were there. Grayson isn't just a criminal, he's a victim. He's a teenager, afraid of his father.

I've lived with violence long enough to know that fear makes you do crazy, desperate things.

"How many people have you accidentally run off the road?"

I sag, and Caleb's hands move to my shoulders. His grip is

warm and steadying. I want to fall forward into him. To rewind to before Grayson got here.

"I'm sorry," he says. "I just . . . I don't like it."

"I know." But there's nothing I can do about it. Grayson is here, which means I'm on, and the sooner I can get what Dr. O needs, the sooner everything will go back to normal.

"It's going to be fine," I say, maybe for him. Maybe for me. "Grayson trusts me. He won't hurt me."

"You're sure of that?" Caleb's arms drop. "How well do you really know him?"

"Are you kidding? I probably know him better than I know you."

Caleb scowls.

I was joking. We research our marks extensively before setting up a con—Grayson is no exception—but what Caleb and I went through last summer with the Wolves goes deeper than any amount of digging. He has to know that.

I step closer. "You know what I—"

"Brynn?"

We both turn sharply to find Grayson and Henry coming down the hallway that leads to the third floor where the boys sleep. Grayson, now wearing black jeans and a Vale Hall shirt marked with a raven, slows as he approaches. His eyes flick from Caleb to me.

"You've met Caleb and Brynn," says Henry anxiously, cutting around Grayson in order to herd him toward the steps. "Come on, I'll show you downstairs. We have a pool, did I mention that?"

"Can we talk?"

Grayson's words hang between us, tense and weighted. Caleb and Henry might as well not be here; with three words, Grayson's cut them out of the conversation.

Reality catches up with me in one hard lurch. I need to make him comfortable. He needs to feel safe here.

I smile and step away from Caleb, putting another foot between us. "I was just looking for you," I tell Grayson.

Caleb's arms cross over his chest, wrinkling the button-down shirt he wore to the test.

"I was giving him the tour," Henry jumps in.

"I'll finish it." I reach for Grayson's arm. Caleb gives a small cough, and the sound punches through me. I focus on the downward pull of his lips and remember every time I've kissed him. The first time at the river, and in the gardens, and last week, in a frenzied moment in the laundry room downstairs.

What Caleb and I have is strong enough to weather some temporary storm.

I lock him deep inside, and let the con take over.

"The director wants to see you," I toss over my shoulder as Grayson and I take the stairs down to the first floor.

Dr. O may have set this assignment, but it's time to get some answers of my own.

HERE'S THE KITCHEN," I say, motioning to the cooking show setup of marble and stainless steel as Grayson stumbles to keep up. A couple of underclassmen are milling about, but after a few waves and hi's, they make themselves scarce, leaving only our silent housekeeper, Ms. Maddox, dusting in the dining room. She might not be able to speak, but she's always listening, and I don't chance talking freely until Grayson and I are out the back doors, beside the pool.

That's when I grab his elbow and drag him down the stone steps toward the lawn.

"You want to tell me what's going on?"

"I was just going to ask you the same thing." He shakes free, raking his hands through his shaggy hair. "That guy, Min something . . ."

"Belk."

"Yeah. He found me in Nashville."

"Tennessee?"

Grayson nods. "Who is Odin? Is he a cop? Are *you* with the cops?"

"Do I look like a cop?"

His scowl draws my focus. I've forgotten how hard his expressions can be—the sharp lines of his jaw and nose, the intensity of his glare. I've prided myself on the ability to fit in, slip in and out of groups unnoticed. But Grayson is no chameleon. He wears his anger like a weapon.

"I don't know. Private security maybe? Did my dad set this up?"

"No."

He exhales, pacing in a short arc in front of me. "If he finds out I'm here, I'm dead."

"I know."

"I won't go to jail, he'll kill me."

"Grayson, I *know*."

Dr. O thinks Matthew Sterling made that intern, Jimmy Balder, disappear, just as he did the truth about Susan. Grayson's right to be afraid of him.

This whole mission is a bad idea. I've met the senator—I still remember the look on his face when he told me Grayson was a *troubled young man*. If I remember him, then he might remember me. If he sees me on the job, he might think I had something to do with Grayson running away.

Which I did.

It doesn't matter. This is my assignment.

I reach for Grayson's shoulder, a gentle squeeze to let him know I'm on his side. When his hand raises, I expect him to brush me off, but instead he grabs my fingers and holds them against his arm.

I go still.

Grayson does seem fond of you.

"What am I doing here?" he asks.

I close my eyes for the briefest second, then step closer. "Dr. O wants to help."

As I speak, his gaze darts to my mouth.

"You told me he couldn't help. You said he couldn't protect me."

"I know I did, I . . ." I scrunch his shirt in my fist. I'm walking the edge of a blade. Grayson is my assignment, but he knows more truth than any mark.

In some twisted way, he's my friend.

"I thought he couldn't help you, but that changed."

"How?"

I'm not certain how much I can say. Friend or not, Grayson's part of Dr. O's larger scheme, and saying too much may put his safety at risk.

"What did Dr. O tell you?"

Grayson releases my hand, but he doesn't back away. We're close enough to touch, too close for casual conversation.

I need to play into this, to secure his belief that I understand.

"He said he's been looking for me since you and I split up," Grayson tells me. "He wants to help."

"What did you tell him?"

Grayson kicks at the ground, unearthing a plot of grass. "Nothing much."

"Elaborate."

"He knew Susan Griffin died in the . . . crash. The *accident.*" He tilts forward, like he might be sick. "I didn't know they were related—that he's her brother. He has that picture . . . that giant painting on his wall." He shudders as Susan's self-portrait fills my mind. "God, does he want to kill me?"

"No," I say, squeezing his arm before his panic takes hold. "He's a school director. He looks out for kids in trouble. That's all."

It's not exactly all.

And Grayson doesn't exactly look comforted.

"Does it look like we're in danger here?" I motion to the mansion and give a small, encouraging smile. "What else did Dr. O say?"

"He knows what my dad will do if he finds out I leaked what happened. Basically, he knows everything you told him."

I can't tell if he's angry or resigned to this reality. "Does he know I told you to run?"

Grayson's eyes turn to the ground. "He thinks I ditched you. I didn't correct him."

He's helped me without even realizing it, which makes how I'm going to play him even worse.

"Thanks."

He kicks another clod of grass. "He says my dad's going to answer for his crimes, and that I can go home if I testify against him."

His voice wobbles the faintest bit, and I can tell this hurts, even if it's what's best.

"What do you think?" I ask.

He shakes his head. "It would be nice to go home."

Use his pain, I think, even while my chest clenches in genuine sympathy.

I reach for his hand, and he takes it, weaving his fingers with mine. I can feel his fear in the heat of his palm. His loneliness in the clench of his grip. It hits me then: I may be the reason he's in this position, but I'm also the only anchor he has.

"Grayson, does the name Jimmy Balder mean anything to you?"

His head jerks toward mine, wariness flashing in his blue eyes.

"No. Who is that?"

"A guy who might have worked for your dad. An intern."

"I don't know any of the interns. They do the grunt work. Open his mail and plan his events and stuff. Why are you asking?" Worry tightens his tone, but there's no recognition in his voice.

"I think he might be missing."

Grayson's head falls forward. "Great."

Just because he doesn't know Jimmy's name, doesn't mean he hasn't heard of him. I make a mental note to revisit this once I know more.

"So what's in Tennessee?" I ask.

He groans. "Cowboy hats and terrible music."

I angle toward the gardens, and soon we're walking down the path, away from the main house. He doesn't let go of my hand, and I'm aware of how stiffly I hold his, and the unevenness of our gaits.

"Have you been there this whole time?" I ask.

"The last three weeks."

Another pang behind my ribs. I had no idea Grayson was in Nashville. I've checked my phone excessively since he left, hoping to get some sort of message, but none ever came.

"Doing what?" I ask.

"Laying low," he says. "Watching standard cable. I stayed in a motel outside the city."

I think of him in his blue suit, sitting in a dingy room, but the image isn't quite as clear as before. Things have changed since the last time I saw him. Then, I was the poor girl from Devon Park pretending to be rich like him. Now, Vale Hall is my home, and he's the one scraping to get by.

We reach the entrance to the gardens, where Barry Buddha sits, but I hesitate before going in. That's my place with Caleb; even if I'm supposed to make Grayson comfortable, it feels strange being here with another guy.

I glance back at the house, wondering what Dr. O's telling Caleb right now. Surely he'll mention our relationship. Caleb knows better than to challenge him.

"You've been gone three months," I say. "Where were you before that?"

"Louisville for a while. But they found me there," Grayson says quietly, gaze fixed somewhere in the distance.

A chill prickles over my arms.

"Who found you?"

"My dad's guys. I went to get something to eat and when I came back there were two men in my hotel room."

"Maybe they were just trying to bring you home."

"They had guns. Why would they need guns to bring me home?"

He's got a point. Maybe Matthew Sterling hasn't killed anyone himself, but there's a reason Dr. O's sending me in to look for a missing intern. Grayson's already admitted his father will do anything to keep the secret of Susan's death from affecting his political career.

I need to tell Dr. O this information—if men with guns are hunting Grayson, they could come here.

He clears his throat. "After that I went to some hick town in Indiana. I sold my car for cash, but I've been running low."

"How'd you get around without the Porsche?"

"I rode the bus."

I almost laugh.

"What?" He snorts. "I can ride a bus."

"I'm sure."

"Okay, I hired a car for most of it. People piss on busses. Like, right on the seat."

"There he is. Welcome back, Prince Grayson. I missed you."

"I missed you, too."

Grayson's tone lacks all teasing, but he can't be serious. The last few months must have added a layer onto his sarcasm. You don't miss someone who lies to you the way I lied to him.

"I mean, not at first." He digs his hands into his back pockets. "At first I hated you. But after a while, I don't know. You did something I couldn't."

I glance over at him, but his face is hard to read.

"What's that?"

"You going to make me spell it out?"

I raise my brows expectantly.

"You got me away from him," he says quietly, and again, an image of his oil-slick dad flashes through my mind.

The sarcasm is definitely thicker, because right now it almost sounds as if he's grateful. In all the time I've spent thinking of him, my worry has been laced with guilt. I faked who I was to force a secret from him that he didn't want to share. I offered protection in exchange, and then, when I couldn't deliver, I sent him away.

I figured he wanted me dead.

And because I have no idea what to do with his forgiveness—if that's what it is—I say, "That almost sounds like a thank you."

"You'd like that, wouldn't you?"

I wait.

He glances back at the house, the scowl cutting deep lines between his thick brows.

"I didn't think anyone would believe me—my dad said no one would buy it was an accident, that's why I couldn't tell the cops. But you believe me, right?"

His tone is stripped clean, raw and vulnerable, and I feel like something inside me has cracked open, spilling hot liquid through my chest. I don't know what to do. This pain is real, but is it deserved? It wouldn't exist if he hadn't run someone off the road.

But I've done stupid things, too, when I've been angry, and worse, I've deliberately tricked people knowing they might be hurt.

One moment of recklessness ruined Grayson's entire life. That doesn't make him a murderer.

"Yeah," I say. "I believe you."

His steel-blue gaze locks steady on mine, and in that moment, I get him, in a way I haven't before.

All my life, I've been defined by my zip code. It didn't matter if I was smart, or dedicated. It mattered if I was pretty like my mom, because when you're a poor girl, that's the only way to get ahead.

No one believed I was more than that until Caleb. Until Dr. O. Until this place became my home. Now I'm never looking back.

But Grayson doesn't get that luxury. Once word of this accident gets out, he will forever be defined by that night. It won't matter who he is or what he does in the future because people will only see the boy who killed Susan Griffin.

He's more than that, just like I'm more than Devon Park, and he deserves a shot at something better, like I got.

"I'm going to help you and Dr. O put your dad in jail," I say. "Soon, this will all be over." Matthew Sterling covered up Susan Griffin's death, and threatened his own son to save his career. If he had something to do with that intern's disappearance, I intend to find out.

Grayson's jaw twitches. His gaze roams over my face, as if searching for truth.

Slowly, he nods.

CHAPTER 4

By the time I make it to the girls' wing, the sky is black, and my fingertips are numb from the bite of the autumn air. It's Saturday, which means half the student body is out on assignment or in the pit playing video games—even the radio that normally thumps from Paz's room is silent. As much as I want to find Caleb and my friends and tell them what's going on, I need a few minutes alone to adjust to my new reality.

Also known as Grayson Sterling.

But Geri's door is cracked as I pass, and with a jolt I realize we need to talk. Grayson was her mark last year, and when she failed to get the truth from him, he was reassigned.

To me.

Geri and Grayson have a history, and it's going to look suspicious when he learns that both of us go to the same school. We need to get on the same page before that happens.

I stick my head in her room, but the lights are off, and when I call her name, no one answers.

It's strange—Geri never leaves her door open. I flick on the lights, but the room is empty. Kind of a mess, too. Geri's normally meticulous about keeping things orderly, but there are shoes left in the middle of the floor and half an outfit on the bed, as if she left in a hurry.

I wonder if that had something to do with Grayson's surprise arrival.

A silver spray-painted piggy bank sits on a luxurious dog bed in the corner. She won the famed porcelain pig last quarter in our conning class competition, much to Charlotte's dismay. I give Petal a wary look, but she's not talking.

I make my way down the brightly lit hallway to my room, and am inside with the door shut before I register the figure stalking toward me from the bed.

With a yelp, I brace for a fight, but drop my arms as the redhead stops an arm's length away, fists planted on her hips.

"What took you so long?" she demands.

"Charlotte," I groan. "Why are you hiding in the dark?"

"I'm being covert." She points a finger in my face. "Don't change the subject."

Reaching behind me, I flick on the light, and she blinks like some kind of cave dweller who's never seen the light.

"I've been outside. With Grayson." Judging by the way she's jumped me in my room, I take it she's already heard he's here. I rub my hands together, trying to warm up.

"Yes, I know that. I've been watching out your window."

The window beside my bed has a full view of the pool, the lawn, and the gardens that stretch to the brick wall on the back of the property. Walking toward it, I can see the place on the path, beneath the red oak trees just before the garden entrance, where Grayson and I spent the last few hours.

"Congrats," I say. "Your status has just been upgraded to full creeper."

"The Ginger Princess does not approve of your sarcasm," she tells me. "Sam said Belk gave him the room next to Henry's. I told them to lock their doors before they go to sleep tonight."

"Take it down a notch, Ginger Princess. Grayson's not a serial killer."

"That you know of. Where is he anyway?"

I sigh, sitting on the edge of my bed. Charlotte, a bundle of energy, stands before me, arms crossed over her chest. She's wearing her pajamas—a big pink sleep shirt over fleece pants. Her neongreen toenails peek out from beneath.

"Moore came outside to get him. I think they were going over the rules and everything."

Her fingers tap against her biceps. "So this is real. He's actually living here."

"For a while." I wiggle my toes inside my worn Chuck Taylor's— it feels like they're being jabbed with pins and needles. "Were you sleeping? It's six o'clock."

"Belk took everyone who wasn't working to a movie. I only got out of it because I said I was sick. My performance was so convincing Ms. Maddox came in special to make me soup."

My stomach grumbles. Dinner's on your own on the weekends, but our housekeeper always leaves something to heat up in the fridge. I bypassed the kitchen after coming in, too distracted by the current situation.

"Did Caleb go?"

"Belk basically dragged him out the door."

I gnaw the corner of my lip and kick off my shoes. I wish I knew what Dr. O said to Caleb after Grayson and I went outside—if it was the same decree that we keep a friendly distance or something more.

"Geri went, too, I take it." I think of her open door, and the mess in her room.

"She didn't even have a chance to do her makeup. You know how well that went over."

I shiver. I know from personal experience not to get in the way when Geri wants something. Over the summer, when she was upset I'd taken over with Grayson, she planted enough narcotics on me to send me to jail for drug trafficking. Of course, that was on Dr. O's orders, but I doubt he twisted her arm much.

"I guess the director wants the house quiet while our new guest settles in," I mutter.

Charlotte's bitterness warps into worry. "We're on DEFCON 5. Dr. O told us we're all steering clear of Gray-brynn, and operating on happy student mode until otherwise notified."

"He said all that, huh?"

"I'm paraphrasing."

My head falls into my hands. "This shouldn't be weird at all."

"Especially for me. It's going to ruin my birthday, I hope you know that."

Charlotte's planning a big party for her eighteenth in a few weeks—I made her a puff-paint T-shirt that says *Ginger Princess*. It's not exactly designer, but she'll love it.

Everyone playing pretend for Grayson's sake will definitely put a damper on things.

She sits beside me, one arm linking through mine. "So what did the son of Sterling say?"

"That he missed me."

She raises a brow. "Hello. This just got interesting."

With a shake of my head, I tell her the things he said outside, feeling lighter as she absorbs my words.

"So you're playing BFF with your old mark. That's not terrible." She's trying to sound hopeful, but all I can think about is my new job at The Loft, and Jimmy Balder, and if Matthew Sterling has covered up an intern's disappearance.

And what he'll do to me if he knows I'm onto him.

"That's not all," I say.

"Do tell."

Charlotte's twirling the ends of her orange curls around one finger. I can't tell her about my new assignment, even if I want to.

If I do, I could be done here, and having her around knowing half the truth is better than not having her around at all.

"Caleb and I are off until Grayson leaves."

She cranks her head my direction. "You're not seriously breaking up!"

"We aren't officially together," I say, but the look on Caleb's face when I said I knew Grayson better returns to my mind and pinches something inside me. What we have is real, with or without the title.

"Of course you are," she says, the pink pout of her lips contrasting the paleness of her cheeks. "Everyone else knows it even if you don't."

"What happened to *watch out for Caleb*?" When I started at Vale Hall, she'd warned me to be careful around him—that he'd gotten his last girlfriend, Margot, kicked out because he was jealous.

In reality, Margot had gotten herself kicked out by falling for her assignment and telling him all about the program. Caleb had tried to talk sense into her, but it was too late.

"Like you could even hear me through all the hormones." She presses a hand on her throat, and I wonder if that sickness was feigned for my benefit. "Good luck hiding that from Grayson. Any cat in a twenty-mile radius spontaneously goes into heat whenever you two enter the same room."

"Gross," I say. But my cheeks are warm.

Chemistry is not a problem with Caleb.

Charlotte shrugs. "He left you a note."

I throw my hands up. "Seriously. You couldn't lead with that?"

"I was saving it in case I had to torture the truth out of you." She pulls a folded piece of paper out of her fuzzy pocket and passes it my way. I practically snatch it out of her hand, hiding it against my body as I unfold the creased paper.

There are only two words, etched in his perfect penmanship.

Midnight. Roof.

"Trysts are so romantic," Charlotte stage whispers in my ear.

I shove her off. "How am I supposed to get on the roof?"

"Go through the attic. Duh."

I blink at her. "I'm sorry. Where's the attic?"

She smirks. "It delights me that I can be the one to corrupt you. Henry will be so jealous."

AT 11:55, I close the door to the supply closet behind me, guided only by the light on my cell phone. To reach the pull-down cord in the center of the ceiling, I have to climb on the bottom shelf, nudging aside the boxes of tampons with the toe of my shoe.

The higher I go, the more my nose crinkles at the smell of moth balls, but finally, after two attempts, my grip closes around the brass ring hanging from the cord. With a victorious smile, I give it a small tug, but the squeal of the falling attic ladder catches me by surprise, and I slip off the shelf. My feet hit the floor with a thump.

"Shut up," I hiss at the slowly unfolding rungs, groaning loud enough to wake the dead. Finally, the ladder stops, and I hold my breath, listening for anyone who might be coming to check out the disturbance.

The hall outside the door is quiet. I snatch my phone off the floor from where I dropped it, and make my ascent, wincing at each creak the dowels make beneath my weight.

The attic air is frigid; passing into it feels like I've crossed an invisible barrier, and I instantly wish I'd brought a coat to go over my sweatshirt. There's no turning back, though, and I feel a grin tugging on the corners of my lips as I pull myself onto the dusty beams and bring the ladder back up like Charlotte told me.

By phone light, I creep beneath the underside of the circular spire, passing boxes marked *Christmas,* and *Halloween,* and *Fourth of July.* The ceiling is draped with cobwebs, and I duck lower to keep them out of my hair.

"Caleb?" I whisper, but there's no response.

After a few more steps, I find the wooden scaffolding wall Charlotte told me about, and the insulation that's been moved aside to create a hole large enough for a person to get through. Pulling my hood over my ponytail, I climb through and shine my light ahead into the darkness.

A rectangular window is ten feet before me, propped open by an old shoebox. Relief trickles through my veins as I rush toward it, stopping when I see a note card taped to the dirty glass.

My favorite color is green.

The writing is definitely Caleb's; each letter is absurdly straight and symmetrical, but I'm not sure what this means. If this is a code, or a game of some kind, no one told me the rules.

Taking the card, I squeeze through the low window, placing the shoebox back against the frame.

The night air is bitter, the sky black and painted with stars. A fingernail moon hangs over the spire I crept under, and directly in front of me, taped to the slanted shingles, is another note card.

Doughnuts > Pancakes.

I smirk, taking this card as well and pressing it into the palm of my hand with the other. A few feet to the right is a metal air vent, and hanging from the side is a third note.

Birthday: May 17.

I didn't know his birthday, and as I place this card on the others, I'm confronted by a greedy kind of guilt. This is a basic cornerstone of knowing someone. How have I gotten this far without asking?

The notes keep coming, creating a path along the narrow cement walkway between the sloping arches of the roof.

Greatest achievement: Lego Death Star (4,000 pieces).

Nose broken, 2 times.

First pet: bat in attic. Name: Battic. Length of ownership: 12 hours.

Before I know it, I'm hurrying on to the next note card, starved for his writing and any hint of the boy he was before I met him.

Girlfriends: 3 (4?).

Vocational Goal, age 7: professional wrestler.

First crush: cartoon lioness (confusing).

Greatest Fear: failing.

I stare at the words, feeling them resonate through me. I am afraid of Grayson and letting Grayson down. I'm afraid of his father and this internship in his office. But I do whatever I have to, because I'm most afraid of throwing away this chance.

I know what happens if I fail here. I go home to Devon Park. I reenroll at a high school that spends more time busting kids for drugs and fighting than prepping them for college. I try for night school, but in the end, it's too expensive, so I work a job like my mom, at a bar, and pray the tips are enough to pay the power bill.

I want more.

There's another note ahead, and when I see the words, I wilt in the bitter night air.

I have a new assignment.

CHAPTER 5

I bundle this note with the others, tucking them into the front pocket of my sweatshirt as the cold air bites my nose and cheeks. From my right comes a scuff, shoe soles against concrete. I turn and find Caleb, sitting on a ledge in front of another sharp spire. He's half-silhouetted by the lights on the front of the house and the fountain, his black leather jacket and dark jeans blending with the night.

My stomach does a slow flip-flop, and my breath comes in a staggered, hot puff of mist against my lips.

He's holding another card, and when I shine my light toward him, I read the single word.

Trust.

He passes it to me as I approach, and though it's the same as the other cards, this one feels heavier. More important.

He's giving me his trust.

"Hi," I whisper.

"Hi."

There's a space on the ledge next to him, and a folded blanket. When he tilts his head toward it, I sit beside him, and he wraps the wool around my shoulders.

For a few minutes we say nothing. We look at the stars and listen to the breeze rattling the dry leaves below. The knots slowly untie from my muscles, and my shivering ceases beneath the blanket.

"I like green, too," I say after a while. "Bright green. Like the trees that grow near the fountain in Millennium Park."

He smiles.

"Pancakes are greater than doughnuts," I continue. "But I'll settle for greater than or equal to."

I shift closer, and he does, too. Our thighs are aligned, the outside of our knees separated by two layers of denim.

"I fell down the steps in the fourth grade and broke my tibia. No one signed my cast." It was after my dad was killed, and the kids in my class wanted nothing to do with me. Like getting shot in a mini mart is somehow contagious. "How'd you break your nose?"

"I got punched," he says. "First time by Skylar Galotti when he stole my skateboard. Second time by Skylar Galotti when I stole his girlfriend."

The smirk severs my old grief. "Is this girlfriend four, question mark?"

He's leaning forward over his knees and looks back at me, a faint smile dimpling his cheek. "No. That's you."

My smirk fades.

"Sophie Gomez was girlfriend two," he goes on, as if my heart didn't just trip over itself. "We were in the seventh grade. She asked me to the Winter Ball, and then broke up with me when I didn't dance with her."

I'm still stuck twenty seconds ago, on the whole *that's you* comment.

"Why didn't you dance with her?" I manage.

"Are you kidding? Girls are terrifying."

So, apparently, are boys.

We haven't talked about labels, and even if I've wondered what it would be like to call him my boyfriend, we can't now. Dr. O made it clear that my assignment comes first.

Caleb has an assignment, too, now. As much as I want to know what it is, I can't bring myself to ask.

"Bella Cho and I dated in the sixth grade for three days," he continues. "We spent the majority of that time pretending to ignore each other."

"And after Sophie, your next girlfriend was Margot."

He nods slowly. "The years between were not so great."

That's when his dad got hurt, and when the spinal surgeries started, and when they had to move from Uptown to White Bank.

"You know me better than anyone." There's a strain to his voice. Now that Grayson's come to Vale Hall, we only get one role to play. Home and work have become the same, and if these stolen moments are all we have, I don't want to waste them.

I want him to know me, too.

"I've only had one other boyfriend," I say, picturing Marcus the way I always do now, grinning like a fool, pointing to a road sign that says *Baltimore*. "Technically. I did kiss Steve Jamison in the seventh grade, but only to get him to stop throwing paper airplanes at me in woodshop."

He doesn't look back at me, but the lines of his neck move, like he's working to swallow.

I imagine him as a kid, building Legos and skateboarding. Blushing when a girl takes the desk across the room. I know the real him, and he knows the real me, and maybe that—remembering we're more than Dr. O's assignments—is more important than the work we do.

"I can't believe Grayson's here," I say.

Caleb nods.

"I think about him all the time," I go on, and even though Caleb stiffens, I don't stop. "I have dreams that he's dead and it's my fault."

After a long beat, he says, "I have dreams like that about Camille."

His mark, the mayor's daughter. She sent the Wolves of Hellsgate motorcycle club after Caleb when she learned that he was behind her mother's fall from political grace, but he doesn't mention that, just like I don't mention Grayson's part in Susan's death.

The guilt doesn't make sense. Maybe we're just messed up.

"Dr. O wants me to work him while he's here. He seems to think Grayson likes me."

Caleb's hands clasp together, squeezing tightly. His head hangs forward.

"It's a job," I tell him. "That's all."

But it was more than that when I held Grayson's hand earlier. That was real, too, as much as I tell myself it was part of the con.

I huddle tighter into the blanket.

"That sounds familiar," he says.

My teeth clench together. "I'm not Margot."

His ex-girlfriend got close with her mark, too, only she forgot that it was pretend, and when it came time to choose, she picked him, not Caleb.

"I know," he says, though a muscle tics in his neck. He doesn't need to say it out loud; I've been through enough with him to know when he's worried.

He looks at our hands when I intertwine my fingers with his. The air is cold outside the blanket, so I pull his arm underneath, resting his wrist on my thigh.

"What if there was no question mark after four?" I say.

Slowly, his thumb arcs around the heel of my hand, sending warm tingles up my arm.

"Dr. O won't be happy."

Apparently the director told Caleb to back off on our relationship, too.

"He doesn't have to know. And neither does Grayson. Anyway, we only have to hide it until he's gone."

I'm afraid Caleb will say no. That he doesn't want to be hidden, and I don't blame him—I don't, either. But he squeezes my hand.

"We'll have to be careful," he says.

A giddy relief floods through me. "I can do careful."

I know what's at stake. If I alienate Grayson and he runs, or refuses to testify against his father like he said Dr. O mentioned, Caleb and I are both in trouble. If I don't convince Grayson he's safe here, that he can trust me, he'll be out on his own, facing the wrath of a man Dr. O believes killed an intern.

We all have to play this safe.

"Of course," I say, sliding my knee over Caleb's. Beneath, I can feel the muscles of his thigh tense in response. "If you blow me off at the Winter Ball, we're done."

"Noted."

His hands find my waist, and mine, his chest. I unzip his coat until there's enough room to slide my fingers beneath, over the waffled fabric of his thermal shirt.

His eyes, lit only by my upturned cell light, grow dark. It stirs a wanting deep in my belly.

"So if you're my secret girlfriend," he says, the word tingling over my skin, "I think that means you get to kiss me as much as you want."

His fingers fan over my back, easing me closer.

"Lucky me."

He cranes his head from left to right, then he smiles, and I smile, and I know without a doubt he's the best secret I've ever kept.

It doesn't matter if I've done this before. There's a burst of nerves beneath my breastbone just before we touch, a flare of heat that streaks out to my fingertips. I lean in and he meets me, his lips cool and feather soft as they brush from side to side. Tilting my head the slightest bit, I press closer, my eyes drifting closed as I revel in the firm feel of his lower lip between mine.

I deepen the kiss, gasping at the warmth of his mouth and the cold of his nose and cheeks. His hands fist in the back of my shirt and drive me closer still, sensation rioting through me at the feel of his tongue and his teeth. My muscles feel like pulled taffy, stretching and reforming and drawing even tighter, until both my legs are over his and I'm sitting on his lap, locked in the circle of his arms.

Pulling back just a little, I press my lips to the corner of his mouth, and his jaw, and just beneath his ear. He tenses, and his breaths grow uneven.

I feel like flying.

He can turn me upside down with the whisper of his fingertips on my back, but I can do the same to him. There's power in that, and safety in knowing I'm free to try. To experiment. That there's no judgment or doing this wrong.

I find the zipper of his coat and pull it down, pushing open the sides so I can spread my hands over the flat plains of his stomach. The blanket has fallen, pooling around our waists, and I slide deeper into his coat, seeking warmth, seeking him. He drags me into another searing kiss, and my fingers curl around the bottom of the back of his shirt, skimming over the smooth skin above the waistband of his jeans.

He breaks away with a jerk.

"Cold!" he howls. "Cold, cold, cold, cold!"

I erupt in giggles and take the only logical course of action, which is to spread my freezing hands over his bare stomach.

He looks at me with shock, then digs his fingers into my ribs. It tickles so much I nearly shriek. Then we're wrestling, tickling each other, burying our laughter in each other's necks.

"Shh," he says. "Shh!" But I squeeze above his knees and in his writhing he nearly knocks us both off the ledge.

From below comes the click and suction of the front door opening, and we freeze, hands over each other's mouths, still fighting the laughter that's making us both quake. When we've gotten ahold of ourselves, he looks over the side of the roof and backsteps quickly, one finger over his lips to keep me quiet.

"Moore," he whispers.

With a smile, he motions back toward the attic window, and though I don't want to go, he's right. We've been away awhile, and we can't chance getting caught together after curfew, especially with Grayson here.

Bending low, I retrieve the cards that have slipped out of my pocket off the ground, and he settles the blanket around my shoulders. I follow him to the attic window, and he holds the glass panel up so I can slip through.

Inside, I align the cards to put back in my pocket, but the top one is staring up at me.

I have a new assignment.

My stomach plummets. "I do, too," I say, as he squints to read the letters in the dark. To hell with Dr. O's orders. Caleb gave me his trust, and he's got mine in return. "I'm working at a club where Sterling's campaign staff hangs out."

Caleb's mouth opens, but before he can object, I add, "He'll never be there when I'm there. I'm just going in to ask some questions about a missing intern. Dr. O's trying to get as much evidence as he can to get the senator put away." I take his hand and press it to my lips, feeling his grip slowly relax. "When Matthew Sterling's in jail, Grayson will go home, and you can say good-bye to the secret part of girlfriend."

He gives a reluctant sigh.

"What are you doing?" I ask.

"What? Oh." In the dim light, I can see his brows scrunch. "Nothing big. I'm tailing a new recruit. Some girl in Sycamore Township."

The blanket slips off my shoulder.

What do I tell them?

Tell them I've asked you to investigate a potential student.

Caleb's followed recruits before—I was one of them. His job was to watch me work, see if I could pull a con and keep a secret.

He had to give an opinion on whether I would be a good fit at Vale Hall.

I am only here because of Caleb's good report.

But it can't be coincidence that Dr. O just told me to give the same exact excuse when asked about my current assignment—one he very much wants to keep secret. Caleb pulls the blanket back over my shoulder, tucking me firmly inside and rubbing his hands over my arms.

"You all right?"

I search his face for truth, but find nothing suspicious.

But Caleb is good at lying. We all are. That's why we're here.

I nod.

"You'll be careful, right?" he asks, worried.

"Of course."

His hands slow on my biceps. His arms drop to his sides.

We walk back along the planks, fitting ourselves through the gap in the insulation. He takes another exit, one that climbs into a crawl space and drops into a bathroom at the end of the boys' hallway.

Caleb and I promised we'd always tell each other the truth—that what was between us needed to be real if everything else was fabricated. I was honest about my assignment—I risked getting busted without a second thought. But what if Caleb lied? I want to believe that he really is checking out some girl in Sycamore Township, but what if he's not? What other assignment would Dr. O give him?

His trust weighs heavy in my pocket.

"Are you all right?" he asks one more time before we part ways. His brows are drawn together, his eyes filled with concern.

His worry neutralizes mine.

He wouldn't give me his trust just to break it. I've spent so much time doubting people, I've forgotten where to draw the line.

This is Caleb—*my* Caleb, if only in secret. I know him better than anyone. I've trusted him with my life.

I would again, if it came to it.

"Yeah," I say. I kiss his cheek, and his lips relax into a smile. "I'm good."

CHAPTER 6

The next morning, I wake up late, echoing worries about Grayson and the senator lingering on the edges of my mind. By the time I roll out of bed and go downstairs, Sunday brunch is over. People are either in the pit hanging out or on one of the many couches or chairs in the study, finishing homework for this week.

All except Charlotte, Henry, and Sam, who are waiting in the kitchen in various pajama ensembles, ready to pounce.

"Hey sleepyhead," says Charlotte with a knowing smirk. "You look tired. Late night?"

My cheeks warm. Last time I saw her she was giving me instructions on how to get on the roof.

"Where's your boyfriend?" asks Sam, and I nearly choke. No one is supposed to know about my secret status with Caleb, especially those with a direct pipeline back to Dr. O like Ms. Maddox. If she thinks I don't see her meticulously washing a clean plate at the sink behind Charlotte, she's wrong.

"I haven't even met him," Sam goes on. "He snuck into his room when I was out and hasn't emerged since."

Grayson. Not Caleb. Of course that's who they're talking about.

Ms. Maddox makes a close inspection of the plate, and then begins scrubbing again.

"I haven't seen him since you guys went outside," says Henry, an uncharacteristic frown tugging at his mouth. "I don't think he likes me. He barely looks at me when I talk to him." He keeps raking his fingers through his strawberry-blond hair—a nervous tell.

"Who cares if he likes you," says Charlotte. "I like you and that's all that matters." She pets his arm, and he immediately stops with the hair.

"He's got a lot going on," I say. "Has anyone seen Caleb?"

"Left early," Henry says quietly, so even our nosy housekeeper can't hear. "On a job for Dr. O. A new recruit, I think."

I nod. Any lingering doubt that Caleb's assignment is not what he said vanishes and is replaced by a smudge of guilt. I shouldn't have questioned him. I have his trust, and he has mine.

"I guess I'll go find our new friend," I say.

Charlotte gives me a wry salute. "Have fun."

Before I leave, Sam tugs on my ponytail.

"He gives you any trouble, you know where I am." He's smiling, but his deep brown eyes are fierce.

A steadying breath, and mine are, too.

I'M ON THE landing in front of the staircase to the third floor when I run into Moore. His room is on the opposite side of the residence, and I rarely see him over here unless he's doing room checks after curfew.

"Where are you going?" he asks flatly.

Girls aren't normally allowed in the boys' wing, and vice versa, but I'm guessing they'll make an exception for me since everyone at school is adjusting their entire life to accommodate Grayson.

"Our honored guest has yet to rise," I say. "I was going to see if he wants breakfast."

Moore studies me a moment, dark eyes sharp. He nods once.

"Door open," he says.

"Yes, sir."

His gaze pinches at the corners. "Watch yourself with him. Stay public as much as possible. And cell phone on."

"Did I say yes, sir? I meant, yes, Dad."

He makes a face like he just caught me eating roadkill.

"Your new job starts tomorrow."

My shoulders drop. How delightful that I've broken out of Devon Park only to work the same kind of minimum-wage, back-busting job Mom's had all my life. At least the cover shouldn't be too hard to fake—I know the lingo.

"We'll leave at three, after class. Dress nicely. I'll fill you in on the rest in the car."

I'd look more believable if I could drive myself, rather than have a security guard deliver me in a black SUV. I could take one of the cars from the garage, cruise down the highway. Go wherever I want.

But as I proved with Caleb, I can't even circle a parking lot without nearly running into someone.

"Okay," I say, and he motions for me to continue on my path.

Because he doesn't seem to be leaving, I head up the stairs and turn right, steps leading me over the beige carpet past the white doors. I stop outside Caleb's room, just across from Henry's. The first night I came here after Grayson told me about Susan Griffin, I found Caleb awake and waiting, and spent half the night lying beside him in bed, staring at the ceiling and thinking about what I'd done.

I wish I could crawl back into his bed now and forget it all.

Moving on, I find the room next to Henry's and knock twice.

A groan comes from within.

I knock again.

"Go away."

"You're supposed to say, *who is it?*"

The seconds pass and I knock again.

"Good God. Come in already." His voice is muffled, like he's shouting through a pillow.

With one final glance over my shoulder at Caleb's door, I turn the knob and step inside.

The room is much like Henry's—square, with a bathroom on the right and a window over a queen-sized bed. Tangled in the gray comforter is a body, and there's enough skin showing that a warm blush starts creeping up my throat.

"Please tell me you're not naked," I say, averting my eyes.

"Please tell me you are." He does not sit up.

Striding to the base of the bed, I grab the blanket and give it a hard tug, flipping it over his body. He is wearing boxers, thank everything holy, but that's about it.

"My therapist says I'm supposed to talk about my feelings," he says, covering his head with a pillow. "I'm unhappy. This makes me unhappy."

I cross my arms over my chest. "I'm so sorry."

"You don't mean it."

"You don't say. Get up. Let's go eat something."

He groans again.

"You can't stay in bed all day," I tell him, sitting on the edge of the bed.

He mumbles something that sounds like "time."

"Almost noon." I don't tell him that I haven't been awake that long, either.

His leg moves, and it hits my hip. For a second I think he's playing footsie with my thigh, but after a dedicated shove, it's clear he's trying to push me off the edge.

"Come on." I stand, skirting around the corner of the mattress. His back is revealed below the pillow covering his head, the angles of his shoulders sharp and triangular. "You can meet my friends."

"No friends."

I wrestle the pillow away, and he glares at me through red, bleary eyes.

"Then let's go be antisocial. Either way, I'm hungry."

"I've been hungry for three months," he says. "I'll live another day."

Then he rolls over and pulls the blanket over his head.

This is a problem. If I push too hard, I run the risk of burning our friendship. If I leave him alone, he—and Dr. O—will think I don't care. I need to find an in, just like I did at his party last summer. Something to get, and hold, his attention.

Grayson doesn't want Brynn. He wants Sarah, the girl who reeled him in when we first met.

"Want to play a game?" I ask.

He doesn't answer, but I can feel him holding his breath.

"One of the girls here has something I want. A silver piggy bank she keeps on a ridiculous dog bed in the corner of her room." I picture Petal the Platinum Pig on Geri's throne and make a note to warn her. Any other time, I'd let someone stealing her stuff be a fun little surprise, but she, and Grayson have history. "It would be really nice if that could find a way to me—without her knowing who took it of course."

A muffled snort comes from beneath the blanket.

"What do I get out of it?"

I stand, fighting the urge to drag him up with me. Grayson may be having a rough time right now, but he's still Grayson. He's driven by the game.

He likes it when I walk away.

"You get to choose the next game," I say.

Play, I will him. *Play.*

He flips onto his stomach, the blanket still over his head.

I walk to the door and close it behind me. When I look up, I see Moore's back as he heads down the stairs and wonder if he's there to keep me safe, or to report my lack of progress to Dr. O.

GRAYSON DOESN'T COME out of his room for the rest of the day. After our failed pep talk, I distract myself with homework.

I've finally caught up with the assignments I need to keep pace with the other seniors, but that doesn't mean I don't have to work my ass off. Henry and I commandeer the dining room table and trudge through physics and pre-calc, but by the time we're done, it's afternoon, and Grayson has yet to leave his room.

Monday morning isn't any better.

I'm starting to doubt this whole game thing will work. Maybe he's changed since I saw him last. Maybe he's too far gone to play.

I'm trying to think of what to do next when the upperclassmen line up in the gym, facing Belk and the mirrored wall for PE.

"The votes have been tallied," announces our bulky security guard. He also teaches the fitness classes, though there's some debate as to whether he is, in fact, fit.

Beside me, Henry is crossing all his fingers on both hands and whispering a prayer. Sam is on his other side, drumrolling his hands on his thighs.

"Come on yoga," Caleb says, smirking my way. "I was not made for competitive sports."

Thanks to Moore's increased security measures in the boys' wing, Caleb and I weren't able to meet on the roof last night. We texted, but at a school like this, we're fools if we think someone won't hack into those messages. Still, through his vague texts, I managed to piece together that he found the new recruit in Sycamore Township, but doesn't have a good read on her yet.

He's trying again this week, which puts both of us out in the city. My new hostess job starts this afternoon.

"You do have the legs for yoga shorts," I say.

"Eyes up here, Devon Park," he says, motioning toward his face.

I elbow him in the side. Automatically, I look for Grayson, and feel guilty when I'm glad he isn't here.

We had three choices—yoga, basketball, or a fill-in option—after we finished the kung fu segment last quarter. This is the first school I've ever been to where the students actually have a say in what they're going to learn, and since sports aren't exactly my jam, I happily voted for yoga. Everyone I talked to did. I even wore my stretchy black pants in preparation.

"Ballroom dancing," says Belk.

"Yes!" Henry screeches beside me.

Sam's drumroll stops short. "What?"

Charlotte starts to laugh.

"Failed democracy," calls Geri.

"Ballroom dancing wasn't an option." I try to imagine myself in a silky, feathered dress, spinning around a dance floor, but stop when I'm pretty sure smoke starts to come out my ears.

"Nine people wrote it in on their ballots," Belk says. "Caleb wrote it twice."

"Did I?" Caleb gives a weak smile, then narrows his eyes at Henry.

"You must really want to dance!" Henry's voice wobbles in excitement.

I groan, seeing now that Henry must have somehow gotten his sticky fingers on our ballots and written in his own choice. Charlotte and Sam have realized the same, but no one has yet over-ruled Henry's efforts.

With a shrug, Caleb steps forward. "It's been a deeply hidden dream of mine for some time."

I can't help smirking. If Caleb's on board, few people will argue.

"Mine, too," says Charlotte, grinning at Henry.

Belk rolls his eyes. "Majority rules. Suck it up, kids. We're doing this."

"It's going to be so great," Henry assures the rest of us as a collective groan fills the room.

Since Belk isn't a dancer, he turns on the television over the mirrors and cues up an instructional movie on beginning ballroom dancing. For the next ten minutes we practice our posture and the box step, which is a three count move that involves not tripping over your own feet. Then Belk orders us to pair up for the waltz.

Caleb and I always partnered together in kung fu, but with my new assignment, I hesitate before taking his hand.

"He's not here," Caleb whispers, as everyone else joins together.

He's right. Grayson's in his room. It can't hurt for us to dance together—not when everyone else is doing it, too. We take our places. His hand finds the dip of my waist, his other grips mine, and I shiver when his thumb circles the thin skin on the underside of my wrist.

I am not a ballroom dancing expert, but Caleb looks good like this. Regal. Tall, and proud. Even with his black-rimmed glasses and messy hair, he's like someone out of another time.

The starting pose is where it ends. As soon as the music starts, his posture collapses, his chin falls forward, and his full weight ends up on my right foot.

"Ow." Behind me, Charlotte is giggling as she tells Sam to focus. The only one who seems to have it together is Henry, who's dragging Geri around the floor with full grace, but absolutely zero attention to his rotating box step.

"Again," calls Belk. "One, two, three. One, two, three. Henry!"

I snort as Henry gets berated. Caleb and I try again, with similar results.

"Sorry." He winces.

"It's okay," I tell him. "I didn't need toes anyway. Balance is way overrated."

He stomps on my left foot.

"You really suck at this," I say.

He pinches me lightly in the ribs, right in my ticklish spot, and I squeak and curl into him.

Then immediately back away. Even if Grayson's not here, Belk is, and he could easily report my behavior to the director.

Caleb's still scowling at his feet.

"Try thinking about something else," I say, pulling his arm up again.

"Like what?"

"I don't know. Something you like."

His eyes lift to my lips, and the want in his gaze sends a warm, velvet wave through me.

"Yeah," he says. "That doesn't help."

"Tell me about a building." Caleb's dad was an architect before he got hurt on the job, and even if Caleb doesn't talk about it often, he knows all the buildings in Uptown, down to the year they were created and the materials used to build them.

"Morrison Crossing," he says as we take the first three steps. "On the east side, by the curve in the river. Built to be a boat depot but converted to a restaurant in 1967."

We've made it through a full rotation without hurting each other or knocking someone over.

"See? Do it again."

With a small smile, he tells me about the first hospital in the city. His back is still round, and he can't keep his chin lifted, but we're still upright.

"You should be an architect," I tell him.

He slows, focusing on his feet again. "I can't."

"Why?"

His eyes shoot to mine, deep with hurt. "You know why."

Because his dad broke his back on a job, and his family lost everything. Now Shrew has him focused on med schools, and his sights are set on becoming a spinal surgeon.

"I know," I say. "It's just that your sketches are so good. And you love talking about it. Your mom would understand if you talked to her."

His grip tightens around my hand.

"I know she would."

"So?"

He steps on my foot. "What do you want to be? What happens once you get your big fancy scholarship?"

I go to college. I get out of Sikawa City. I never really planned past that, probably because deep down, I never really thought it would happen.

My chest clenches, and suddenly I'm thinking of my mom.

I can picture her sitting on the blue couch in the living room at home, alone, since Pete's in jail. She's eating cold chicken wings from Gridiron Sports Bar as she watches *Pop Store* and talking back to the host of the show like he's speaking directly to her.

We haven't talked in a month, since I told her about Parents' Weekend, this coming Saturday. I don't even know if she's coming—she wasn't sure she could get off work.

You sound good, she told me. *Now quit bugging me, I've got stuff to do.*

We both know she didn't, but that's how we do love in my family.

"Don't change the subject," I tell Caleb.

He sighs.

"When my dad got hurt, we didn't know what to do. My mom had to make all these decisions, but we couldn't even grasp what parts of his back were broken. She wonders all the time if we should have done things differently. She can't go through that again."

I imagine his family gathered in the hospital, trying to decide what to do. Wondering if they made the right decision when Caleb's dad didn't wake up. I picture his mom, blaming herself, and Caleb blaming himself for not being able to help her.

It's why he's here. Why he works for Dr. O.

He's doing what he can to keep his father alive.

As long as I can remember, I've been trying to get out of Devon Park. I've conned, stolen, and fought tooth and nail for what I need. I've never faced the burden of caring for another person—of someone depending on me for their survival.

"None of this is your fault," I say.

"It's my fault if I don't do anything about it." The outside of his foot bumps against mine. "Sorry."

But I barely felt it, because my heart is suddenly too big for my chest, and all I can think of is how he's putting his family in front of himself, and how noble and unfair that is.

"Architecture's more like a hobby anyway," he says, and if there's any regret in his tone, it's swallowed up by a practiced smile.

The door behind us opens and Moore strides in, looking more annoyed than usual.

"You have a new student," he says to Belk.

Behind him stands Grayson, wearing a rumpled Vale Hall sweatshirt, jeans, and a look of simmering rage.

CHAPTER 7

I jerk back from Caleb, clasping my hands before me.

"Come on," Belk says when Grayson doesn't move.

Grayson, hair mashed up on one side like he's just rolled out of bed, trudges after him.

"Your new partner," Moore says. "Caleb, you're with Geri."

With a jolt, I realize I've yet to touch base with Geri or tell her about my little challenge with Grayson. I don't think he's stupid enough to try to break in while she's sleeping, but I need to warn her just in case.

"Hey," Caleb says to Grayson, words light but gaze hard. "Heard you were here. Welcome."

Grayson glares at his outstretched hand. "I know you from somewhere."

My breath catches. Moore was backing away, but pauses, looking to Caleb.

Grayson knows Caleb because they were both at Grayson's house when I passed my initiation test. I danced with Caleb to make Grayson jealous.

"I went to a party at your place once," says Caleb, clearly prepared for this. "Some friends of mine know your sister."

"Oh yeah." Grayson turns toward me, deliberately angling Caleb out of the conversation. "This is bullshit."

"Have fun," says Moore, and walks away.

Caleb gives an awkward wave, then makes his way around a whispering Alice and Beth to Geri, who's pretending like Grayson's presence here hasn't upset her in the slightest.

I know better, though. She may have tried to con him before me, but she was the one who walked away feeling used.

"That guy's a dick," Grayson says, nodding toward Moore.

I remind myself that I'm supposed to be the supportive friend, but sarcasm wins.

"Because he rolled you out of bed? Poor baby."

The rest of the class pretends not to stare at us as they fumble through the waltz.

"I'm not doing PE."

"It's dancing," I tell him. "It's fun."

Grayson's glare narrows on Henry, who's taking a turn around the floor with Charlotte. After a complicated spin that ends in a dip, they both fall over.

"I'm not drunk enough for this," says Grayson.

"Typically the man leads, Geri," calls Belk.

"Tired of your antifeminist agenda, Mr. Belk," Geri answers. Grayson's gaze shoots her way, but she's already spinning away, her back to us.

Jealousy whispers through me as I see Caleb's hand on Geri's waist, and her fingers curling around the back of his neck. He's smiling like he's having a good time, but I know he's only pretending. He and Geri aren't friends. She was close with his ex, Margot, before she was booted, and has been nothing but cold to Caleb since.

"Come on," I say to Grayson. "Think of it as an easy A."

"I'm not a student."

"Maybe not, but I am, and you want me to get a good grade, right?"

I take a step closer and grab his hand. To my relief, he doesn't bolt away. Placing it on my waist, I show him how we're supposed to stand, but the weight of his grip is heavy and unfamiliar on my side as I siphon in a tight breath.

"See? Not so hard," I say.

Sam, now back with Charlotte, bumps into us.

Grayson's hands drop as he spins toward them. "Watch it."

"Sorry, man," says Sam as they waltz away.

I hurriedly return Grayson to the proper stance.

"Look at that guy," he says, lifting his chin toward Caleb. "He's a train wreck."

Maybe. But he's my train wreck, so Grayson better watch his mouth.

"He's trying," I say.

Grayson's cold stare, still directed at Caleb, makes me nervous. It's as if Caleb has wronged him and Grayson's looking for an excuse to fight.

"You could try, too, you know," I say.

He finally looks at me and gives, just enough.

"This is ridiculous," he mutters.

Grabbing my waist, he straightens my arms, and then pulls me across the floor in a perfect rotating box step, just like on the instructional video. With him leading, my feet are forced to follow, and his strong frame holds me up even when I start to get dizzy.

Holy crap. Grayson can *dance*.

The music stops, and I try to catch my breath as we slowly pull apart.

"There," he says. "Happy?"

I grab the wall, my head still spinning. "Where'd you learn to do that?"

Everyone is watching us. Henry claps, and then they all join in. My skin heats as I search for Caleb and find he's now the one staring warily at Grayson.

Grayson's gaze bounces across the room like a cornered animal's.

"My mom made us take lessons ever since I was six."

His tone has changed, and I follow his line of sight to Geri, who's checking her phone in her bag at the other side of the room. He squints a little, then spins away, his mouth pulled tight.

"I know that girl," he says.

Alarms blare between my temples. Geri will have prepared for what to do when she's inevitably recognized, but I'm unsure how Grayson will react.

"Oh yeah?" I say.

He scowls. "We used to . . . hang out."

"Right," I say slowly, because with an explanation like that we both know it was a little more than "hanging out." I glance toward Caleb, hoping Grayson doesn't find it suspicious that he knows three people in a school composed of twenty students.

Might be better to poison that idea before it takes root.

"At least you know people here already," I tell him, as shouts for an encore performance rise around us. "When I came, I didn't know anyone. I guess you rich kids all run in the same circles."

He huffs, enough to tell me he buys this answer. Still, he seems offended by the smiling faces and applause of the others. His jaw sets, and his hands ball into fists. With a shake of his head, he strides toward the exit.

I race after him.

"What's going on?" I ask. "You were great back there."

He keeps walking, shoving through the glass doors.

"Grayson." I jog to keep up. "Everyone wants to meet you."

"I'm sure."

"They do. They're nice. You'll like them. Just give them a chance."

He stops, and his glare is searing. "I'm not here to make friends." With that, he stalks away, and doesn't look back.

AT THREE O'CLOCK, Moore drives me to Uptown. On the way, I get a new ID that says *Jaime Hernandez* and a reminder that my phone both records conversations and takes pictures.

Thanks, Dad.

I pull at the hem of my sweater, hoping that I'm dressed nicely enough in these fitted charcoal pants and tall black boots I borrowed from Charlotte's closet. It's not exactly the low-cut T-shirt Mom wears to the Gridiron Sports Bar, but neither is the clientele. According to The Loft's website, club members pay a yearly fee that could buy me any one of the cars in the garage at Vale Hall.

These people have money, and power, and the sooner I find what Dr. O needs on Jimmy Balder, the better, because I'm making exactly zero headway with Grayson.

"The office workers usually come up for drinks around six," Moore says as he pulls the SUV up against the curb. The Loft is in the business district, several blocks away from the lake and the shops on the Riverwalk. It sits on the roof of a gleaming silver office building with tinted windows and doormen that look suspiciously like Secret Service. "You'll be looking for a guy named Mark Stitz. He's Sterling's intern supervisor—came straight out of his own college internship a little less than a year ago. He would have worked with Balder."

I'm already looking up pictures on Mark's social media feeds. Mostly ridiculous selfies of him in suits, white-blond hair gelled back in an attempt to look sexy. Judging by how perfectly staged these shots look, I'm guessing he's not as confident as he's trying to appear.

I file that away for later.

"The evening manager at The Loft is a woman named Jessica Barton. If she wonders why you didn't interview in person, it's because your aunt went to college with the senator's wife."

I nod, letting the cover story evolve in my mind. My aunt's name is Lucia. She lives in Michigan now but still exchanges Christmas cards with Mrs. Sterling.

"Your application says you're eighteen and have experience working in a diner," he says.

"The good senator won't be making a surprise visit, will he?" I eye the door, trying to catch a peek inside of what looks to be a very fancy lobby. I can't forget that the senator knows my face, and has seen me with his son. If he senses I'm here for the wrong reasons, he might send the same people after me he sent after Grayson.

"He's in Washington."

I snort. "Guess he's not so worried about his kid."

Moore's quiet a moment.

"Men like him let other people do the worrying."

I can't help but think he might be talking about Dr. O.

With a nod, I'm out the door, ankles wobbling in the stupid heels of these boots as the doorman ushers me inside. The lobby is glass and metal, not unlike the Sterlings' house, and behind a front desk is a sign that says, *Macintosh Building, a Sterling Property.*

Of course it is. He already has his campaign headquarters and private club here. Social programs, restaurants, even various historic buildings are part of the senator's renovation and revitalization plan. Matthew Sterling has embedded himself so deeply into the heart of Sikawa City, you can't go very far in any direction without seeing his name on a plaque, or a fountain, or a billboard.

But right now, being here, it feels like I've just been swallowed by a monster.

In front of the elevators, carefully tucked out of view, is a metal detector. A woman in a green suit jacket checks my ID, then types the name into a laptop on the desk behind her.

"First day at The Loft?" she asks after a moment.

"That's right." I can convince anyone I'm someone else, but lying to people with badges makes my palms sweat.

She motions me through the machine and scans my bag with a wand. It's more like the gateway to prison visitation than the entrance to a political office.

"Have a good afternoon, Jaime," she says, and hands me a temporary pass to hang around my neck.

Head high, I stride toward the elevators, exhaling only when the mirrored doors close and I'm alone inside.

I've got this.

Get in, and get out.

With a chime, the doors open on the roof above the tenth floor, and I step out onto a terrace walled with cascading vines and exotic plants, and covered by a vaulted glass ceiling. A stone walkway leads past a koi pond, and with an appreciative whistle, I walk over the small arched bridge toward a hostess station.

And am immediately thrown back by Grayson's face.

The framed picture hangs from the wall behind the dark wood station. His father's featured, too, one arm tossed comfortably over his son's shoulder, but my gaze bounces off Matthew and lands back on the boy with the sharp blue eyes. He's smiling, and without the pinch of his jaw or the subtle strain in his neck, he looks younger, and happy.

This must have been taken before Susan Griffin died.

"That's his son, Grayson."

I turn sharply to my left to find a girl about my age approaching from the kitchen door. She's pretty—model pretty—with dark eyes and long lashes, and the kinds of curves people write songs about. A slim white button-down meets a short black skirt, black stockings, and heels higher than mine.

She sizes me up, then focuses on the picture.

"But I guess you probably knew that already, didn't you?"

CHAPTER 8

All the blood seems to rush to my head, and I grip the strap of my bag a little tighter.

"Why would I know that?" I ask the girl now standing beside me admiring Grayson and his father.

"I mean, he looks just like his dad, right?"

Right. I deliberately take the edge out of my voice and force myself to breathe.

"He does," I say. "It's kind of spooky."

She makes a sound of agreement, and glances to my temporary badge. "You must be our new hostess. Jessica said to keep an eye out for you. I'm Myra Fenrir."

She holds out a hand. I shake it.

"Jaime Hernandez." I glance up as a waiter comes speeding out of the kitchen to the left, carrying a fancy cheese tray and wearing the same white-and-black ensemble as Myra. He's older than us, and gives me a fake smile as he passes.

"Pierre, this is Jaime, the new girl," Myra says.

"Great," says Pierre. "Another cute college girl to steal my tips."

He does not sound pleased. I get it. Mom always complains when new waitresses come in and take her regular tables.

"Relax. She's taking the hostess position." Myra rolls her eyes as Pierre snorts and hurries away. "You go to Sikawa State?"

I'm not sure what exactly my application has said about my availability, so . . . "I do."

"Me too." She smiles and steps out from behind the hostess stand. "What's your major?"

I take a subtle glance around the floor for anyone who might work for Sterling's campaign seated in the pavilion beyond. "Political science."

"No way, me too!"

Great.

"Have you had Professor Garrison? I had her for diplomacy in the fall. She broke down foreign trade with Europe into song form and it changed my life."

That seems a bit dramatic, but sure.

"I haven't had her yet," I say. "I've just taken the intro classes. But my mom campaigned for the president, and it kind of got me hooked on government."

Her eyes light up. "Well, you're in the right place. Senator Sterling's staffers come up here for meetings like every day."

Cue excitement. "Really?" And since we're already nerding out on poli-sci, I add, "Do you know any of them?"

"A few." Her lips pinch together so quickly I almost miss it, then she smirks. "They're great tippers. Well, most of them."

I smile, genuinely. I've just made a new fake best friend.

She tilts her head toward the kitchen. "Come on. Jessica—she's our manager—got stuck in traffic, but she said I could get you set up."

I follow Myra through the swinging doors into a brightly lit kitchen, filled with steel appliances, savory scents, and servers in the same outfit as Myra, bustling around.

"Watch it," snaps a woman carrying a basket of fancy breads, and Myra and I smash against the doors of a walk-in fridge to get out of her way.

"Don't take it personally," Myra says. "People have to move fast back here. Have to keep the customer happy."

"I get it," I say. "It was the same at the diner I worked at."

"Oh good," she says as we turn a corner around an empty office, into a hall lined with lockers. She opens the second one and pulls out a giant to-go cup of coffee from the shop I saw across the street. "This is basically the same thing except everyone you seat probably owns a private jet."

"Then I'll fit right in," I say.

She chokes on her drink, then laughs as she puts it away. "Jessica had your uniform brought up. I hope it fits—"

"Myra!" shouts a man from the kitchen—Pierre, I think. "Where are you? There's no one greeting!"

Myra winces and rushes to a locker at the end, where she pulls out a black dress wrapped in plastic on a hanger. I wasn't aware there was a uniform involved—Moore better have gotten my size right when he submitted my application.

"You're supposed to get a full orientation and training, but we're kind of in a crunch today . . ."

I take the dress off her hands. "I'll be out in five."

She nods gratefully as Pierre shouts her name again, then races back toward the kitchen.

The bathroom is opposite the lockers, and I quickly change out of my outfit and squeeze into the black wrap dress that falls just above my knees. It clings to curves I didn't know I had, and when I shimmy into the black tights and slide my feet into the heels, I feel my new alias slide into place.

Jaime Hernandez is ready to work.

I stride out of the bathroom, chin high, stash my clothes into the locker, and hurry back through the kitchen. This time no one snaps at me to get out of their way. I look like I belong, act like I belong, and in a con, that's all that matters.

Myra's at the hostess station when I arrive, and she gives me a thirty-second rundown of the menu, the layout of the pavilion, and the guest list, organized by photo on the electronic screen out of view and cued by the member's card. Everyone is to be greeted by name and given their choice of table when possible, and if anything goes wrong, I'm to apologize immediately and profusely, and grab one of the senior serving staff to make it right.

Sounds easy enough.

I've seated Mrs. Morris, a woman with a rat-like dog named Belvedere in her handbag, and am returning from escorting two men in designer suits to a table by the indoor fountain when I see three guys waiting at the front. One is engrossed in his phone. The other two are arguing, and I hope that doesn't have anything to do with my brief absence.

I set my smile as I approach, and feel the kick of adrenaline when the guy with the phone glances up and meets my gaze.

Mark Stitz.

The pictures online don't exactly do his sour expression justice. He looks like he's been waiting two hours, not two minutes.

"Mr. Stitz," I say, reaching for the menus. "I'm Jaime. How are you today?"

"We have a room in the back," he says bluntly. The two behind him barely look up, still engaged in a heated discussion.

"Of course." I grab the menus, just appetizers, or *tapas*, according to Myra, and lead them through the pavilion, beneath the glass roof I'm told opens in the summer. The meeting room is blocked from view by a wall, and the heavy oak table isn't set like the others.

"Let me get some plates," I say as Mark sits down. He doesn't look up from his phone.

"Hello boys." Myra glides into the room, pushing a silver tray of tapas—fancy flatbreads with fresh herbs and meatballs in a delicious-smelling sauce. The plates and utensils are on the shelf beneath it. "I see you've met Jaime."

She's not talking to Mark, but to the two guys still arguing just inside the entrance. The taller one, wearing a snug University of Illinois shirt and a cardigan, waves in my direction.

"That's Ben," Myra says as I help her unload the plates on a table in the corner. Her chin tips to the other guy, who has a patchy beard and a beret. "He's Emmett. They're interns at UI. They've been fighting over flower arrangements since lunch."

Ben sets his laptop on the table. I can practically see the steam coming out of his ears.

"Emmett says they should be white. White tulips. For a parks benefit, outdoor, on the lake." Ben scoffs like this is unheard of.

"Who doesn't like white tulips?" argues Emmett. "They're classy. Matt's classy. It fits his image."

I stiffen at the casual use of Sterling's name.

"It would if his image were smug and pretentious," mutters Ben.

Myra gives me a look that says *told you so*.

I stifle a small laugh, and Ben wheels on us.

"What do you think? What does Senator Sterling stand for? White tulips or stupid pink Easter tulips?"

I glance between them, not wanting to say the wrong thing five minutes into my first contact. From the back of my mind, I dredge up my weekend's research about the bills Sterling supports and what his campaign is about.

"I thought he stood for family first values and revitalizing the city," I say.

Emmett nods, impressed. Ben cheers and gives me a high five.

Mark looks up from his phone.

Bingo.

"We've got a new intern," Emmett tells him.

"I hope she does a better job than you two," he says. He returns to his phone, but as I head toward the door, I catch him watching me out of the corner of his eye, his gaze settling a bit too low for comfort.

"For what it's worth," I say quietly to Emmett as I pass, "I'm not sure dead flowers are a great way to promote parks. What about something you can plant?"

Emmett points at me. "*Sustainability.* I like her. I like her more than you, Ben." He pulls his phone out of his pocket and dials a number.

"Same," says Ben.

Step one, establish rapport. *Check.*

"Well you certainly made a good first impression," Myra tells me outside the room. "You even got Mark Stitz's attention. I've been working here since the beginning of summer and the most he's done is checked out my legs."

I cringe. This explains her tension when she'd told me some people were good tippers, and some weren't.

"How many interns work for Sterling?" I ask.

She stops at the bar and grabs a dewy carafe of water. "Six or seven. They rotate in from different colleges. I helped out on the Greener Tomorrow initiative last summer for one of my classes. That's how I met Emmett and Ben."

Her enthusiasm is clear, and it makes me think of Jimmy Balder. Was he this passionate before he disappeared?

"I'm sure they needed your help with all the staff coming and going."

She glances at me over her shoulder, one brow quirked, and I kick myself for not having a smoother transition. I just met Myra; I need to build rapport before she tells me anything.

But I don't want to be here longer than I have to be.

"The interns, I mean," I add. "You said they rotate through a lot. It's got to be hard to count on people knowing they don't stick around."

She's heading to one of her tables, but slows at this, and I swear, there are shadows beneath her eyes that weren't there before.

"They leave when their internships end. I'm sure they all don't quit or something."

She's defensive. That's a good sign there's something there, but I can't push until I know her better.

"Sorry," I say. "Just wondering if I actually have a shot as one of Sterling's interns."

She nods slowly, then her eyes brighten. "I'm sure you do. And if not, there's a ton of volunteer positions."

"Great," I say, then excuse myself to greet two women in Senator Sterling T-shirts approaching the hostess station.

The conversation may have hit a wall for the moment, but Myra Fenrir knows something, and I intend to find out what.

CHAPTER 9

We hit traffic on the way home, which adds another hour onto the drive. Because we're starving, Moore swings into a fast-food drive-through and grills me on what I learned over chicken strips and fries.

"Nothing yet," I tell him.

I met Jessica, the manager, after Sterling's group left. She's a gorgeous redhead who has some strong feelings about me using my supposed connections to get the job, and made it clear that she doesn't have to keep me just because of who I know. For the rest of my shift, she watched me very closely, correcting my posture when I walked and reminding me to smile until my jaws ached. The night ended with a lecture on confidentiality.

You'll hear all kinds of things said in The Loft, she said. *They're not gossip material. The reason our members feel safe talking openly here is because they can depend on the staff's discretion. Understand?*

No problem. I'm only reporting everything I find to a man building a missing person case against the senator. I'm sure that won't upset her in the slightest.

Back at Vale Hall, everyone has eaten and scattered, and I dodge upstairs to change clothes before I run into Grayson and have to make up a reason why I'm dressed this way.

When I'm back in sweats and a long-sleeved T-shirt, I head

upstairs to knock on his door, but his room is open, and he's not lying in the unmade bed.

Pulse racing, I jog back down the stairs, looking for Charlotte, or Caleb, or any of the others who might have seen him. I check the kitchen, but it's empty. Joel and Paz are making out in the study, which I didn't really see coming, so I duck outside, but I don't see Grayson on the path to the garden where we talked before.

Worry quickens my steps. PE did not go well earlier—I never should have left when he was upset. He could have waited until the house was quiet, then snuck out the front door. Or maybe he came downstairs searching for me and instead faced a room full of staring faces. I've seen Grayson in social situations—like at his party, the first night I met him. He doesn't do small talk. I should have told him I was going out for a little while.

He could be gone already, and even if I was working, I can't help feeling like that's on me.

Voices filter up from the pit—maybe someone down there has seen him. I hurry through the dining room toward the basement steps, the familiar engine growl of *Road Racers* growing louder as I descend.

Everyone's gathered around the TV, cheering for cars six and eight as they round the final stretch of the muddy track. Their backs are to me, but I don't have to see their faces to know who's playing.

Car eight is Henry. Car six is Grayson.

I come up behind them, but no one looks up except Geri, who flicks her straight, dark hair over the shoulder of her designer tee, and gives me a look that says *nice of you to show up.*

My gaze shoots to Grayson, who's sitting forward on the couch, banging his thumb against the controller like a drummer in the midst of a solo, and actually grinning.

Like he's having fun.

As I watch, Henry pushes his shoulder, a deliberate attempt to unseat his lead. Grayson mutters a curse but wins anyway.

He throws his arms up in victory while Henry groans and falls back against the cushions. Beth, Alice, and Bea, all juniors with Geri, cheer on one side, Charlotte whoops on the other. Sam, sitting on the floor between Charlotte's knees, reaches up to give Grayson a fist bump.

Caleb is nowhere to be seen.

Grayson is hanging out with my friends. I have had dreams that aren't as surreal as this moment.

"Nice job," I say.

At this, everyone turns around to face me, and my cheeks light up like a stoplight. Apparently I was wrong to think Grayson couldn't handle this place alone. He's blended in just fine—too fine, and now everyone's staring at me like I'm the one who doesn't belong.

"What's up?" Grayson's ears turn pink, and he tosses the controller on the cushion like he just got caught stealing it.

Charlotte glances to Henry. Henry sinks in his seat. Geri's grimace could rival the Wicked Witch of the West's. Everyone seems to be waiting for my response.

This may be awkward, but Grayson's doing exactly what he should be—fitting in. He's comfortable, and I can't chance ruining that, so I push whatever weirdness I feel aside and play the part.

The grin comes easily. I tie my hair back with a band around my wrist.

"I call next," I say.

The room breathes a collective sigh of relief.

"This should be good," says Geri as I come around the front of the couch. "Brynn's barely better than Henry."

"Hey," objects Henry, but he passes me the controller. I wedge between him and Grayson, sandwiched so tightly our thighs are all touching. Geri hands Grayson the controller, which he takes, elbowing me playfully, but tentatively, out of his way.

We pick our cars, and as the engines rev, he leans close and whispers, "Where were you? I got a note in my pocket to meet here."

"A note?" My gaze switches to Henry, who has a fun habit of planting things on other people. When he catches me looking, he smiles broadly, and tips his head toward Grayson, as if I should be impressed with what he's accomplished.

"Ah. That wasn't me."

"You don't say." Grayson's staring at the screen, irritated, and it occurs to me I misjudged how difficult it is for him to put on a show. This good time might very well be a cover.

"I had to run out," I say. "Got stuck in traffic. Why? Did you miss me?"

He gives the smallest shrug. "I met the hotel chain heiress and the game coder."

My eyes widen as he nods to Charlotte and Sam. Wonderful. They've chosen aliases. Grayson clears his throat as his eyes flick to Geri. "And I've been catching up with old friends."

Panic flutters in my chest as I pick our track—a snow course through the Alps.

I know why he's unsettled. River Fest, when Geri planted a bag full of drugs on me, wasn't the first time these two met. They knew each other before. They've slept together before.

But Grayson doesn't know I know that.

And Geri would probably cut out my tongue if I let that secret fly.

"I can hear you, you know," says Geri, examining her nails. "Yes, imagine my surprise to find Grayson cruising through the girls' wing. Turns out it's a small world after all."

Charlotte stomps on her foot.

Henry sings the Small World song.

"I told you," Grayson says, "I got turned around."

"I'm sure you did, creeper," says Geri. "Sometimes I get turned around and end up outside a hot girl's bedroom, too. Spoiler alert: it's not going to happen."

Grayson glares at me. I glare at Geri.

"Take it down a notch," I tell her. "I'm sure you got lost in this giant house when you were a new student, too."

Geri sighs. "Loving the female solidarity, as always, Brynn."

"I'm not a new student," Grayson says. "I'm just staying here for a little while so my dad doesn't kill me."

"Oh, me too," says Henry. He pauses a moment later, looking around at the faces all glaring his direction. "I mean . . ."

The room falls silent but for the trucks revving their engines on the television. The sound crackles across my nerves.

Grayson hunches over his knees. "What? It's not like people aren't talking about it."

I think I hear the pipes groan across the property.

"Well, this is fun," says Geri. "While we're discussing homicide, I'd like to remind everyone that if Petal is not returned to me by noon tomorrow, I will be issuing a formal complaint to the director and poisoning the food."

I swallow a cough. Everyone seems to have already heard this threat, including Grayson, who has trained his eyes on the TV in front of him.

Well, well, well. He wasn't cruising through the girls' hall looking for me. He was snatching Petal. That sneaky bastard.

"Maybe you misplaced her," says Charlotte sweetly.

"Don't think you aren't top of my suspect list, Ginger Princess," Geri replies. "Those eyes are green for a reason."

"Because she was born that way?" I can't help smiling. Grayson took the pig. He is the same Grayson, still driven by competition.

And right now he's spinning the controller in front of his knees by the cord. I better get this show on the road before he drowns in small talk.

I bump my knee against his. "So are you ready to lose, or what?"

He grunts, and as the female voice counts down, "Three . . . two . . . one . . ." the others pick their sides and place their bets.

Then we're off, and though I'm not the best at this game, I know how it works now, and even where a few of the extra fuel packs are located. I charge ahead, but Grayson's strategy is different. He aims his car straight at mine, trying to knock it off the road.

"Cheater," I say, making a tight turn around a corner. Grayson slides on the ice out of bounds, but in seconds is back on my tail.

"Go, go, go!" chants Henry, leaping up to point to a jump on the right side of the screen. I take it, but Grayson plows through the wall, taking a hidden shortcut none of us have seen before.

"What is that?" Sam objects. "Hold on. What just happened?"

"It's a shortcut," Grayson says. "Aren't gamers supposed to know this stuff?"

"Not everyone's trying to rush to the finish line," says Charlotte, wiggling her brows.

Out of the corner of my eye I watch Sam drag her to the ground, and her squeals of laughter rise over the game.

"Trying to focus here," I call.

We're in the final stretch, the finish line in view, when Grayson reaches across us with his left hand and covers my eyes.

"No!" I elbow his arm away, but he's laughing, and we both spin out. My fingers tap against the buttons as fast as I can. My tongue sticks out the side of my mouth in concentration. By the time we're back on track, the others are shouting our names. I know Grayson's going to try to knock me out again, so I scramble up to my knees and block his view of the TV with my back.

His left arm latches around my waist, but he doesn't toss me back to my seat—he pulls me down on his lap, holding me there so he can see over my shoulder.

Part of me knows I shouldn't be doing this—that my back

against his chest, and my legs over his, isn't right, but I can't stop. This is the game we're playing, both on the screen and in real life. My number eight car can still pull this out, and with one final effort I beat both thumbs against the controller, chanting, "Come on, come on, come on!"

He hits me from behind at the last second, and we both explode inches from the finish line.

It's then that I realize Charlotte and Sam are quiet, and Henry's back to finger-combing his hair.

I feel Caleb's presence before I see him. It's like a change in the atmosphere, a thinning of the air. I know he's watching me, that he sees me half-strewn over Grayson's lap, and I'm sick now with what this looks like.

"What was that?" His voice is different. I've heard it before—it's the tone he uses when he's on assignment. When the people he cons call him Ryan.

Trying not to make a big deal of it, I slip off Grayson's lap, carefully putting a few extra inches between us. Henry smashes himself against the armrest to make room.

"That . . . was awesome," says Sam, recovering faster than the rest of us. "He found a new shortcut."

Everyone exhales.

Caleb comes around the couch, taking Charlotte's old seat at the edge. "Who's got next?" He barely looks at me.

Henry loosens at my side. This is fine. Caleb knows how to play this.

Grayson tosses him the controller, and Caleb and I battle it out on the desert course. This time I win by a mile, but I'm pretty sure he lets it happen.

We take turns playing again and again until nightfall. We cheer for each other, and laugh, and eat the celery and carrots and chips that Ms. Maddox has left on the bar at the back of the room.

If Caleb notices Grayson's hand on my knee when he gets up to switch seats, or how he keeps glancing at me while we play, he doesn't say a thing.

And neither do I.

CHAPTER 10

I tell Caleb to meet me on the roof that night, but he texts just before ten to say Belk is working on a leaky faucet in the guest bathroom on their floor, which means his path to the attic is blocked. I heard Joel talking about the dripping sound that kept him awake last night, but I can't help thinking it has something to do with what happened earlier in the pit.

I know he's not mad—this is my assignment—but it can't be easy watching me flirt with someone he hates right in front of his face.

I'm making myself blush with creative ways I'll make it up to him tomorrow when there's a quiet knock on my door just after midnight.

Already in my sleep shirt and flannel boxer shorts, I turn on my nightstand light and tiptoe toward the sound, careful to avoid the creaky spot in the carpet near my desk. A giddy rush fills my veins as I peel back the door.

Caleb's snuck out to see me after all. And he's going to be in my *room*.

But Caleb isn't standing in the threshold. Instead, glowing in the pale light from my lamp is a small silver pig, waiting, like a dog, to be let in from outside.

"Petal?"

From the hall comes a creak in the floor, and when I crane my head outside, I find Grayson leaning against the wall beside the door.

"That's a relief," he says. "I had your room narrowed down to one of three. If you didn't answer, I was going to make a run for it."

I snatch Petal off the floor, then grab Grayson's shirtsleeve and drag him inside.

"Quiet," I hiss, shutting the door behind him.

"Wow." His gaze makes a slow path down my body. "Unexpected, but I'm game."

He steps closer. I cross my arms over my chest, halting his approach. Petal's locked in the death-grip of my right fist.

"We have a curfew, you know. You're not even supposed to be in this hall."

"You came to my side earlier."

It isn't his "side." He's only here for a little while.

"That was different."

"How?"

His steel-blue eyes gleam in the low light. From only a foot away, I can see the sharp lines of his jaw, and how his slim T-shirt fits against his chest and waist. He's still wearing jeans, but his feet are bare.

He crosses his arms, mimicking me.

"I was seeing if you were all right," I say.

"The pig and I were doing the same," he replies. "We thought you might be lonely."

Still wary, I drop my guarded stance, holding Petal between us. Grayson's here now, which means I'm on.

"How'd you do it?" I ask.

He grins. "Waited until everyone went to class, then snuck into her room."

"Not very sneaky," I say. "She caught you."

"After the deed was done."

I smirk.

I've never actually held Petal, and doing so now, in my dark room in the middle of the night, feels wrong in all the best ways. The coveted Platinum Pig, the prize of Vale Hall, is currently in my possession.

"What are you going to do with it?" Grayson asks.

"Her," I correct.

"Weird," he says.

My finger trails over Petal's pointed ear, where the paint has grown thin, revealing the pink plastic beneath. As much as I'd like to keep her, I have no doubts Geri will find out and report me for stealing.

"I've got an idea," I say, and add, "You wish," when he glances hopefully at the bed.

Grabbing a scrap of paper and marker from my desk, I use my left hand to write a note, hoping no one will be able to read my penmanship, then show it to Grayson.

"Again," he says. "Weird."

I giggle and grab his elbow, leading him into the hall. One finger pressed to my lips, I urge him on until we're both jogging toward the catwalk opposite the girls' wing, which leads to Belk's and Moore's rooms.

The house is quiet now, all the lights off. The carpet is soft beneath my padding feet as I slow to a stop. Hunkering against a wall, I pull him beside me and point to the nearest door.

"Put it outside that one," I whisper.

"Why am I doing this?" he asks, but in the dark I can see the gleam of his teeth and I know he's smiling.

Taking the pig and the note, he creeps toward Belk's door and places them on the floor before it. Then he knocks once and runs.

A dark thrill surges through me—I didn't tell him to knock, but now that he has, we need to get out of here before we're caught. Running for the stairs that separate the two wings, I hear his stifled laughter and swear under my breath when a door behind us cracks open.

Dodging around the bannister, we huddle on the steps as Belk appears in the threshold of his room, shirtless. His gut overlaps the waistband of his basketball shorts, and his loose black hair hangs down his neck.

With a grunt, he looks right, and left, then down at Petal. He scratches his belly, then picks her up.

A moment later, he's back inside his room, door closed.

"Nice," I whisper, and then realize I'm alone, in the dark, with half my body pressed against a guy who is definitely not my secret boyfriend.

Subtly, I put a few inches between us.

"What now?" he asks, his voice floating through the dark.

"Now we go to bed. Our *own* beds," I add when I hear him snicker.

"No way," he says. "I passed the test. I get to pick the next game."

Wariness crawls over my excitement, and I sink onto the steps.

"It's late," I say.

"Technically, it's early."

I think of Caleb, asleep in his bed right now. He didn't try very hard to sneak out to see me. If Grayson, the king of subtlety, could manage it, I'm sure a trained con artist could make it happen.

I push the thought away.

"What'd you have in mind?"

Again, I see the dull glow of Grayson's teeth as his mouth cracks into a smile.

"The director's office."

Cold fingers trace down my spine.

"What about it?"

"Let's go check it out."

"It's locked."

"You scared?"

"No," I say, genuinely irritated.

"So let's go."

There's no way I'm getting out of this. If I refuse, I ruin the fun. But if I do it, and we get caught, I'm in trouble.

Dr. O's office is off-limits to students when he's not around. He's made that clear.

But Grayson's not really a student. And if I'm helping him, it's only because I'm following Dr. O's orders of making him comfortable, anyway.

"Fine," I whisper.

We make our way down the spiral staircase, and when we reach the bottom, the cold from the marble seeps through my feet and up my legs. The outside light sends a glimmer through the foyer, highlighting the twin black ravens on the pillars bracketing the office door. Maybe I'm being paranoid, but I swear their black stone eyes are watching every move we make.

Grayson pulls something small and metallic out of his pocket, and as I step closer, I see that it's a hairpin.

"Where'd you get that?" I whisper.

"Piper's room." He frowns. "I mean . . . Geri? She said she goes by her middle name now."

"She changes names like she changes outfits," I say with a weak laugh. "You'll get used to it."

"A lot of that going on here," he says, giving me a look that says he hasn't forgotten that I used to be Sarah.

"Don't you ever want to be someone else?" I ask. He doesn't seem too suspicious, but I need to steer him away from the truth about this place, just in case.

"Just every second of every day," he says quietly.

He stares at the curved door handle, trying to find a place to stick the hairpin. Kneeling, he nudges me out of the light with his elbow and examines the lock more closely.

I wonder how many movies he's seen where this actually works. "You need a credit card," I finally tell him.

"How do you know?"

"It's a spring lock." I sigh, remembering our bathroom door at home that always managed to lock from the inside. Mom taught me how to get it open when I was five years old, a skill that may or may not have come in handy over the years.

Grayson stands and pulls a leather wallet out of his back pocket, slipping one of the many cards free. I glance over my shoulder, almost hoping to hear Ms. Maddox on some midnight cleaning mission so we can call this off.

I'm out of luck. She probably went to sleep hours ago.

"I'm not sure it'll work." I can always fake it and pretend I can't pop the lock. He'll never know the difference.

"Is that defeat I hear?" he whispers. "If you're not good enough . . ."

It's an echo from our past, from the first night we met. His party, when I planted licorice on Caleb while we were dancing and challenged Grayson to find his own mark.

I snatch the card from his hand. "I didn't say that."

He wants to play, fine. We'll play.

But he's not taking anything.

I press the card between the jamb and the door until it bumps against the lock. Then I push away, the card nearly breaking as I jiggle the handle.

With a click, it opens.

Beaming, Grayson strides through the door.

I check back over my shoulder, hugging my arms against my body. It's colder down here, the air like an icy breath over my skin. Passing the tablet with the school's motto, he heads toward the desk.

"What are you . . ."

We both freeze at the same time, caught by a soft snore near the fireplace on the opposite side of the room. My eyes have adjusted to the dark, but even so, it's hard to make out the figure lying on the couch in front of Susan Griffin's portrait.

Another murmur, and this time I'm certain it's the director. He's hidden by the back of the couch, but a blanket drapes over the side beside his pale, limp hand.

He's asleep, and I don't ask myself why he's crashing here when he has a house across the property. I back away slowly, keeping my feet silent and my breath still. Grayson's doing the same, his eyes pinned on the director.

Slowly, carefully, we retreat, my heart pounding in my throat as we reach the door and close it softly behind us. I don't breathe until it's shut, and even then, I stop Grayson from speaking with a pointed look. We shouldn't have done this. Even if I have a built-in excuse, it feels like tempting fate. Dr. O gave me a future; I can't risk it doing something stupid like breaking into his office in the middle of the night.

I motion toward the stairs. We climb each step in silence, and once we reach the top, my pulse has slowed enough that I can think.

I didn't know Dr. O slept here—if it was a onetime thing, or if he does it often. All I know is Grayson broke into an office just to see if he could do it, and he looks like he won a million bucks. The boy who's running from his father couldn't be farther away.

This might not have been so stupid after all.

He leans close, and this time I don't back away when he whispers, "I guess you get to pick the next game."

With a grin, he rolls his shoulders back, and leaves me staring at his back as he heads upstairs.

CHAPTER 11

Caleb's waiting for me the next morning at breakfast, but we don't get a chance to talk. Grayson rolls in like a hungover zombie and sits beside me at the dining room table. His presence creates a shift in the atmosphere, turns us all into actors in some reality show. Charlotte, still keeping up the hotel heiress front, complains about the food, saying her private chef in their Boston penthouse only uses organics and non-GMOs. Sam puts on headphones and challenges Joel and Paz to his newest fake game. Caleb asks Grayson about cars, and Grayson grudgingly admits he had a Porsche, which cues Caleb to launch into a story about how his father liked to sketch car engines in his spare time and taught him all the parts by drawing them.

I'm not sure if it's made up or not, but I kind of want it to be true. Still, I'm not sure which is worse—holding on to those memories when your father's strapped to a hospital bed on life support, or barely having any memories of him at all.

"Yeah, that's a sweet story." Grayson leans over his bowl of cereal, resting his head in his hand as he cuts Caleb out of the conversation. "So, last night was fun. What are we doing today?"

My toast gets lodged in my throat, and I cough to swallow. Grayson's tone, and the way his eyes are dipping a little too low, makes it seem like something less than innocent happened last night, but just as I'm about to correct him, my brain overrides the reaction and the words stay trapped behind my teeth.

I've always been able to call Grayson out when he's acting like a jerk, but things are different now. Despite last night, he is more fragile, and he's on my turf. I can't push him away.

Caleb's jaw clenches, then unclenches, and in a blink, the annoyance has vanished from his face. He's good at this—pretending things are fine when they're not, when our home is being invaded by an intruder whom he believes is an active threat to the safety of his girlfriend.

Secret girlfriend.

I shove Grayson playfully. "First, don't be rude. Second, this is a school. I have class."

Caleb leans back in his seat, gaze narrowed on my mark. "You should come."

Grayson scoffs. "No thanks." Lifting his chin, he glances across the table to Caleb, then turns a razor-sharp smile my direction. "Ditch. I'll make it worth your while."

There's a clear intent to his voice, a challenge I'm almost sure isn't reserved for me. Three months ago we were friends—at least, kind of—but it seems he's forgotten that.

I should say something clever, or flirty, *anything*. But I feel pulled in two different directions, and any way I lean will be wrong.

"Students, listen up."

I turn to find Belk striding into the kitchen. He's wearing a shirt, thank everything holy, but I still can't quite shake the image of him answering the door topless last night. From his right hand hangs a plastic supermarket bag.

"First of all, I'd like to remind everyone that curfew is eleven p.m., and you're to be in your rooms, lights out, by midnight on weekdays."

"Yes, sir," says Henry, standing beside him.

"Also, upperclassmen, you need to be working on your form for PE. Next week you'll be tested on the waltz before moving to the paso doble. The winning couple . . ." He pauses to remove the item from the bag he's holding, and a collective gasp fills the room when the silver pig appears in his broad palm. ". . . will be the proud new caretakers of our little mascot."

Henry gasps loud enough to make Belk startle. "Petal," he whispers reverently.

"Wow," says Grayson. "You're all weird."

"Where did you get that?" Geri's voice rises above the others. She's standing in the living room, face beet red, an apple in her hand. Belk better duck—I think she means to chuck it in his direction.

"Anonymous donation," Belk says, clearly not entertained or believing that this is true. "She showed up in the middle of the night with a note that said, *I'm ready for a new home, Love, Petal.*"

Henry gasps again.

I am shaking, trying not to laugh. Beside me, Grayson catches my eye and his mouth tilts in a mischievous grin.

Geri's making serious strides toward making applesauce with her right hand. Her face right now is the stuff dreams are made of.

"There's been a mistake," Geri snaps, but to her credit, doesn't point fingers.

"Take it up with your classmates," says Belk, and then he leaves us to our breakfast.

I can't hold it in any longer. As questions layer one over another of who stole Petal and gave her to Belk, I lower my head and bust up laughing. I don't even care if we get caught at this point. Maybe it's a childish way to get back at her for planting pills on me last summer, but it was worth it.

Grayson's laughing, too, though mostly at me.

"What was that all about?" asks Caleb, his gaze flicking between the two of us. My stomach sinks, the laughter drying in my throat.

"I can only imagine what's so funny over here."

Geri strides in from the living room, still gripping the apple in one hand. Having classes the same place where you live generally means everyone dresses casually, but today she's in a bubblegum-pink sweater that matches her lipstick and jeans that look painted on.

She stops behind Caleb, resting one hand on his shoulder, and immediately I sit up in my chair.

They're not close enough to touch like that. She's up to something.

"Good morning, Geri," says Caleb carefully, glancing at me before looking up at her. Her smooth, dark hair drapes over her shoulder as she grins down at him.

"Hey handsome. We going to practice that dance later? Looks like we have a lot on the line now."

My fork drops on my plate, making a loud clatter.

She's mad about Petal, and she's trying to get even by flirting with Caleb while I can't do anything about it.

Typical Geri.

Grayson relaxes back in his seat. "Are you seriously competing for that plastic pig?"

"Platinum," Geri corrects, then mock pouts at him. "You're not scared, are you?"

"Of that guy?" Grayson motions toward Caleb, then laughs. "You're kidding, right?"

Caleb's jaw flexes.

"Not at all. Caleb's got moves you've never seen." Geri combs Caleb's black hair back with one hand and I scoff. He stares at the wall behind me.

Grayson's arm stretches over the back of my chair.

"Good luck," Geri adds, winking at me. "May the best couple win."

I've got to hand it to her. Geri may be a demon straight from hell, but she just diffused the tug-of-war between Grayson and Caleb. Whatever threat our guest felt from Caleb is eliminated while his attention's focused on another girl.

I still have to kill her, though.

Charlotte can pet Caleb all she wants. Henry can share a sleeping bag with him for all I care. But Geri? No. I don't think so.

Without thinking, I stretch my leg out beneath the table, feeling with my toes until I bump into Caleb's socked foot. His alarmed gaze flicks my way, then back to Grayson.

Feeling brave and reckless and a little stupid, I reach farther until my foot can flex and rise up beside his ankle.

As Geri talks about some ridiculous assignment she has for junior government, Caleb's hand tightens around his fork. I watch, victory simmering into doubt when he doesn't respond. But just as I'm pulling back, Caleb's leg stretches toward me, and his foot slides up my insole, streaking heat up my leg.

I smile at Grayson, but it's for Caleb, and when he brushes the arch of my foot, I give a tiny, inaudible gasp.

I glance across the table, but Caleb's staring intently at his Eggo waffles.

"Okay. It's better than sitting around all day, I guess."

Grayson's words snap me out of my trance, and I pull my foot back beneath my chair.

"What's better?"

"Your stupid class," he says. "I'm going. Just don't expect me to stay awake."

"Great," I say quickly. The flutters in my belly from Caleb's touch turn to a sledgehammer. I glance across the table for help, but Caleb's now cutting his waffles into eight billion microscopic pieces while Geri massages his shoulder with one hand.

Rising, I take my plate to the kitchen. Caleb follows, leaving Geri in the dining room. He doesn't say anything, but I feel his fingertips skim across the small of my back when he passes, and as I take my place beside Grayson, my own hand lingers there, trying to re-create his touch.

WE MEET IN a room on the first floor—the usual location for the junior and senior classes. Instead of chairs and desks, there are sofas and discussion tables. A TV hangs on the wall opposite the door, and opening the burgundy drapes is a birdlike woman in a black frock with gray wavy hair.

"Find a seat," she says as the seniors filter in. There are only five of us—Charlotte, Sam, Henry, Caleb, and me. Six counting Grayson. "We have a lot to cover today, so let's get started."

"Is this it?" asks Grayson, looking around at the empty couches.

"It's a small school." I'm still irritated at him for the way he brushed off Caleb at breakfast and for acting like we're more than what we are.

That's my job.

"You have perfect timing, Mr. Sterling," Shrew says. "We're starting a new section today."

"Lucky me," Grayson mutters, taking a seat on the sofa in the very back of the room. I motion him up. The cool-kid-in-the-back routine doesn't work in a class of six.

With a groan, he rises, then collapses beside me on a couch in the middle of the room. Shrew has already tasked Henry and Caleb with turning the one in front of us so we can all face each other.

"Our next reading includes love and betrayal, jealousy, discrimination, and lies. It involves a decorated military general, a woman who has the gall to stand up to her father to be with him, and a friend, bitter enough to see them both dead." She passes out a stack of paperback books, and I'll admit, my interest is piqued until Charlotte mutters, "Oh good. Shakespeare."

"*Othello*," says Sam, poking her in the side. "You'll like this one—the premise, anyway."

His arched brow makes her chuckle.

"You've read it?" I ask.

"He devours the classics for fun," says Charlotte. "He has a secret spreadsheet where he catalogues and cross-references his favorite literature themes."

Sam balks. "How else are you supposed to keep them straight?"

"Yes, how else?" I ask, making Charlotte snort. Sam probably has the biggest brain here, hence the old SAT gig. I should have paid him to take mine. The longer I wait for results, the more convinced I am I bombed it.

We're tasked with reading through the first few acts aloud, which, due to the Shakespearean phrasing, is kind of like driving off-road without a seat belt. Still, it's going well enough until we reach the third act, when Caleb stands and quietly tells Shrew he has an appointment.

"Carry on," she tells Grayson and motions Caleb to the back of the room, where her roller bag sits beside a table.

As Grayson stumbles though the first few lines, and the way Shrew and Caleb talk, his hands dig into his pockets cues a frown on my lips. Though I can't hear what they're saying, it looks like he's in trouble for something.

Then he nods, and as he heads toward the door, his eyes meet mine. His expression may be serious, but that wink is all for me. It sends a flutter through my chest and reminds me I'm not the only one straddling this line of truth and lies.

He's got his assignment, I've got mine, and when we're done, we'll have more than secret winks and rooftop trysts.

"You're up, Desdemona," says Henry.

My eyes snap back from the door to the book, and I struggle to find my place as Grayson's stare narrows on the side of my face.

My pulse begins to gallop as I struggle.

"Here," he finally says, pointing to a stanza halfway down the page.

"Right. Thanks." I take a deep breath, still aware that he's watching me. I need to be more careful.

"My noble father," I begin.

"Yes?" says Henry in a dignified voice.

"I do perceive here a divided duty. To you I am bound for life and education. You are the lord of my duty, and I am hitherto your daughter."

"But," says Shrew, holding up one finger. *"Here's my husband."* With that she snaps the book shut. "A divided duty. A woman, split in two by loyalty to two different men she loves—her father . . ."

"And her fine black husband," finishes Sam.

"I get it now," says Charlotte, tapping her nose.

Shrew casts them a firm look. "Finish act one tonight on your own, and come up with three discussion questions for tomorrow."

She segues into group time, but I'm still thinking about the look on Caleb's face when he left the room, and the pinch in Grayson's gaze when he saw me staring, and the words I read aloud to the others: *I do perceive here a divided duty.*

TO MY LUCK, Myra is scheduled that afternoon, and I help her fold cloth napkins and refill the salt and pepper shakers in the lull between lunch and dinner. Under the overlord Jessica's watchful gaze, we don't have much chance to talk, and when Sterling's campaign staff shows up at four for a staff meeting, I know it's time to get creative. I need time to get closer to Mark and the staff, and I need Jessica out of the way so I can do it.

Lucky for me, I have a mom who works in food service.

At Gridiron Sports Bar, when you have a rude customer or a bad tipper, things happen to their food. It's not pleasant, or particularly mature, but that's how restaurant life works. So when Mr. Jefferies at table nine orders albondigas soup, and a Band-Aid—a clean one, I'm not a monster—tucked into my sleeve makes it into the bowl as I pass on my way to the employee restroom, The Loft goes into high alert. Jessica is consumed with calming him down. Pierre is screaming at the chef, who's screaming back at Pierre.

And Myra and I have the Sterling staff to ourselves.

The back room is buzzing with activity, and no one seems to notice Myra and me as we hurry to refill waters and the veggie tray against the back wall. From what I gather, they're coming up short on cash for the park fund-raiser, and they need money fast. Half of the staff are on their cell phones making calls, Mark included.

I squeeze behind Emmett and Ben near the wall, listening as Mark flat-out asks for a donation and then stares, annoyed, at the phone when the person hangs up on him.

"Ouch," Ben says quietly. "That's embarrassing."

"Begging for money or making the calls at all?" Emmett asks, his finger trailing down a list of numbers on a printout.

Ben and Emmett already like me—this is as good an entry point as any.

"It might help if he warms them up first. Makes sure they're relaxed."

"I think that's called foreplay," says Myra, clearing empty dishes from their other side.

I snort. "It's called sales."

"We're supposed to ask for money," says Ben with a cringe. "It's so awkward."

"It doesn't have to be." Before Grayson, we all took Vocational Development, aka conning class, at Vale Hall, which involved a lot of sales training.

As it turns out, working a mark is not so different from closing a deal.

"You want to do it, be my guest," says Ben.

"She's too polite," says Emmett, sinking in his chair.

"Only when I have to be." I flash him my best grin. He chuckles. Myra and Ben laugh. Across the table, Mark watches us, his stare pinched.

I lean across Emmett to fill Ben's water. "I bet I can get a bigger tip from one table than you can get in the next hour calling for donations."

"Uh-oh," says Myra. "This sounds like a challenge."

"Deal," says Emmett. "What do I get if I win?"

"I'll donate my tip to your cause." I grin. "And if I win, you all have to buy me dinner."

With a smirk, Emmett picks up his phone. "You're on."

"Careful," Myra warns as I head toward the door, but she's smiling. As soon as I'm out, I've picked my mark. "Mrs. Morris!" I head toward the gray-haired woman in a red blouse, feeding her tiny dog the crust of her bread. "How's Belvedere today?"

An hour later, I've earned a hundred-dollar tip for walking Belvedere and praising Mrs. Morris's hair, and am getting reprimanded by Mark for the effort.

"I don't know why my interns put you up to this," he says, like he isn't only a year or two older than them, "but this is campaign business. We don't need a waitress—"

"Hostess," I correct with a smile. Even though Emmett didn't make a dime, I still handed over my profits in good spirits. I need an in with the team, and now that I've got their attention, I need their secrets. Still, this wasn't exactly the response I was hoping for when I handed a cheering Ben my earnings. So much for impressing the boss.

"Whatever," he says, losing a little more of my respect. He's shorter than me by an inch, with a sliver of a goatee that probably took him months to grow and enough gel in his blond hair to chip a tooth. "What would your boss say if I told her you were soliciting club members on our behalf?"

I cringe internally, positive that Jessica would fire me before she even heard my side of the story.

I can't lose this job—not yet, anyway.

"Please don't tell her," I say, amping up my worry. "I'm so sorry if I screwed up."

He's pulled me out of the meeting room, into the hallway that leads to the bathroom. We're out of sight from the others, but it's just a matter of time before Jessica catches us and asks what's going on.

"I didn't solicit anyone," I continue. "I wanted to donate money I'd earned, that's all."

With a sigh, he pulls me deeper into the shadows, letting his hand linger on the back of my arm. I glance down at it, feeling my pulse tic in my ears.

"Look, you're sweet," he says, and I catch a glimpse through his professionalism to the slime just beneath as he glances over his shoulder to make sure we're alone. "And we could use someone with your . . . skill set."

I bet.

"But . . . and don't take this the wrong way, but a waitress making the guys look bad? It's not good for morale, you get me?"

No, I don't *get* him. First, I'm pretty sure I told him I was a hostess. Second, if I was a wait*er* I doubt we'd be having this conversation right now. Third, he can't honestly think Ben or Emmett or any of the others were threatened by my rake. Emmett gave me a high five and asked me to teach him my Jedi mind tricks.

But I can't challenge Mark and risk him telling Jessica before I know about Jimmy Balder. I'm not here to burn bridges; I've got do whatever I can to make friends.

"I get you." I summon my best puppy dog eyes, because that's clearly the response Mark's hoping for. "I didn't mean to make anyone feel bad. You don't think . . ." I swallow. "You don't think they're mad at me, do you?"

Mark's expression softens. His hand, still cupping my arm, squeezes before sliding away.

If this wasn't a job, I would flatten him.

"I'll talk to them. Smooth it out. And don't worry, I won't tell your manager."

My hero.

But in that instant, I see an entrance that's evaded me up until this moment.

"I knew you'd be a nice guy," I tell him. "Jimmy said I'd like you."

If a weasel could smile, it would look a lot like Mark Stitz, right now. "Who's Jimmy?"

"A friend that used to work for the campaign. Jimmy Balder?"

Mark scoffs. "You should pick better friends."

Pretty solid advice coming from this guy. Still, Mark remembers who he is, and that means I'm on the right track.

"Why do you say that?" I ask.

Mark takes a step back. His dress shirt is too wide for his skinny body, and it makes wings beneath his arms when he puts his hands on his hips.

"I really shouldn't be talking about it, but the guy wasn't exactly Sterling material. Got booted halfway into our primo donation season."

I try to place the timeline in my head. Dr. O said he disappeared before Susan Griffin died, which would have been a year ago, sometime before Christmas.

I frown. "Seriously? I always thought . . . well, given the way he spoke so highly of you . . ."

Mark lifts his chin, staring down his nose at me. "He was decent before he left, I'll give him that."

"So why'd he get fired?"

"You're his friend. You ask him."

I cross my arms over my chest. My concern isn't part of the show.

"It's been a while since I've seen him," I say.

"You and me, both."

"You're the intern supervisor," I say. "You didn't let him go?"

"That's confidential." He's still standing close enough I have to press my back against the wall so I don't accidentally touch him. He may be small, and pathetic, but he's got power here and he knows it. That makes people like him dangerous.

"I'm starting to worry about him. I didn't know he'd been fired. He hasn't answered my calls in a couple months."

Mark's eyes roam to my mouth. The hair rises on the back of my neck.

"What a jerk. You deserve better."

I hide my grin in my shoulder, but only because I know it would look more murderous than flattered. Mark is a necessary evil. I can handle him. I've dealt with worse.

"Some of the interns asked if I want to go to dinner later. I was going to go, but maybe now it's not such a good idea. Unless . . ." Cue pouty look. "Maybe you could come to smooth things over?"

To his credit, a wary look passes over his face. He considers this for half a beat, then nods. "I had plans, but for you I'd make an exception."

I smile. And as I excuse myself to return to my post, I hope that anything I can get out of Mark will be worth the trouble.

CHAPTER 12

We meet at Risa's, a taco joint just around the corner from the Macintosh Building, right after my shift. Since she's already friendly with the interns, I drag Myra along. Most of us walk over together, but Mark insists on driving, either because he's afraid the wind will bust through his concrete-gelled hair, or because he likes the idea of parking his Mustang in a thirty-dollar-an-hour lot where the rest of us can see.

"Please tell me he isn't your date," says Myra.

"Not my date," I assure her. "Needed to make amends after the whole donation scandal." I also need to get to know Mark a little better, and I'm not going to be able to do that in a meeting setting, where he's busy playing top dog. An activity away from work might help him relax a little, and I have exactly zero interest in meeting this creeper alone.

"Good, because if it was, we were going to have a serious talk about setting a higher bar." She links her arm through mine as Mark hits the key fob three consecutive times, making his car honk so we all know it's his. "Wish my daddy bought me a Mustang for Christmas."

"Wish I had a daddy."

Her face snaps my direction. "Ouch." She laughs.

I smirk, grateful that this rolled off without question. For a second, I forgot that I was Jaime Hernandez, college girl and senator-intern wannabe.

"Seriously, though," she says. "Careful being too friendly with him. Ever wonder why there aren't more female interns?"

I had noticed that there appear to be a plethora of white males in the meeting room, with the exception of Myra and me.

She leans closer. "I heard they all quit because they can't stand him."

"Maybe he's misunderstood," I try.

"Yeah. I'm sure that's it." Her sarcasm is heavy enough to drown us both.

As we head inside, I'm hit by a blast of hot air and a wave of regret that this friendship with Myra is only pretend. In some alternate universe, I can see us hanging out, getting one of those snooty coffees she likes or going to the movies.

But that's not my life, and I'm playing her just like I'm playing Mark.

"Table for seven," Mark says, pushing through the line to join our group. Ben hasn't even reached the hostess yet to tell her, but I'm pretty sure he could have managed that simple math without Mark's help.

The hostess only smiles, the way I'm sure I must have the first time I escorted Mark to the meeting room at The Loft. Though I never would have noticed or cared before this job, I watch the way she bobbles the menus and think of how Jessica would run me up the wall for appearing so disorganized.

We remove coats and gather around a large table near the front window. Outside, Moore is waiting somewhere in his car for my call, but I can't see the SUV in the street traffic. If I could drive, he wouldn't have to watch over my shoulder all the time.

Not that I mind. The truth is, I don't hate having him around.

Mark takes the head of the table and I sit to his right. Myra sits beside me, and while Emmett runs over margarita options with our supervisor, she pulls the chip basket between us.

"So," she says, taking a crunchy bite. "What's going on? How're your classes? I can't believe I've never seen you on campus."

I take a chip. "I'm taking a lot of the intro courses online."

"I've never done online classes. You still have to do fieldwork, right?" she asks, tying her long black hair into a bun. She steals the salsa from Ben just before he dunks a chip and sets it next to our private basket.

I nibble on the corner of my chip, an image of Dr. O, standing in front of the portrait of his sister, flashing through my head. "I will eventually. Right now it's just me and my laptop."

She's looking at me, brown eyes round and inquisitive. I focus on the chips.

"Seems like a lot of pressure," she says. "Just you and your assignments every day."

The word rings through my body, like an out-of-tune string plucked on my stupid guitar.

"It's not that bad."

Myra grins. "I guess there is the added benefit of going to class in pajamas."

I force a smile. Myra's controlling the conversation. I need to shift the tide.

A girl with a nose ring and thick black eyeliner comes by to fill our waters. She's goth from head to toe with the exception of a red T-shirt that says *Risa's* in curly script.

"You want something to drink?" Goth Girl asks.

"Water's fine," I tell her.

"She goes any slower, you girls are going to have to take over," mutters Mark, loud enough that Goth Girl can hear over the piped in music. She stiffens, eyes narrowing the slightest bit.

Myra and I laugh weakly.

The guys order drinks, and when Goth Girl is gone, an uneasy quiet settles over the table. The college interns keep checking their phones. Myra chats with Ben about the finale of *Pipes*, the singing competition on TV Geri, Beth, and Alice never miss. Mark keeps making snide comments about the service and how we should get the waitstaff in line. I get the sense things would go a lot easier if the boss wasn't here, which doesn't exactly set me up for the Most Likable New Friend award.

But I need more information, and Mark's already admitted to knowing Jimmy Balder.

"I called Jimmy," I tell him. Beside me, Myra goes still, probably wondering what I possibly have to talk to Mark about.

"Good for you." He laughs unsteadily and looks to Emmett, who's still staring at his phone. The others don't see Mark's insecurity, or how much he wants to be liked. They just see the jerk in charge.

Which he is.

"He didn't pick up," I say. "I called his house, but no one answered there, either."

"Sounds like he's trying to tell you something."

Another waitress comes back with their alcohol, delivering both a drink and a shot to Mark. As Goth Girl returns to refill our waters, Mark downs the shot in one gulp. He slaps the small glass on the table, which surprises Goth Girl, and she spills some of the water she's pouring, splashing Mark in the chest.

"Are you kidding me?" he hisses. She hands him a napkin, which he snatches out of her hand.

Bad idea to be nasty to the people who serve your food—you might just find a Band-Aid in your soup. Still, I wince, like I'm sorry that it happened.

"I don't think he's dodging me," I say when Goth Girl's gone. "I think something's wrong."

"Wrong with what?" asks Ben from the other side of the table.

Mark is still dabbing at the water on his shirt like it's permanent black ink.

"I can't get in touch with a friend of mine," I say. "He worked on Sterling's campaign last year."

"Yeah?" asks Ben. "What's his name? I started after Christmas."

"Jimmy Balder."

"Jimmy? Yeah. I remember that guy," says Ben. "Tall guy. Super funny." He bumps Emmett on the shoulder. "Wasn't Jimmy the one who got that lady to donate five thousand dollars at the art gallery fund-raiser last spring? Didn't even know her, and by the end of the night she was writing a check."

Myra chokes on the water she's drinking, her face turning red. "Wow," she manages. "And I thought your hundred-buck tip for walking the dog was good."

My gaze shoots to Mark, hoping he didn't catch that.

"I think it was more," says Emmett. The two interns at the end—Beckett and Nick—break from their conversation to join the party.

"Fifty-five hundred," says Mark flatly.

No wonder Mark's pissed that Jimmy left during donation season. The guy was raking in the dough.

"Heard he got a job in Washington," says Emmett. "Working for some House Republican."

I glance to Mark, who's staring at his empty shot glass. Apparently not everyone knows Jimmy was fired, which seems odd with a tight group like this.

"No," says Ben in disbelief. "He wanted to do social programs, didn't he? No way he'd sell out for Washington." He frowns, then whips out his cell phone, typing at lightning speed with his thumbs.

"Maybe he pissed someone off," I suggest.

"No way," says Ben without looking up. "Everybody liked that guy."

"He was the best intern I trained," Mark interjects.

"Didn't he start before you?" asks Emmett. Ben laughs down at his phone as they high-five.

Mark's lips pull taut across his teeth. He pounds back his drink fast enough to make even the boys cringe, then raises his hand to the waitress for a refill.

Mark may be a sleaze, but I can't let him be eaten by wolves. Not until he gives me what I need.

"Careful," I say. "Your boss is going to make you answer Sterling's hate mail if you talk enough smack."

Emmett chuckles dryly, as if this is probably true.

I kick Mark under the table. He jumps, then looks my direction.

I tilt my head toward the others. If he wants to be liked, he should at least try to make himself likable.

"That's right," says Mark. "And . . . and I'll send you to Mrs. O'Leary's house to personally invite her to the Greener Tomorrow benefit."

Ben tosses his head back and cries, "No!"

Emmett cackles. A happy, booze-fueled flush rises in Mark's cheeks. Everyone's smiling but Myra, who's staring blankly at the others like she hasn't a clue what just happened. Even Goth Girl, who's back to bring more chips, doesn't look quite so annoyed as she squeezes by Mark to get an empty basket.

Probably because, with a subtle turn of her wrist, she lifts his wallet right out of his back pocket as she moves past.

I quickly look away, torn by what just happened. I need Mark on my side, but there's code with cons. We don't rat each other out.

"Who's Mrs. O'Leary?" I ask as Goth Girl speeds back to the kitchen.

"One of Matt's favorite people," says Mark, and again I'm thrown by the use of the senator's first name. "She comes to all the events to donate her bingo money and has been known to—"

"Accost the interns," says Ben.

"That's an exaggeration," Mark says.

"She sat on my lap!" He covers his face with his hands. "An eighty-year-old woman sat on my lap."

"Most action you've seen in a while, I guess," says Emmett.

"Well, yes," says Ben, and even Mark laughs. "Here it is." He shows Emmett his phone, and Emmett grins. "That's him. Jimmy B. Good guy."

I nearly leap out of my chair reaching across the table for the phone, and when I accidentally lock the screen he has to give me the keycode to open it back up.

The photo shows three people in black tuxes, arms slung around each other's shoulders. Ben is on the left, Emmett in the middle, and on the right is a good-looking guy about the same age. He's leaning forward a little, his mouth half open as if laughing.

I'm here because of him.

Because he disappeared.

This guy, that everyone liked. That Mark fired for some reason.

In a beat, it becomes hard to look at him. I peel my gaze away, realizing I was staring. Beside me, Myra was, too.

She clears her throat. "You all look nice. Was that at a party?"

I glance down again, seeing there are other people behind them in the photo. A woman in a yellow gown. A man with slicked-back black hair whose arms look like sausages stuffed inside his suit jacket.

"A fund-raiser at the art gallery on Fifth," says Ben. "I don't remember a lot about it, if I'm being honest." He takes another drink, and everyone laughs.

I pass the phone back to him. "Can you send me that? Jimmy looks great in it." He gets my number as the waitress returns with another drink for Mark.

The front door opens, and from the corner of my vision, I catch the profile of a guy with raven-black hair and glasses. In an instant, my lungs cram straight into my throat, and I jerk so hard the opposite direction, my chair screeches on the floor.

"You all right?" Myra asks.

"Yep. Yes. Why?"

She looks back toward the door, but Caleb is gone.

Panic rises in my chest. It's not just that his presence could potentially blow my cover on a job, it's that there's no reason for him to be here, now, unless he followed me.

As the waitress comes back to take our order, I tell Myra to get me pork tacos. Then I excuse myself to the restroom. Cutting through the growing crowd by the door, I search for Caleb, but he's not by the hostess stand or down the hallway to the restrooms. I scan the bar, but he's not there, either.

Stepping outside into the cold, I look up and down the street. It's almost dark, but the sidewalks are crowded, and there's enough light from the restaurants and shops to see.

A hand closes around my biceps, making me jump, but it's not Caleb, it's Mark.

"What are you doing out here?" he asks.

"Nothing." I look behind me, but no one's followed. There's now a crowd gathered outside Risa's and enough voices raised in conversation to block out ours. "I thought I saw someone I knew. I was wrong, though."

"Oh." He glances back at the door. "You having fun?"

"Yeah." I smile.

Where the hell is Caleb? Maybe I didn't really see him. Maybe I'm imagining things.

"Good," Mark says, as if he's the reason why. There's a goofy smile on his face, and I remember he's been drinking. "I didn't want to say this in front of the others, but you were right about Jimmy."

He's got my full attention now.

"How's that?"

"Matt didn't like him."

A couple standing in line to get inside bumps against him, and he motions us toward the street.

"The senator told you that?"

"Let's go over to my car," he says. "I don't want anyone else hearing this."

He must think I'm pretty stupid to fall for that one.

"No one's listening here," I say, motioning to all the people on their phones or talking to their friends.

He shakes his head. "This isn't something Matt wants getting out."

Damn. Damn it all to hell.

"Just across the street," I tell him.

He heads into traffic without looking both ways, and I throw up a hand to wave at a driver who stops before running him over. We make it to the opposite sidewalk without dying and soon are standing in the shadowed lot, behind his Mustang.

Out of habit, I keep my eyes roaming, and stand more than an arm's length from Mark. I wish I had my knife, but I can't take it through the metal detector at the office. It's just me and my cell. At least Moore can track it and knows where I am.

I look around again for Caleb but don't see him. Maybe he wasn't following me after all.

"You have to be eighteen to work at The Loft, right?" he asks.

"That's the rule." A chill crawls over my skin. Nothing about this is okay. "So what happened with Jimmy and the senator?" I flash to Jimmy's face, warped with laughter.

"Shh." Mark holds a hand to his lips and beckons me closer.

Reluctantly, I lean in.

"He told me not to tell anyone."

"Who? The senator?"

Mark reaches for my arm, sweaty hand closing around my wrist. I jerk back automatically, but he doesn't let go.

"Come here," he says. "You want to hear or not?"

A warning pounds through my temple. I try to shake his hand free, but he grabs on with the other and laughs, like we're playing a game.

"Let go," I tell him, trying to wrangle free from his hard grip. My joints crack as I try to get loose.

"What's wrong with you?" he says, worry warping his expression as he searches the lot. "You're making a scene."

He drags me out of the light, telling me to calm down.

"Mark, let go!"

A rushing fills my ears, so loud that I miss the sound of footsteps running toward us until they stop right behind me.

"She said let her go."

I turn, and there in the streetlight, wearing his leather jacket and a look of cold, hard fury, is Caleb.

CHAPTER 13

This is bad.

Like plane-crash-on-a-desert-island bad. Like just-fell-down-a-mine-shaft bad.

Caleb shouldn't be here. He and Mark should not cross paths.

"We're good." I put on a cheery smile. "Thanks for stopping by."

"Maybe you didn't hear her." Caleb's tone is light, conversational, but laced with threat.

"Maybe *you* didn't hear her," Mark tosses back. "She said get lost."

He slings an arm over my shoulder. Now I can smell the alcohol on his breath, and I can't help turning my face away. He smells like volatility, like ticking time bombs. Like my mom's old boyfriend, Pete.

"What's wrong with you?" Mark asks for the second time in two minutes, only now the question's directed at Caleb. It makes me think of this thing my mom used to say. How if you wake up in the morning and someone's a jerk, they're the one with the problem. But if you wake up and everyone's a jerk, surprise! Time to take a look in the mirror.

"Let go of her," Caleb says.

I glare at him. He can't blow this for me. I can turn this around. I've dealt with worse.

At the same time, there's a sob burning my throat, and all I want to do is shove Mark away, grab Caleb's hand, and run until I can't breathe.

My words are automatic: "Really. We're good here."

He steps closer.

I hold a hand out, and it stops him in place.

"We're friends," I say clearly.

"That's right," says Mark. "If you don't get out of here, I'm calling the cops."

Caleb's stare tears from Mark to me, questions and anger in his eyes.

"Can I walk you back to the restaurant?" Caleb reaches a hand toward me.

I stare at it, jumping when Mark slaps it away.

"You followed us over here. You a . . . a stalker or something?"

I need to get him out of here before he does something stupid.

"Let's go back inside," I say.

"I'm not sure it's safe with all these stalkers roaming around." Mark looks back at his car slowly, his moves more exaggerated with each moment that passes. He probably pounded back the second drink just as fast as the first.

"Let's go." He pulls his keys out of his pocket, still keeping his arm over my shoulders.

"Mark, that's not a good idea."

"Come on." His voice is louder. More irritated.

Caleb tilts his head. "You're drunk."

"No one asked you, stalker," spits Mark.

He tries to turn me toward the car, and when I resist, he pushes me. It isn't hard; I don't even fall, but it's the last straw for Caleb.

He's between us in a second, shoving Mark into the back of his car. Mark bounces off the trunk and hits the ground hard, but Caleb doesn't wait for him to get up. He turns to me, one hand cradling my face.

"You all right?"

I nod quickly, but I'm not okay. Nothing about this is okay.

Mark lunges from the ground, taking out Caleb's legs. Caleb falls to his knees on the asphalt, then spins, kicking blindly to dislodge Mark's hold on his calf. His foot connects with the side of Mark's head, and with a howl, Mark flops back onto the ground.

Reality slams into me, freeing me from the shock of the last few seconds.

People are running toward us; I can see them cutting through the shadows as they cross the street from the restaurant.

"Fight," I hear someone say. "Hurry! Check this out!"

I catch a glimpse of someone's phone as they raise it to record the action.

Scrambling to Mark's side, I pull him up to a seated position by the now dirt-stained collar of his shirt. His lip is bleeding. He blinks at me, a little dazed, though I think more from the alcohol than Caleb's kick.

"Jaime? Jaime!" Myra's voice cuts through the dark. She and Ben are pushing through the gathering crowd, running toward us.

Caleb is frozen, perched on one knee, halfway to a stand. He's fallen into a shadow, his face hidden in the dark.

"Go," I call desperately to him. He doesn't move.

"*Go,*" I beg him. "Please."

He lurches to his feet, teeth flashing in a stripe of white light from the overhead lamps as he grimaces. Then Myra and Ben are crouched beside me, asking what happened, and if we're okay, and who did this.

I look over Myra's shoulder, but Caleb is gone.

"I don't know," I tell them, the shaking in my voice one-hundred-percent real. "He came out of nowhere. I think he was going to mug us or something."

Myra's face lifts, her dark eyes peering into mine in disbelief before her gaze flicks to Mark's car, and his keys, now strewn on the ground between us.

This looks bad, but even bad is better than reality.

Ben helps Mark up, and I tell him he should go home. He can't drive. He's had too much to drink. Again, Myra's gaze settles on me, seeking answers I'm not prepared to give.

Ben agrees to take Mark home—he's got a car in the garage down the street. Hooking Mark's arm around his shoulders, they take off, while Myra and I cross the street to tell the others what happened.

I'm so jumpy, I can hardly keep my steps even, but for once it's all right. It's okay to look like you almost got mugged if you're sticking to a story that you almost got mugged.

We're across the street and outside the door to Risa's when Myra pulls me to a stop. I'm shivering now; the cold has finally needled through my thin sweater, and my teeth are chattering.

"What'd he do?" she asks flatly.

"What?" I need that heater on me stat. Maybe that will stop me from trembling.

"Mark." She steps closer, arms on my forearms. "Why were you in his car?"

"I wasn't." I bite the inside of my cheek hard, trying to focus on the story, but I can't help looking around for Caleb. Is he still somewhere in the crowd? Did anyone else see him, or catch the fight on video?

"Then what were you doing in the parking lot?" she asks.

"Nothing." My voice breaks. "Nothing, all right? I thought I saw someone I knew outside. I didn't. Mark met me out here. He said he needed to get something in his car for the interns, and I could help him carry it in."

"And you believed him?"

I shrug. "I'm trying to make a good impression. He's still mad about the donation thing."

She folds her arms over her chest. "Did you hit him?"

I can tell by the set look on her face that she's not going for the mugging story, and any attempt to convince her is only going to make this worse.

I nod.

Her hands move to my biceps, squeezing tightly. "That lousy piece of trash. I knew he had the hots for you. We have to tell his boss."

"No!"

Her eyes widen. "Jaime, if he attacked—"

"He didn't. He . . ." I need to get control of this. *Think.* "He tried to kiss me. I hit him. End of story. He won't try it again."

"He needs to be fired."

He can't be. Not until I figure out what he knows about Jimmy Balder. My rapport with him is already in jeopardy. If he thinks I'm the reason he's losing his job, he'll never tell me and any strides I make toward finishing this assignment for Dr. O and getting Grayson out of Vale Hall are ruined.

"He's not at work, and neither am I. This is a social thing."

"The senator's staff needs to know they've hired a scumbag."

"Come on. It's not a big deal."

"Are you serious?" Her hands drop. "Since when is sexual harassment not a big deal? Did he tell you not to say anything? Did he threaten you?"

"No. Myra, no, it wasn't like that. I overreacted."

She throws her head back and groans. "Do you even realize what you sound like right now? This is how guys like him become men like . . ." A strained breath hisses between her teeth. "They get away with one little thing, and then another, and then they're trying to shove underage interns in their car, and . . ."

She stops her rant, closing her eyes for one forced breath. Her face transforms to the same pained expression she had yesterday when I asked about interns not sticking around.

"What do you mean, Myra? Men like who?'"

"No one."

She's pulling on the sleeves of her coat.

"Like the senator?" It's a guess, but the hard light in her eyes tells me I'm pressing a nerve. "Did he do something?"

"He did nothing." She sighs. "And when you do nothing, you're complacent. People get hurt."

"How? How do people get hurt?"

She stares at me, locks me in a standoff of secrets where neither of us are willing to give in. Slowly, her arm lifts, motioning to the lot across the street where Mark's car will now sit overnight, tallying up an enormous bill.

"Like this," she says, then quietly adds, "The senator isn't the problem. It's those who let people like him get away with things that are the problem."

I shrug it off, but it hurts being called out like this, even if she doesn't have the right story.

"I'm not letting anyone get away with anything." If she only knew why I was really here. What I've gone through to keep my position at Vale Hall.

"Then do the right thing," she says. "Or I will."

At that, she goes inside. I follow a moment later, but the cold has soaked through my skin and left a lingering numbness even the heater can't blast away.

I am doing the right thing. I'm doing what's best for me, and for Caleb, and for Dr. O and Grayson. I'm helping to put a man behind bars that's hurt and frightened his son. Who is responsible for covering up one, maybe two, deaths.

But by letting Mark off the hook, I'm telling him it's okay to mess with seventeen-year-old girls. I'm showing him we won't fight back. That we're weak, and that he can do whatever he wants, without consequences.

If I weren't working tonight, I would have kicked his ass.

Or maybe he would have kicked mine, and that makes me feel a million times worse.

I will stay on until I know everything there is to know about Jimmy Balder, and then I will report Mark.

But I need him first.

Which means I need Myra to give me time before she turns him in.

Emmett wants to hear details when we get inside, but I stick to the almost-mugging story and tell him I didn't see the face of the attacker. Myra sits quietly in her chair, growing more sullen and furious as the hour progresses, until neither of us can sit any longer.

I have to fix this with Mark.

I have to find Caleb.

As I say good night and make my way to the door, I'm stopped by the busgirl with the nose ring. She's holding Mark's leather wallet in her hand and trying her best to look like a hero.

"Your friend leave?" she asks. "Someone found this by the door. Picture in the ID looks like him."

I grab it out of her hand and head toward the door.

"Hey," she says. "He didn't pay his bill."

"I'm sure whatever purchases you charged to his cards after you picked his pocket should cover it."

Her mouth makes a small O.

"We good?" I ask.

She nods quickly, and I'm out.

CHAPTER 14

Just after curfew that night, I climb the attic stairs to meet Caleb on the roof.

The wind has grown even more bitter than it was earlier, and it threatens to toss me over the side on my way to the spire. When I see him sitting on the ledge where we met last time, my steps slow, and I'm torn between wanting to punch him or to curl up in his arms.

He stands when he sees my expression, his hands in his pockets.

"Wasn't sure you were coming," he says.

We didn't have a chance to talk after I got back from the internship, and texting that I was going to be late might have alerted Moore or Belk, who have access to our phones.

"Grayson wanted to play another game of *Road Racers*."

A muscle tics in Caleb's neck, and he looks to the ground, hiding his expression.

"Are you okay?" His question is steady, too practiced.

"Yes. Are you?"

"I'm fine."

Fine. The word digs beneath my skin.

I step closer. He does not.

"Why did you follow me tonight?" I ask.

A shocked sigh slips out of his lips, like he didn't see this coming. It puts me even more on edge. He should have expected this question, and acting like he didn't confirms he's hiding something.

He zips up his coat, putting a leather shield between us. "I thought you were working at a restaurant, not hanging out at one."

He isn't even going to try to deny he was tailing me. I don't know if that makes me feel better or worse.

"I am. At least, I was until you decided to show." Mark's going to be mad when he sobers up. Any chance I had of hearing what he knows about Jimmy is gone. For all I know, he could be planning on telling Jessica about the donation game and getting me fired.

"Seriously?" Caleb stares at me. "Sorry. Didn't realize you guys were having such a good time."

Now it's my turn for the shield. I feel Devon Park Brynn slide over my skin, lifting my chin and straightening my spine.

"I had it handled."

"Maybe you did," he says. "But I see anyone getting dragged around a parking lot by a guy like that, I'm going to say something."

Myra's words echo in my head: *It's those who let people like him get away with things that are the problem.*

Caleb wasn't trying to mess things up on my job—aside from touching my face, he never even acknowledged that we knew each other. He was protecting me the way he'd protect anyone, and even if that makes me feel like the worst kind of scum, that still doesn't explain why he was there tonight.

"What were you doing with those people?" he asks before I can, and there's a carefulness to his tone that sets me on edge. "Those older guys. That girl . . . Do you even know who they are?"

The anger in his voice catches me off guard. "Do you?"

He shoves at his glasses.

Dread snakes through my veins.

"Why were you following me?" I ask again. "Why do you know them? Shouldn't you be on your own assign—"

"I *was*." He hesitates, and I see the truth in his struggle. He knows who the people I was with are because they *are* his assignment. He said he was following a new recruit, a girl.

But he was following me.

A sudden pressure pulses between my temples. It wouldn't be the first time I was the focus of someone's job—Geri's whole purpose last year was to play me according to Dr. O's bidding. Caleb himself tailed me before I was accepted to Vale Hall to make sure I was suitable for the program.

But the recruitment angle is over. Dr. O said to keep my assignment a secret, to tell the others I was following a potential new student if anyone asked. He must have told Caleb the same.

Caleb followed the rules, and I didn't. And now Caleb's asking questions he already knows the answers to, like this is some kind of test to see what I'll give up.

"They're just interns," I say. "Or coworkers. But I guess you knew that."

He's quiet a moment, and then he closes in on me, fast enough that I step back. He's different now, back to himself. He reaches for my hands, grasping them tightly. Worry is etched into every line on his face, and his frown pulls at my heart.

"This is me," he says. "I'm not some mark."

But I am.

Caleb and I faced the Wolves of Hellsgate together. We sent Pete, the man who made my life a living nightmare, to prison. I've met his mom and his brother. I've seen his dad.

We don't have secrets.

"Just tell me what's going on," he says.

But he already knows. I told him about The Loft. About Sterling's missing intern.

And he lied.

"I can't talk about it," I say.

He releases my hands.

"What *can* we talk about? Everything's off-limits because Grayson's always crawling all over you."

Irritation prickles between my shoulder blades. He gets to pull this after following me to work? After spying on me? "That's kind of an exaggeration, don't you think?"

"He likes you."

"I'm making him like me. It's part of the job."

"The job," he repeats, and then laughs coldly. "Yeah, it's more than the job. He looks at you like . . . I don't know. Like he owns you or something."

"So kind of the way Geri's been looking at you."

"That's different," he says. "She's just—"

"Being Geri, I know." It irritates me that he thinks I let her get to me, even if I have a little. "Grayson doesn't own me."

"I know that."

"Do you?" A gust of wind howls through the pointed mountains of the roof, throwing me off balance. Caleb grabs my elbow to steady me, but his gaze is flat, hiding secrets, and it makes me doubt myself yet again. Did he follow me tonight as part of his assignment? Or was it personal—he wanted to see for himself what I was really up to?

His arm falls slowly to his side, and I feel my insides twist.

"Do *you*?" he asks quietly, and I know he isn't just talking about Grayson, but Dr. O as well.

Do they own me?

The fight drains out of me as the words from *Othello* ring in my head.

I do perceive here a divided duty.

On one side I have school—my assignment, my "education." On the other, I have Caleb. I have Charlotte and Henry and Sam. SATs. College. My real life.

Which is becoming more of a lie every day.

It's like jamming two wrong puzzle pieces together until they fit.

Caleb takes a step back, brows drawn together. His frustration, his worry, is replaced by something heavier, something I can touch through the wall that's just lifted between us.

"This doesn't work if you don't trust me," he says.

It feels like my chest is caving in. "Do *you* trust *me*?"

He flinches. "You need to be careful, Brynn." He doesn't say Margot's name, but I feel her presence between us. He thinks I'm in too deep with my mark. That I'm going to betray him, like she did, or maybe that I already have.

He really doesn't trust me.

"That's not an answer," I say quietly.

"Yes, it is," he says. "It's just not the one either of us want to hear."

He won't look at me.

"So that's it?" I say, seeing red. "We're doing whatever Dr. O says now? We don't get our own lives?"

"We're doing this so we can have our own lives."

"No," I say. "*You're* doing this because you're afraid."

"Of course I'm afraid!" he shouts, and for one second, I'm relieved that this is hurting him as much as it is me. Then he says, "We should take a step back for a while."

A fist clenches around my heart.

"You're breaking up with me?"

He looks like *I'm* the one who just hurt him. "Maybe for now . . . it's for the best."

"For now? Is there a better time for you? You can pencil me in for next spring, how about that?"

He doesn't answer.

I want to rage at him. I want to tell him we're better than this. Stronger than this. That Grayson, and our assignments, and Margot's stupid memory aren't enough to shove us down.

But they are, because Caleb's hands are tied. He needs Vale

Hall more than I do, more than any of us do. If he doesn't follow Dr. O's directives, he gets kicked out of school. His dad loses his medical care. His mom can't afford it on her cleaning job wages.

My future depends on this place, but Caleb's family's *lives* are counting on him.

If he's lying to me, he doesn't have a choice.

But if he's lying to me, we can't trust each other.

I lift my chin, unwilling to let him see me suffer.

"I have to get back," I say. "Henry heard Moore say he's doing room checks after curfew."

Caleb's head falls forward. He doesn't try to stop me.

MY FEET FEEL like cinder blocks as I trudge through the attic and down the ladder into the storage room. I keep looking back, like he's going to be there. I keep waiting to hear him call my name, to hear him say this was a mistake.

But he doesn't follow me. He doesn't confess anything.

And I don't turn back, either.

I try to move faster, to escape the fist squeezing my lungs, but I can't. He gave me his trust, but it came with strings attached. A disclaimer in the fine print I didn't bother to read. He was mine, as long as it didn't interfere with his job. He could only be honest to a point.

And the worst part is, I knew it the whole time. I never would have asked him to put me before his family.

As I open the storage room door, I run smack into someone and bite back a surprised yelp.

It's Sam, but he rebounds off the door without looking at me and mumbles something I can't make out as he disappears around the corner.

It hits me wrong, and so instead of going straight to my room at the end of the hall, I stop next door, at Charlotte's.

Quietly, I knock twice, and before my knuckles strike the wood a third time, the door jerks inward.

She's wearing a tank top and flannel pants, and her pale face is streaked with tears.

"Oh." Her disappointment is obvious. As she turns away I slip inside her room, closing the door behind me.

"What's going on?" I replay Sam's hurried departure and grumbled words in my mind. They must have had a fight. Maybe she thought he was coming back when I knocked.

"Nothing," she says. Then, "Life just sucks, you know? It's like a giant vacuum cleaner in a black hole, inside a supernova black hole."

She buries her face in her hands and starts to sob.

I'm not very good at the whole comforting thing, but seeing Charlotte in pain sucks worse than my own double black hole vacuum cleaner. In a few strides, I'm sitting beside her on the bed, one arm wrapped around her shoulders.

"What happened?"

"Oh, you know," she says. "He loves me."

"Okay," I say slowly. "I'm missing the part where this is a problem."

"NYU doesn't have a good law school," Charlotte says on a hiccup. "Southern Cal has a great pre-law placement, but we can't do this three thousand miles apart."

I'm surprised it's only college madness. With the kinds of lives we lead, it could be anything.

"People do long-distance relationships all the time."

Of course, I can't even manage one with a guy who lives in the same house, but whatever.

She shakes her head, which makes me think there's more to

this story. If they decide to break up, they still have almost an entire year together before they go their separate ways.

"Unless that's not what you want," I say.

Her bottom lip quivers as she looks to me. "I don't know what I want."

The part of my heart Caleb hasn't crushed breaks for Sam.

"This might be harsh," I tell her. "But if you aren't all in, he deserves to know."

She stares forward at the door, a blank expression taking over her face as her shoulders stop quaking. "I get a life, don't I?"

"Of course." I squeeze her shoulder. Now I'm feeling rotten for both of them. "If it helps, I think Caleb and I just broke up."

Charlotte's head snaps my direction, and she blows out a long breath.

"Your call or his?"

"His," I say. "I don't know. Maybe both."

I am heavy enough to sink through this mattress and through the floor below. My eyes burn and I blink back the tears. If I cry it will be real. It will be over.

"This calls for chocolate." She pulls out the giant bag of M&M's from her nightstand and spills them on her comforter. I eat about fifty before I realized Charlotte hasn't even had one.

I stay with her until we hear Moore's steps outside, then I return to my room and lie awake, leafing through Caleb's drawings of skyscrapers, hospitals, and me, sketched into his copy of *A Tale of Two Cities*. I bury the book along with his trust in the bottom of my nightstand drawer and then press the heels of my hands to my eyes until I can't hear Charlotte crying through the wall anymore.

CHAPTER 15

The week stays in that supernova vacuum of suck.

We have tests in physics and precalc, as if some of us didn't just finish studying our asses off for the SATs. Charlotte and Sam set up camps on opposite corners of every room—Charlotte throwing herself into party planning like some kind of manic birthday fairy, and Sam plucking at his guitar or staring forlornly into space. Caleb and I are pulled into sides—girls versus boys, just like on the grade-school playground. I tell myself this is because Charlotte needs me right now, and I'm sure Caleb is telling himself the same thing.

We both know it's just a convenient excuse.

Focus on Grayson, he said. Like to do my job I can just turn off the way I feel about him.

Maybe he can, and that makes me feel even worse.

I go back to The Loft Thursday, but Myra isn't scheduled, and when the campaign staff comes up for their afternoon meeting, I learn that Mark has called in sick. Ben and Emmett are consumed with raising the donations for their park event, which leaves me with nothing to do but apologize for Mr. Haruki's lukewarm salmon pâté and clean up Ms. Dalton's spilled gin and tonic.

Jimmy Balder is on hold until everyone is back on Monday, which is something I'm looking forward to about as much as running my knuckles over a cheese grater.

The rest of my time is spent with Grayson.

We play *Road Racers*. We pick the lock on the music room door and play drums like rock stars, and sneak desserts from Ms. Maddox's stash after curfew. We even go running on the treadmills in the gym.

Which is less fun than running from the cops.

He sits by me at every meal and blocks out everyone else but Henry and Charlotte, whom he somehow deems nonthreatening. We practice our waltz, but only when Caleb's rehearsing with Geri.

Grayson plays the cool guy in front of the others, but as soon as they're gone, he asks me if I've heard anything new about his dad, or if Dr. O has a way to put him in jail yet, or what he's supposed to say when he testifies against his father.

I tell him the truth: I don't know.

Whenever I'm with him, I can feel Caleb watching me. But he doesn't send me a single message, or ask me to meet him on the roof again, or run his fingertips over the small of my back as he passes. So I pretend it doesn't matter. I pretend that our assignments really are the most important thing. I pretend to be the girl Grayson likes until it's so natural, I forget the real me is still inside, ripped open and bleeding.

SATURDAY MORNING IS sunny and uncharacteristically warm for late September. After we finish breakfast, everyone is sent to clean their rooms in preparation for family visits. The residence has been a flurry of emotion all week—a crackling blend of excitement and wary anticipation.

We have to convince our families—those that are coming—that this is nothing but an elite boarding school. We can't let anyone close to us become suspicious of what we're really doing here.

For some, that's the biggest con of all.

I know I should have called Mom to remind her about this weekend, but I didn't want to pressure her—I know she's happy for me, but hearing about this place and seeing it are two different things. She lives in a run-down house in the slums. This would make her feel weird.

I give my room a half-assed once-over, but pick my best jeans and a raven T-shirt. I may not have anyone here for me, but Caleb's mom, Maiko, is coming, and even if Caleb and I haven't really spoken since that night on the roof, I want to make a good impression. I do my makeup carefully, and even fix my hair.

It can't hurt looking nice.

For Caleb's mom.

Most of the other students are downstairs when I finally get the courage to come out of my room. Charlotte is wearing a dress with a black ribbon tied around the waist. Her red hair is in perfect spirals, and her makeup is impeccable. As I go sit beside her, she swears down at a chipped nail.

"You all right?" I ask.

"Don't I look it?" She swears again. "Ten bucks says she tells me to get a manicure."

I'm curious to meet Charlotte's parents, if only so I can put faces to the terrible people that believed a rapist's word over their own daughter's. Charlotte tried to tell them what their friend had done when she'd been called over to "house-sit," but they'd called her *dramatic,* and when she'd taken matters into her own hands and set his living room on fire, they'd given her over to the courts.

And eventually, to Dr. O.

"Why did you invite them?" I ask.

"Oh, I didn't. Dr. O did. He thinks it'll be therapeutic."

I wince.

"Also, he needs them not to accuse him of holding me captive and throw a giant lawsuit his direction. It's twice a year. Whatever."

But her face is pale, and her brow is dotted with sweat.

"I'll stay with you," I say. Out of habit, I look for Sam, but he's absent. Belk left early this morning to take him to the train station so he could take it Bennington Max, the women's prison north of the city, to see his mom.

Charlotte squeezes my hand. "I love you too much to subject you to that." Her eyes fix on something behind me. "Besides, you might be needed elsewhere."

I look over my shoulder to find Henry bypassing the living area to head straight into the kitchen. His head is down, his back slumped. He's wearing jeans that are baggier than normal and a long-sleeved T-shirt with a hockey logo on the front. His hair is combed straight back, and there's even some yellow stubble on his jaw.

Charlotte and I both rise and make our way to the kitchen. Henry's getting an apple out of the basket on the island, but stops as we approach.

"Hey," he says.

"Hey yourself," says Charlotte.

My eyes narrow at the fierce ice-skating penguin on his shirt. "Since when do you like hockey?"

"Since when do you curl your hair?" He scowls, pulling at a wrinkle in the bottom of his shirt while I self-consciously run my hand over my coiled ends.

Behind me, Caleb enters the living room, his gaze only glancing over us as he moves to Paz and Joel. My hand drops from my hair, and I will myself not to think of his drawings in the book in my room, how he drew the long lines of my neck, and how curling my hair shows them off.

He's not looking at me.

"Is this day over yet?" Charlotte asks. We all know what this is about. Henry's mom and stepdad don't know the Henry we do. They know this version, this toned-down creature who can't even hold his back up straight.

I pity them.

"So I guess I'm not invited." Grayson strides into the room, cutting in front of Charlotte to grab an orange for himself. She sighs and steps out of his way.

"Oh hey," says Henry, lifting a little. "You're not missing anything, don't worry." His cheeks go a little rosy, highlighting his golden stubble.

Grayson glances over at him, then narrows his eyes. "Wow. You look interesting."

Henry sags again.

"Be nice," I tell Grayson. I hadn't thought of him this morning, but of course he wouldn't be around for Family Day. No one's supposed to know he's here, and anyway, it's not like anyone needs his dad showing.

"I'm missing the inevitable drama that comes when adults are forced to remember they're parents." Grayson grins at Charlotte. "I was looking forward to meeting yours. Don't they own a fast-food chain?"

Charlotte's eyes narrow, but I catch sight of her hand balling into the side of her dress and my teeth press together. I doubt she expected Grayson would still be around when she made up her little alias.

"A hotel chain," she corrects. "Too bad you'll be on room arrest. I'm sure they would have loved you."

I'm not sure she's lying about that part.

Grayson chuckles. "I'm supposed to get food for the afternoon before I go upstairs." He nudges Henry with his elbow. "Want to make me a sandwich?"

"Sure," says Henry a little too eagerly.

I'm not certain what's happening here, but I don't like it.

"Can't you make your own sandwich?" I grab a plate off the counter and shove it in Grayson's direction.

"I could, but it wouldn't be as good." He winks at Henry and passes him the plate.

Definitely not loving this, but I don't say anything, because Geri's just strutted into the room, wearing a short pink dress and a string of pearls around her neck. It's not that her outfit's particularly unusual, but the way Caleb stops his conversation with Joel and Paz to go talk to her is.

I can't hear what they're saying, but he leans closer to speak in her ear, and when she smiles a pure, unscheming, uncalculating smile, flames sear across my skin.

"That guy's got it bad for her," says Grayson, following my line of sight. "Hope he knows what he's doing."

"What's that supposed to mean?" Curious is what I'm going for, but the words come out far too harsh.

Grayson doesn't appear to notice. "She's like those praying mantises that eat their mates' heads after sex. Only hot."

"That's disgusting," says Charlotte.

"She's not that hot," says Henry.

I suppress a groan. "How'd you escape alive?" Geri made it sound like he used her, not the other way around. If he actually did like her, Geri would have exploited that to get what she needed.

I never would have been brought in to take her place.

There's more to this story; I can see it in Grayson's bitter stare. Whatever actually happened, she hurt him, and that's something not many people can do.

"Emergency eject button," he says. "Don't worry. You're better than her anyway."

I'm not sure if I'm supposed to say thanks or laugh. But as Grayson's blue eyes find mine, I realize he doesn't just think I'm better than Geri, he thinks I'm better for *him*.

He smiles, and it's small, but unguarded, an echo of what Geri just gave Caleb. It's exactly what I've been aiming for this entire week—his comfort, his trust.

Which means now is when I should try to find out anything else he might know about Susan, or his father, or Jimmy Balder.

But I don't ask, because we're not alone. And because even though he's a spoiled brat, driven by competition, he's becoming a real friend, and when he finds out I'm lying again, it will destroy him.

AN HOUR LATER, the families begin to arrive. Joel's foster parents arrive first, bearing chocolate chip cookies for all the students. Paz sticks by his side the whole time, and when they hold hands, his foster mom hugs her.

Geri's dad comes next, pulling into the drive in a BMW. He's got her dark hair, but lacks the face of Satan I was expecting. Instead of being smooth and small like her, he's huge. Her waist is as big as one of his biceps, and when she hangs on his arm while they walk, she looks like a little kid.

There's something familiar about him I can't quite place. Maybe he's an actor or something.

If he was, I'm sure Geri would have mentioned it.

Charlotte's parents come next, and they spend an extra five minutes outside by the fountain arguing before they even reach the front steps. After that, Belk shows up in the SUV, and out of the back pour seven more adults—those who met him at the train station.

Mom is not included.

Soon, the house is alive with conversation and laughter. A few more cars arrive bearing parents and kids. People go upstairs to show off the bedrooms, or down to the pit. They head outside to the pool area or walk to the gardens. Ms. Maddox has made a feast of fancy finger foods and little desserts, and Dr. O, dressed down in a collared shirt and dark jeans, positions himself in the living room, where he can visit with everyone.

When Charlotte's parents finally make it inside, she greets them with an awkward hug and brings them into the kitchen for snacks. Her father wears the kind of glasses that sit on the tip of his pointy nose, which makes him lift his chin as he peers around the room.

"Where's the boy you were hanging all over last time?" asks her mother, waving off a dessert while she pats the updo of red hair she shares with her daughter.

"He's at the jail, I told you," Charlotte says.

"Well, it was just a matter of time, I suppose."

Maybe this fanfare is all necessary for our continued survival as a program, but right now I hate Dr. O for making Charlotte go through this.

I go in for the rescue, or maybe to pick a fight. Her mother acknowledges me with a superficial smile, aided in part by Botox, but before I reach her, I'm stopped by a Japanese boy half my size dodging around a crowd of people to skid to a stop in front of me.

"Christopher!" I haven't seen him in a month, since Caleb and I snuck out to visit his family at the hospital, but he's at least two inches taller.

Realizing we might not do that again makes me sink a full two inches.

He grins up at me, pointing to his missing bottom tooth.

"Oh man," I say. "I hate to be the one to tell you this, but your teeth are rotting out."

"It was loose," he explains.

"The tooth fairy come?"

He nods. "She brought me a potato."

Beside me, I hear a snort, and I turn to see Jonathan combing his black hair forward with his hand.

"You wouldn't happen to know this potato fairy, would you?"

His cheeks turn pink, and when he jams his hands into his pockets, I'm so reminded of Caleb my chest hurts.

"He doesn't know the difference. He's just a kid," says Jonathan, as if he isn't only twelve himself.

I jab him in the shoulder but can't help laughing.

"Mom wanted us to find you." Christopher loads up a small plate of fancy cheese and crackers to my left. "She's over there."

I follow his pointing finger through the crowd to the entryway, where Maiko stands on the tile, wearing a black dress and high heels. Her inky hair is brushed back today, and she's put on some lipstick that brightens her proud smile.

Without hesitating, I head toward her, glad she's finally here. Last time I saw her, we talked about Barry Buddha, and she asked if I would take her to the garden when she came.

But as the crowd clears, I see that she isn't talking just to Caleb, but to Geri and her dad. Geri's hand is on Caleb's forearm, and when she laughs, she rests the side of her head on his shoulder.

Then Caleb shifts, placing his hand on her lower back, the way he used to do with me.

My mouth goes dry. A knot forms behind my collarbone. Grayson's not here, so Caleb has no reason to pretend he and Geri are together for my benefit. It's like he doesn't care who's watching at all.

"Who's that?"

I approve one hundred percent of the disgust in Jonathan's voice.

"Geri," I mutter.

"That's a boy's name."

It's not the most creative insult, but I give him a high five anyway.

"Is that his girlfriend or something? I thought you and he were going out. You're all he ever talks about. Brynn this. Brynn that."

My gut clenches.

"We're friends," I say.

"Oh." Jonathan rolls back his shoulders but refuses to meet my eyes. "You got a boyfriend?"

"Why, you got someone in mind?" I give him a sideways look, and his face turns stoplight red.

I don't want to be here anymore. All these people in this house feel like an invasion. I should go up to my room. Or better, go to Grayson's and dig around in his head for more information. The sooner Dr. O has what he needs to put Matthew Sterling away, the better.

But that means Grayson will leave.

It's for the best—he's not a student here, and he said himself that he wants to go home. But I'm getting used to having him around.

He's not awful once you get to know him.

Giving Jonathan a fist bump, I head toward the stairs, but the collision is unavoidable. Maiko spots me and waves, then excuses herself from the conversation to come see me.

"Brynn!" She holds her arms out and there's no avoiding it. I bend down to hug her. She squeezes the perfect amount, and pats my back, and tells me how glad she is to see me. My stupid eyes betray me and get all glassy and wet, and I have to clear my throat just to say hi.

When I pull back, Caleb's standing there, staring at me like I just punched him in the chest, while Geri still hangs on his arm.

"I have to run upstairs for a minute," I lie. "I'll be right back."

"I'll save you some dessert," Maiko says.

I smile and try to edge around Caleb, but he breaks free from the Geri leech and grabs my hand.

"Can we talk?" he whispers, his palm warm against mine.

The room around him wavers and falls out of focus. I don't care about Geri then, or Grayson, or whatever rift has formed between us over our stupid assignments.

I miss him.

"Meet me tonight?" he asks. Behind him, I catch a glimpse of Geri clearly eavesdropping before looking away.

Part of me wants to say no. To remind him he followed me. To remind him he lied, and put Dr. O's orders over us.

But I nod.

And he smiles.

And it feels like hope.

Then the pause button is released, and we're back to our regularly scheduled program. He's with Geri and his mom, his back to me as he introduces Jonathan and Christopher around. The inertia drags at me, pulling me into motion when I'm still stuck in place, until finally my feet are able to move.

I head toward the stairs and am halfway up when the door opens and Moore steps inside. He's not alone; there's a woman with him. She's my height, with my color hair, and my face, only lighter.

"Mom?"

My voice cracks.

I can't believe she's here.

I didn't think I cared, but I do. I care so much I think I might break open.

"You could've warned me you live in a castle," she says.

"You wouldn't have believed me," I tell her.

She grins and clutches her bag close against her side, as if she's afraid she might bump into one of the fine pieces of art on the walls. She got dressed up—the kind of dressed up that turns heads in Devon Park, but averts stares on the North End. Her blouse is too tight, and her skirt is too short. Her silver heels look straight out of a club.

But I don't care, because she came.

"Work kept me late and I missed the train," she says. "Hugh was kind enough to get me at the house."

Hugh? What exactly happened in the car? She wasn't giving

him the flirty smile she is now when he picked me up to bring me to Vale Hall for the first time.

"I could have met you." I wish I could have driven to get her. Used one of the fancy cars in the garage. That would have blown her mind.

"It was my pleasure." Moore takes a subtle step away, then looks up at me. "You want to show her around?"

Stupid me is still standing on the stairs like some kind of Southern belle. I hurry toward them, taking Mom's arm to lead her toward the living room and kitchen.

"Wow," she mutters when Moore's out of view. "If my school police looked like that, I never would have dropped out."

"Gross. You want to eat first, or see the house?"

"I think . . ." She takes a deep breath. "I think we should go somewhere to talk. There's something I need to tell you."

CHAPTER 16

Instead of meeting the others, Mom and I go upstairs to my bedroom. She gawks the whole time, saying things like, "I was just about to get this marble statue for *my* hallway," and, "Our place looked just like this before you were born. Kids ruin everything." By the time we reach my room, my meeting with Caleb is shoved to the back of my mind. I'm braced for the worst, and she's wound tighter than a copper coil.

"What happened?" I close the door behind her while she stares, in awe, around my room. "Is it Pete? Did he contact you?"

Her ex-boyfriend's been in jail for three months, unable to make his hundred-thousand-dollar bail. At least—that was the last I'd heard. If he did manage to pay it, he could be home, messing with her again.

Coming after me.

"No, he's gone," she says. "They repossessed his place downstairs and everything. Do you seriously have your own bedroom?"

I blow out a tense breath. The cops must have found more than enough Wednesday Pharmaceuticals pills and illegal gambling money to put him away for a long time.

"Mom." I move in front of her, blocking her from wandering further.

"He's gone," she says again, this time meeting my gaze. "I wanted to tell you in person that I'm gone, too."

"Which means?"

"I'm moving out of the slums, baby."

It takes a second for this to sink in. She's never talked about moving before. Even when I begged her to leave with me. Even before Pete. She said Devon Park was home, and she couldn't see herself living anywhere else.

"Well, say something," she says.

I shake myself out of shock. "Where? Why?"

Side-eyeing me, she continues her assessment of my room. At the closet, she flips through the clothes, feeling the material of each one.

I wish she'd just sit down.

"An apartment opened up in Edgewater."

Edgewater is a suburb on the east side of the city. It's not a step up from Devon Park, it's a ride in a rocket ship to the moon.

"Edgewater."

"That's right. Two bedroom, two bath. You can come back and stay with me whenever you want."

"How much does it cost?" I don't want to rain on her parade, but I'm not sure how this is going to work.

She waves a hand, moving to my bathroom, where she hoots when she sees the rain shower and stone tiles. "Don't you worry about that. I got a new job."

"What?" She's waitressed at Gridiron Sports Bar since I was in fourth grade. "Another restaurant?"

She pulls a towel off the rack and holds it against her cheek. "These are like cotton candy."

I snap my fingers. "Focus."

She sets down the towel and straightens her blouse, holding her chin high as she says, "Meet the newest member of the Wednesday Pharmaceuticals team."

It feels like I've just missed a step going down the stairs.

"They hired me as an administrative assistant in the east side office. Salaried position, with benefits, thank you very much."

"Hold on," I say. "Wednesday Pharmaceuticals is . . ."

The company that makes the drugs Pete stole and later sold on the streets.

The company that Dr. O owns.

"I know," she says. "Obviously I'm not telling them how my ex made an income."

"How did you get this job?"

"I interviewed for it." Pride is evident in her voice, her posture, even her little smirk. Clearly she has no idea that my employer is also her employer.

"How'd you find out about it?"

"Guy came into the bar the other night saying he was looking for someone to fill the position. I guess my service impressed him." She flicks her hair.

"A guy from Edgewater came to a sports bar in Devon Park and just happened to offer you a job?"

Her lips pull into a frown. "He was in the area. Who cares? I start next week. I put the house up for sale yesterday!"

Nostalgia bites into me, bringing memories of the bedroom I haven't seen since the beginning of summer, and the kitchen where Mom makes birthday cupcakes, and the blue couch by the front window that will forever be stained by a fruit punch box I spilled when I was six. She's selling the house we lived in with my dad, where we cried together after he'd been shot. Where I grew up.

The house I ran away from.

I don't care. I won't. Because it's a dump. It smells like ashtrays, and the carpet's threadbare. The floors creak, and the windows are so thin you freeze in the winter. It doesn't even have air-conditioning.

It's just a stupid house.

She's never going to sell it, anyway.

"What about all our stuff?" I ask.

She shrugs. "The company's covering the move. They gave me the name of the realtor and everything. She's really classy. Thinks someone will snatch it up in the next couple weeks."

Because everyone's dying to move to Devon Park.

She's so happy, and I want to be happy for her. But this isn't the random stroke of good luck she thinks it is. This is Dr. O's doing, and everything he offers comes with a cost.

"Congrats, Mom," she says out of the side of her mouth.

This is a huge deal for her—an opportunity that doesn't come along every day. But how could Dr. O have done this without asking me? Why did he pull my mom into his web? Is this some kind of reward for my work?

"Congrats, Mom," I say. It's not like I can tell her to turn the job down or break the contract on the apartment. Regardless of where this came from, it's too good to pass up.

"I owe it to you," she says. "If you hadn't come here, I'd still be doing the same old routine. You inspired me."

I hope she doesn't see the hesitance in my smile.

"People often call me the Great Inspiration," I say. "You want something to eat? There's appetizers and stuff downstairs."

"Ooh." She gives her best this-is-fancy smile. "Yes, please."

THE KITCHEN IS still bustling with activity as we make our way down the spiral staircase, but before we leave the foyer, there's a loud *thunk* against the wall behind me. I turn, assuming it must be someone outside the front door, but no one is visible through the glass panes on either side.

"Hold on a second." Mom waits as I step beneath the twin columns holding up the black marble ravens and turn my ear to Dr. O's closed office door. He's not inside; I can hear his laughter filtering in through the open back door, where Ms. Maddox set up a marshmallow toasting station in the outdoor fireplace beside the pool.

It was probably nothing. A car door slamming outside, or a painting that fell off the wall. But as I listen, there's a screeching sound, as if a heavy piece of furniture is being dragged across the floor.

"What's in there?" Mom asks, creeping up behind me. "Please tell me it's a wine cellar."

"Shh."

No one's allowed in Dr. O's office without an invitation, and the smart move is to tell Moore or Belk what I've heard, but they're busy playing tour guides and it's only a quick look.

As I turn the knob, the wooden door creaks and pushes inward. I'm surprised it opened—usually if Dr. O's not inside, it stays locked. My surprise doubles when a figure on the opposite side of the room ducks behind a burgundy armchair.

In an instant, I'm ready for anything. I look around for a weapon, eyes landing on the metal pokers on the fireplace mantel. I should run and call for help.

But this is Family Day, and no one's breaking in on Family Day. It's probably just some kid who went exploring. My shoulders unbunch as Mom steps beside me, whistling as she takes in the museum of art and antiques that Dr. O surrounds himself with.

"Whoever's in here shouldn't be," I say to the still room.

There is no movement.

I stride toward the monstrous chair, but no one stands up. "I already saw you. There's no use hiding."

When I round the corner, I see long, denim-clad legs and socked feet. Another step, and the rest of the intruder comes into view.

"Grayson?"

He winces. "No Graysons here. Move along."

I fold my arms over my chest.

"What are you doing?"

"Playing hide and seek?"

"By yourself."

"No one else wanted to play."

I reach out a hand, which he takes, and he nearly drags me to the ground as I attempt to pull him up.

"You picked the lock?"

He holds a credit card up between two fingers.

I ignore the swell of pride inside me.

"Dr. O catches you in here, you're dead, you know."

"That seems to be a theme these days."

I glance to the edge of the mantel beside him, where the love seat has been dragged aside to reveal an opening in the stones—a small door, blending with the rock, hiding a silver safe.

My gut sinks. "Please tell me you weren't trying to break into that." Whatever curiosity I have over what might be inside is overridden by the growing idea that this office wasn't just a game for him, but an end goal.

"Of course not," he says. "I was just admiring it."

I slap his arm.

"I know you." Mom's voice surprises me—I'd forgotten she was here. "You're Grayson Sterling. The senator's son."

Grayson wilts.

"Just a look-alike," I say.

"No." Pure delight is radiating off her as she wags a finger at him. "I saw that picture of you two on *Pop Store* a few months ago. I asked you about it, and you said it was someone else."

"It was," I say, Grayson's wariness now infecting me. "It was this guy. He looks like Grayson, but really his name's . . . Billy."

Grayson glowers at me. I glare back. No one's supposed to know he's here. Men—sent by his father—are looking for him. Why didn't he stay in his room like he was supposed to?

Mom taps her nose with one finger. "Top secret. I get it. I know how you celebrity types are."

Because watching *Pop Store* makes her a celebrity expert.

There's no use denying it now. I rush toward her, leaving Grayson shifting from side to side behind me.

"It's important no one knows he's here, Mom. Grayson's hounded by the press, all the time. He wasn't even supposed to come out of his room today."

"I get it." As I put my arm around her shoulders to turn her away from Grayson, she whispers, "Was there an assassination attempt?"

"What? No!"

"They do this kind of thing with the president's kids," she says. "People make threats, so they hide these kids in private schools, or homeschool them. They hardly have a life at all, poor things."

I dig my thumb into my temple. "Okay, yes. It is something like that. Which means it's absolutely crucial you tell no one he's here."

Behind me, I can hear the screech of the couch as Grayson pushes it back in place. I'm sure that won't leave any scuff marks on the floor, or look at all suspicious.

"I got it, I got it. So are you and him . . ." Mom weaves her fingers together in front of her face.

"We sure are." Grayson's suddenly over my shoulder, leering in on our conversation.

My mom shrieks.

"Celebrity romance!"

"Look what you did," I tell Grayson, but he's beaming, like he did in that picture with his father that hangs on the wall in the campaign office. There's something magnetic about him when he looks this way. His happiness swallows you up, just like his despair, or his anger.

"You must be Mom," he says, taking her into his arms. "You two could be sisters."

Mom blushes.

I want to gag.

I haven't forgotten why we're standing in this office, or the safe Grayson's revealed in the fireplace. I'm not sure how he even knew it was there. But I can't say anything now, because Mom's already reached her gossip quota for the day.

"Tell me everything," she says. "How'd you meet? What do you guys like to do? All the details."

"I'm not sure you want *all* the details," says Grayson, in a way that makes my mom snicker rather than roll her eyes. "I met your daughter at a party. She was dancing with this other guy, but when our eyes met . . ." He clutches his heart, leading her toward the door. I gape at them, then hurry to follow, and close the door behind.

"That's so sweet," Mom croons.

"I took her to this music festival downtown for her birthday," Grayson continues. "I was so nervous she didn't like me as much as I liked her."

"She's hard to read sometimes," Mom agrees.

I scoff.

"Turns out she found a way to get us backstage passes, and while we were waiting for the band to finish, she kissed me."

Mom squeals.

"It wasn't exactly like that." I distinctly remember River Fest involving a game of pickpocketing, a bag filled with stolen pills, and security chasing us from backstage after Grayson punched one of the guards in the face.

"All the emotional stuff embarrasses her," says Grayson.

"She gets that from my ex," says Mom. "He was never good at showing love."

"Pretty great at showing anger, though."

Mom glares back at me.

Grayson's still got one arm over her shoulders, and he's talking to her with a smoothness I've never seen him possess. It's like watching a con at work—he's figured out what makes Mom tick, and is feeding her, line by line.

He probably learned this from his dad.

"You should head up," I tell him as we reach the stairs. He doesn't need Dr. O figuring out he's broken his room arrest.

"It was wonderful meeting you," he says to my mom, but before he finishes, a man in a black wool sweater comes storming past, dragging Henry by the back of his collar. They nearly run me over on the way out the door.

"Henry?"

Charlotte's running after them, but no one else seems to have noticed they're gone.

"Get out of here," I snap at Grayson, then chase after Charlotte. "What happened?"

"I don't know! They were talking, and then Henry walked away, and his stepdad just grabbed him."

Outside, Henry's stepdad is dragging him toward a white Camry. In Henry's struggle to get away, he finally loosens the older man's grip and shoves him into the trunk.

"What's gotten into you?" his stepdad shouts.

"You need to go, Luke." Henry's voice wobbles. *"Leave."*

Luke looks up at me and Charlotte, and then behind us, to where my mom and Grayson are now standing. I'm ripped in three different directions—staying still, running to Henry's aid, or physically shoving Grayson up the stairs.

"Get in the car." Luke juts a thumb in the direction of the backseat, but Henry doesn't move.

"No."

"Get in the damn car."

My feet are taking me closer before I even command them to walk. I don't know what's going on, but Henry was there for me once when I needed it and now it's my turn to repay the favor.

"He said no." I'm two feet behind Henry, close enough to see his shoulders shake as he inhales.

"This isn't your business, sweetheart. Go back inside."

"Call my daughter sweetheart again and they'll find your balls on the side of the road," says my mom.

I smirk. Waitressing at a dive has taught her a thing or two about jerk management.

Henry's stepdad opens the nearest door, which happens to be the back passenger side.

"You think this is what your mother wants?" he hisses at Henry. "You're lucky she isn't here to see you like this. It would break her heart."

Henry takes a step back, and another, as if pushing against some magnetic force.

"She's lived through worse, believe me."

His stepdad lunges toward him, jaw flexed, but before I can grab Henry's arm to pull him back, Grayson is between them. With the pounding of my own heart in my eardrums, I didn't even hear him approach.

"I wouldn't do that if I were you." Beneath the threat in Grayson's voice is relief. He wants this fight.

I've seen him when he gets riled up. This can't happen here, or now.

"Go," I tell him. But he doesn't even flinch.

"This is him?" mutters Henry's stepdad. "This the one who turned you?"

"No!" Henry's face is scarlet.

My hands are fists. I'm going to pummel this guy myself if he doesn't get out of here soon.

"Turned you into what?" asks Grayson with a laugh. "This is going to be good. Let's hear it. Come on."

I'm scared then—not just for Grayson getting in a fight, but for how he might hurt Henry through this dare.

"Stop," says Charlotte. "Let's go back inside."

"No, he's right. Say it, Luke." Henry's words draw my stare. His jaw is set, his shoulders back. He's feeding off Grayson's darkness, and I'm not sure if that's good or dangerous. "What am I? What did I turn into?"

Luke's gaze flicks between us, but none of us back down.

"This isn't any of your concerns."

"Henry's our concern," I say.

Luke's gaze compresses. He turns to my mom. "A little help?"

"Looks like they've got plenty."

"Your mom's a badass," says Charlotte.

"Did you expect any less?" I reply, but I'm glad she's found her backbone again. When Pete was around, he had a way of making her soft.

Luke leans around Grayson, hands open, pleading with his stepson.

"You need help, Henry. There are people that deal with this. Scott Barrow's daughter had the same thing. She went through this program that changed her life."

"I bet it did," says Henry flatly.

Sickness rolls through me as his meaning takes hold. I've heard of this kind of therapy, meant to straighten gay kids. As if there's something wrong with them.

"I'm going to give you to the count of ten before I hit you." Grayson raises his fist. "One . . . two . . . three . . ."

"Seriously, we need to go inside," says Charlotte, glancing at the front door. "If Dr. O sees this, we're dead."

She's right.

"Come on," I warn, grabbing Grayson's shoulder.

"You have my permission," says Henry.

"The countdown's only fair," Grayson explains. "Five . . . six . . . seven . . ."

"I feel sorry for you," says Luke, slamming the Camry door. He stalks around the front of the car. "I feel sorry for all of you. My boy's sick. He needs help. He doesn't deal with this now, it's going to become permanent."

"Whatever will we do then?" says Charlotte, backing toward the house.

"Nine," announces Grayson.

"I don't need your help," Henry tells Luke. "And neither does Mom."

Luke's in the car before the count gets to ten. But Grayson slams his fist into the roof of the car anyway.

We're sprayed with dust and bits of gravel as the Camry goes careening down the driveway.

"Damn," says Grayson. "Guess you told him you don't like hockey."

Henry turns and stalks inside, alone.

CHAPTER 17

Grayson finally goes upstairs, promising to stay hidden in his room for the rest of Family Day. My mom talks with Charlotte's parents for thirty seconds before giving me the sign it's time to move on, and we spend the rest of the hour wandering around the grounds. She talks about people from the neighborhood, but I can only half listen, my mind still on Henry, and if he's okay, and Grayson, and what the hell he was doing with that safe in the director's office.

Then we gather in the gym, where Belk announces that a few of the students have prepared a surprise, a demonstration of what they've been learning.

Irritation wells inside me as Caleb steps into the center of the circle with Geri at his side. She's grinning up at him, all swinging hips and perfect hair and fresh makeup. Her black dress matches his black jeans and raven hair, and when he gives her a nervous grin, I feel my ribs turn brittle around my throbbing heart.

"Aren't they a cute couple," says Mom.

"Not really," I mutter.

The waltz music is piped in through the speakers, a sliding, three-beat cadence that now reminds me of Grayson's hand on my waist and his square shoulders. I shove him from my mind as Geri takes her place in front of Caleb and smiles, like she did earlier when he left Paz and Joel to talk to her.

Probably about this.

The parents love it, of course. They're already oohing and ahh-ing. Caleb's mom is wiping away a tear. Geri's dad is pointing her out to other nearby parents, as if they don't already know she's his. They make sure they show how impressed they are—no one's stupid enough to blow off a guy who could bench press double their body weight.

Again, I get the strange feeling I know him from somewhere, but I can't place it.

Mom clasps her hands over her heart as they begin their slow curve around the floor. Caleb's still terrible, but it's obvious they've been practicing. He hardly looks at his feet, and though his gait is stiff, he doesn't run her over.

"Can you do that?" Mom whispers reverently.

The sudden memory of Grayson sweeping me across the floor fills my mind, and it's stupid, but I wish she could see us. We're a thousand times better than these two.

As Geri tilts her head back like the women in the training videos, I suppress a groan, and try to hold on to the feel of Caleb's hand in mine. But I can't stop staring at his ink-stained fingers on the back of her black dress.

"Mrs. Hilder."

I jump as Dr. O comes up beside us. As he takes my mom's hand, my focus shifts away from Caleb and Geri to the director. I'm excruciatingly aware of how her silver shoes and red lipstick stand out against his deep, quiet tones, and the way she sizes him up like he's a customer who'll leave a huge tip if she plays her cards right.

I'm dead if Dr. O saw Grayson talking to her.

"I'm so glad you could make it." Dr. O takes Mom's hand in both of his, smiling warmly as Geri and Caleb finish their dance. "Your daughter has proven to be a wonderful addition to our school."

Nerves flutter beneath my sternum. My nails press into the heels of my hands. This can't be about Grayson—Dr. O would have talked to me about it, not her. He's just doing the good director thing and making the rounds.

Still, I'm nervous for what she might say. Is he going to bring up the job with Wednesday Pharmaceuticals? She won't—she has no reason to see the connection.

Which leaves it to me. But if I say something, then it ruins it for her. This leap that's taken her all my life to make will be nothing more than a favor, and she'll turn it down because Hilder women don't take handouts. We earn our keep.

Even if it means stealing.

"She's always been smart, I'll give her that," says Mom. "This is a gorgeous place, sir."

"Please, call me David."

"David," she smiles, and it's at full Allie Hilder wattage. "It's really good of you to do this for her. No one believes my girl made it out—they all think I'm lying and she's in juvy or something." She laughs so hard she slaps his shoulder.

I want to die.

"They should know she was bound for greatness being raised by someone like you." Dr. O's all charm, and it reminds me of the way Grayson turned it on with her earlier.

Mom waves a hand. "Oh, you."

"Anyway, it's me who should be thanking you," says Dr. O. "I'm not sure what we'd do without Brynn here. She's the very definition of hard work."

"That's my girl." Mom grins at me, but when Dr. O does the same, my gaze falls to the floor.

Maybe this is all coincidence, and he had nothing to do with her new job or place, but right now it feels like the worst kind of reward—the one that comes with an IOU.

He may have handed my mom a winning lottery ticket, but

the payout isn't tax free. The responsibility of it falls on my shoulders, and if I fail to complete my assignments, I don't just lose my future, but hers as well.

I owe Dr. O nearly as much as Caleb does now.

THE AFTERNOON ENDS with a thank-you from Dr. O, and Belk and Moore driving the parents who took the train back to the SCTA station. Caleb borrows the Jeep to take his family home and pick up Sam from the jail, and Charlotte, claiming to be sick so she doesn't have to face him, returns to her bedroom.

I go on a hunt for Henry.

He's not in the pit or in his room, and since I'm already upstairs, I knock on Grayson's door. Even though he should have stayed in his room today, I'm not mad at him. He risked his secrecy, but Mom swore she wouldn't say anything, and Henry's stepdad didn't seem to recognize him.

Plus, he stood up for Henry. I didn't think he cared about anyone enough to do something like that.

He calls me in, and I'm surprised to see Henry sitting in a chair next to his bed. They're watching something on a laptop, and judging from the creases around their eyes, they've been laughing.

"Brynn, come here." Henry motions me over, but there's nowhere to sit, so I end up squeezing on the side of the bed next to Grayson.

He doesn't move much, which means our hips touch, a fact he acknowledges with a wicked tilt of his lips.

They've picked some old movie about a bomb on a bus, and a hot policeman who has to keep the driver going above fifty miles per hour. The freeway's halfway built, though, and when they run out of road, they jump a forty foot gap.

In a bus.

I see now why they're laughing.

"You okay?" I ask Henry as the bus careens around another turn.

He's wearing a school shirt again, fitted to reveal his slender torso and the lean muscles of his arms. His hair is damp, like he's recently showered, and brushed over the side.

He looks like the old Henry again.

"I'm good," he says.

"He's going to hockey camp," Grayson says. "Where he can learn all about knee pads and scoring triple doubles."

"Hat tricks," says Henry. "Triple doubles are in basketball."

Grayson and I stare his way.

Henry gives a sheepish shrug. "I actually do like hockey."

"That's all right," says Grayson. "I actually like to dance. No-body's perfect."

I glance between them. Despite Grayson turning Vale Hall into a social experiment, it seems they've actually managed to become friends.

"Where's your mom?" The second I ask, I wish I could take it back. On the chance that they are pretending, I don't want Henry to feel awkward by me asking this question in front of Grayson.

"Probably at church. Or at home. Or doing whatever will make Luke happy." Henry slouches over his knees.

"Sounds like a winner," says Grayson.

"She's great," says Henry. "Really. She would do anything for anyone. She once gave all our clothes to this shelter because they put out a sign saying they needed donations." He gives a small smile. "She used to bring home dogs and cats that looked hungry because she felt bad for them. Animal control had to come clear out our house when the neighbors complained."

"So she's crazy," says Grayson.

Henry's cheeks darken. "She likes taking care of people."

I think of how Henry's always the first to give a hug, or praise, or to point out all the positives when something goes wrong. His mom's not the only one who puts others first.

"Sometimes she tries to help the wrong people," he says. "They're not always so nice. To her."

He doesn't say *or to me,* but I see the haze of memories in his eyes—the kind of things you wish you could forget. Experiences that wake him up at night and have him crawling into Caleb's room until they pass.

I reach for his hand, and he takes it and holds it against his chest. Even though we're with Grayson, even though Dr. O plays us like chess pieces, I'm glad we have this place. Henry needs it.

We all do.

"Well, if I had to live with all that, I'd be drunk all the time."

I hit Grayson hard in the shoulder.

"What? It's more fun than talking about feelings." He closes the laptop, which none of us are watching anymore. "And less fun than punching someone in the face."

"So half-drunk, all the time?" Henry asks, giving my hand a little squeeze.

"Or full drunk, part of the time," Grayson says.

I sigh. "Would you settle for ice cream, some of the time?"

Henry stands. "I would. Who's going to be my enabler?"

"I'm in," says Grayson. He sends me a wolfish smirk. "Who's going to be *my* enabler?"

I roll my eyes. "I don't even know what that's supposed to mean."

But I stand up and follow them toward the door.

We play video games through the evening. One by one, the others join us—all except Caleb, who still isn't back from picking up Sam at the train station.

One by one, they all go to bed.

"Goodnight, friends," says Henry with a yawn. He pats me on the knee and then stands. "You guys are the best."

"Have sweet dreams of me," says Grayson.

"Maybe I will."

"For sure you will."

I snort.

Henry blushes.

It's late, and I should go, too, but there are things Grayson and I need to discuss, and we haven't had a chance alone all day.

"So," I say. "About that safe in Dr. O's office."

His grin is reflected in the television as we change to a mountain track and pick new trucks. "About that."

"What were you doing?"

"Looking for the phone."

I pause.

"What phone?"

"The phone that was on . . . you know. That was in the car."

The warmth of the room falls steadily, one degree at a time.

"Susan Griffin's phone."

Grayson took it off her after he found her dead in the car. He hid it in a hollowed-out tree near the accident site and gave it to me when he told me he'd been the one to run her off the road.

He nods.

The game starts, but my fingers slip off the right buttons on the controller, and he jumps into the lead.

"How did you know it was there?"

"Deduction," he says. "Your director said it was in a safe. Henry said there's a safe in his office, hidden in the fireplace. It's where he keeps all your student files."

Why Henry is telling Grayson, who doesn't even really know what we do here, about our student files is beyond me.

"If there is, it's locked by combination."

"You don't need a combination if you've got an axe."

"You have an axe?"

"I was working on that part."

My monster truck takes a dive off the road, and I drop the controller into my lap. "Why the hell do you want that phone?"

He shrugs. "Insurance."

"Explain."

"What's your director doing?" he asks. "He knows Dad covered up what I did, and he's just sitting on it. Why? What's he waiting for?"

More information on Jimmy Balder.

Urgency rises in my veins.

"He's letting me stay here without question until I testify against him, but when will that happen? Dr. Odin hasn't made any reports. He hasn't done anything."

"I know."

"He's up to something," says Grayson, tossing the controller on the couch beside him. "And unless I've got my own insurance, I'm the one who's going to get screwed here."

He says *screwed* as if he weren't the one to run Susan off the road.

"So what's the plan?" I ask, shifting in my seat. "Get the phone, then what?"

"Keep it. I never should have given it away."

A wave of guilt washes over me, a reminder that I betrayed him by passing the phone along to Dr. O. Never mind that I was trying to protect Grayson by doing so. Never mind that I could have turned him in to the director, or the authorities, and didn't.

"Without that phone it's his word against mine that I actually . . . you know." His brows are furrowed, and his tone is thin with unease. "If my dad admits I did it, it will destroy his reputation, and since he's not talking, the only evidence I was there that night is that phone, with my fingerprints."

"You want to get rid of it," I realize.

He looks back at the television.

"Grayson, I . . ."

"Before you say anything, tell me you wouldn't do the same."

I swallow my breath, feeling it burn in my throat. If I had done what he had, and the only thing standing between me and jail time was a stupid cell phone with my prints on it, I would get rid of it, too.

I'd burn this house to the ground if it meant making my guilt disappear.

"Somebody died," I say.

His eyes flash to mine, and in a snap, a desperate anger sizzles across the room. "You think I don't know that? You think I don't think of it every second of every day? I tried to make it right, but I couldn't. Now it's just me. I've got to look out for myself."

He is scraped raw and aching. I can hear it in his voice. I can feel it in the throbbing tension between us. This is the boy who went to his father after the accident. This is the boy who tried to tell the cops and was sent home.

This is what exists beneath the anger, and the privilege, and the sarcasm.

"You're not alone," I say.

For a while, he doesn't respond. Then, he reaches for me, his hand closing around my calf. I stare at his fingers, glowing red and green and brown in the reflection from the television. The weight of them burns through to my muscle.

"Help me," he says. "You helped me before. Help me get that phone."

"I can't."

He starts to pull back, but I stop him. My hand over his.

"I will help you. I just need some time to figure out a plan."

"What kind of plan?"

I don't know. I squeeze his hand, but it feels too heavy to move. "I need to know everything you do about Susan Griffin."

"I told you everything I know."

"What about Jimmy Balder?"

He looks confused. "The intern you were talking about? I don't know anything about that."

"What about your father? Is there anything else he's done? Anything we can use to make a case against him?"

He flinches.

I wait.

"He called her," he says.

"You father called who? Susan?"

He nods.

"On that phone?"

He nods again.

This doesn't seem that important—*Pop Store* had already reported that Matthew Sterling and Susan were likely having an affair. Of course he'd call her.

"They were talking on the phone when it happened."

"When you hit her?"

He grimaces.

"How do you know that?" I ask.

His hand slides from my calf. He crosses one ankle over his knee, then sets both feet back on the floor.

"I heard someone talking on the phone when I got to her car. It was sitting there on the seat."

He bows forward, head in his hands. "He kept saying her name. *Susan? Susan? Talk to me. What's going on?* That kind of stuff. I knew it was him."

"What'd you do?"

"I picked up the phone."

"You what?"

Sweat has blossomed on Grayson's forehead, and he swipes it away with the back of his hand.

"I said there'd been an accident, and she wasn't moving. He didn't understand why I was there."

The scene is playing out in my mind in bold colors. Susan's car, smashed against a tree. Grayson reaching across her to pick up the phone off the seat, while she lays there, still as death.

"I said I needed to call the police, and he told me not to. That I had to come home. I shouldn't stop anywhere or do anything. Like I'd take a detour and catch a movie or something." His heels are drumming against the carpet. "When I got home, he was crying. *What'd you do?* he asked me. He kept saying it over and over. *What'd you do? What'd you do?*"

"He was crying?" I can't picture this, but maybe it was part of the act.

Grayson closes his eyes. "Then he got mad."

He pounds one fist lightly on his thigh. It takes a second to adjust to this new version of his story. It's like earlier, when he made it sound like Geri was the one who hurt him instead of the other way around. When I thought he was shallow, it was easy to assume everything he did was reckless, the actions of some spoiled brat. But the more time I spend with him, the more I realize there's so much beneath the surface that no one, not even his father, has bothered to explore.

"Does that help your plan?" he asks.

"I think so. But tell me if you think of anything else."

He exhales. "Okay."

Tilting forward, he stares at the floor, his jaw working back and forth.

"Do you think I'm a terrible person?"

"No."

He snorts, like he doesn't believe me.

"I don't," I say. "It was an accident. It could have happened to anyone."

"Not to you. You're too smart."

It's not meant to be a compliment, but a fact. Even if it's not true, it means something that he thinks that way about me.

"It was one night," I say. "A few minutes. There's more to you than that."

He's quiet.

I reach for him, my fingers spreading on his hard shoulder, feeling the breath move his back. With a pang, I remember the night Caleb called me down here, after the Wolves had beaten him up. How he looked at me, like I held all his secrets. Like I could crush him.

I remember the way he put his hand on Geri's back earlier.

I remember that he chose Dr. O's assignment over me, and even if I understand why, I still hate that he did it. He may have given me his trust, but he's been taking mine, piece by piece, since my first night at Vale Hall. Now I can't get it back, and the armor I've worn all my life is riddled with holes. It lets in too much. I feel *too much*.

As the minutes pass, a change comes over Grayson and me. I focus on the white of his shirt between my tan fingers. On his slowing breath.

On the way mine quickens.

I try to push Caleb from my mind, but the wounds are too deep, and a pulsing ache remains behind my ribs.

"I haven't always been here," I say. "Before this place, I lived in Devon Park, and it was all anyone ever cared about."

He looks over his shoulder at me, the light from the TV washing over his face.

"You'll break through this, just like I did," I say, and then I look away, embarrassed. I didn't want to tell him that. It's too personal. It's in the past.

He leans across the cushion and lifts his knuckles to my cheek. I don't move, frozen by the idea of what's happening, and whether I want this or don't, and if it even matters because if it's what Grayson needs, it has to be what I need.

My pulse jumps in my throat as his hand turns, cupping my jaw. He stares at my lips, the dark blue in his eyes turning stormy gray with an angry kind of need. A slick fist of warning closes around my lungs, but there's heat in my belly.

I don't want it to be there. I want Caleb. I *miss* Caleb.

"Grayson," I whisper. *We can't. We're friends.*

I say none of it, because all I can feel is that hole inside me that Caleb left, that keeps ripping more every time I see him outside Risa's, following me. Every time he touches Geri, and I picture that card with his trust, and I hear his voice whispering *we should take a step back.*

We're supposed to meet tonight. Fix things. Tell each other the truth.

But what if he doesn't want to fix things? What if he just wants to ask more questions about my assignment?

What if I can't trust him again?

What if this place that brought us together has broken us for good?

Grayson leans close and kisses me.

It isn't gentle. There is no question in the press of his lips, no tentative exploration. Only a heated, desperate desire, a demand to fix all the broken things inside him, to sand away the razor-sharp points.

And I answer with my own hurt and doubt and anger.

Until I can't smell Caleb's soap, or hear his breath, or feel his glasses nudge my nose.

Until there's only Grayson.

His other hand rises to my cheek and he kisses me hard again, his eyes closed tightly, the force of his grief threatening to swallow me whole.

I place my hands on his chest to steady myself, or push him back, I don't know, and he responds by grabbing my shirt and bunching it in his fist, dragging the fabric tight across my chest.

"Grayson," I say, gasping for breath. This isn't right. He's my assignment. Kissing him makes me no better than Geri, no more immune to his callous brush-off than any one of his conquests. Doing this isn't a job requirement; there are a dozen other ways to make him feel safe and comfortable.

I don't want this.

Only . . .

Only I kind of do.

"Brynn."

I shove back at the low voice that rumbles from the foot of the stairway. Humiliation scalds me as I register Moore's stiff posture, his jaw flexed in anger. Beside me, Grayson slumps back in the couch, running a hand down his jaw. He stares at the television, avoiding my gaze.

"Go to your rooms," Moore says. He's furious, though my thoughts are flying too fast to think why.

I kissed Grayson.

I can't even say it was all for the job. I was hurting, and he was hurting, and for a moment, the lines blurred. I stopped thinking about Caleb. I stopped thinking about how this was supposed to accomplish my assignment for Dr. O.

It's what Margot, Caleb's ex-girlfriend, did. She played her assignment, and then fell for him, and told him everything about Vale Hall.

I try to swallow, but a knot has formed in my throat. I stand, trying to look innocent. Failing miserably.

Grayson's thumbs punch the game controller. "I thought curfew wasn't until—"

"Upstairs. Now." Moore isn't playing.

Grayson doesn't even look at me as he shoves to a stand. Without turning off the game or the TV, he heads toward the stairs. Realizing he needs this quick escape as much as I do doesn't exactly make me feel better.

He shoves by Moore without a word.

I shut down the game console and walk toward Moore, palms damp. I don't know what I'm going to say. In the end, it doesn't matter; I don't have to say anything.

"I told you to watch yourself," he growls. "I told you to stay public."

My hands ball into fists inside my sleeves.

"Get in your room. I don't want you leaving until morning. I don't want you calling him or sending a single message. I don't want to see you looking at him again until you remember this isn't a game."

Moore's never talked to me like this before. He wasn't this angry when he caught Charlotte and Sam in the hot tub after curfew. This is a step above security officer. This is dad territory.

A wave of shame crashes over me.

With a nod, I hurry up the stairs, through the kitchen, up to the girls' wing. I close my bedroom door and sit on the edge of my bed. My heels bounce against the floor. My hands fist in the comforter.

I should be heading to the roof to meet Caleb right now, but I'm stuck in my room. Moore said no texting, and if I had to guess, he's checking my phone. I could probably get a pass if I went to Dr. O and told him Moore's interfering in my mission, but I don't want to. Last time I blew off Moore's orders I ended up careening down Route 17 in a Porsche, half-convinced I was going to die.

No wonder Moore's touchy when it comes to Grayson.

No wonder Caleb wants me to focus on my assignment.

I can't even tell him I'm not coming tonight. Maybe it's better that way. I don't know what I'd say to him.

My head falls into my hands.

I kissed Grayson.

I'm not sure what to say to him, either—he didn't exactly look pleased that I'd bolted back when Moore caught us.

This isn't a game.

I close my eyes, my lips still tingling from Grayson's searing kiss. My chest still aching from Caleb's lies. I go to my nightstand, shoving aside my books and notes until I find the card labeled *Trust*. Gripping it in one quaking hand, I trace the word with my finger, feeling its meaning slip out of reach.

I don't even know if I trust myself anymore.

CHAPTER 18

Caleb is gone when I wake up Sunday—out on assignment again, according to Henry. He left early and didn't say when he'd be back.

I can't help thinking his absence has something to do with me.

I start to text him, but delete it, because what can I say? *Sorry I blew you off, I was making out with my mark. By the way, did you get what you needed from me for Dr. O?*

I don't know what came over me last night. I never intended to kiss Grayson. He's a friend, one who doesn't even know the whole truth. He's angry, and complicated, and messed up right now.

And maybe I am, too.

But that's no excuse. If I don't help put his dad away, he's going to do something crazy, like try to steal Susan's phone again. Moore was right, this isn't a game. Grayson's an assignment, and I have a job to do.

Which is made slightly impossible when he won't even look at me.

I try to sit by him at breakfast, but he gives me the cold shoulder. I tell him I've got a new challenge, but he and his new best friend Henry are going to play *Road Racers*. Every time I try to corner him, he avoids me. It doesn't help that Moore is watching both of us like a hawk.

I have screwed this up, and I don't know where to go from here.

Caleb comes home that afternoon and joins the other guys in the pit. Geri squeezes next to him on the couch, smiling at me over his shoulder while I try to read *Othello* on the other side of the room. If he's annoyed by this, he doesn't let on. He barely acknowledges I'm there.

I am shunned, and every day I don't figure out a way to fix this situation is another day it feels more permanent.

MONDAY AFTERNOON IS a teacher in-service day, so Charlotte rounds up the girls and Belk drives us to Uptown for the afternoon to shop. Charlotte's birthday party is this weekend, and even though she's ordered four different dresses online, none of them fit right.

"We have to look perfect," she says as we head into a shop on Lakeside Avenue. "It's the last chance we have to be young and beautiful."

"Except for the holiday dinner at New Year's, and the spring formal you made us all do last year, and graduation, which Dr. O insists we all dress up for." Geri throws up her hands as Charlotte casts a glare her direction. "Not that I'm complaining. You're just being mildly dramatic."

Charlotte groans, tearing off her knit cap and stuffing it into her bag. Her red curls are an explosion today, but her makeup is on point. She wants to make sure she gets an accurate representation of what she'll look like next weekend when she sees herself in the dressing room mirror.

"Why did she come again?" I ask, glaring at Geri's back.

"Because if I didn't invite her, she'd probably be back at Vale Hall sticking her tongue down Caleb's throat."

I stop.

Charlotte winces. "I didn't mean that."

I know she didn't, just like I know Geri and Caleb don't really like each other. But thinking of them kissing makes me want to tear every little dress from the racks in this store and light them on fire all the same.

Not that I have any right to be jealous after what happened with Grayson and me in the pit.

"I'm in a pissy mood," Charlotte continues. "I'm sorry. Can we try on dresses now?"

I follow her to the nearest rack, covertly checking my phone in my pocket. After this I'm heading straight to my job, just a few blocks south of here, where Mark and I are going to have a little talk about Jimmy Balder and appropriate behavior with female interns.

"So, black for mourning?" She holds a small satin dress in front of her. "Or black for my soul?" She switches to a skirt with a slit straight up the hip.

"Either are good."

She rolls her eyes. "You're supposed to say, *Black's not your color, Charlotte. You need something vibrant. Green, or blue. Gold even.*"

"Sounds like a solid plan."

She lowers the hangers in her hands, mouth pulled into a thin line. "You aren't very good at this."

"Sorry."

"Look." She points to Paz and Michone, who are oohing and ahhing as Lila holds up a purple formal gown and smiles like a porcelain doll. "That's how it's done."

"Ooh," I say. "Ahh."

"Have you ever been shopping?"

"It hasn't exactly been a priority." I shoot her my best side-eye. "Not everyone gets to be a hotel heiress."

"Don't I know it." She sighs heavily, and sets the hangers back on the shelf. "Normally I'd just call James Wan to design me an original piece, but I know he's swamped working on Damien Fontego's suit for the Met Gala." Her haughty tone makes me smirk, and my cheeks warm at the mention of the Vale Hall alum that kissed my hand at my recruitment rally in the train yards. "So here I am," Charlotte continues, "slumming it in Uptown with a girl who thinks clothes *aren't a priority*."

I snort. "You poor thing."

She curtsies, pleased with her own performance. "But really, what are you wearing?"

I hadn't much thought about it. "There's a dress in my closet." It was there when I arrived, just like all my clothes.

I wonder if Mom's going to have her closet stocked in her new apartment, too.

My teeth tap together.

"Wrong," says Charlotte. "This is my eighteenth birthday. It's got to be exactly right."

"Why?" I don't mean to challenge the issue, but she's putting a lot of pressure on it. She asked Dr. O to have a tent put up in the field behind the pool, and there's going to be dancing and everything.

"Because it just does, okay? Everything changes after this."

Her head falls forward, and I know she's thinking about Sam again, and college. Everything that will be different next year.

I grab a blue dress off the nearest shelf and hold it in front of me.

"Well?" I make a kissy face and kick out one heel. "Not bad, huh?"

She snorts and puts it back on the rack. "Blue's my color. You, my friend, are wearing red."

I gulp, heading after her to a corner of the store where the necklines get lower and the hemlines get shorter. She grabs a gown the color of cherries, ankle-length but open across the shoulders, and grins mischievously at me.

"Uh-huh," she says, tossing it over her shoulder.

Fifteen minutes later, I'm standing in an oversized dressing room while Charlotte lounges on a purple velvet armchair. The dresses she's picked for herself are hanging on a hook, but she doesn't make a move for them.

"I'm not doing this unless you are." I swipe my palms down my jeans, staring at the explosion of red fabric before me.

She's pulling at the end of one of the skirts she's picked out—a blue satin scrap that'll show off her three miles of legs. In this lighting, it's easier to see the bruises beneath her eyes and remember the sound of her crying through the air vents in the wall.

"So how are things with Sam?" I ask.

"Huh?" She looks up. Scowls. "Oh just peachy. Like mealy peaches. That are rotten. With worms coming out of them."

"That good, huh?"

"I'll be okay. It was just a fight."

I give her a look, then take a deep breath and peel off my shirt.

"You're not eating." I've watched her at breakfast and dinner, pushing the food around on her plate like a five-year-old. "You look like you haven't slept in a week. Just talk to him."

She won't look at me, just like Caleb won't look at me, and Grayson won't look at me. It's like I've turned into a damn solar eclipse or something. Stare into my eyes and I will burn your retinas to blindness.

"It's not that easy," she says.

"It's Sam. You can tell him anything. Just figure out what you want, and go get it." But the words grow heavy on my tongue.

My fingers go to my lips, pressing them, the way Grayson's did. I wish I'd gone to the roof and met Caleb that night, but part of me wonders if what happened with Grayson was inevitable—if we have always been two trains from opposite directions on the same track, bound to crash.

Whatever the case, I know what I'm risking. That kiss with Grayson is going to stay locked in the vault until the day I die.

Charlotte stands, and then we're hugging, and I forget about my problems with Grayson and Caleb. It's awkward for a second that I'm in my bra, but she doesn't notice or care.

"Thanks," she says, her tears damp on my shoulder.

Pulling back, she wipes her eyes and turns to the mirror to hurriedly fix her makeup. Then we're trying on dresses, and our giggles turn to laughter when we see how ridiculous or sexy some of them look—how Moore will send us back to our rooms for a cover-up if we wear something too low-cut, or how we're supposed to dance in something too short without our underwear showing. We practice different moves in front of the mirror to see how we look, and then crack up all over again because it's not the dresses that are ridiculous, it's us.

But then I try on the last one, the red, strapless dress she picked out first, and Charlotte claps her hands over her mouth.

"Holy hell," she says.

It can't be any worse than the others, but I strut to the mirror anyway, and stop short.

The silky red fabric makes my shoulders glow a deep copper, and the wells behind my collarbone stand out like shadowed pools. My waves of hair seem darker and more vibrant in this color, and the way the dress clings to my waist gives me an hourglass shape I didn't know I had. At my ankles, the soft skirt fans out and ripples with every movement of my legs.

This dress is beautiful.

I am beautiful.

"Hold on." Charlotte digs into her bag and pulls out a gold tube of lipstick. Twisting it open, she makes me pucker my lips and paints them an apple red to match the dress.

I look in the mirror.

I'm not just beautiful, I'm hot.

"Whoa," I say.

"Girls!" Behind me, Charlotte's opened the door and is motioning for the other girls to come see.

"Damn." Paz is closest, and nods appreciatively. Lila is next, barefoot and wearing a lacy pink dress, and she leans into our room to give me a high five.

Charlotte should shut the door—this is embarrassing. But I don't move from the threshold, and when Alice and Michone howl their approval, I blush and laugh.

"Look at Cinderella, all cleaned up for the ball."

The way clears to reveal Geri, pure sin in a black halter dress that hugs her thighs and reveals her slender pale legs. Her hair swishes over one shoulder as she swivels her head to examine me.

I send her a patronizing grin. "Are you one of the little mice that turns into a horse and pulls my carriage?"

"Nice try." She saunters toward me, taking measured steps so her backside doesn't fall out of her short skirt. "I'm your fairy godmother, and if you don't do your job, I take everything away when the clock strikes twelve."

I straighten. The other girls meander closer, listening in.

"What's that supposed to mean?"

"Your new friend needs to go."

"That's not exactly her call," says Charlotte, hands on her hips.

"Sure it is," says Geri. "If you're so good, seal the deal already. Get him out of here. Playing hotel heiress and captain coder was fun for a while, but it's exhausting enough pretending I like you. I'm over pretending I like Caleb."

Her lips twitch, and even her condescending smile can't hide her true feelings. She worked with Grayson—failed with Grayson—and having him around is a constant reminder of that fact.

"So quit pretending," I tell her.

"Take it up with your ex." She steps closer and whispers so only

I can hear. "He's the one driving that train. He was pretty torn up about your breakup. I know he's rebounding, but I didn't have the heart to let him down. Need an A in PE to keep on honor roll, you know how it is."

I want to shove her away. Call her a liar. Caleb wouldn't go to Geri if he was upset about me. He'd go to Henry, or Sam, or even Charlotte.

But however much I hate to admit it, Geri's flirting hasn't been one-sided. I've seen him smile at her, touch her, and it's been different since we broke up.

No. He isn't really into her. This is another one of Geri's twisted games, and I'm not falling for it.

"I'm working on Grayson," I tell her. "Thanks for the concern."

"Clock is ticking, Cinderella."

She strides back to the dressing room, the other girls glancing between us as if expecting a bigger fight. Disappointed I didn't give them one.

"Show's over," says Charlotte. "Go back to being gorgeous."

I stomp back into the dressing room, fighting with the zipper on the back of the dress. Charlotte closes the door and helps me before I rip it.

"She's just being Geri." Charlotte carefully drapes the dress over the back of the chair. "Don't let her get to you."

"I know." In a hurry, I jerk on my jeans and check the time. I need to leave for the club.

"Caleb's just humoring her," she says.

"I *know.*" But I don't. Geri's putting the pressure on me through Caleb, so I'll hurry and get Grayson out of Vale Hall, but does he actually like her?

I turn on Charlotte. "Why would he do this?"

She shrugs. "Because you're taken. He's trying to get your attention, I don't know."

He didn't need Geri to get my attention; he already had it. He's the one who broke up with me, and now he's upset about it?

"Put the dress on your card, yeah?"

Charlotte nods, and I head out to my job, forcing Caleb aside so I can focus on Grayson, and Jimmy Balder, and slimy Mark Stitz.

CHAPTER 19

When I get to The Loft, I head straight through the kitchen to the lockers so I can change into my hostess dress. Myra is on break, sitting on the bench beside the bathroom door, sipping another giant to-go cup of coffee. She's wearing a loose braid today, and tendrils of black hair surround her face.

I say a quick hello, grab my uniform, and head into the bathroom—I want to be ready when Sterling's staff shows up today. But as I lock myself in a stall, I hear the main door open and swing shut.

"Got a minute?" Myra asks. It sounds serious, and even though I didn't hear anyone else in here, I check under the stall door to my right just in case.

Just us.

"What's up?" I pull my shirt over my head and hang it on the back of the door.

"I've been thinking about what happened."

I pause, then get to work on my jeans. "Yeah, me too."

I hear a quiet drumming, as if she's tapping her fingers on the paper cup. "I didn't mean to make you feel bad about what happened with Mark. I should've been more supportive."

The problem isn't that she wasn't supportive, it's that she was, but I can't take her support because there's too much wrapped up in this that she doesn't understand.

I need Mark to tell me about Jimmy Balder, and his inappropriate behavior, obnoxious as it was, may be just the leverage I need to get some answers.

"It's okay," I tell her.

"You can trust me."

My chest pangs as Caleb flashes through my mind. I wish it were as easy as that.

"We're friends. Or we're going to be, anyway," she says. "Sometimes you just know about people."

Her need to make this right is so sincere, so eager, that I regret keeping my true identity from her.

"Thanks." I slide the black dress over my head and pull it down my hips. Before, it gave me confidence, but now, at the prospect of facing Mark again, I wish I wasn't wearing something so tight. I hate that he's made me question a stupid uniform.

One issue at a time.

"I checked into that friend of mine who's missing," I say. "The one who used to work for the campaign."

My exterior may be the picture of calm, but inside, my nerves are humming. I'm on a time limit right now—I need to get to Mark quickly—but Myra knows something. I felt it when I first started here, and again that night at the restaurant. I can't dismiss that.

"Jimmy something, right?" Again, I hear her fingers drumming on the cup.

"Jimmy Balder. No one's seen him in a year." Ben never sent that picture of him, Emmett, and Jimmy after the whole "mugging" debacle. I make a mental note to remind him.

"Really?" she asks.

"I think something may have happened to him. With the senator." I pull on my tights, then crack the door so I can see her face when I add, "I called the campaign's human resources department on my way in. They've never heard of him. No file. No record of employment. Nothing."

Her brows knit. "Isn't that confidential information?"

I shrug. "I can be persuasive." It wasn't difficult—I just told the woman on the phone that my supervisor needed his mailing address to forward a letter of recommendation since the email Jimmy gave was no longer active.

"Maybe they get rid of a person's information once they leave. Or maybe he split on bad terms—got fired or something." She takes another sip of coffee as I fix my hair in the mirror. "That's why you were so concerned with the interns coming and going your first day, wasn't it?"

"Maybe."

HR wouldn't get rid of an intern's profile. They'd need it, especially if he got fired. That kind of stuff is always documented, even at Mom's job at Gridiron Sports Bar.

No, Jimmy's not in human resource's files because Sterling found a way to get rid of him—to make him disappear. I couldn't find anything online about him, either—no address, no missing person stories.

"You knew Sterling's campaign met here before you got the job, didn't you?" She sighs. "Jessica mentioned the other day that you got the job because your aunt and Mrs. Sterling are friends."

Time to tread carefully.

"I did," I say. "I do need the job, but I want to know what happened to Jimmy, too."

She sets the cup on the counter, but her hand is shaking, and she knocks it over. Quickly, she rights the cup before too much spills.

"Sorry," she mumbles as she grabs a handful of paper towers to wipe it up. "This is my third refill. Too much caffeine."

Or she's nervous about something.

"You haven't heard anything about him, have you?" I ask.

"No," she says without looking up. "Why would I?"

My frown is reflected in the mirror as I fix my eyeliner with the pencil in my bag. Maybe she's hiding something, or maybe she really was nervous about talking to me about what happened at Risa's and drank too much coffee.

"I think Mark knows something," I say. "He was starting to tell me at the restaurant when things got a little . . . weird."

"And you hit him."

I nod.

She blows out a breath. "You think he had something to do with it?"

I hadn't considered this.

"How do you mean?"

She scowls. "Maybe Mark killed him. Maybe he dragged him into some dark parking lot like he did you."

I shiver.

"He's not a killer."

I don't think. A scenario plays through in which the senator has Mark do his dirty work. It's not impossible that Mark played a personal role in Jimmy's disappearance.

"He kills my joy every time he shows up," she says.

"He's not at the top of my favorite people list, either."

"So what are you going to do?"

"Find out what he knows," I say. "However I have to."

She's stirring the drink slowly, staring at the cabinet in front of her. "That doesn't sound very safe."

"I've dealt with worse."

She takes a slow sip of her coffee. "I've said that before, too."

There's a heaviness in her tone, that festers under my skin, a wound you can't scratch.

"And?" I say.

"And I was wrong." She turns toward me. "There's always someone worse."

I'm about to ask what she means when the door shoves open, and Jessica is framed in the threshold. Her perfectly painted lips form a thin line as her gaze narrows on us.

"Break time's over," she snaps. "Half of the senator's group is already here for a meeting."

I frown as Myra scurries away. The campaign staff usually doesn't meet for another half hour. I can't help wondering if something's happened.

As I rush to the front of the restaurant, I see three staffers I recognize bypassing the hostess stand and making their way to the back room, brows drawn and frowns tight. Myra's already hustling that direction carrying a water jug, and I grab another on the bar and hurry after her.

Inside, every seat around the oak table is filled, and people are filling in behind the chairs.

Everyone is talking. Hands are moving, faces are red.

Fear makes my heartbeat stutter. They know about Susan. They know about Grayson. There wouldn't be this much frenzy over what happened between Mark and me the other night.

Something big has leaked, and I need to warn Dr. O.

My eyes catch on Mark, standing in the front of the room, nodding grimly as a man with orange hair reads something off his cell phone.

"What's going on?" Myra asks Ben as we start filling glasses on the table at the back of the room. There's so much commotion, no one else seems to notice we're there.

"The news just broke," says Ben. He shows us the open screen on his phone, which has Senator Sterling's smiling photo on one side, and a news anchor on the other.

Illinois Senator Pulls 180 on Vote says the caption below.

"He was presenting the drug bill today," says Ben, pulling anxiously on the collar of his shirt.

"The what?" I ask.

He tucks his phone into his pocket. "Decreasing the price of pharmaceutical medication."

"Right," Myra says with a weak smile.

Ben lowers his head so we can hear what he has to say.

"It's been a huge deal getting the support in-house. All the other politicians are funded by big money—big drug companies, like Pfizer and Biotech and—"

"And Wednesday Pharmaceuticals," I say.

"Yes," Ben whispers. "Exactly. And those big companies are going to lose a ton of money by supporting this bill, so they've been buying out their senators so they'll vote against it."

"But not Sterling?"

Ben shakes his head. "Are you kidding? Sterling consistently votes for the people. He'd never be bought out by some giant company like Wednesday. At least, until now."

"He was bought out by Wednesday?" I ask, panic fluttering inside me. Dr. O owns Wednesday Pharmaceuticals. Why would he bribe Sterling when he wants to see the man in jail for covering up Susan's death?

"No one knows," says Ben. "That's why everyone's freaking out. He was supposed to propose this bill today that would save people millions of dollars countrywide on their medicine, but he changed his mind last minute and voted with the opposition."

"In support of the big drug companies?" I ask.

Ben nods. "Someone got to him. The staff had no idea this was coming."

Someone got to him. There are millions of people who could bribe or threaten Sterling, but only one I know of who's connected to a big drug company—who would stand to profit off a bill that gouged the public on medicine prices.

Dr. O.

As the man with orange hair stands at the front of the room, I think of Vale Hall, a giant mansion supported by a rich benefactor that gives away laptops and clothing like candy, and sends students to college without breaking stride.

I knew Dr. O's money came, at least in part, from Wednesday Pharmaceuticals, but I never thought about how much he needs that money to continue his operation. We only con for him because of what he does for us, and all he provides comes down to money.

If someone tried to take away his money, how far would he go to stop them? Would he use Wednesday's wealth to bribe a senator he would rather see rot in jail? Or would he threaten that senator with intimate knowledge of a covered-up murder, provided by me, and a missing family member, now hidden away in Vale Hall?

I keep my head low, filling water glasses slowly to make my presence here warranted.

It's too coincidental. Dr. O wants Matthew Sterling to pay for what he did to Susan. He wouldn't let the senator walk the streets if he could crush him, even if Matthew Sterling could vote in ways that would bring Dr. O more money.

The man with the orange hair—Lewis, the campaign manager, from what I gather from people talking—is telling us to expect an uproar from Sterling's constituents. People will be calling—constituents, press, donors—demanding an explanation for this betrayal. The staff needs to stick to a consistent message and keep things vague until "Matt" returns Lewis's calls. Yes—Greener Tomorrow is still on. Yes—the senator still fights for the working class.

The sound of cell phones ringing is already filling the air, overriding the raised voices. Ben joins Emmett and a few other interns huddled around their phones, while Myra heads out of the room. She waits a moment for me to follow, but I hesitate, holding my gaze steady until Mark Stitz looks up.

His cheeks turn rosy as his eyes hold mine. A moment later, he rises and slips through the crowd in my direction.

"You shouldn't be here," he mutters, leading me outside the room.

Instead of crossing the pavilion, I tilt my head toward the hallway where we talked before, and after a reluctant moment, he follows me in that direction.

"This isn't . . ." His nostrils flare as I pull to a stop, not far out of sight. "This isn't a good time, Jaime."

"We need to talk." I step closer.

He eases back.

An echo of fear ripples through me—a memory from his drunk fumbling in the dark parking lot across from Risa's. He's come to his senses now, but that doesn't mean all is forgiven.

"I want to know about Jimmy Balder."

He glances back as a cacophony of strained voices stretches around the corner. "Not now."

"I think now is perfect, actually."

"In case you haven't noticed, we have work to do."

"I heard," I say. "It's hard when people don't do what you want, isn't it?"

The muscles of his neck pull tight.

I smile grimly. "Let's make this quick. You said Matt didn't like Jimmy. Why?"

"Did you not hear me? We have a crisis . . ."

"Remember what happened in the parking lot last week? How that guy had to step in because you wouldn't keep your hands to yourself? I'm not sure your team could handle more drama today."

The color drains from his face.

"What did Matt tell you about Jimmy?" I ask.

"Is this extortion?" He looks shocked that I could even think of it.

"That's a big word, Mark. I'm only eighteen. But then, you knew that, didn't you?"

His nostrils flare as he exhales. "Nothing happened."

"You sure about that?"

His hands lift to the sides of his face. "You bitch."

"Careful," I tell him. "Don't want to add any more fuel to my harassment complaint."

He's crumbling, panic seizing him, but I feel no pity. He played his cards from the beginning and took advantage of his power. Myra was right; if we let people like this get away with mistreating us, they'll continue to do it.

"Jimmy," I tell him. "The senator didn't like him. Why?"

"I don't know."

"Try harder. He was a rock-star intern. He pulled in tons of donation money. What did he do to piss off the boss?"

Mark blinks up at me as if I've transformed into a monster in front of his eyes.

"That guy with the red hair is your boss, right? Lewis? Convenient that he's here today. I'd love to meet the people in charge of this operation."

"Okay," says Mark, holding up his hands. "Okay. Fine. Matt has limited contact with the interns. I didn't even know he knew who Jimmy was."

I hold Mark's gaze. I will not be bullied, intentionally or not, by him again. He needs to know that.

"We were working late one night. It was after that fund-raiser at the art gallery." I picture the photo on Ben's phone. Jimmy, rocking forward in laughter.

Mark scratches the back of his head. "Some of the staff and interns came back here to count up the donations. Matt showed up as people were starting to leave. He and the artist wanted to thank everyone."

My pulse spikes.

"What artist?"

"Some woman, I don't remember her name. All the proceeds from her paintings went to the campaign."

Susan Griffin was an artist. She painted the portrait of herself that hangs in Dr. O's office.

"When was this?"

"Last year sometime. I don't remember."

"But you could look it up."

"Probably. I guess. What does it matter? I thought you wanted to know about Jimmy."

"I do," I say. "What happened then?"

"They thanked people, and everyone headed out. It was late. After midnight sometime. I was packing my stuff up when I heard voices in Lewis's office." Mark glances down the hall. "Matt and Jimmy were in there arguing."

"About what?"

"I didn't catch all of it. Just that Matt wanted him to leave. That night. He told Jimmy he should never come back."

"Why would he do that?"

"I don't know. Jimmy must have said something at the gallery. Offended him or made the campaign look bad. I'd never heard Matt so upset."

"But Jimmy was a good intern, everyone says so."

"I'm just telling you what I heard," Mark says. "I can't be everywhere at once."

This doesn't fit. Why would the senator tell Jimmy to disappear when he could *make* him disappear? If Sterling wanted Jimmy gone, he wouldn't warn him. Giving a head start wouldn't have worked in the senator's favor.

"Why didn't Matt talk to you about it?" I ask. "You're the internship supervisor. If Jimmy messed up, wouldn't you be in charge of discipline?"

"Normally, yes." Mark's face warps with annoyance. "Matt has control, though. If he doesn't like what he sees, he can make the call to fire someone."

I tap my fingers against my thigh. Jimmy couldn't have been fired. Something else was said in that room, or Mark misunderstood. If Jimmy had been cut loose, human resources would still have his file.

"So Jimmy didn't come back after that?"

"That night was the last time I saw him."

"Where was the artist?"

Mark groans. "In the room with them. Are we done?"

"She didn't say anything?"

"Not that I heard."

"Well, what did she look like? Was she mad? Was she offended? Did Jimmy say the wrong thing to her?"

"I don't remember what she looked like. This was forever ago."

"What about she and Sterling? Were they together?"

"He's married."

"And?"

Mark's hands rest on his hips. "They weren't messing around in the office if that's what you're asking. Look, we have things to do, so if you're all done, go smile and take people to their tables."

A good con knows when the ice is growing thin. Mark's done talking, and I've gotten what I need, even if I'm not sure what it means.

I've turned and am striding away when I hear him say, "You think you're so smart, but you don't have nearly the power you think you do."

I glance at him over my shoulder, mildly amused by the wings in his shirt sleeves and the daggers in his glare.

"You're a minimum wage waitress," he says. "And we were out. No one's going to believe your word over mine when I tell them you were the one acting inappropriately—that I tried to spare your feelings to be nice, but you couldn't keep your hands off me."

"Is that your defense, Mark?"

"It's my offense."

"Oh." I crinkle my nose. "To be your offense, wouldn't you have had to tell someone before I made the complaint?"

His jaw drops open.

"Did I forget that part?" My smile is pure ice. "I called your human resources department on my way in and reported your behavior. Apparently I'm not the first girl you've known to make this kind of claim. I'm sure they'll be calling for your side of the story at some point, once the smoke clears from the current *crisis*."

As I stride back to the hostess station, I catch Myra's worried expression and give her a reassuring nod.

Mark will no longer be a problem.

CHAPTER 20

At the end of our shift, Myra and I walk to the parking lot together so I can fill her in on my report to HR, but before we step onto the sidewalk she pauses, digging through her purse.

"Can't find my keys," she says, then glances up. "Fancy car waiting over there. Must be for Lewis."

I follow her gaze to where Moore, bundled in a long wool coat the color of ash, is leaning against the outside of a gleaming black sedan parked behind a utilities truck. With a wince, I consider taking a lap around the block so she won't see me get inside. This wouldn't be an issue if I could just drive myself.

"Actually, that's my ride," I say.

She stops digging, brows hiked halfway up her forehead. "Seriously?"

I ball my hands inside my sweater, pulling the sleeves into my fists. A year ago, I never thought being waited on by a driver and a fancy car would make me uncomfortable, or that I'd feel anything but pride that someone could feel jealous over something I had. But judgment, whether intentional or not, is painted all over Myra's face, and I wish I'd told Moore to meet me around the corner at the train station.

"My mom's kind of paranoid about safety," I say as Moore glares at a bike messenger who rides too close.

"That's . . . awesome," she says, though I can't tell if she really thinks so. "I think I left my keys in my locker. Fill me in tomorrow on what happened."

She's already walking back inside.

"I'll help you," I say.

"No, it's cool. See you tomorrow."

The driver thing has made it weird. Definitely need to work on my own ride.

With a sigh, I walk around the utilities truck that's blocked Myra and me from Moore's watchful gaze. My security guard gives me a curt nod, then slips into the driver's seat and starts the engine.

Awkwardness prickles between us. He's still mad about my boundaries with Grayson, and I'm still trying to pretend he didn't catch us kissing. It's going well. Every time I glance his way, I feel the need to sink deeper into my seat.

We're nearly out of Uptown before he speaks.

"How'd it go today?"

I have more information about Jimmy Balder than I did three hours ago—maybe enough to stop this job. But I keep thinking about Matthew Sterling's change of heart, and if his support of companies like Wednesday Pharmaceuticals has anything to do with Dr. O's interference.

And what it means for Grayson if it does.

"All right."

Moore's not one for small talk, but since Grayson's arrival, he's been around a lot. It was nice when the tether was longer, but the truth is, apart from the kissing Grayson debacle, I don't mind so much. Picking up my mom for Family Day was a stand-up thing to do, and even if Moore's got the personality of an icicle, he's from my neighborhood, and he gets me in a way other people can't.

He grunts, and we drive on.

Twilight is bruising the sky as he pulls off the highway. I think he's trying to avoid traffic—this isn't our usual route—but when he pulls into a high school parking lot, I lean forward in my seat.

"What are we doing here?" There are no other cars in the lot, and the yellow lights paint the cracked asphalt with oval shadows.

"Got a flat," he says.

"No we don't."

Is this a test? What has Dr. O put him up to?

Moore grabs his coat from the backseat, giving me a look when I don't move.

"You want to learn how to drive or not?"

I gape at him.

He shakes his head, the equivalent of a Moore eye roll.

"Get out," he says.

I get out. I'm in such a hurry to zip up my coat, I get my sweater caught and fray the bottom of the white knit.

I'm sure I've cared less about things, but I can't think of what they are now.

"If you're doing this, you're going to be responsible about it," he says, and I get the sense he's not talking just about the car, but my assignment.

He pulls on his leather gloves. "Rule number one. You want to learn how to drive, ask an adult with a license. Don't steal someone's car unless you're asked to do so."

"Yes, sir."

Images of the day I took the SATs slide through my excitement, reminding me of Caleb and how things were before Grayson came.

Before everything got screwed up.

I can't think about that now.

"Rule number two," says Moore. "Driving's a privilege. You get it when you learn to take care of a car."

"I'll feed it twice a day and tuck it in every night, scout's honor." I hold up three fingers.

"I'm regretting this already," he says.

I follow him to the trunk, where he pulls out a metal crossbar and hands it to me. Each beam is the length of my arm, and it's heavy enough to knock someone out if you swing it right.

"Tire iron," he says, then opens a wide plastic case. "Jack. Wedges. Jumper cables. Road flares."

"Not to be confused with firecrackers."

"A car's a weapon, Brynn," he says. "This stuff's important."

I glance over at him, finding it suddenly hard to swallow. I know a car's a weapon. I remember every time Grayson lets me see beyond his shield to the brokenness beneath.

"Right," he says grimly. It's an apology, and we move on.

Removing the jack from the trunk, he sets it behind the front driver's side tire. He calls for the wedges—twin metal triangles hanging from thick rope handles—and tells me to put them behind the back tires to make sure we don't roll.

"Cool," I say. "Can I have the keys now?"

"Once you get that tire off and the spare on."

He's not kidding.

Under his direction, I successfully position the jack. By the time I'm removing the lug nuts from the front tire, I'm sweating, but he doesn't lift a finger to help.

"You want my keys, you'll figure it out."

I do. I drag the spare out of the trunk myself. I jack up the car and slide it into position. And after thirty-five minutes, I have changed my first tire.

I rise, arms raised victoriously as I take a victory lap around the car.

Then he makes me change it back.

I tell him this is why we have cell phones. This is why tow trucks were invented. There is a whole profession of people dedicated purely to roadside assistance.

He doesn't seem to care.

And honestly, it is kind of interesting.

He shows me how to open the fuel lid, and turn on my flashers, and pop the hood. There, he points out the main pieces of the engine and where, if I touch, I'll get shocked or lose a hand. We walk through the process of jump-starting the engine, and when I pass his little quiz, I'm pretty damn proud of myself.

Only then does he give me the keys.

It's different than driving with Caleb. First, the lot is empty, which does wonders for my self-esteem. Second, Moore sets up a system where I'm constantly checking my mirrors and the road as I move forward. I still ride the brake hard, but after a few stops and starts, I'm actually driving.

"Thanks," I tell him as we switch back to our regular seats. Almost two hours have passed, and it's time to get back to school.

"Someone's got to teach you."

Caleb said Dr. O taught him. I wonder if they went through the same process—if Dr. O crouched outside the car beside Caleb as he sweated to turn the tire iron. If Caleb could relax, or if he was only thinking about what mistakes he was making because of what hung in the balance.

Even a driving lesson is weighted when the man teaching you is responsible for keeping your dad alive.

"Mom got a job at Wednesday Pharmaceuticals," I say.

Moore doesn't respond, but that doesn't mean he didn't hear me. If there's one thing I've learned about Moore, it's that he hears everything. He's worse than Ms. Maddox.

"I keep thinking I should tell her not to take it," I say.

We've never talked about Dr. O's ownership of Wednesday. By Moore's non-expression, I doubt he's surprised I know about it.

"What happens if you do?" he asks.

We're back on familiar roads now, and the properties are growing larger, with more distance between each massive house.

I think of Mom's face when she told me about the job and the new apartment. How much this could mean for her.

"She stays in Devon Park."

"Is that so bad?"

She deserves more. Now, with Pete gone, she has a chance to move on. If she doesn't, she could meet someone new, maybe worse, and get tied to the neighborhood all over again.

"She could do better."

"Like you did?"

The way he says it makes me squirm in my cushioned leather seat. I am doing better. I live in a mansion.

Filled with lies and complications.

Doesn't matter. It's better than what I had before, and it's going to get me somewhere so far up, I can't even see the slums anymore.

"Devon Park's just a place," he says. "Can't make you any happier than anywhere else."

I cross my arms, and my legs for good measure.

"Are you happy?" I ask.

"Don't I look it?"

Shadows flicker across his brown skin as we make the final turn toward our drive. He reveals nothing, as always.

I can't tell Mom not to try for something better. Aiming high is what got me where I am today. She'll be safer out of that run-down house. She'll have more money in her pocket with a new job.

But what if I screw up with Dr. O and he takes it all away?

An ache pounds through my chest, hard enough I have to rub the top of my ribs with the heel of my hand to ease the pressure. These are questions Caleb lives with every second of every day, and right now I miss him so much I can barely breathe.

These stupid assignments pitted us against each other. I thought we were strong enough to withstand them, but how could we, when he was spying on me? When Grayson now stands directly between us?

Right now, Caleb feels farther away than ever.

Headlights appear in the distance, at the iron gate that marks the private drive to the mansion.

"Who is that?"

As we approach, a beige car comes into view. Two men are already standing outside, one of them in a black, knee-length coat, the other in a brown suit. They hold their hands up to block our lights, hiding their faces.

My blood turns cold.

"Stay in the car," Moore tells me.

He stops beside the car, which has blocked the keypad access to the gate, and gets out, standing in the open hinge of the door.

"This is private property," he calls.

I lean forward in my seat, wariness crawling down the back of my neck. A flashlight is lifted and shined in my face. I quickly block the beam with my forearm.

"Perfect timing," says one of the men. "No one's answering the speaker. I was just about to call for someone to knock down this gate."

"Why would you want to do something like that?" Moore's voice is hard, sending prickles of fear over my skin.

The man in the brown suit moves closer to the car and becomes visible again through the crack in Moore's open door. He opens his jacket, and I swallow a gasp as a gun is revealed in a leather holster beneath his left arm.

He takes a folded piece of paper out of his pocket and holds it in front of Moore's face.

"Sikawa City Police Department," he says. "We have a warrant to search this property."

CHAPTER 21

The beige car backs up so that we can pull forward, and when Moore enters the code, he holds his finger on the last button for a long time, until the box makes a series of beeps and then goes black.

As many times as I have been in and out of this gate, I've not seen it do this. It must be some kind of a warning.

The gate pulls open, and Moore drives down the lane. The headlights of the car behind us reflect in my rearview mirror, urging my pulse faster.

I pull out my cell to text the others what's coming and find a blank screen. A picture of Charlotte and me is usually my background, but it's missing now, and when I search for my speed dials, the menu is empty.

It's like my phone has been reset.

"Put it away," Moore says. "They'll ask to see it."

My breath is hot and raspy in my throat. I can't hold still; my whole body is twitching, a live wire.

"Leave your ID in my glovebox," he orders.

I rip the *Jaime Hernandez, THE LOFT* employee card over my head and pop open the glove box, stomach turning to water when I find a gun beside the car registration.

I place my card on top of it and close the box.

"What's going on?" I whisper, as though they might hear. "Why are the cops here?"

"Relax." His voice is the same, but the muscles in his jaw flex around the word. "If this were a raid, there'd be more than just two."

A raid? I picture twenty FBI agents and police officers storming the mansion, throwing smoke bombs and tackling students to the ground.

"So what do they want?"

He doesn't answer.

It could be anything. Beneath the surface, we operate in everything from fabricated IDs to political manipulation.

"Where is everyone? Why didn't someone answer the speaker?" I ask.

"Dr. O has a meeting in the city," Moore says. "Mr. Belk took him."

Which means the only adult on the property would be Ms. Maddox, who can't speak and wouldn't be able to answer the gate comm.

"What are we going to do?"

His eyes flash to me, as dark as the shadows in this car.

"You're going to do what you always do and act like a professional."

I straighten in my seat. The guy who taught me how to change a tire is gone, and in his place is the same scary security guard everyone on the outside must see.

Each crunching rotation of the tires grates against my raw nerves. Where is Grayson? He needs to hide. All of us are documented students, with parental consent, but he's a fugitive. A runaway. A senator's son.

Hiding him has to be illegal.

Parents were just here a few days ago, but this is different. This is the police. If we're busted, we'll be lucky to share a juvy cell while Dr. O and the adults take the pipeline to prison.

"Thirty more seconds," Moore mutters, checking his watch.

"Until what?"

He doesn't answer.

We pull around the fountain, but the other men have already parked and are out of their car. Moore hurries to unbuckle his seat belt, no doubt wanting to reach the door before they do.

"You are a professional," he reminds me one more time, and then he's jogging after them. He passes them on the front steps and keys in the door code. I am close behind.

"Don't think we don't know what you're doing," says the man in the suit. He's agitated now, his voice rippling with tension as he grabs the graceful, S-shaped handle of the door.

"What's that, officer?" asks Moore.

"Detective Morales," corrects the suit. "You have a secret knock, too? We'll be checking your cell phone records to see who you've called to warn."

"Then you'll see I didn't call anyone," says Moore calmly.

I've come through this front door dozens of times since I moved to Vale Hall, but now I'm unsure what I'll find inside. Moore said he needed thirty more seconds. He must have been giving Ms. Maddox and the others time to prepare for our arrival. It's been three, maybe four minutes since he keyed in that strange code on the gate box. What's happened since then?

The lock clicks and Detective Morales shoves inside, followed by his friend, who looks harder in the bright light of the entryway, cut by deep wrinkles that line his eyes and mouth and stretch to his thin, silver hair.

They both look like they've been at this game for some time.

Ms. Maddox comes hobbling toward us, plump cheeks flushed, her favorite poppy dress swishing around her ankles with each labored step. She looks to Moore, eyes wide.

"Ma'am, we need to see the director," says Detective Morales. His silent friend has already passed and is snooping his way toward the kitchen.

Ms. Maddox shakes her head.

"He's not on the property. You'll have to come back," says Moore.

"I didn't ask you. Ma'am?"

Ms. Maddox looks worried. She taps her neck and shrugs.

"She can't speak," says Moore. "Throat cancer."

"Well isn't that convenient?" mutters Morales.

"Not really," I say.

His gaze cuts to mine. I turn and try to walk as casually as I can toward the kitchen, to where his friend is now asking Paz and Alice where the rest of the students are.

"Studying? I don't know," says Paz, motioning toward her homework laid out across the table. "Why? Someone in trouble?"

Sounds are coming from the pit. If Grayson's down there, I need to warn him.

As quietly as I can, I walk toward the dining room and the basement stairs.

"That depends," says the wrinkled detective. "Do you know a boy named Grayson Sterling?"

My heart stops.

Restarts with the force of a punch.

Alice looks to Paz, and then to me, frozen in my tracks. Paz grins. "Yeah, I know him."

My stomach drops through the marble floor.

"He was on the *Pop Store* website, right? I think he was standing on a car or something."

"Oh yeah," says Alice, with a half smirk. "I remember that."

"Is he here?" asks the detective.

"Why would he be here?" asks Alice. Paz looks confused.

Gold stars, all around.

I resume my walk toward the pit, but the detective is following me. How did they know Grayson was here? My mind flashes to his arm, linked with Mom's. Did she say something? She loves gossip, and her daughter dating a senator's son is prime material. It could have been Henry's stepdad, too, though he didn't seem to realize who Grayson was.

"My name is Simon," the older man says. "What's your name?"

My mind shoots through half a dozen aliases I've used in the last year. Jaime? Sarah? I don't know which one I can use that will look the least suspicious if they do a background check.

"Am I under arrest?" I ask.

"No."

"Then I don't have to talk to you without the director present."

He gives a quiet chuckle. "That's technically true."

We're at the edge of the dining room, the empty kitchen open behind us. I can still hear Morales talking to Moore as they make their way down the hall on the first floor. Each door opens as he looks inside the rooms where we have class.

"Who's the guy you came in with?" He's using the friendly voice cops use when they're trying to trick you into spilling your secrets.

"Mr. Moore," I say. This seems harmless enough. "He's a security guard here."

"Do you have many security guards here?"

"That sounds like a question for him."

He chuckles again, and just as I'm preparing to turn back toward the kitchen and lead him back to Moore, the basement stairs creak. Someone's coming up.

I hide the panic swelling in my chest.

I am a professional.

Henry appears, and when his eyes land on the man beside me, he scrubs a hand through his strawberry-blond hair.

"Hello," he says. "Are you someone's dad?"

Simon pulls open his jacket, revealing a gold police badge hanging on his hip.

"Oh God," says Henry. "Okay, is this about the candy bar I

took from that gas station? Because I was only twelve, and my mom made me return it when she found out what I did."

"She sounds like a good mom," says Simon, and Henry beams.

I am going to dissolve in a puddle of sweat.

"This is about Grayson Sterling, the senator's son," Simon continues. "Have you seen him?"

Henry shakes his head. Someone else is coming up the stairs, and when Caleb appears, he edges very carefully in front of Henry. Sam isn't far behind, and he stands on Henry's other side, a wall against the detective and me.

"Did you say Grayson Sterling?" asks Caleb. Despite everything, I'm glad he's here. We've pulled off worse than this with the Wolves of Hellsgate.

"I did. We're looking for him. Heard he might be here."

"Like *Senator* Sterling?" asks Caleb.

"His son, actually."

"Why would he be here?" I ask.

"Thought you don't talk to cops," says Simon with a smile.

I sigh, but inside, I'm dying.

"Got a tip someone saw a boy who looked like him here on parents' weekend," says Simon.

"Family Day," says Henry with a scowl. "That's only for students and their families."

Sam puts a hand on Henry's shoulder, lowering it a full inch. "That guy isn't a student here, if that's what you're asking."

I'm standing slightly behind Simon, at an angle so I can see Caleb blocking Henry's clenching fist. Caleb's gaze finds mine just long enough for me to mouth *where?* and his eyes to lift.

Grayson's upstairs.

It's just a matter of time before these detectives go that direction.

Slowly, I back up, one step at a time, and when Simon starts to turn, Caleb moves closer to him, asking what the senator's son has done and why they think he's here. It's a deliberate cover for my escape, and I take it.

"We can ask around downstairs," I hear Caleb say, jutting a thumb toward the pit. "Some of us were just watching a movie."

Silently, I backpedal through the kitchen, speeding toward the staircase that leads to the bedrooms. Moore, Ms. Maddox, and Detective Morales are in Dr. O's office; I can hear the harsh opening and closing of desk drawers within.

I take the steps two at a time, heart pounding by the time I reach the first landing. The girls' wing stretches to my right, and at the end of the hall I see a flash of red hair as Charlotte sticks her head out the door.

Motioning her back inside, I take the short hall before me to the second set of stairs, which will lead me to the third floor and the boys' dorm. Each creak of the carpet beneath my footsteps is a bomb exploding in my ears. Every time I glance back, I'm sure the detectives will be right behind.

As I reach the first step, there's a flash of movement above, at the turn in the stairs. I look up in time to see a figure dodge out of sight.

Grayson.

I take the steps two at a time, and when he sees me, he steps out from behind the corner. His face is pale, his brow furrowed. He's wearing jeans, running shoes, and a Vale Hall sweatshirt with the words *Vincit Omnia Veritas* printed across the chest.

His eyes land on mine, and my nerves are swallowed by his fear.

He doesn't have to say a word; I know he's leaving.

We both jump at the sound of voices on the stairs. Detective Morales and Moore are arguing about something, though it's hard to decipher what over the static in my ears.

"Go," I whisper, pointing my finger up the stairs. "Go. Now."

He's frozen in place, staring, horrified, down the hall behind me.

Moore and the detective have reached the top of the first set of stairs, and I dodge out of sight as they turn toward the girls' wing.

"It's them," Grayson whispers.

"They're cops."

A drop of sweat slides down his temple. "They're the ones who followed me to Tennessee."

The men with guns.

As I shove him up the stairs, it hits me that they might not be real cops. These men could have lied about their warrant, flashed fake badges. Any kind of bounty hunter might be on Grayson's tail.

But Sterling has the power and money to bribe real cops. To twist the law to his advantage, the way he did today with that vote.

It doesn't matter where these men came from. If they're here to bring Grayson back to his dad, they're dangerous.

We make it to the top of the landing before Grayson stops again. My hands fist in his shirt as I try to drag him toward his room, but he's fighting me, pushing me out of his way as he tries to go back down.

"There's no way out there!" He tunnels his hands through his hair, voice cracking over the words as I attempt to quiet him.

"You have to hide."

"They're going to find me. I can't get out the windows; we're too high up."

He's right. Caleb's and Henry's windows aren't near any trees, any branches he might use to escape. If he's under his bed or in his closet, they'll find him. He's too big to fit in any of the cabinets beneath the bathroom sinks.

The bathroom.

"Come on." Grabbing his hand, I run toward the guest bathroom at the end of the hall. It's the only one up here not attached to a bedroom, and it has the attic access that Caleb uses to get to the roof.

When we're inside, I close the door quietly and stare up at the ceiling.

"What are we doing?" Panic sharpens Grayson's voice.

The outline of a large rectangle is etched directly over his head, above the marble vanity and sink. There's no string to pull it open like in the girls' storage room, but there's a small hook on the far side, lying flush against the ceiling. If I hadn't known it was there, I never would have seen it. Grayson follows my gaze, lines deepening between his brows.

"There." I point overhead. "It's a ladder to the attic. You can get up to the roof. Hide until they go."

He's shaking his head. "I have to leave. If they find me, I'm dead. My dad—"

"You'll never get past them." I climb onto the counter, my black Converse squeaking against the emerald-green surface. A chair would be better, but we don't have time for that.

"If I can get to the garage, I can take one of the cars."

I swipe for the hook, but I'm not tall enough, and my fingers just miss it.

"They'll see you leave and follow you. You'll be hunted for the rest of your short life, and everyone here will go down for lying to the cops."

"I can't stay!"

I crouch on the vanity, one hand on his shoulder, then his jaw. For a moment, I see my mom, her arm linked with Grayson's while he smiles smoothly down at her. She wouldn't have hurt him—us—on purpose, but all the same, I hope she's not responsible for bringing the cops here.

"You have to trust me," I tell him. "I'm going to get you out of this."

His teeth press together in a wince, but his blue eyes lock on mine.

He nods once.

"Good. Help me pull this open."

I reach again for the hook, but this time Grayson steadies me, hugging my thighs with the side of his head against my hip. My fingers peel it off the ceiling and pull, and with a squeal, the ladder descends.

He lifts me down to the floor like I weigh no more than ten pounds, and when I fold the ladder down, he starts to climb.

From down the hall comes the slap of a door against the wall, and Caleb's voice resonates off the walls in warning.

"Why do you have to search our rooms?"

"Go," I hiss at Grayson, holding the ladder steady. "Get up!"

"What about you?" he asks as he reaches the top.

Another door opens, and this time it's Joel's voice, muffled through the walls.

"Hey! You can't take our phones." A pause. "Moore! Can they take our phones?"

"Dammit." There's no going back, and no reasonable explanation of why I'm here in the boys' hall before them.

On Grayson's heels, I hurry up the ladder, and together we pull it up, trying our best to move slowly so it doesn't squeak. Breath locked in my lungs, I point ahead to an open area in the attic. We scramble through the small space, past the dusty cardboard boxes.

Below us, the bathroom door opens. We both freeze.

"Why was this shut?" comes a male voice from below. Grayson starts to move again, but I grab his ankle, forcing him to be still. If the ceiling creaks beneath our weight, they'll know we're up here.

He holds still.

Neither of us breathe.

Moore's voice is quieter; he's farther away, and I can't make out what his response is.

Seconds pass. A minute or more. Then the voices below move the other direction, and we head for the open area of the attic where we can both stand.

Creeping down, we're careful not to disturb any of the boxes or step off the solid wooden beams onto the thinner wood panels. Our path is pitch black except for the yellow circle of my phone's light.

The last time I was here, I was with Caleb.

I need to get downstairs before they notice I'm missing.

"That way." I point left to where the beams will lead Grayson to the window outside. "Go to the roof. Wait there until one of us comes to get you."

"You're not staying?"

"The detectives have already seen me. They'll notice if I'm not there."

He glances ahead, peering into the darkness toward the window. He doesn't have a phone, and without the light, he chances falling or getting lost in the maze of twisting rooms.

I give him mine. "It's going to be fine. You trust me, right?"

"Yeah," he says. "Yeah, all right."

He goes toward the window, and I head to the girls' storage room exit, feeling my way with my outstretched hands, cringing at every soft brush of cobweb that dances across my knuckles or cheek. My other senses are sharper without my vision, and I can hear more voices coming from downstairs as I breathe in the dusky scent of mothballs on the cold, stagnant air.

My feet shuffle over the planks, but still, I almost trip and go crashing across the insulation.

I catch myself with a muted yelp and move on.

Finally, I make it to the ladder. Wiping my damp palms on my thighs, I hustle down. The ladder goes up with another metallic groan, and I press my ear to the seam of the storage room door, listening for any sound outside.

When none is heard, I slowly turn the handle and tiptoe out into the hall. I head toward my room, eyes down, hoping they haven't already searched it while I wasn't present.

"Hey, you. What's her name?" I turn sharply to find Detective Morales standing with Moore and half a dozen students at the end of the wing. Geri stands on his right, her stare as cold as death. To his left, Caleb is passive, mildly interested.

But I know him better. This is a show. He is coiled and ready for anything.

"Brynn," says Moore evenly.

"Brynn, where are you heading off to?"

I jut a thumb over my shoulder. "My room."

"Where've you been?"

I work to swallow. "With Detective Simon. Downstairs."

He nods, walking toward me. "You didn't hear we were searching your room? Thought you might have wanted to be around for that."

Caleb meets my eyes, waiting for my response so he can play off it however necessary.

"You searched my room?" I turn, and feigning annoyance, stomp toward my door. Sure enough, it's been tossed. My laptop is missing off my desk, and my mattress has been pushed aside. Both closet doors are open, as are my nightstand drawers, and my bathroom door. Some of my clothes have been strewn across the carpet.

I cross my arms over my chest and summon a worried, angry expression.

"Did you think I shrunk him and hid him in my dresser? Sorry."

Morales smirks, his neat black beard crinkling with his cheeks.

"I've seen your face before," he says, and my knees begin to shake. "You know Grayson, don't you?"

Behind him, Moore's stare narrows. "You have a warrant for the premises, Detective. Not to harass the students."

"I'm hardly harassing her," says Morales, stepping closer. His eyes move over my face, confirmation lighting his smile. "I've seen you somewhere with him, or in the news, perhaps."

My throat goes bone dry.

"It's the *Pop Store* photo." Charlotte, standing inside her cracked door, steps out, her face flushed. She's already wearing pajamas, and she looks pale. My heart lurches at these words, though I'm not sure where she's going with them.

"The *Pop Store* photo?" The picture of Grayson and me in his house comes to mind. I'm standing on the stairs while he writes his number on my wrist.

I'm beaming because I've just earned my place at Vale Hall.

"Yeah, remember last summer?" says Charlotte, giving me a meaningful look. "There was that picture on *Pop Store* that Geri swore was you."

"Oh." I groan. "She looked nothing like me."

"Yes, she did," Geri calls out from the back of the pack. "She totally looked like you."

I grin. "Enough that you believed I was a celebrity for a week." She rolls her eyes.

Morales frowns. "I need your phone, Brynn."

I cringe. "I don't have it."

"It's an anomaly," says Morales. "A teenager without a phone. I didn't think there were any of your kind left in the world."

"I mean, I lost it," I say.

"Where is it?" Moore steps around Morales, his mouth a flat line.

I look at my feet, repentant.

"It was in my bag! I must have dropped it sometime after music class."

He says nothing for a moment, and I'm suddenly afraid that he's actually angry with me. That my innocence will hinge on a stupid flashlight I gave to Grayson so he wouldn't come crashing through the ceiling.

"That's the third one in two months," Moore finally says. "You pay for the next one, that was the deal."

I gape at him. "I don't have that kind of money!"

"Neither do I," he says.

"Morales!" Simon yells from downstairs. "Got someone here to see you!"

Morales takes his time sizing me up with his cop glare before he turns and heads toward the staircase. We all follow, pausing on the steps when Belk and Dr. O come into view. Simon's standing beside them, holding a plastic bag filled with cell phones.

Dr. O's cheeks are ruddy. He's still wearing his black, knee-length coat and leather gloves, though he rips them off now and flicks them onto a side table beside a vase.

"Detective Morales," says the director. "If you'd like to step into my office, I'm sure we can work out whatever problem you *think* you might have."

Morales descends the stairs slowly. "We're just investigating a lead, Director. A concerned father reported there was a kid here we know to be missing."

Henry's stepdad. He's the only father that saw Grayson at the house this weekend. He must have been angered enough by Henry's refusal to leave that he went to the police.

Henry's at the bottom of the stairs, still with Caleb and Sam, and at this, his head lowers, hiding his face.

I told Grayson he should have gone upstairs that day.

"Students, go to your rooms," Dr. O says.

Those on the first floor move slowly toward the stairs.

"Now." Dr. O bites down on the word.

We back away toward the corner, while those who were downstairs come up. No one goes to their rooms, though. We stay out of sight, in the alcove beside the stairs, smashed together like sardines to eavesdrop.

Henry squeezes beside me, his cheeks still glowing red. I think of that safe in Dr. O's office—the one hidden in the fireplace. It might have Susan Griffin's phone. It could have all our student files.

Who knows what kind of information Dr. O is hiding in this place.

"My security tells me you're looking for Senator Sterling's son? He's not here. This is a school, Detective, a private institution, approved by the state. We abide by regulatory procedures and do not steal unenrolled children from their parents."

"I don't know," says Morales. "That dad seemed pretty concerned you were holding his stepson hostage."

"And yet, you aren't here for him, which leads me to believe you took no stock in his claim."

"There's nothing to be angry about," says Simon. "Not unless you're hiding something."

For a moment, there is silence downstairs. Geri's elbow presses into my side. Charlotte's hand is on my back. Henry leans against my side, shoved in place by Sam.

Caleb is right in front of me. My eyes fix on the stripe of bronze skin between his black hair and the collar of his gray T-shirt. A week ago I would have touched him there without thinking, but now I'm not sure if it's okay, so I'm perched forward on my toes, trying not to fall as I listen to what's being said below.

"Detectives," says Dr. O slowly. "These students are my responsibility, and you have breached the security of their home while I was not here to assure their safety. If you have questions, you take them up with me, otherwise we can discuss this at the station, in the presence of your supervisor."

"Damn," whispers Charlotte. "Nicely done, Dr. O."

"No kidding," says Sam.

Their eyes meet across the heap of us, then deflect away.

Not much else is said, and when the front door closes, we break apart, breathing a collective sigh.

All except Caleb, who turns on me, mouth pulled in a thin line. "Where is he?"

Automatically, my defenses rise. He can't blame Grayson for this; Henry's stepdad's the one who turned him in.

Of course, Grayson never should have been downstairs.

But it's Dr. O's fault he's here at all.

And it's mine that he isn't gone already.

"On the roof," I say.

Hurt flashes through Caleb's eyes and echoes back through me. I sent another guy to our place.

"I'll get him," says Henry, trudging off alone. I should do it, but I have the feeling Henry needs a minute alone to tell him why this happened.

"Sterling's going to blow this for all of us," says Caleb roughly.

"It isn't his fault," I say.

His eyes widen. "You're defending him? Now?"

"Why not? No one else will."

We're standing close enough that I can feel the anger steaming off him. Everyone has gathered around us, hungry for the show, but I don't care. Caleb's anger becomes mine, and as my skin heats, I edge closer.

"There's a reason for that," he says, shoving his glasses higher on his nose. "Maybe you forgot why he left you on the roadside last summer, but I haven't."

"He didn't leave me. I sent him away."

"Brynn," hisses Charlotte, and it's only then I realize what I've said. I told Caleb that Grayson threw me out of his car and ran. I told everyone that, Dr. O included.

Now everyone knows that I tried to protect him.

"You sent him away?" Caleb asks.

I swallow. "It was an accident. You've made mistakes that hurt people, too."

Like Margot, when he told Dr. O that she was in love with her mark.

Caleb looks at me like I've just switched to some foreign language, and something inside me breaks.

We were on the same side, and now we're not.

He shoves his hands in his pockets. "Grayson needs to go. If you don't get rid of him soon, I will."

With that, he turns and strides away, leaving me bruised and hollow, while the rest of the students stare and whisper.

All but Geri, who squeezes my arm in understanding as she heads back to her room.

CHAPTER 22

D ue to the security issues, we're all on lockdown for the rest of the week. No one goes to their assignments or off campus for any reason, and after a couple days it starts to feel like one of those social experiments where guards place bets on which inmates will shank each other first.

Everyone blames me for the cabin fever, whether they say it or not.

But so far no one seems to have told Dr. O that I set Grayson free three months ago.

The morning after the detectives left, Dr. O gathered us—Grayson not included—in the living room for a debriefing. He apologized for the inconvenience and assured us that everything would be all right. Moore signaled Ms. Maddox to initiate a code when he saw the police, which wiped our browsing histories and phone messages clean. All alternate IDs were collected and moved into his safe—Charlotte found mine in my desk drawer and turned them in. Moore would be retrieving our devices from the station the following day. He promised the detectives would not be back again to bother us.

He also said Grayson wouldn't be leaving anytime soon, and that everyone should support my efforts to complete my assignment. Which did not make me the most popular girl on the playground.

And yet, I still haven't told Dr. O what I know about Jimmy Balder.

I've started to at least a dozen times this week, but whenever I head toward his office, I think about my mom taking that job for Wednesday Pharmaceuticals and selling the house to get a new apartment. I have to be absolutely certain not to screw this up.

What will Dr. O do if I tell him that Susan and the senator approached Jimmy together the night of that fund-raiser? What did they say to him before he disappeared? If this information is what Dr. O needs to bring a case against Matthew Sterling, will Grayson have to testify? And if he does, will he be safe, or a necessary casualty in Dr. O's mission for justice?

I know Grayson's wondering the same things. Since the detectives came by he's been humbled—I actually heard him thanking Paz and Alice for having his back—but I can hear the tapping of his heel against the floor when we eat in the dining room, and see the wariness in his eyes during class.

I told Grayson he could trust me, but the man I work for may be using him to blackmail his father into changing his political stance away from things that might actually do this city good. I can still hear Ben telling Myra and me that Matthew Sterling might have been swayed by a big drug company like Wednesday Pharmaceuticals.

Dr. O could be behind this, but if he is, I don't know why he'd buy the senator when he wants him behind bars.

I don't need to know. I only need to do my job, even if it means everyone hates me.

Even if Caleb can't look at me.

Even if Grayson goes to jail.

Because staying in is my only way out.

• • •

SATURDAY NIGHT, I get ready for my first dance.

The day's been a rush of birthday preparations and decorating the tent that's been set up in the backyard. Henry and I were in charge of hanging twinkle lights, while Caleb and Sam set up the music list and moved in tables and chairs.

Sam and Charlotte seem to have reached an unsteady truce, but Caleb moves around me like the wrong side of a magnet. He's mad Grayson's still here, but there's more to it—I lied to him when we were together. I didn't tell him I'd sent Grayson away for his protection. Part of me is irritated Caleb's upset by this when he's the one following me around town. The other part is relieved he doesn't know Grayson and I kissed.

As the sun sets, I go to Charlotte's room to get ready. Music and laughter pours down the hall, and even Geri's singing along with a song on the radio eases the tension between my shoulders. We've finally caught a break in the storm.

Or maybe we're in the eye of the hurricane.

"Straight or curls?" Charlotte asks as I lay the red dress we picked out the other day over the back of her chair. She's holding a flatiron in one hand, a curling iron in the other, and has already done her makeup.

"Dealer's choice," I say. My fingertips trail over the silky fabric, and I smirk a little, remembering Grayson's four thousand muttered comments about how ridiculous it is to get dressed up for the same people you see every single day.

Her smile is scary. "Come here, my little plaything."

Hesitantly, I pad her way, taking a seat on the desk chair she's pulled into her bathroom. I've brought some of my makeup, but she's got different colors from me, and while my neck warms from the heat of the curling iron she uses, I paint my eyes a dark coal color and line my lips with red.

We don't talk about the boys. We don't talk about school or work. We focus on the party, and the music. We trade lipsticks and I help her straighten the back of her hair while she does the sides. We laugh and make silly faces in the mirror, but all the while there's an unspoken pressure between us.

She's eighteen. This is our senior year. In the spring, we'll graduate, and then Vale Hall will be nothing more than a memory.

For all the times I've wished this assignment would be over, the end is coming too quickly.

I put away those thoughts as we slide into our dresses and snap new pictures on our cleared-out phones. Charlotte looks incredible in her blue dress with her long, straight hair cascading down her back, and when she struts down the hall, I follow behind, awed at how she put this all together.

She's going to love my handmade Ginger Princess T-shirt. It even glows in the dark.

"Pull it in," she calls, and we all gather around her in the hall, giving our best pouty faces as she takes a dozen pictures. No one gives me dirty looks or ignores me for my role with Grayson. We cling to each other and laugh, and even Geri is grinning.

I kind of wish Myra were here. Everyone here would like her.

"To the party tent!" Charlotte cries, and we head down the stairs toward the back door. I'm the slowest in my borrowed heels, and as I reach the bottom step, the door to Dr. O's office opens, and Grayson and the director step out.

My stomach sinks like a stone. A dozen thoughts shoot through my head—is he in trouble? Am I? Did he get caught trying to break into that stupid safe again?

Grayson groans and shakes his head, but he's smirking.

"You look ridiculous," he says.

"She looks lovely," Dr. O amends. He's beaming as he passes by. "I need to wish the birthday girl a happy eighteenth. Have a wonderful night, Brynn."

"Thanks."

When Dr. O's gone, I grab Grayson's elbow, only now realizing he's wearing a hoodie and jeans and doesn't meet Charlotte's required attire for tonight's event.

"What was that about?"

"Nothing really." He sighs. "He's been checking in with me every day to make sure I'm all right."

"And?"

"And I haven't lit anything on fire in the last thirty minutes, so we're good."

I pull him closer. "What about the phone?"

He frowns. "What about your plan?"

"I'm working on it."

The truth is I have no idea what to do about my job or Jimmy Balder, but I have a bad feeling that once I tell Dr. O what Mark told me, Grayson's life will change. He'll either have to testify against his father or go to jail. Either way, he won't be as protected as Dr. O originally implied.

"He's sleeping there every night," says Grayson. "And during the day everyone's here."

Because we're all on house arrest thanks to the visit from the detectives.

"Everyone will be out at the tent tonight," he adds quietly. "I can get into it then."

"With that axe?"

A grin splits his face. "I don't need one. I watched this video online. All you need is a magnet."

He's serious.

I pat him on the head. "You pull one off the fridge?"

He rolls his shoulders back. "Maybe."

"You need a special magnet," I say. "A neodymium magnet. And that only works for safes with a nickel solenoid locking mechanism."

His jaw drops open. I've clearly surpassed his video tutorial.

"That safe has a combination lock," I say. "The best way in is code."

"So, like his birthday. That's what my dad's is."

"You're sweet." Like the director of a secret conning school would use something as obvious as his birthday to lock up murder evidence.

He swears. "How do you know all this?"

I tried to break into Pete's safe a few times before I came here—thought I could use some of that gambling money to get out of Devon Park. I cracked it once, but was too chicken to take anything.

"Call it a hobby," I tell him. "You're not going to the party?"

He scoffs, and his eyes dip down to my lips for the briefest moment. It's enough to spark a memory of our kiss, and we both take a quick step back.

Awkwardness settles between us. We haven't spoken about what happened, and if I have my way, we never will. I need to be more careful around him. I let my feelings about Caleb interfere and lost sight of the boundary between mark and con.

I put my future at risk.

I put Grayson's future at risk.

That can't happen again, even if there's something settling about being close to him. Even if sometimes I'm not sure it was as wrong as I thought.

"Parties aren't really my scene," he says, scowling at the back door, where the girls are now waving good-bye to Dr. O.

"They aren't mine, either. That doesn't mean Charlotte won't murder us if we don't show."

"Murder you, maybe. Nobody cares if I'm there."

"What are you talking about?"

His head tilts forward. "I'm not stupid, you know. Henry wants me. The hotel heiress tolerates me for your sake. Everyone else is *nice*."

I brush off Charlotte's alias, really hoping he's not right about Henry. "And?"

"My dad's been in politics all my life. Nice is code for talking shit behind your back."

His blunt explanation takes me by surprise. I never took him to be the most popular kid at school—whenever I saw him with others he was always rude and aloof. But people still surrounded him, either because his father is a big deal or because they wanted to see what stupid thing he'd do next.

Here, he's nothing special—we pull the kinds of stunts he does for fun every day for work. Now that he's become a burden to our security, no one is impressed.

My hands find my hips. "Since when do you care about what everyone else wants?"

He shrugs. "I don't."

"So come."

He sighs.

"Come with me," I say. "We'll figure out the safe later."

He glances over at my bare shoulders, and I swear I can feel his lips against mine again. I look away.

"It's kind of sweet how desperate you are for me," he says. "I mean, it's a little pathetic, I can't even get a single night to myself. But it's cute, too."

I punch him in the shoulder.

"You hit me a lot," he says.

"You say a lot of things that make me want to hit you."

He smiles. "I'm not dressing up."

"You don't look that good when you do."

He barks out a laugh, then holds out his arm. I link mine through his.

"Try not to drool all over me," he says. "It'll make everyone uncomfortable."

"I'll try."

By the time we reach the back doors, everyone is already inside the tent. It glows in the night, pulsing with light from within. The steady thump of the bass echoes through my bones, even from a distance.

Grayson stiffens with each step, but I pull him forward. I don't want him digging through Dr. O's office while we're all dancing. I don't want to think of him upstairs, alone in his room.

I want him here. With us.

As we approach the tent, nerves flutter through my chest. I know everyone inside, and like Grayson said, it's stupid to dress up for each other, but I feel like a different person right now. A girl who wears satin, not a knife. Who has friends, even if they're not all speaking to me.

But I shouldn't feel this way. Not when I'm standing next to my mark.

"Ready?" I ask.

He blows out a breath. "I guess."

We step inside, through the vinyl flaps pulled open like drapes. Twinkle lights line the upper corners of the tent and crisscross over the sloped ceiling. Votive candles are lit on every round table. A sign reading *Happy Birthday Charlotte!* hangs on the side of the room. Beside the entrance, Ms. Maddox stands beside a table, serving sparkling cider in fancy stemmed glasses with a smile stretched across her face. Dr. O and Shrew are making a terrible attempt at dancing the twist in the corner. Moore is beside them, eyeing the students in the center of the tent suspiciously.

When he sees us, his gaze narrows, but I send him a small wave to let him know there's nothing to worry about.

"Good," says Grayson. "Food."

He leaves my side to head to a table to the left, covered with appetizers, small bites of pizza, and an enormous chocolate cake adorned with sugared flowers. Charlotte is there talking to Sam, and to my relief, neither seem to be combusting in each other's presence. Henry is beside them, wearing a full tux and posing like a blond James Bond.

When Grayson walks by, Henry immediately stops and pulls at the bottom of his jacket. He looks like he's going to say something to Grayson, but then bows out at the last second, double-fisting the appetizers.

Grayson was right when he said Henry wanted him, and though I'm mildly amused, I can't help worrying Henry's about to get his heart stomped on.

The music is loud, the beat fast and hard-hitting. Soon my knees are bouncing the smallest bit, and my hips are swaying, just a little. A self-conscious heat rises up my body as I watch the other girls on the wooden floor in the center of the tent, their arms raised, their gorgeous dresses and perfect hair already forgotten as they dance.

I'm envious of how they let go.

I can't do that, not with Grayson here. Not ever.

I'm not sure the exact moment it starts, but soon I become aware of a heat on the side of my face. It travels down my neck and bare shoulder, over my arms to my fingertips, and down my leg to my toes. It's the feeling of being watched, and when I turn my head, my breath catches and the small movements of my body cease.

Caleb stands across the dance floor, wearing a black suit and a crisp white button-down, open at the collar. His lips are parted, his black hair casually mussed. His glasses reflect the twinkling lights, hiding his eyes.

I can't move.

The heat of his gaze deepens until my insides feel like pulled taffy. I remember the way his hands feel on my face when he kisses me, and the way his eyes always flick to my mouth when I talk. I miss the smell of his soap, and his hair in my hands, and the way he adjusts his glasses when they slide down his nose.

How he bites his top lip when he's studying. How his jeans hang off his hips.

I can see every word he wrote on the notes he taped to the roof our first night there. I've traced his drawings of my face in his book with my fingertip dozens of times.

I miss him.

"We're dancing!"

I'm jolted out of Caleb's hold by Charlotte, who grabs my hand as she sweeps by and drags me onto the floor. I lose sight of Caleb for a second, going through the motions with the other girls as I search for him through the sea of bodies.

Then he's there again, on the outskirts, watching me with a cockeyed smile. I shake my hips and he laughs a little, holding my gaze. I spin in a circle, and he moves, and mouths *wow* when I flip my hair back.

Sam joins us, and then Grayson's there, too, dragged by Henry. There's something liberating about the dark, and the music, and the moving people all around us. Charlotte and I hold hands and jump around, and then Sam spins me, and Henry and I waltz.

Grayson's hands are on my waist; we're close, but it's not weird. It's fun, and when he turns to Henry and they start bouncing off each other like a mosh pit, everyone laughs and joins in.

Then Caleb's in front of me, and his hands fall automatically to my hips. I step closer, into the circle of his arms. He leans forward to whisper, "Is this okay?" and when he looks up I know he's searching for Grayson.

No one's watching right now, and even if they were, it would be weird if we didn't dance—everyone else is. So I sling my hands around his neck and swing my hips, and try not to think too much about his eyes on my shoulders, or all the places we're pressed together, or that he isn't mine anymore, even in secret.

"See?" I say back, and he tilts closer to hear. "Girls aren't that terrifying."

His grin stretches into a full smile, and I know he's thinking of the roof, the night he told me about Sophie Gomez and how she broke up with him for not dancing with her at the Winter Ball.

We're smashed together by the people jumping behind us. His stomach and chest press against my stomach and chest. His belt buckle digs into my belly button, his fingers spread over my lower back. We should back off—people will see, people will know—but we don't.

"Sorry," he says. When my eyes lift to his, his mouth flattens. He leans close, his lips brushing the shell of my ear as he whispers, "I'm sorry," again, only this time it isn't about us jostling together.

"I'm sorry, too," I say.

I watch his Adam's apple rise and fall as he swallows. His fingertips press into my waist. One hand rises and skims along the bottom of my hair.

My heart slows, then pounds harder, thunder booming within my ribs.

I move closer, watching his lips.

"Brynn." I can't hear my name, but I feel it, pounding through me with the bass. I move closer, gripping the collar of his shirt.

We're shoved apart as Grayson and Henry crash through us, and as I lift my chin, Henry's pointed stare says I need to check myself. If he can see what's happening between Caleb and me, everyone can.

I need to be more careful. I don't know what I was thinking.

The music changes to a slow song.

"Boo," says Grayson, but I pull myself together fast enough to grab him and drag him against me.

"Shut up," I tell him.

"All right." He pulls me closer, and I adjust his hands as they sink too low on my back.

I rest my head on his shoulder. He stiffens for a moment, surprised, no doubt, by my sudden affection, but soon he's with me, swaying to the beat, moving his hands as if he never quite knows where to put them.

Beside us, Charlotte and Sam arc kissing, and Paz and Joel are *really* kissing, and Henry is rocking from side to side with Alice and Beth and Bea, singing at the top of their lungs.

And behind all of them, Caleb and Geri are dancing.

I watch as she pulls him closer and moves his hand to the base of her spine. Her fingers play with his hair and slide down his neck. She's made it clear she's not into him, and he's made it clear he's still into me, but the song still feels like it lasts a million years.

Finally, it ends, and Caleb quickly retreats, heading toward the front of the tent.

As he passes me, his hand slides over the side of my hip, but he doesn't slow. A glancing touch, and then he's gone. Outside.

I wait until Grayson and Henry are loading their plates with food, and then I follow.

CHAPTER 23

I go to the gardens.

I'm not positive that's where Caleb went, but it's close, and private, and people will see if we head back to the house alone.

In silence, I pass under the trellis, rubbing my hands up and down my arms to fight off the chill in the night air. Muffled music blasts from the tent behind me. I glance back to make sure I haven't been followed.

A wall of brush and ivy soon blocks my view of the party, and I hurry down the stone path, searching for movement in the darkness.

"Caleb?" I whisper.

There is no response.

When I reach the statue of Barry Buddha, my heart sinks. We've met here before, studied here, made out on the park bench behind me. But he's nowhere to be seen.

Then, a crackle of leaves behind me, and I turn, swallowing a gasp.

He's half silhouette, shadowed by the tent light over the wall to his back. He looks like a black-and-white movie star in his suit, and like before, my heart throbs at the sight of him.

All the things I want to say are swallowed by the want pulsing inside me. In a breath, we connect—mouths and hands hungry for touch. He tastes like apple cider and feels like home, and as my hands fly over his back and beneath his jacket, all I can think is *finally*.

His heart pounds against my flat hand as it slides up his chest. His teeth nip my bottom lip and the sound I make seems to spear more urgency through him. His hands lower over my hips, sliding over the soft fabric like water, pushing it aside when my knee hikes up his hip.

We stumble toward the park bench, and then I'm straddling his lap, and his lips are on my neck, and the rasp of his tongue below my ear drives me crazy. I pull at his buttoned shirt, and he gives a low groan as my fingers ride the ridges of his abs.

I am burning up. My blood is turning to steam. My need is so blinding I forget why I was mad at him. That we're lying to each other. That I kissed another guy.

Almost.

I all but tear off Caleb's coat, because I don't want to think about those things now. This is simple. For one second, I just want to stop thinking.

His glasses are crooked and his hair's a mess. His breath is hot as he mumbles words against my throat.

"I miss you," he says.

I open my eyes, head tilted back, and the stars are a spray of glimmering salt on a black sky. I don't feel the cold, but I feel the steam on my lips, and when his hands slide up the outside of my thighs beneath my dress, I press closer.

"Okay?" he asks, and I nod frantically. *Okay. Yes. Yes.*

My dress is draped over us, hiding his forearms. My fingertips press into the hard planes of his chest.

The music changes in the tent behind us. I don't know how I hear it over the roar of my blood, but I do, and it reminds me that we're outside, on a bench, fifty yards away from our friends and the school faculty.

Hiding.

And if I keep saying okay, this could go further, and further, and it's not like I haven't gone all the way before, but Caleb's different.

I don't want to sneak around. I don't want to go back to pretending he means nothing to me while Geri sits on his lap and I flirt with Grayson.

And now the rest of it is coming, things I can't block out anymore. Questions of if he's still been following me, and why he couldn't tell me, and why I can still feel Grayson's grip on my cheeks when Caleb's hands are in my hair.

"Brynn?" Caleb pulls back, searching for my gaze.

I can't look at him.

It hurts now, that slash in my shield. It feels like something in me is tearing open, and I can't stuff it back in. Not here. Not in this stupid, beautiful dress.

My head gives a quick shake, and his hands flatten on the outside of my hips.

"Slow down or total stop?"

I try to say something, but my breath comes out too rough, and I hate that sound as much as I hate myself for lying to him, and him for lying to me.

His eyes widen, and then his hands are off my legs, smoothing down my dress. Hiding my skin, even while I'm still on his lap. He holds my face in his hands, and when I tilt forward, his forehead rests against mine.

"We need to talk," I whisper.

His breath expels in a hard whoosh, and of all things, he smiles. "There are about a hundred things I need to tell you."

"Yeah?" Hope sears through my chest, knitting together the edges of my wound.

"Yeah," he says. "But first, you're killing it in this dress."

My lips curve into a smile. "You like that, huh?"

Now he's smiling, too. "A little bit."

It's going to be all right. He'll tell me about his assignment, and I'll tell him about kissing Grayson, and we'll figure out what to do. We always figure out what to do.

A sound to my right yanks us out of our bubble, and both our heads snap toward the figure standing at the edge of the garden. A boy in jeans and a Vale Hall sweatshirt.

"Brynn?" Grayson's voice is quiet, but sharp as a blade.

I feel as if I've been shoved out of an airplane with no parachute.

"Grayson."

"Wait," says Caleb as I scramble off his lap. I step on the hem of my dress, causing the fabric to tear as my feet find the ground. When I try to lunge after Grayson, I trip.

Caleb catches me before I fall.

"Let go!" I twist out of his grasp. Grayson's already gone. I've ruined this. I have to try to fix it before it's too late.

"Don't," says Caleb. "You don't need to—"

"Stop."

He falls back a step.

"Don't go after him," Caleb pleads. "He's dangerous. And if he's mad right now, you don't know what he'll do."

"He'll leave is what he'll do." I jerk my skirt up, but the leather strap has fallen off the back of my heel and kicks off when I take a step. With a groan, I snatch it off the ground.

"Brynn, someone is dead because of him!"

"It was an *accident.*"

"You can't possibly believe that. That woman was running from him when he drove her off the road. She was afraid of him."

"She had no idea who he was." Grayson told me this part of the story. He was trying to talk to her about the affair with his father. She wouldn't pull over. He opened his window to tell her to stop, and he didn't see the curve in the road in time.

"She'd been attacked," he says. "The police report said she had head injuries not caused by the accident."

"What are you talking about? There were no reports filed. Matthew Sterling covered the whole thing up."

"I know, but, I . . ." He stammers. "I've been looking into it. The pieces don't add up."

He's not making sense. If there was a police report filed, I would have seen it.

"What pieces? What are you talking about?"

"I . . ." He gives a pained wince. "I can't tell you everything yet."

I balk. "So this is not one of the hundred things you were going to say?" I step closer. "What about why you were following me? Was that included?"

His shoulders drop, along with my stomach.

"I guess not," I say.

He snatches his coat off the bench, and the sight of his shirt, half tucked in, reminds me that I look just as guilty.

"At least let me come with you," he says. "We'll talk to him together."

"Not a chance."

Hurriedly, I fasten my shoe and smooth down my dress, pulling the clip free from the side of my messy hair.

"Just stay," he begs, his jacket hanging limp in one hand.

He doesn't get it. Trust is not a one-way street. He can't convince me I'm in danger if he can't even tell me why.

Without another word, I run as fast as these stupid heels will allow, past the all-seeing eyes of Barry Buddha, out of the garden. With my skirt gathered in my hands, I head back toward the tent, but I see Grayson ahead, stalking up the stone steps toward the pool.

"Wait!" I shout, racing up the path after him. "Grayson!"

He doesn't stop.

He's inside before I pass the pool, and by the time I rip open the back door, he's already across the house.

"Grayson!"

My voice echoes off the walls. This level is empty—everyone's outside at the party. Panic seizes me as I pass the hall that leads to the garage. He could be getting a car, racing out of here with no one to stand in his way.

But when I turn, I find him sitting on the stairs.

Heart pounding from the run, I take a steadying breath and sit beside him, on the opposite side of the step.

He picks at his thumbnail, his back hunched.

"That why you freaked out the other night?" he asks.

Sweat drips down my back, sticking to my flattened curls.

"What do you mean?"

"You and him. Is he why you wouldn't even look at me after we kissed?"

Dread pools in my belly. There is no way around this but to plow through.

"First, Moore caught us, in case you forgot." When he snorts, I add, "And yeah. Something like that."

Stars are born and die in the length of silence that follows.

"So you're into him?"

I can't really deny it now. He wouldn't believe me if I did.

"It's complicated," I say.

"So, yes."

I don't disagree.

"Why didn't you tell me?"

I shrug. "Maybe I like you, too."

He shakes his head. "That's not fair."

"I know. I'm sorry."

More quiet, in which I contemplate if I am, in fact, the worst person ever.

"Man," he says. "I wish I could go home."

My heart cracks in half.

"You will soon," I say.

I'm so good at lying now, I don't even have to think before I do it.

CHAPTER 24

The next morning, Belk knocks on my door.

"Director's office. Five minutes." He doesn't explain why I'm being summoned before 8:00 a.m., only stares expectantly at me until I say, "Okay," then retreats down the hall.

In a heartbeat, my bleary eyes clear and last night's guilt is washed away by panic.

I've blown it with Grayson. That's the only explanation for this early Sunday morning order. As I scramble to throw on clothes and wipe away the dark rings of makeup beneath my eyes, I think of the look on Grayson's face when he left me on the stairs last night.

Broken.

There was no way to fix it. Nothing to do but let him go.

He trusted me. He *liked* me. And I couldn't keep my hands off Caleb, who followed me and broke up with me and can't tell me the truth even after his lips have been on mine.

I hesitate outside Charlotte's door on my way to the stairs. I heard her come in late, but didn't go over to say happy birthday, or ask how the cake was, or see how her night went. I didn't even give her my present.

Good thing there's enough room on my wall for the All Around Great Person Award, because I've just clinched it.

My socked feet pad down the steps I sat on just hours ago with

Grayson. If Dr. O wants to see me now, it can only be because he knows how epically I've screwed up my assignment.

Wariness is gnawing at my gut as I place my hand on the office door. Whatever Grayson's told him, I can fix. It's what I do.

I wish I knew what Grayson told him.

"Brynn, come in." Dr. O motions me toward the chair in front of his desk as I enter the room. With heavy steps, I walk toward it, ignoring the Latin motto carved into the stone tablet in the corner. *Truth conquers all.*

This is my first time alone with him since Mom told me about the new job with Wednesday. I should bring it up, thank him maybe, but I have a feeling that isn't why I'm here.

The closer I get, the rougher Dr. O looks. His eyes are bloodshot, the thin, pale skin beneath smudged by exhaustion. His button-down shirt is wrinkled, tucked into his belt unevenly. Automatically, my gaze shoots to the fireplace and the safe hidden in the stones beside the chair, then bounces off.

"I'm sorry for the early wake-up," he says. "I have business in the city today, and wanted to check in with you before I left."

I wonder if he slept at all last night. My mind is already shooting through reasons why that might be—if it has to do with Grayson, or those detectives that searched the house, or something else.

"No problem." Half a dozen papers litter his desk, but they're not neatly organized as usual. My worry stretches thin as he frowns down at them. "Sir, are you all right?"

He coughs into his fist. "Yes. Thank you."

I wait.

"Is it that obvious?" His smile is genuine, but pained. "I suppose so."

His hands rest on his waist as his gaze lifts to the portrait of his sister in the white dress behind me.

"I miss her deeply. There are some nights . . ." His hand lifts so that his thumb can press into his temple. "I've had a hard time sleeping lately."

"Since Grayson's been here." I've overstepped by saying this, but he doesn't call me on it.

"His presence hasn't made it easier." He sighs. "My sister was a good woman. Kind. I keep remembering these little things I haven't thought about in years. She had this uncanny ability to predict the weather." His laugh is thick with memories. "You'd mention plans for this weekend, and she'd say, *Better wait until Sunday—it's going to rain,* or *Bring a coat, just in case.* I never believed her, but she was always right."

I'm not sure why he's telling me this. It feels too personal, and I've learned my lesson not to get too close to the fire. Dr. O has tricked me before.

But everything he's done, he's done for a reason.

It wears away at me to see him like this. He may be a con like the rest of us, but he's not immune to pain.

"She loved children," he says. "She always wanted kids. This school was her idea."

"Really?"

He nods. Opens his mouth to say more, then frowns. "I'm sorry. You're not here to listen to an old man's sad story. How are you? How is the job going?"

"I'm fine. The job . . ." I catch myself right before I tell him what Mark said about Jimmy Balder and Susan the night of the fund-raiser. The words are right on the tip of my tongue, but something stops them from spilling out.

"Sterling's staff has been busy," I recover quickly. "They were getting ready for a fund-raiser for the parks, but things kind of fell apart when the senator changed his mind on some vote."

Odin's gaze lights with recognition. "I saw that. I imagine some people were . . . upset."

The way he says this makes the hair on the back of my arms

stand up. A minute ago he was broken up over his sister's death. Now apathy has flattened his tone.

He doesn't care if people are upset.

Maybe that's what he wants.

"Did you have something to do with that?" I ask.

It shouldn't matter if he did. My job is to gather information about Jimmy Balder and pass it along. But if he is bribing or threatening Sterling, that affects Grayson, and until I know how, my lips are sealed.

Dr. O lifts his brows, impressed. "What makes you say that?"

I hold his stare, though I'd be lying if I said my knees weren't shaking. It takes an iron will to call Dr. O out on the floor.

So I sit, crossing my legs, like I planned it the whole time.

"I don't know," I say. "Sterling's leading the charge to lower the price of medicine, then gets bought out by some big drug company and changes his mind. You still own Wednesday Pharmaceuticals, don't you?"

You know, the company that just hired my mom.

A muscle in his jaw tics.

"It almost sounds like you think I'm the one who's corrupted him," he says.

"He was already corrupt." The rest of the question hangs between us.

Were you?

Dr. O hums thoughtfully. "And you're wondering what I stand to gain by blackmailing him."

I uncross my legs. Then cross them again.

"I think I know what you'd gain."

He nods. "Ah. Money."

"It's got to come from somewhere."

"Indeed it does. But I'm doing just fine without tax cuts and government assistance."

"Then why?" I ask.

He glances to the painting, then back to me. "If I did have something to do with this—and I'm not saying I did—it would be because that bill Sterling was going to propose would have cost a lot of people their jobs in the pharmaceutical business. Cheaper medication for all comes with a price. Matthew Sterling's change of conscience has helped a great many workers in our city."

By the righteousness in Dr. O's tone, there's no *if* about it. He did it, and he plans to do it again.

I sag, disappointed, even if I have no right to be. "That's why you didn't turn over Susan's phone to the cops and send him to jail. You wanted to use him."

"That bothers you."

I pick at my thumbnail. "I thought this was about justice for your sister."

"It's about justice for all of us. A senator doing what's best for Sikawa can help a lot of people, Brynn. Surely you can see that."

Maybe. But the way Ben was talking at the club, it sounded like Sterling was already helping people.

Either way, it feels wrong. Like all that stuff about Dr. O's sister wasn't real.

I try to picture what he did to make the senator change his mind—if Dr. O left a message saying he knows the truth about Susan, or if he claimed to have her phone.

If he said he's talked to Grayson.

Dr. O wouldn't have done that, though. If he had, then Sterling would have bombed Vale Hall just to keep the secret hidden.

Or sent two detectives with a warrant to snoop around.

But they didn't find Grayson, which means that Sterling doesn't know Dr. O has him, or at least has him *here*. And that means that Dr. O is keeping his word to protect the boy who ended his sister's life.

But for what purpose? And for how long?

Dread creeps over my skin like a spider, crawling up my arms and down my legs. I'm ready for this meeting to be done.

"Have you learned anything about Jimmy Balder yet?" asks the director.

My heart trips over the name. How does Jimmy fit into the puzzle? If Dr. O plans on blackmailing Sterling, he clearly has enough to get the job done.

"Not much," I say. "The senator's internship supervisor remembers him, but they weren't close."

Dr. O examines me through a narrowed gaze. Our places have switched—now he's the one trying to gauge if I'm giving the full story.

"What does that mean? Were they at odds?"

"Not from what I can tell."

Dr. O knows I'm stalling. I have to give him something.

"He said he heard Sterling talking to Jimmy before he disappeared. Told him to leave and never come back."

"When?"

"After some fund-raiser. That's all I know so far."

I look away so he can't see the truth on my face—that Susan was there that night, too.

"Keep at it," he says. "If anyone can bring light to the truth, it's you."

"Is there a possibility that Sterling didn't kill Jimmy Balder?" I blurt. "That he was just fired, and skipped town?"

Dr. O scoffs, then flips open the top of his laptop. After clicking a few buttons, he turns the screen to face me.

On it are a couple in their forties, dressed in coats and scarves. The woman is crying, her head tipped forward. The man is holding her tightly against his side, a grave expression painted on his face.

"Those are Jimmy's parents," says Dr. O.

I guess not all the devices were wiped clean when the detectives came through.

A closer look at the couple reveals that they're walking down a set of stone steps in front of a columned building in Uptown I recognize. The police station.

"They insisted their child had been abducted, but the police—cops in Sterling's pocket—never investigated the case. Jimmy was nineteen when he disappeared—legally an adult. He'd packed a bag of belongings. Withdrawn some money from an ATM. If he wanted to leave town, nothing was stopping him."

Dr. O turns the laptop back around, staring at it with something between pity and anger in his eyes before closing the screen.

"He had straight As at the university. Friends in the dorms, who cared enough to organize a search when he didn't come home. He'd never shown signs of depression or other mental health issues, and saw his parents for dinner every Sunday night. If he'd lost his job, why didn't he go to them? Why does a boy like that abandon everything?"

The answer is clear: he doesn't.

Still, this seems impossible. "No one saw anything suspicious? None of those friends? What about a girlfriend or boyfriend?"

Dr. O's gaze lifts to mine.

"He wasn't dating anyone. Not seriously, anyway."

Which leaves me back with Mark, the senator, and Susan Griffin. How do they all connect? Where did Jimmy go? And why were the cops so quick to drop the case when his own friends seemed shocked he was gone?

I slouch in my chair. I'm not a detective, and it's not my business. My job is clear: find out what people know about Jimmy and tell Dr. O. But something's wrong about all of this. I can feel it.

A knock on the door makes me jump in my seat.

"Come in," calls Dr. O.

The door opens to reveal Henry, standing in the threshold. His hair is neatly combed, but he's wearing the same clothes he did on Family Day. A hockey shirt and jeans, too baggy for his usual style.

He straightens when he sees me and walks over, a nervous bounce in his step. "Hey."

I eye him suspiciously. "You all right?"

He looks away.

"Henry," says Dr. O, voice stern. I wonder if he blamed Henry for those two detectives showing up. I never asked Henry what came of that.

I am seriously failing at this whole friend thing.

"Sorry to interrupt," Henry says. "I need—"

"Of course." Dr. O's tone softens. "Excuse me, Brynn. This will only be a moment."

Henry stands beside me as Dr. O steps around his desk toward the fireplace. My breath catches in my throat as he carefully moves aside the chair and crouches on the ground in the exact same position I caught Grayson in on Family Day.

He's going into the safe.

"What's he getting?" I whisper. Is Susan's phone in there, like Grayson said? Are our files?

"Henry, will you need identification?" asks Dr. O.

Henry's gaze flicks to mine. "Um. Yes. I should take it just in case."

It takes me a moment to realize Dr. O's talking about our fake IDs—the various aliases we use on a job. I'd forgotten Mrs. Maddox hid them when the detectives came.

Henry's going out on an assignment.

My blood begins to hum as I wonder where he's going, but that worry is quickly chased away by curiosity. Henry plants things on people—I've witnessed this firsthand when he planted the pills in

Grayson's house last summer—but he doesn't have the best poker face.

Before I can get Henry's attention, there's raised voices in the hallway, followed by a loud crash, heavy enough to vibrate the floors.

Sparing Henry a bewildered glance, I spring toward the exit, Dr. O on my heels. Outside the door I find Sam and Grayson, staring at a fallen statue—one of the black marble ravens from the twin pillars bracketing the outside of Dr. O's office—on the floor between them.

"Someone should anchor that thing," Grayson says, a line of sweat racing down his temple. "Could have knocked someone's head off."

I look to Sam, who is glaring at Grayson.

"How did it fall?" asks Dr. O, brows furrowed. He kneels beside the statue, cradling its stone head like a beloved child.

Neither boy answers immediately.

"I bumped the column," says Sam. "My bad."

"Are you all right?" I jump at Henry's voice, finding him suddenly behind me. His gaze bounces off Grayson to the raven.

"Fine," says Sam evenly.

Dr. O stands, bumping the pillar with a flat hand as if testing its stability.

"I'm sorry, gentlemen," he says. "I'll have this looked at immediately. I'm glad no one was hurt."

Grayson backs away, probably wanting to disappear before he gets in trouble.

Sam's tight glare says there's more to this story, but I'm smart enough not to ask in front of Dr. O.

"Sam, can you ask Mr. Moore or Mr. Belk to take care of this? Make sure they secure the statue. I'm a little busy at the moment."

"No problem," says Sam.

No, there's definitely a problem. No one accidentally bumps

these columns unless they were shoved into them, or crowding at the door to eavesdrop. The raised voices I heard before the statue fell make me think there was some kind of fight, and by the way Sam's seething, my bets are that Grayson started it.

I'll deal with that later.

Back inside the office, Dr. O strides toward the safe, and when Henry goes to follow, I snag his arm.

"What are you doing?"

His cheeks are already stained red.

"Cleaning up my mess," he answers.

My worry multiplies by a hundred as Dr. O shuts the safe door. He passes Henry three stacks of green bills and a small, rectangular ID card, which Henry tucks into his large pockets, out of sight.

What is Henry going to do with that kind of cash?

"We'll talk when you get back," says Dr. O, replacing the stone in front of the fireplace.

"Yes, sir."

Henry heads toward the door. I try not to make a huge show of following him, but that's exactly what I intend to do.

"Is that all you need from me?" I ask Dr. O.

"No." He runs a hand over his jaw and waits for the door to close behind my friend. "I actually have a concern I'd like to talk to you about."

My stomach goes rigid. This *is* about what happened last night with Grayson. I knew it.

"What's that?"

"I'm concerned about Caleb."

Of course he is. Dr. O wanted me to put our relationship on hold, and I didn't. Now I'm busted. My concern over Henry's assignment, and whatever is going on between Sam and Grayson, is put on temporary hold while I scramble to figure out how to save my own ass.

"Have you noticed anything . . . off with him lately?"

Caleb's words from that night on the roof echo through my head. *This doesn't work if you don't trust me.*

Something's definitely off. A week ago he wouldn't have said that. He would've known I did, and he would've been right.

"How so?"

"You remember that everything said in this room is confidential."

I nod.

Dr. O frowns down at the papers on his desk. "He's been distant lately. Troubled. He says he's going somewhere, then heads another—you know how important our tracking system is for your safety."

"Yeah." I may have deliberately left my phone someplace once or twice in order to avoid being followed by security.

"It's not like him to be dishonest. If he's struggling with his assignment, I need to speak to him about it."

I nearly choke.

I suspect Caleb's assignment has something to do with me— that's why he was at the restaurant that night when I was with Mark and the other interns. But Dr. O's just thrown it out as if it's common knowledge what he's doing, which makes me wonder if I misjudged the entire situation, or if he has some greater, twisted plan that I can't see.

"What is his assignment?" I ask.

Dr. O makes a sound in the back of his throat. "That's between him and me."

Damn.

"I haven't heard anything," I say.

"No problems with school?" Dr. O asks. "I know Ms. Shrewsbury keeps you all on your toes with your classwork. Any big projects he's been having a hard time with?"

If Caleb were struggling in school, I would know. We study together. We talk about that kind of stuff.

At least we did, before Grayson came here.

"Nothing out of the ordinary," I say.

Even if there was something going on, I'm not telling the director. Caleb and I might not be in a good place, but I'm not about to snitch on him.

"You're sure?" Dr. O is nearly pleading now, and it makes it even harder to balance on those eggshells he's put under my feet. "Caleb's been here a long time. He knows things about this program—about you and the other students—that could be very . . . damaging."

I bite hard on the inside of my cheek.

"I want to make sure he's doing all right," says Dr. O. "That he's making good decisions."

Fear seeps over my doubt, bringing on a new layer of suspicion. What is Dr. O talking about? What wrong decisions could Caleb possibly be making? Everything he does is with the purpose of maintaining his position here and protecting the rest of us.

If he's struggling with his assignment, I need to speak to him about it.

Something's been going on with Caleb since Grayson got here. He's been following me. Hiding things. After the detectives came, he was angry that Grayson was still here, and after Caleb and I kissed in the garden, he couldn't even tell me where he'd gotten the information about Susan Griffin.

The police report said she had head injuries not caused by the accident.

I researched Susan Griffin's death extensively. If there had been a police report filed, I would have seen it. Dr. O may not have told me everything, but this wouldn't have slipped by without his knowledge. He would have told me about it so I could see what Grayson knew.

Was Caleb lying to me?

There are about a hundred things I need to tell you.

Why can't he say them?

"I'll talk to him," I say.

"Thank you."

Finally excused, I head to the door and reach the foyer just in time to see a black SUV pulling around the fountain. I can't see who's inside the passenger seat on account of the tinted windows, but my money's on Henry.

CHAPTER 25

Henry doesn't return by noon, and when I ask around, no one seems to know where he went or if he's gotten a new assignment from Dr. O. I keep my phone on me at all times, but he doesn't answer my texts. He's as good as any of us, but the way he said *my messes* makes me think he's in trouble, and that plus the load of cash he stuffed into his pockets feels like a recipe for disaster.

He's been hanging out a lot with Grayson this week, though Grayson has yet to come downstairs—probably because he's avoiding me after last night's train wreck. I'm just getting up the nerve to confront him about his fight—if that's what it was—with Sam, when I see Caleb coming down the stairs. He's not in his usual Sunday morning lounge pants or sexy white V-neck T-shirt, nor does he have a bag hooked over his shoulder like he's off somewhere to study.

He's going out.

Every worry Dr. O expressed comes alive in my mind as I follow Caleb to the front door. He grabs his coat off the rack, and like he knows I'm tailing him, he looks back over his shoulder.

I step into view, racked by a sudden burst of nerves.

"Hey," he says, a guarded hope in his eyes as he shrugs into his coat. He looks over my shoulder, probably for signs of Grayson, and stiffens when the stairs above my head begin to creak.

"Heading out?" I ask.

He nods. "I have to go meet someone."

"The new recruit from Sycamore." I can't hide my sarcasm.

A brief hesitation trips up his flow. "Yeah."

He's lying. It's so clearly painted across his face and posture, I doubt anyone would believe him. There is no recruit from Sycamore. It was all a story to cover for the fact that he was tailing me.

But I'm here and he's leaving.

He says he's going somewhere, then heads another.

It's one thing that he's hiding why he followed me and how he knows anything about Susan Griffin, but it's another if he's got Dr. O worried. Caleb wouldn't put us all in danger—he needs this program too much.

So what is he doing?

I step closer, steeling myself to that magnetic pull that's always between us. "How's it going with her?"

"All right. She doesn't seem very careful. What happened last night . . ." He trails off. Someone's close now, rounding the bend in the stairs.

"Want some company?" I ask.

He pulls his phone out of his back pocket and scowls down at the clock on the screen. "Maybe next time? I'm kind of in a hurry."

"Sure." My smile is thin.

He adjusts his glasses.

Charlotte comes down the stairs, pausing when she sees both of us and then continuing with a thin-lipped smile.

"Oh look. My friends."

I cringe. She's not pleased, and I don't blame her. She was jacked about her birthday, and for all she knows, we ditched.

I have to fix this, but I can't right now with Caleb lying to my face.

He's wincing. "Great party last night."

"Oh." She feigns surprise. "Were you there?"

Guilt worms its way through suspicion. I shouldn't have left with Caleb. If I hadn't, Charlotte wouldn't be pissed, Grayson wouldn't be mad, and it wouldn't sting quite so much that Caleb's lying to me now.

With a muttered, "Sorry," Caleb gives her wide berth and strides down the hallway toward the garage. Worry works down my spine as I consider what he has to lose—what we all have to lose—if he's breaking the rules.

Charlotte tries to pass, but I dodge in front of her.

"Want to go for a ride?"

She tucks her still straightened hair behind one ear. I'm already slipping on my shoes and grabbing my jacket off the rack.

"Not particularly."

"Please," I say. "I need your help."

"And where were you when I needed you last night, huh?"

My heart gives a hard, breath-swallowing pang. She needed me last night? As soon as I settle this with Caleb, I'm officially figuring out a way to kick my own ass.

"I'm sorry," I say. "I'll tell you if we can go somewhere right now."

Outside I hear the crackling of gravel as a car pulls out onto the roundabout.

"I wouldn't ask if it wasn't important."

She sighs.

"Fine," she concedes. "Where's security? We need to tell them—"

"I'll call Moore from the road." I usher her toward the door. She's still wearing her pajamas, so I grab a coat off the rack. It's not hers, but it'll do the job.

Muttering complaints, she grabs the keys to the Jeep, and I all but shove her through the garage into the driver's seat.

"Come on," I tell her. "We have to move."

With a bitter look, she starts the ignition, and we pull out onto the driveway.

I need my license ASAP.

"You want to tell me where we're going?" she asks. "I'm guessing this isn't school-sanctioned, otherwise you'd ask Moore to take you."

"We're going that way. Hurry." I point to the end of the long driveway, where Caleb's car is passing through the gate onto the street.

The Jeep slows.

"Are we seriously stalking your boyfriend?"

I press a hand on her knee, and when her foot slams down on the gas we lurch backward.

"It's just some light stalking," I say.

"Why?"

"Call it curiosity."

Her frown unlocks, and soon enough, we're racing after the black car.

"So what'd he do?" she asks.

"I don't know yet. He's just acting funny."

"You think?" she deadpans. "That dance at Family Day with Geri? What the hell was that?"

Jealousy prickles through me. "Don't ask me."

We follow at a close distance—close enough I begin to wonder if Charlotte's done this kind of thing before.

"Where'd you guys go last night?"

I grip the door as she swings around a turn.

"We had to talk."

"Is 'talk' code for 'make out'? Because don't think I didn't notice that Grayson was missing, too." She smirks across the car at me.

"You're right," I say. "We definitely snuck out to have a threesome."

"How was it?" She makes another turn, Caleb's bumper in view three cars ahead. "Kind of awkward? Seems like there'd be a lot of elbows and knees involved."

I groan. "So many knees."

As we come to a stoplight, the comfortable silence grows brittle. I clear my throat. "Caleb and I kissed, and Grayson caught us."

"Oh shit."

"That's what Caleb said."

"What'd you do?"

I slump in the seat, my heels tapping against the floorboards. "Chased after Grayson. Told him I'm the worst."

"You kind of are."

I'm not forgiven for the party, but I think she might be joking.

"What'd he say?" she asks.

"He agreed." I grip my knees, wishing this part wasn't so hard. "I'm sorry I missed the rest of your party."

Her right shoulder lifts, then falls. "Whatever. It's fine."

We both know it's not.

The light turns green, and we pull forward. But Caleb's turn signal is already on, and he's heading into a lot marked Sikawa City Transit Authority.

The train station.

"I'll make it up to you," I tell her. "We'll go out dancing. I'll buy you a whole cake."

Her green eyes light up in a scary way. "And a new cashmere sweater?"

I think of the Ginger Princess T-shirt I made, still sitting in a wrapped box in my closet. I'd intended to give it to her after the party, when she could try it on as we ate M&M's and hung out, but maybe that wasn't a good idea after all. "Sure."

"And some earrings. Good ones. Platinum."

Danger, danger, danger. "I guess?"

She slumps in her seat. "You sound like the girls on my assignments."

The rich girls, she means. I feel something tear inside me. Charlotte barely knew me on my birthday, and she still threw a basement party, with a homemade cake, and gave me a lei made out of construction paper. It's not about stuff, it's about being there.

She's been there, and I haven't.

But still, her party was for fun. This is serious. This is Caleb, possibly jeopardizing all of our positions at Vale Hall. If she knew what was at stake, she wouldn't be so upset.

She pulls into a spot in the back of the lot. "Have fun stalking."

I open the door to get out, eyes trained on Caleb's car as he finds a closer spot.

"Pick me up later?" I ask, guilt spreading. I know what it looks like—like I'm that girl who ditches her friends for a boy—but this is different. Caleb's gotten himself into some kind of trouble. Dr. O thinks he's endangering the program. When I get back I'll explain everything. Charlotte will understand.

She points to the front of the building. "There he goes."

With a quick good-bye, I race after Caleb, tugging my coat on as I run. My eyes stay trained on his glossy black hair and his leather coat as his stride picks up speed. Inside, he bypasses the pay stations and heads straight toward the turnstiles. I race after him, digging through my pockets for a leftover ticket.

With fifty cents left on my pass, I make it through the metal arm and keep a careful distance behind Caleb as he takes the escalator to the upper level. At the top, he waits near the edge of the platform, checking his phone with a scowl creasing his brow.

Did someone send him a message, or is he just checking the time?

Who is he in such a hurry to meet?

Gripped by a sudden change of conscience, I fall back into the crowd. This is Caleb I'm following. The same boy I was making out with last night. The guy who brought me into the fold of Vale Hall, and taught me the ropes, and drew pictures of me alongside skyscrapers in a copy of *A Tale of Two Cities*.

This is the same Caleb who introduced me to his family. I have hugged his mom, and laughed with his brothers, and seen his dad pinned together by metal and machines.

This is the Caleb I've wondered if I'm in love with.

Following him breaks something between us. This is a line I'm crossing, and if I continue, whatever trust is between us will be gone.

I wonder if he thought this same thing when he followed me to Risa's.

My resolve hardens as the train pulls into the station. With a hiss, the doors bounce open. Caleb gets inside one car, and just like he did the first day he followed me back to Devon Park, I get in behind him.

He doesn't see me—I make sure of it. I keep to the back of the crowded compartment, standing with the other passengers, my face to the window. I watch him through the reflection in the glass, his face warped with worry as he checks his phone again.

Doubt needles through my suspicion.

By the time we reach our first stop, I'm wondering if he really is going to Sycamore Township to follow some new recruit, or to his father's care home in White Bank. He could have told security he was going out on assignment as a cover, but really something happened with his dad, and he didn't tell me because he knew Grayson might be listening. The story's so built up in my mind, I'm almost shocked when he gets off the train at Lake Street in Uptown.

I follow fifteen feet behind him as he skips down the stairs and walks quickly into the heart of the business district. I've come to recognize these streets since I began my internship, and as we pass the police station on my left, I shiver, thinking of Jimmy Balder's parents walking down the steps in that picture on Dr. O's laptop.

A block past the station, before we get to the Macintosh Building where The Loft and Sterling's campaign headquarters are located, Caleb turns. The sidewalk is crowded with commuters, and I nearly lose him as he ducks through a restaurant's outdoor seating area, past a metal cylindrical heater, and cuts into an alley. Near the edge, I pause, reluctant to follow with so few people to hide behind.

He doesn't go far. As I wait beside the heater, warming my hands with the other customers waiting to get in, I see him slow beside the restaurant's kitchen exit. He walks hesitantly forward, then stops and rolls back his shoulders. His next steps are steady, more confident.

I've seen this change in him before—right before he runs game.

Repositioning myself on the other side of the heater, I can make out the shadowed profile of another person—a girl, I'm guessing, based on the curves and height. A cold readiness washes over me before I consider the options of who this might be or why Caleb's meeting her in some shady alley in Uptown. If he's in trouble, I'm close enough to step in.

He stands two feet away from the other person, his head tilted down as he listens to what she has to say. His hair hides his eyes—I can't make out his take on the situation—and when she slides toward him, I edge closer to the corner, prepared to come to his defense.

The way he did when I was with Mark.

I swallow my shame. This can't be his assignment—he was supposed to tail the new girl, not make contact. She was in Sycamore, not Uptown.

I tilt my ear toward the alley, but it's impossible to hear him over the noise off the street. The girl is twisting her finger through her hair, drawing Caleb's gaze there. Then she reaches for him, toying with the collar of his shirt.

I wait.

His hand covers hers.

My stomach twists.

She leans in, whispering something in his ear, so close she could kiss him.

I fight the urge to look away.

My heart counts the seconds until she finally pulls back.

Then Caleb is leaving, heading straight toward me. I should stop him and say something, but I don't know what. Instead, I turn toward the heater, hiding my face, trying to make sense of what I just witnessed.

Caleb passes without noticing me, heading down the street in the same direction we came. I feel like I've done something awful, like I've drunk poison and am waiting for it to take hold.

I wait until the girl leaves the alley, needing to see who Caleb's come all this way to meet in secret. I tuck my chin into the collar of my coat and keep my head turned as she approaches. My hands fist in front of the heater. I have no right to be angry with her, not after what's happened with Grayson. But I am.

Then she steps into the light, and I feel as if the ground has given way beneath my feet, and I'm falling straight through to the sewer below.

Long black hair braided over her shoulder.

Copper skin and dark eyes.

A black skirt and a wool coat, open to reveal a white button-down top with a snug black tie.

Myra Fenrir.

CHAPTER 26

The train ride home takes approximately forty-seven years. I miss my exit and don't have enough cash to refill my ticket, so I end up waiting for a hard turn on the train, then falling into a man to snag a ticket from his coat pocket just to get back.

Being right has never felt so awful. Caleb *has* been following me. Lying since the first night he told me about his new assignment. He was never tracking some potential recruit in Sycamore Township—he was using Myra to spy on me. And that's even worse, because she doesn't deserve to be conned.

I doubt she thought twice before trusting him. She's a nice person, and that's what nice people do. But it's also what makes her a perfect mark.

People like her never see people like us coming.

Why couldn't it have been anyone else? I like Myra. We're friends—kind of.

Which is exactly why he chose her.

I can't figure out what he's trying to learn from her. Whatever he said to win her over must have been smooth. I saw the easy way she approached him. How she flirted with him. I wish I could unsee it.

Distant, the director said. *Troubled.*

Because Caleb's conning me, and working my contacts for information. Maybe at Dr. O's orders.

My mind keeps churning out more questions. How long, and why, and how could I have been so blind? He said he needed to tell me something in the garden, but we'd been kissing awhile before he got to that.

Would he have mentioned Myra, or was that off-limits?

What game is he playing?

I call Charlotte to pick me up from the train station, but I don't tell her what's going on. She's in her own world anyway, and when we get to the house, she goes to study, and I head up the stairs to my room. I don't see Caleb at dinner, but Henry is back, tight-lipped about his day and the stacks of cash he no longer seems to have. As he and Grayson head into the study to finish the reading on *Othello*, Sam asks if I've heard the news.

"What's that?" I say.

"Caleb's on an overnight pass," he tells me. "Something with his dad. I think he might be in the hospital."

Worry clenches around my spine. "Who told you that?"

"Heard Moore telling Belk about it." Sam pulls at the brim of his hat. "I never knew his dad was around. He only talks about his mom."

Because he's afraid of jeopardizing his father's care by screwing up here.

So afraid he's stealing my marks to get information on me.

I picture his mom and his brothers. Even if I'm on the wrong end of this, I can imagine the sickness Caleb must feel on their behalf if his dad is really going downhill. I hear Caleb telling me about right after the accident, when he and his mom had to make decisions about his dad's care without knowing what they were dealing with. The powerlessness they all felt when they learned he would be paralyzed and on life support.

And then, with a punch of guilt, I wonder if this overnight pass story is true, or if it's just some cover for the bigger con he's really pulling.

And I hate myself for wondering.

I text Caleb as soon as I get back to my room.

What happened? Is your dad ok?

But he doesn't respond, and the doubt spreads, like a cancer, through my mind.

THE NEXT DAY, Moore drops me off ten minutes early for work. I expect to see Myra waiting tables or downing another giant coffee near her locker when I arrive, but she's nowhere to be found. Pierre tells me she hasn't called in, though, so I take my place at the hostess station and wait for her arrival.

I intend to find out everything she knows about Caleb, and what exactly he wants to know from her.

When Mark arrives for the campaign's afternoon meeting, he barely looks at me, buffering his presence with four other staffers. I'm not sure if human resources has contacted him about his behavior yet, but either way, he's scared.

Good. He should be.

"What about that church?" one of the senior staff asks as I lead them to their room. She pulls out her phone, scrolling through stories as she weaves around tables. "That man was just arrested this morning for embezzling all that money from them."

"Perfect," says the woman behind her, wearing a royal blue *Greener Tomorrows with Senator Sterling* shirt. "I'll schedule Matt to speak to the congregation. Something about the importance of community involvement. Standing together in times like these. That should get the press off his ass about the medication bill."

I stand aside as they filter into the room, catching sight of the first woman's phone screen as she passes by. A familiar face fills the box on the left side of the screen. The man is pale, grimacing in his orange jumpsuit. His hair is thin and uncombed, and I start as I recognize Luke, Henry's stepfather.

I only see part of the caption below, but it's enough. *Cash Found in Car* . . .

I see the money Dr. O handed Henry from the safe—the stacks of green bills Henry stuffed into his pockets. I hear Henry's voice, whispering that he's cleaning up his mess.

Luke deserved it. He hurt Henry. He went to the cops. Maybe he recognized Grayson before, maybe they showed him a picture once he got there; either way, he threatened everything we have at Vale Hall.

But this feels wrong. Henry was mad at his stepdad, but not mad enough to send him to prison. Dr. O must have pushed him, threatened expulsion maybe.

And Henry went to Grayson last night when he came home. Not to me, or Charlotte, or Sam.

The family I've found is unravelling, and I don't know how to stop it.

I reach for my phone, and I'm scrolling through to find Henry's name when Myra walks through the door. She's wearing her heavy coat, her hair windblown but her eyes bright. She smiles at me, and I make myself smile back.

"Is it too much to hope that Jessica hasn't noticed I'm late?" she says quietly, glancing around the pavilion for our boss. "There was a huge pileup on the highway."

Two days ago, I would have believed her without question. Now I'm not sure what is truth and what is lie.

"I think she's too busy to care," I say. Jessica is in the kitchen, inspecting every plate before it's served to make sure there are no more health code violations. She got lucky—Mr. Jefferies agreed not to report the Band-Aid due to the long-standing good service he'd received from the club, but Jessica isn't about to allow another slipup on her watch.

Myra nods and starts to head toward the lockers, but I step in front of her before she can pass. Everything in me is screaming to ask about Caleb.

"Wait," I say. "Jessica will come out in a minute to recheck the bar—you can slip through the kitchen then."

She nods. "Good call. Thanks."

"We should go out sometime," I say. "You and me."

Her brows arch. "Why?"

Not exactly the response I was hoping for.

"Um, because it'd be fun to have a girls' night?"

"Yeah." Her cheeks take on a pink glow. "That would be awesome. When? Tonight?"

"Tonight's good for me."

She does a little shimmy. I wish I didn't have an ulterior motive.

"Is there something going on?" she asks. "Is there a reason you wanted to get together?"

There's intention in her tone, and it occurs to me a beat later that she might think this is a date.

"Not really."

She's nodding. A lot. "Okay. Cool. Food? Coffee? Ice cream?"

"All of the above? I just thought we could talk."

"About what?" She's stopped nodding and is holding my gaze as if expecting a confession of some sort.

I may have approached this wrong.

"I don't know. We always talk about me. I don't know anything about you. I don't even know where you live." I lean a little closer. "Or if you're dating anyone."

She slumps, and I'm positive now I've said the wrong thing. Her expression locks down, and a chilly distance fills the space between us.

"No boyfriend," she says. "Definitely no boyfriend."

"*Definitely*." I lean against the wooden stand. "That sounds like a story."

"It isn't. There was a guy. Now there's not."

I think of the way she touched Caleb's collar. I'd been so sure she was flirting with him, but maybe I misread what had happened. Was he turning her down?

"I'm sorry," I say.

"Not nearly as sorry as I am."

"What happened?"

She takes off her coat. Folds it over one arm. "I screwed things up."

I can't help feeling bad for her. Caleb might be playing her, and she's the one thinking she messed up.

How many people have we screwed up while working a job? I don't want to add Myra's name to the growing list of people who hate me.

"He was kind of perfect." She unbraids her hair and runs her fingers through the black strands. "I miss him."

Her words echo through me, evoking an image of Caleb on the roof, with a card against his chest that says *Trust*. I wish I could go back to that moment, before I saw him with Myra when he was supposed to be tailing some recruit in Sycamore Township. Before he and Geri danced together at Family Day. Before I kissed Grayson.

"How'd you meet him?"

Her mouth curves in the tiniest of smiles. "It was at this coffee place near the Rosalind Hotel. He was arguing with the barista about how the building was used in *A Love to Remember*, you ever seen that movie?"

I shake my head.

She waves a hand. "It's old. Anyway, he was going on and on about how the building had been used in something like fifteen movies—you could always tell because of the gargoyles hanging off the sides. He was so into it he elbowed me in the arm, and I spilled my coffee all over him."

"You did?" I laugh, but inside I'm crumbling, because knowing a building by the gargoyles, by the architecture, sounds exactly like Caleb—the real Caleb. The boy I know, not the con.

"Didn't you know I'm super smooth?" She ducks her head suddenly. "Watch out. The chicken has flown the coop. I repeat, the chicken has flown the coop."

I follow her gaze to find that Mark is out of the club's meeting room and is rushing toward us, phone in hand. Everyone he passes stands or follows in curiosity, and though I brace for whatever might come, he continues right by us.

The elevator dings as he reaches it, and Lewis charges out, surrounded by a horde of staffers. Mark pivots as they shove by, trailing after like a stray dog.

"Meeting room!" Lewis barks. The group doesn't wait for me to seat them today—they storm past, half of them on their phones, all of them looking rattled.

Myra stuffs her coat inside the hostess stand. She's already wearing her uniform.

"Come on," she says. "We'd better get over there before Jessica sees us."

We rush after the group.

There are more people crammed into this room than ever before—I'm sure we've got a fire code problem on our hands—and as Myra and I rush to serve waters, even more pack in after us. In a matter of seconds, we're trapped against the far wall, shoulder to shoulder.

"What's going on?" I whisper to Myra, as if she would know any better than me. I look for Ben or Emmett, but they both have ended up on the opposite side of the table.

"Quiet down!" calls Lewis.

"I thought he was in Washington," whispers a middle-aged woman in a *Sterling Reputation* shirt to a guy in front of me.

"That's what I heard," says the guy. "Maybe he snuck out so the press wouldn't hound him about the bill."

The heat in the room seems to rise twenty degrees. Sweat beads on my hairline and between my shoulder blades. I don't think they're talking about Lewis.

I am trapped in the back corner of this private room, unable to get out, as Jessica escorts Matthew Sterling into the room.

He's wearing jeans and a heavy black coat. His baseball cap has flattened his dark hair, and the way he rolls the brim in his hands makes him look anxious, and small. Not at all like the powerful senator I met in his home this summer, or the slick politician gracing the walls of this office.

His skin is pallid. He looks sick.

He's covered up Susan's death, maybe Jimmy Balder's, too. He's threatened and hurt his son. Maybe the pressure is finally getting to him. All I know is he's dangerous, and he has seen me with Grayson, and if he makes that connection now, I'm positive those detectives he sent to the house will be heading my way.

"Quiet. That's enough!" Lewis is standing beside him, motioning for us to settle down. I sink behind the man in front of me, trying to keep out of view.

"Hold still," Myra whispers as I try to turn and hide my face. Her arm hooks in mine, holding me straight.

She has no idea what's happening here.

"Thank you, Lewis," says Sterling, his voice rough. "I'm sorry to take you all by surprise, but I can't help but be moved by the way you've all mobilized in light of recent events."

The room is silent, perched on the edge of a knife.

"I'm sure you all have questions about the recent changes, and I know you've probably heard the talk that I've sold out, or given in to the lobbyists."

"Well?"

All eyes shoot to Ben, whose face is glowing red. He doesn't back down, even when Mark hisses for him to wait his turn.

I keep my gaze on the floor, my heart pounding. Moore told me Sterling would never be here when I was. He was keeping track of when the senator was in Washington and when he was home. Sterling has gotten past everyone to be here today.

I need to get out of here before he sees me, but the door is on the other side of the room, and if I push through the crowd, I'll draw attention to myself.

Myra's arm stays linked tightly with mine, anchoring me in place.

"It's all right," says Sterling. "I deserve far worse for not preparing you. The truth is the bill was flawed, and pushing it through before it was ready would do a great deal more harm than good. Lewis will be sending an email in the next few hours detailing the pros of my new decision. But I wanted to let you know there will be more changes coming in the coming weeks."

More changes. Does Dr. O have something to do with that?

Whispers have now risen to a dull roar. Lewis has to quiet everyone down again.

"What kinds of changes?" someone asks.

"Is this in regard to the Greener Tomorrow initiative?"

"What are we supposed to tell people?"

"Are you all right?" It takes a moment to register that Myra is talking to me.

As Sterling begins answering questions, I swipe at the sweat on my temple. "Claustrophobia."

"It'll be over soon," she whispers.

That's what I'm afraid of.

"Senator? Matthew?"

Sterling's gone quiet, and at Lewis's worried tone, I glance back up. Sterling is staring at the table in front of him, his jaw clenched. A bitter desperation crackles through the air, leading those closest to lean away and whisper to each other.

I didn't hear the last question—someone could have offended him.

He leans forward, hands flat on the table, as if the invisible load he's carrying is suddenly too heavy to continue. What has Dr. O done to him?

"The brief's coming soon." Lewis recovers quickly. "Check your emails. The senator's obviously been working around the clock. We'll reconvene in a few hours, but in the meantime, carry on with your instructions. Keep it positive, people. The senator has everyone's best interests in mind."

In the stunned silence, Matthew Sterling is ushered from the room by Lewis and Mark, and people gradually begin returning to their stations. Even though the space clears, my breath stays thin and shallow, and I hurry toward the door with Myra chasing after me.

"What's going on?" she asks as I grab my bag by the phone bank. I look around for Sterling, but he must be with the crowd, gathering at the bar around Lewis.

"I'm not feeling well," I say. "I'll catch up with you later."

Disappointment drops her shoulders as I pull my arm from hers. "But what about girls' night?"

"I . . . I can't tonight."

Before she can ask more, I'm hurrying toward the door, past the framed photo of Grayson and his father on the hostess stand, into the hallway. My shoes squeak across the stepping stones as I make my way toward the elevator, as I watch the light move from 1, to 2, to 3. But right as the doors start to open, I hear the clatter of steps behind me.

"Hold the door." I turn and see a man with black hair, graying at the sides, wearing a long wool coat. A gold badge gleams from his hip.

Detective Morales.

For one fraction of a second, I weigh my options.

Stay, and talk my way out. He's got nothing on me—if he did, he would have picked me up during or after the raid.

Run, and I definitely look guilty. But these men have come after Grayson twice before and are willing to do anything to bring him home to the senator.

I bolt.

"Stop!" Morales yells.

Heels slapping against the tiles, I race around the elevator to the emergency exit. He's close behind as I rip open the door and run down the concrete steps. Grabbing the railing, I skip the last six, leaping to the turnaround. I'm going so fast, I don't see the other man waiting on the landing of the eighth floor until it's too late.

"Ease up, there." The other cop—Simon—grabs my arm. I struggle in his grip, but he just holds me tighter. Above us, the door squeals open.

"What do you want?" I shout.

"Just a minute of your time," says Simon.

"I told you, I don't talk to cops."

"Then maybe you'll talk to me."

Before us, Matthew Sterling descends the stairs, Detective Morales just behind him.

CHAPTER 27

There are different kinds of fear—being scared of what lurks in the dark, or being surprised by someone hiding around a corner. The wariness that quickens your pace when someone follows too close, or the gripping prison of a nightmare.

Being trapped is its own special kind of terror.

I've known it before, at home with Mom and Pete when he's had a bad night, or lost money at his gambling tables. I've felt that acid streak through my blood and gather in the hinge of my jaw and my locked fists and the coiled muscles of my legs. I've heard the message it screams through my brain: *get out, get out, get out.*

That same urgency pounds through me right now.

Simon's grip is tight on my right arm, and I go stone still, hoping this convinces him to loosen his hold. My exits are all blocked. Sterling and Morales stand in the way going up, Simon is between me and the lower level—he's my best bet. If I can surprise him and break free, I can run. They haven't pulled out their cuffs yet, which means they don't plan on arresting me, and they won't shoot me in an office building in Uptown.

I don't think.

"Brynn, isn't it?" says Morales.

Sterling and I both jerk at the name. I'm not Brynn here. I wasn't Brynn when I was in the senator's house. I'm only Brynn at

Vale Hall, where Morales asked Moore my name before he yelled it down the hall.

Simon's grip loosens by a fraction.

"I know you," says Sterling. "You've been to my house, haven't you?"

His voice is raw, as it was upstairs, but now it's not just exhaustion I see on his face, but a wild, desperate fear.

But that can't be right. He's not afraid of me.

"I don't know what you're talking about."

"Please," he says. "I just need—"

Simon's grip falters and I break free, charging down the steps. His hands snag my bag, but I twist away.

"No!" shouts Sterling. "Don't hurt her!"

I'm halfway down the stairway when I glance up and see Morales aiming a gun at my shoulder. Panic screams through me, and I'm thrown sideways, as if he's actually fired. He hasn't though— it's just the shock of seeing him with the weapon that's knocked me off course. As I rebound off the cold concrete wall, Simon's fist twists in the back of my shirt. In a flash, he's cranked my right arm behind my back, eliciting a yelp.

"*Enough,*" Sterling bellows. His back is straight now, his eyes dark. His hands lift before him, like Lewis's in the meeting room when he was trying to quiet everyone.

"Put it away, Detective," Sterling says, without looking back.

My heart is hammering against my ribs.

Morales puts his gun away.

Simon pulls me back onto the landing.

My phone is in my back pocket. I need to reach it—to call Moore. He'd come. He'd help me.

My mind flashes to the police report Caleb mentioned—the head injuries before the accident. I fully understand now why Grayson's afraid of his dad. Maybe Susan Griffin was, too. Maybe Matthew Sterling hurt her before Grayson ever could.

The senator clearly has the connections in the police force to make a report like that disappear.

"Let go of her," Sterling tells Simon. "She's just a kid, for God's sake."

I see what's happening. The senator's going to play the good cop. He'll act like he's on my side, the only thing saving me from these bad guys. He's probably orchestrated the whole thing so I'll look to him for help.

I may not have a choice.

Simon's hold loosens, and I jerk free. But I don't run again. Maybe Morales is on a leash, but he's still got a gun.

"What's your name? Your real name," asks Sterling. He's too close. This stairway is too bright with the yellow buzzing lights overhead. The walls feel like they're edging closer with each second.

I don't answer.

"Is it Sarah?" asks Sterling. "Brynn?"

Not saying a word.

"It doesn't matter," he says. "Do you work at the club?"

My cover's blown. Sterling doesn't know I'm going by Jaime Hernandez, but he will soon enough—a few simple questions to Jessica will lead him there.

"Okay," he says when I don't answer. "That's all right. All I want to know is if you've seen my son."

The hair on my arms stands on end. Definitely pleading the Fifth on that one.

"The detectives say you go to Vale Hall." Sterling senses my recognition and takes another tentative step forward. "Why was my son at your school?"

I pull the strap of the bag tighter across my chest.

"One of the dads said he'd seen Grayson on campus last weekend. He recognized a picture of Grayson from a lineup of missing teenagers." Sterling scowls. "He claimed his own child was in danger there."

I can only imagine what that conversation with Luke was like. I bet he told Sterling and the detectives that Grayson tried to beat him up.

Still, I'm surprised that Grayson's included in a police lineup. I assumed Sterling hadn't reported his son missing to anyone other than his little detective team. He's more desperate to find Grayson than I thought.

"Please talk to me," says Sterling. "I need to know if he's all right."

His plea is so broken, so genuine, I nearly falter. His Adam's apple is bobbing, his hands open before him. It reminds me of what Grayson said the night we kissed—that his father was crying when he got to the house after the accident.

Matthew Sterling's either a hell of an actor, or he actually misses his son.

"He was all right last I saw him." If I give him nothing, I will look even guiltier than I do now.

A breath escapes through Sterling's teeth. "When was that?"

"A couple months ago, I guess."

Sterling frowns. "Do you know where he was going?"

Grayson told me when he first came to Vale Hall that the detectives had traced him to Nashville before Belk had picked him up.

"Tennessee, I think? He said he was visiting friends there. Then going to Florida."

"What's in Florida?"

"I don't know, the beach? He said he just needed to get away for a while."

"Why?"

"I don't know. Maybe he was looking for an adventure."

Sterling rubs his jaw. "He hasn't been in contact with you?"

I shake my head.

"No texts? No emails, nothing online?"

"No. Why? Is he in trouble?" It's time to up my game now, and I pinch my brows together in worry.

"I don't know," says Sterling. "He's . . . a troubled kid. He left his medicine. He's missed appointments with his therapist. He needs help."

My mind flashes with the image of a boy I don't even know. Was Jimmy Balder troubled? Did he need the kind of help Sterling offers?

But at the same time, what if Sterling isn't lying? Grayson *is* troubled—because of the accident, and what his father did to cover it up. He could need therapy and meds, and he's not getting either now.

"If I hear from him, I'll let you know," I say.

"This is the truth, isn't it?" he asks weakly. "If there's something you think I should know, you can tell me. If he's . . . if he's done something, you can tell me. You won't be in trouble."

Says the man surrounded by two armed detectives.

"I don't know where he is," I say.

He looks toward the ceiling, as if asking for answers, and it reminds me of how Grayson did the same after he first came to Vale Hall.

When the senator looks at me again, his gaze is steady, his shoulders square. "I'm going to give you my personal cell number. I want you to call me if you hear anything—it doesn't matter how small you think it is. Can you do that?"

I nod.

We exchange numbers, and then he shakes my hand. His grip is cold and awkward, though I'm sure he does this all the time.

"Thank you," he says. "I'm sorry for scaring you."

I hesitate a moment and then take a step back, away from Simon. This is it. He's letting me go. When I reach the steps I half expect to turn and see Morales's gun aimed at me again, but it's not. He's talking in a low voice to the senator while Simon watches me walk away.

The senator's head falls forward. He grips the bannister. It's the last thing I see before I race down the steps, all the way to the first floor.

When I shove outside, I gulp down the cool fall air, feeling it bite my throat as I race away from the mirrored windows of the Macintosh Building. I scramble to make sense of what just happened, but the pieces are too slippery to hold and press into place.

The senator was here.

He *recognized* me.

His detectives know where I live.

I sent them all to Florida after Grayson.

I jog toward the train station—it's not the end of my shift yet, and Moore won't be here. I shove through the people, glancing behind me to see if Morales or Simon are following.

My job at The Loft is blown; I can't go back. If Mark knew more, I'm not going to get it now, and whatever secrets Myra's holding about Caleb have slipped out of reach.

I need to get out of here.

But I can't help wondering why he let me go. I just faced a man who's abusive to his own son, who's powerful enough to bury secrets—to bury me—and I'm walking away, unharmed.

It doesn't make sense.

"Slow down!"

I bite down on a scream as a hand closes around my wrist. When I spin back, it's not Morales or Simon chasing me, but Belk.

"I parked over there." He juts a finger across the street.

"Where's Moore?"

We've parted the crowd like a river, now moving around us in both directions. Belk frowns and tucks his hands in the pockets of his slacks, opening his gray coat and revealing the swell of his paunch.

"He's off pickup duty until further notice."

My chest grows tight. I keep my eyes roaming for the detectives—I may not see them, but I know they're watching. Sterling wouldn't let me get away that easy.

"Why?"

Belk's head tilts. "Let's see. Last time you came home three hours late and left the residence to Ms. Maddox's defense. That's not happening again."

Automatically, I reach into my back pocket, fingers pressing against the smooth surface of my phone. I didn't realize how much safer I felt knowing Moore was nearby. Now he's not even close enough to answer a distress call.

I can tell by Belk's expression I'm to blame for this change, and it hits me that Moore must be in trouble. We were late the night the detectives came because he was giving me a driving lesson.

"Fine," I say. "Let's go."

He opens an arm toward the street, where he parked the car. I hurry toward the black sedan.

"Didn't think you'd be done for another hour," he says.

"The manager let me go home early."

I head toward the passenger side, but Belk is opening the back door behind his seat. He expects me to sit in back. Moore never does that.

I slide into the seat.

He takes the front, and when the door closes, I rub at the knot of tension in my throat.

He doesn't drive. Instead, he taps his knuckles on the window. "Is that the intern supervisor?"

"Who? Mark?" I follow Belk's gaze to the hot dog cart on the corner that Mark is passing by on his way to the parking garage.

Belk nods.

A new dread seeps into my veins. "Yeah, that's him. Why?"

Belk starts the car. "Just need to get an idea of who's involved."

I don't buy it—Belk's never taken an interest in my assignments before—but we've got bigger issues.

"I got a visit today from those detectives," I say. "I need to talk to Dr. O."

Belk doesn't say a word. A moment later he hands me his phone over the seat. It's already ringing.

"Yes?" The deep, satin voice gives me only a second to prepare.

"Dr. O," I say. "We have a problem."

CHAPTER 28

'm taken off my assignment until further notice.

Dr. O didn't seem mad when I told him the detectives had followed me, or that the senator had asked where his son was. He seemed more worried that I was all right, and praised me for sending them on a wild-goose chase to Florida.

He said we'd talk more when I got home, but when we reach Vale Hall, he's gone. Caleb's still out, too, and when I look for Grayson, Paz tells me he went to study with Henry in one of the classrooms.

It's not one of Henry's usual study nooks, and even though they've been alone together before, I find my steps quickening as I head down the hall. It's probably just because of what happened with Grayson's dad, but I keep picturing the detectives coming back and dragging Grayson out of here. In my pocket, I feel the weight of my phone, now loaded with the senator's private number.

The door to the senior classroom is cracked, and as I approach I can hear voices coming from inside.

"She seriously fell for it?"

Grayson's snarky laugh makes me pause.

"Of course she did," Henry answers. My back straightens. I know it's stupid to think they're talking about me, but the way my day's going, they just might be.

"She's an idiot," says Grayson. "She believes anything that any-one tells her."

I think of the senator in the stairwell, begging me for informa-tion about his son. Was he playing me? Was the sad dad face an act, so that he can find Grayson and shut him down before he tells everyone what really happened to Susan?

My thumbs screw into my temples. This is ridiculous. Grayson and Henry wouldn't know what happened. Dr. O wouldn't have said anything, and I just got home.

"Maybe she's just hopeful," Henry argues. "Maybe she's trying to see the good in people."

"That's you, Pollyanna," says Grayson. "She's naïve. It's going to get her killed."

Henry's laugh is a little rushed. My throat is dry.

"It's the jealousy that'll kill her, I think," Henry finally says, quieter than before. Sad almost. "He foreshadows it in act three. *Beware of jealousy.*" Henry pauses, and I can hear the rustle of paper, pages being turned. "It's the green-eyed monster which doth mock the meat it feeds on."

"That's dramatic," says Grayson, and with a lurch I realize what's going on. They aren't plotting someone's death, they're reading *Othello*.

A crazy, broken laugh expels from my lips before I can stop it, and I cover my mouth to silence the sound. I am officially losing my mind.

In the silence that follows, I push into the room, fully expecting to find Grayson lounged out on some couch and Henry perched in a chair across from him, book in hand. Instead, I'm greeted by the two of them on a love seat, the book forgotten on Grayson's lap while he and Henry are engaged in a not exactly innocent star-ing contest.

"Brynn? Hey! There you are!" Henry jolts out of his seat, cheeks growing pinker with each passing millisecond. Grayson snorts, then grabs the book and leafs through the pages absently.

"We were just going over discussion points for class tomorrow." Henry looks to Grayson, then to me, then to the floor.

I cross my arms. "Is that so?"

"We were fooling around," says Grayson.

"What?" Henry's voice slides up an octave, until it's high enough to shatter glass. "No we weren't! That's crazy. We were just talking. About Othello. Iago. Desdemona. You know. The whole gang."

"Sounds riveting," I say.

Grayson taps an invisible watch. "Don't you have somewhere to be?"

"What?" Henry crosses his arms. Uncrosses them. "Oh. Yes. I have to go do a thing. Out. In the great wide world. I may be a while, so don't wait up." He laughs.

"You don't have to leave," I say.

He's already heading toward the door, though, and has nearly made it out when Grayson tells him to wait. He's forgotten his backpack on the floor.

"Oh, right." Henry heads back to get it, but Grayson picks it up, and as he passes it over, I swear there's enough tension between them to level an entire city.

My stomach tightens, just as a flush rises up my neck.

I am not jealous of Henry and Grayson. That would be ridiculous.

"See you later," says Grayson, holding Henry's gaze.

Henry nods.

Grayson returns to the couch and sits, turning the pages once again, looking mildly amused.

"What was that?" I ask.

"Told you he wants me." Grayson doesn't look up.

Annoyance flares over my nerves. "Seemed like you were pretty into him, too."

Grayson turns the page. "Jealous?"

He's mad at me for the other night—for Caleb, and for pretending we didn't mean anything to each other when we did.

He can be mad, but that doesn't mean he gets a pass to hurt someone else.

"You didn't have to tell him to leave."

"Did he look like he wanted to stay? I did him a favor. Besides, if you're here, I figure you want my full attention."

He is just as arrogant as the first day we met.

"You can't mess with him, Grayson."

"Who says I'm messing with him?"

I quirk a brow. "If you're trying to get back at me, don't do it with Henry."

"Wow." He grins, impressed. "And people say I'm self-involved."

His words cut through my thinning shield.

I collapse onto the cushion next to him.

He puts the book down. "What's wrong with you?"

Your dad cornered me in a stairwell.

His detective pulled a gun on me.

I'm outed on an assignment you didn't know I had, which could put my position here at risk.

I can't tell him any of it, but if I could, I think he'd probably understand. I slump over my knees.

"Basically everything," I say.

He taps the book on his thigh. "It's that guy, isn't it? *Caleb.*"

I put my face in my hands. "He isn't helping things."

Hurt pangs through me as I picture Caleb's face. Where is he now? With his family? Or on a job? I feel like I don't know him at all, and maybe I never did.

"He giving you a hard time?" Grayson almost sounds hopeful.

"Something like that."

Another pause.

"You want me to talk to him about it?"

I crane my head in Grayson's direction, but he's staring down at the book again, brows furrowed. This isn't a joke—he actually means it.

He's trying to *protect* me.

I refocus back on my empty hands. "It's okay. Thanks."

"What's his problem?"

"It's a long story."

"Sum it up then."

Again, I glance his way. He may be rough around the edges, but he actually cares what's going on with me. I don't know why I'm surprised. I care what happens to him.

"I lied to Caleb, and he lied to me," I say.

"You sound perfect for each other."

I snort.

"You want him back?" Grayson looks up at me as he says this, and I fight the urge to stare at the floor. If I tell him yes, then I chance losing both parts of my assignment today—him and the job. If I tell him no, I add another layer onto the lie he's already exposed.

The truth is my safest bet.

"I don't know."

He inhales, then claws a hand through his hair. "You should tell him the truth. It sucks when someone's lying to you."

For some reason this kindness reminds me of what Caleb told me in the garden—about the police report, and how the pieces of Grayson's story didn't fit.

"Grayson?"

"Yeah."

"When the accident happened, did you see if Susan had any head injuries?"

He stiffens, his face growing pale. "Why are you asking that?"

"I was just remembering something I heard a while ago."

A shudder works its way down his body. "I don't know. How would I know that?"

"You don't remember?"

"She was dead. There were injuries. I didn't look at her head specifically."

Of course. There would have been blood. Broken bones. How would he be able to see if she'd had old scrapes and bruises?

But doubt needles my comfort, and I move my leg another inch away from his.

"What made you think of that?" The anger in Grayson's voice puts me on edge. "You mess with me with Caleb. You mess with me about the accident. Why are you doing this?"

"I didn't mean to press a button. Forget it. It was just a stupid question."

"What about that plan, huh? I suppose you probably forgot about helping me, too."

His voice is raised. I glance to the open door. We don't need other people listening to him go on a tirade about the phone in Dr. O's safe, or my diversion from it.

"I will help you."

"When? My head's on a chopping block, in case you haven't noticed. By the time you work it into your busy schedule, your director's going to have me on the bus to prison. Where do you go all the time, anyway?"

"Nowhere," I say. "Just . . . out with friends and stuff."

Great answer.

"Friends." He snorts. "What are those?"

"Come on, don't be like that." I reach for his arm without thinking.

In a flash, he's shaken me off and pointed a finger in my face. I slam back against the cushion, a sudden fear gripping my spine. He moved faster than I expected.

"Don't." His eyes are like storm clouds. I don't know if he means don't touch him or don't try to placate him with more lies, but I won't do either.

He's dangerous. Caleb's words shoot through my mind, leaving an echo of wariness behind.

Susan drove into a tree trying to get away from Grayson. She had head injuries not from the accident—at least according to some report Caleb's seen.

No. I shake the dark thoughts from my head. That was an accident. I know Grayson. He wouldn't hurt me. He'd know better than to try.

"I'm sorry," I say, even though he's the one who just snapped at me. This whole conversation has gotten twisted up. I should be the one telling him to back off.

He jerks back as if breaking from a trance and jolts off the couch. For a moment he stands before me, an awkward strain warping his brow and rounding his back. He opens his mouth, and I think an apology might be coming.

Instead, he says, "The heiress is having a mental breakdown."

He knows her name. I don't know why he still acts too good to remember it.

"Charlotte? What happened?" I should probably defuse the situation, make sure he and I are good, but I'm as eager as he is for a change in direction.

"How should I know? No one tells me anything around here."

Except for Henry, who told him about the safe. Who's here for him all the time.

I wonder what else Henry is telling him.

By the time I stand up, Grayson's already striding out of the room.

I find Charlotte in the garden, staring at Barry Buddha. She's sitting on the bench where Caleb and I made out, huddled in a blue wool coat, her chin tucked inside a scarf. Her bloodshot eyes flick my way as I approach, though that's the only movement she makes.

I sit beside her, the evening air biting my exposed neck and the backs of my hands. The sun will be down in minutes, though Charlotte doesn't seem to care.

I run through the things I should say—all the things she would tell me if I were in her shoes—but there's no good way to start.

"Sam said you might be out here." I caught him on the stairs when I went up to check Charlotte's room. He was devastated. He didn't even look at me when he told me. It was like someone had died.

I'd thought after the party they'd be getting back together, but it's clear now that isn't the case.

Charlotte doesn't say anything.

A gusty wind makes the dry leaves clatter over the stone walkway, and I glance back, half expecting to see Grayson or the senator and his detectives following me.

"What happened?" I ask.

The sun dips below the horizon, and in seconds, the temperature begins to drop.

"We might freeze out here." I pull up my collar, tucking my chin inside. "Is that the plan?"

No response.

"Death by hypothermia it is," I say. "Not the worst way to go. There was a guy who used to live at the abandoned factory across the street from my house—he died of hypothermia. The crazy part? When they found him, he was completely naked. That's a thing, you know. I looked it up. *Paradoxical undressing.* I guess in some last-ditch effort to save yourself, your brain floods blood through your body and it feels like a thousand degrees. They've recorded it with lost hikers in the Alps and stuff."

"I'm pregnant."

Her words stop me like a six-inch nail in the tire of a car going ninety down the freeway. I screech to a halt. The words bounce around my head for three full seconds before they actually make sense.

"He doesn't know," she adds quietly.

"Oh," I say brilliantly.

I think of the nights she's been crying, all the pressure to make her birthday perfect. *It's the last chance we have to be young and beautiful,* she said.

Before what? She has a baby? Or doesn't?

Charlotte is pregnant.

I close my eyes, dread ripping through me on her behalf. And then I open them, and I hug her. She doesn't hug back at first, but I don't give up. I pull out all the Henry Hug tricks, squeezing until her chin rests on my shoulder and her arms circle my back.

"It's going to be okay," I tell her.

She shudders with a sob. "I can't do my job if I'm pregnant. Dr. O will never send me out on assignment. I'll be done here."

She's right. "Do you want to have it?"

It. A baby. This decision feels a hundred times bigger than anything I've ever faced on a job.

"I don't know," she says.

"Okay."

"I want to go to school. I'm supposed to be a lawyer."

But. I hear the hesitation in her voice.

"You still can be," I tell her. "It'll just be different." Lots of girls at my old school were pregnant. They figured it out, and none of them were nearly as resourceful as Charlotte.

"It won't happen if I don't graduate or get this scholarship." She pulls back, the strain in her eyes accented by the lines between her brows. "If I get kicked out, I'll have nothing. You think my parents will take me back now? Not a chance."

"You'll make it work. I'll help you. Sam will—"

She shakes her head adamantly. "He can't know."

I siphon in a breath. "Why?"

"You don't know him like I do," she says. "He'd quit school for me. He'd blow off NYU. He *needs* NYU."

"He needs to know what you're going through."

"You don't get it." She stands, wrapping her arms tight around her body. "This can't happen. The appointment's next Tuesday. I've already made the arrangements."

"Charlotte," I call, but she's speeding away, locked in her shell, more alone than I've ever been in my life.

try to talk to Charlotte again that night, but she won't let me in. I wish I could say something to help Sam, but I can't face him and pretend I don't know what Charlotte told me. With Henry still hiding somewhere and Grayson playing a *Road Racers* tournament in the pit, I go up to my room to do homework, but I keep the door open, just in case she needs me.

Minutes pass, and the words and images on my laptop screen blur together.

Charlotte is pregnant. Why weren't she and Sam more careful? They never should have let this happen.

The thoughts fizzle as soon as they enter my mind. Maybe they *were* careful. This was clearly an accident.

It could be me in her shoes.

Caleb and I never got that far, but we could've. Closing my eyes, I remember the rush of heat, the way I pushed those paper-thin boundaries. The way his kiss made me hungry for more, and tempted me to forget to be rational.

Caleb always knew when to slow down, though. To ask.

Is this okay? Are you okay?

My insides twist in knots. I wish he were here. I wish I could talk to him about this. I wish I could trust him.

I wish I could feel safe in this house, but at every raised voice down the hall and every creak in the stairs, I'm convinced the detectives are back, this time with a warrant for me.

My head rests in my hands. I don't know how to help Charlotte.

If she keeps the baby, she loses Vale Hall. She's right—Dr. O doesn't need someone who can't pull a con, and there's no way she's blending in with her rich girls with a giant belly.

Keeping that appointment is probably the smart thing to do.

But I'm not sure it's what she *wants* to do.

Every part of me hurts for her. Every part rages against this picture-perfect life for making the decision for her.

I flip through the internet pages, seeing nothing. Finally, a face registers on the screen, and fear sharpens my vision like a blade. It's Matthew Sterling, walking out of a restaurant in Uptown. He's wearing jeans and a sweater, his eyes hidden by the same baseball cap I saw him wearing earlier.

Sweetheart of Sikawa in the Dog House, the article says.

I've unconsciously navigated my way to *Pop Store,* the gossip site where I first learned Susan Griffin had died in a hit-and-run accident.

I scan through the words, my pulse kicking up, sending me back to the stairwell below the campaign office. I can get the gist of the article without reading the entire thing.

The voters are angry with Sterling for changing his stance on two recent bills.

The millionaires who stand to profit from these changes are overjoyed.

I know which side Dr. O falls on, which side is keeping me here, in a giant room inside a mansion, on a laptop, with a cell phone and a limitless credit card in my pocket.

I close the screen.

Picking up my phone, I dial Mom's number. It rings and rings, but she doesn't pick up. I try Gridiron Sports Bar next, but the hostess tells me Mom quit two days ago.

She works for Wednesday Pharmaceuticals now.

THE NEXT MORNING, I stumble through my classes, having spent half the night running dead-end searches on Jimmy Balder, and Mark Stitz, and Matthew and Grayson Sterling. Apart from an old *Pop Store* article, there are still no public records of Susan Griffin's death—whatever report Caleb got his hands on isn't online.

I'm itching to ask him more about it, but he still hasn't answered my texts.

Even if he does answer, I'm not sure I can believe him.

Charlotte's already in Shrew's class by the time I get there, but her gaze only glances off mine. While Sam sulks on a love seat by himself, she talks with Henry and Grayson, playing normal.

This place used to be where we could all let down our guards and act like ourselves, but now everyone is pretending, and I can't tell what is real.

The afternoon finds the rest of the upperclassmen, Grayson included, in the glass-domed exercise building, where we're warming up for our first test on the Viennese waltz. Petal the Pig sits on a gold place mat on a chair in front of the mirror, judging us with her spray-painted, plastic smirk.

It's no secret I'm counting on Grayson to get me through. If all goes well, we switch to something called the paso doble on Wednesday.

"Thank God," grumbles Geri. "I thought I was going to have to do this on my own."

I follow her gaze outside, to where Caleb is rushing down the stone path that connects this structure to the main house. He looks like a tree blown too long by the wind—his back is rounded, his head down. He's wearing the same jeans and sweatshirt I saw him in three days ago.

My heart lurches at the sight of him. But I train my face to reveal no emotion as I slip outside to intercept.

He doesn't see me until he's almost reached the doors, and when his chin jerks up, the exhaustion in his face cues an alarm in my veins.

I have seen Caleb in trouble before. It looked a lot like this.

"You okay?" he asks, tense.

I remain balanced on the balls of my feet, ready for anything.

"I should be asking you that."

"I wanted to call you back, but my phone died. My mom doesn't have the same charging cord."

His dad is ill. This is real. It isn't some cover so he can work a job behind my back.

But Myra . . . What was he doing with her?

Distant. Troubled.

Dishonest.

Says he's going somewhere, then heads another.

I force Dr. O's voice out of my head.

"Is your dad all right?"

He closes his eyes, and it takes an eternity for him to find my gaze again.

"His feeding tube got infected. It led to pneumonia."

I can hear the weight in his tone. What he's not saying is as clear as what he is.

Caleb's father doesn't have much more time.

The lies we've both told clear aside, and in that moment, there's only us.

"You should go back. Be with them."

"I had to see you."

Relief tastes bitter as I try to swallow.

"We need to talk," he says. "Now. It's important."

He looks over my shoulder, through the glass doors. Inside, the music starts. Our test has begun. I know we should be inside—it's not just Petal the Pig at stake, but our grades. With as much as Shrew is punishing us with calculus and physics, we both need this easy A.

"What is it?" I ask.

He steps closer, and I see the tic of a muscle in his neck and the panic in his dark eyes as his gaze lifts to the corners of the door, as if he expects to find a security camera watching us. His glasses have water stains and fingerprints on them, and I wonder absently when he cleaned them last.

"It's not safe here anymore," he whispers.

I think of Grayson, snapping at me last night. Of Sterling's detectives. Caleb's right, I don't feel safe, but I can't tell him this because whatever he's got going with Myra is part of the problem.

"Grayson's into something." His words are coming faster, water from a broken pipe. "Dr. O's no better. The security. Ms. Maddox. All of them. We can't trust anyone."

Adrenaline punches through me.

"What are you talking about?" I try to grasp for reasons why he might be acting this way. He doesn't believe Grayson's story about Susan's accident, but this paranoia is on a new level.

His eyes pinch at the corners. He leans closer. "Next chance you get, you have to leave. Grab some cash and clothes, and get out."

I step back. I don't know what he's talking about. I don't understand his urgency.

"Why would I do that?" My mind flashes from Pete—did he get out of jail?—to the detectives. I've convinced myself they weren't really stalking me outside the gates, but maybe Caleb knows something I don't.

My heart finds a faster tempo.

Caleb's gaze bounces off the mansion behind us. "Dr. O's not who we thought he is."

I plant my hands on my hips. "A closeted superhero in red spandex? Yeah, I got that."

"He's hurt people."

"I know."

"Badly."

I pause as his implications sink in. I know what the director's capable of—he's the first to light the match and fan the flames—but it's not as if he's running around with a sharp knife, thirsting for human sacrifice.

"Look, we do our job, he does his. That's the way this works." Caleb knows this. Caleb taught me this.

"He's out of control."

"That's not our call."

"People are dying."

My stomach sinks like a stone. My body believes Caleb, even while my mind argues that he's officially fallen off his rocker.

"Who?"

"I . . ." Caleb shakes his head quickly. "I can't tell you yet."

And here we are again.

"Yet?" I give a short laugh. "But you will?"

"Of course I will."

"After he strikes again?"

He scowls. "I'm serious."

"He's a twisted old man with money," I say, "not a psychopath."

There was a guy who used to live down the street from my mom and me when I was a kid who talked like this. Jonah. He used to say the security guard at Freedom Hills Mall was a serial killer. He claimed half the murders in the slums could be traced back to that guy, and if we saw him, not to call the cops, because they were in on it, too.

Caleb sounds a lot like him right now, and the way he keeps looking around, like someone's watching, is making my heart hurt.

"What about Charlotte?" Even if I were sure Caleb was right, I can't leave her now. "If we're in danger, what about Henry and Sam? What about you? Why aren't you running for the hills?"

Caleb glances behind us. He lifts his head. Smiles, like you do when you know someone's watching. An icy breeze blows across the back of my neck.

"I can't leave."

Of course.

We're all on the verge of certain death, but Caleb's not going anywhere. He needs to take care of his family. He needs the medical care his work here provides.

But he wants me to get out of here.

Because it's *not safe*.

"You've got to give me more than this," I say. "Whatever it is, just say it."

His jaw bulges. "Why can't you just trust me? Just one time? I don't understand . . ." He shakes his head, frustrated. "Brynn, I gave you my trust. You know how many people I'd do that for?"

My breath comes in a staggered pull.

I want to trust him. I want to know, without a doubt, that this is real. But if it is, why can't he just come clean?

I force myself to be steady for us both. "Where have you been, Caleb?"

He shakes his head too quickly. "With my mom. At the care home. I told you."

"What about the girl in Sycamore?"

"What?"

"Your assignment."

"She's . . . still there, I guess. I don't know. I don't care."

I brace myself for the words I can't hold back any longer. "You never went to Sycamore. There was no recruit. You've been working another job this whole time."

"Brynn . . ."

"I saw you."

The fear drains from his face, and his jaw tints rose red.

"I saw you with Myra Fenrir."

The door opens behind me, and we both jump. In the wedge stands Geri, looking like an angry pixie in her dark ponytail, black dress, and spike heels.

"Um, anytime, Caleb."

The glare I send her could freeze hell.

With a scoff, she looks to him for validation, and when she gets none, she lets the door suction closed behind her.

"I don't know who you're talking about," Caleb says when Geri's out of sight through the glass.

"Don't lie to me." My voice hitches. I know it's wrong to demand the truth when I never offered it about Grayson, but now's our moment of reckoning. It's honesty or nothing.

"I swear," he says.

"I followed you Sunday to Uptown. You met her in the alley past the police station."

His eyes go round.

"Is she a mark? Are you working her for information or just keeping tabs on me?"

"Brynn, that's not who you think it is."

But I'm on a roll now. I want answers, and I'm tired of the guessing game.

"Who is it then?" I ask.

He looks down, ashamed, and I feel a wave of sickness roll through me.

"I didn't know she was back until that night at the restaurant, when that guy you were with tried to drag you into his car."

Absently, my hand slides over my wrist, remembering Mark's grip as he promised to tell me what he knew about Jimmy.

"I thought she was gone," Caleb says miserably. "When she left, I had no way to reach her. I never knew what happened."

His gaze lifts to mine. Holds.

"Brynn, that's Margot Patel," he says.

The name hits, and resonates through me like a strike of a gong.

Myra is Margot. Caleb's ex-girlfriend. The girl who lived in my room before me. Who was kicked out for falling in love with her mark and telling him about the true nature of Vale Hall. Who disappeared when Dr. O erased her, but somehow ended up in a job scouting out Sterling's campaign staff, working alongside me, pretending to be my friend.

I've been conned.

CHAPTER 30

"Margot," I repeat. "No. That's not true."

I picture her sitting on the bench near the lockers at The Loft, sipping her coffee and smiling, her white button-down giving way to her black uniform skirt. I see the excitement in her face when we made plans to hang out, and the pain in her eyes when she told me about the guy—Caleb—who'd gotten away. She was so angry when she suspected Mark had hurt me. She was so intent that I stand up to him.

But in my bones, I feel the truth. Caleb is not bluffing.

How did she know I'd gotten a job at The Loft? What was she trying to get out of me?

She asked so many questions. About my life. About school.

Seems like a lot of pressure, she told me once. *Just you and your assignments every day.*

She'd know all about that, having gone here.

I never saw her coming.

Fury sears up my spine as I remember her hand on Caleb's forearm in that alley. I'd thought he was playing her, but she was playing me—they both were. That dinner at Risa's was over a week ago; Caleb's known she was onto me at least since then, but he said nothing.

"What does she want?" I say between my teeth.

"It's . . . a long story."

"Of course it is." I run my hands down the sides of my face. I can't believe I was so stupid. I can't believe I actually liked Myra.

"I've got to be honest, I'm impressed with her dedication. Not every girl creates a false identity to get their boyfriend back."

"It's not like that," he says.

"No?" I loop my arms over my chest. "How is it then?"

He doesn't answer.

He's right. He gave me his trust. I held it in my hands, on a three-by-five note card, but it was as paper-thin as his intentions.

"Let me guess," I say. "She's the one who told you Dr. O's a serial killer."

"She didn't say serial killer."

I want to shake him, but I can't get any closer. He's a smart guy; how can he not see what's happening?

I think of her hand on his cheek, the way she hugged him. He can't see it because he's still got it for her. It's chemical; we trust people we care about. It's conning 101.

"She's playing you," I say, loud enough for him to lift his hands in an attempt to quiet me. "She got kicked out, and now she hates Dr. O. She wants to scare you and everyone else out of here, too. It's revenge, Caleb, that's all."

"No." Caleb's shaking his head. "She wouldn't do that."

Is he serious?

"Maybe I got the story wrong, but I thought she cheated on you behind your back with some mark. I'm pretty sure she's got the lying thing down."

She tricked me well enough. I didn't even think to run an online search on her. She could have pulled me into that meeting room, arm linked in mine, to out me to the senator.

Did she know the men he traveled with had guns?

"You don't know her," he says. "She wouldn't make up something like this."

"Can she prove it?"

His weight shifts back on his heels. "She's working on it."

"I bet. Did she give you that police report about Susan, too?"

"Caleb!" We both turn sharply to find Moore standing in the back door of the house. His sunglasses are pulled down, hiding his eyes. "Dr. O wants to see you."

Despite my anger, worry crashes down over me. If there is some sliver of truth to Caleb's claim, he's the one who isn't safe. Margot's gone for a reason, and if Dr. O finds out she and Caleb have reestablished contact, he'll be gone, too.

Still, he paints a weary smile on his face.

"Watch your back," he whispers before turning toward the house.

I stare blankly after him. In all the times I wondered what he was actually doing on assignment, hanging out with Margot never crossed my mind.

She's poisoning him. Tearing down the program from the outside, piece by piece. But even if all the evidence points this way, I can't align the facts with the girl I met at Sterling's club. I know a con when I see one—my radar can't be that far off. Maybe Margot changed her name and lied about her school, but our conversations seemed real.

If she'd told me, to my face, Dr. O was dangerous, I might have believed her.

I need to hear the truth from her mouth of why she's working me.

The music inside changes, and with a start, I pull open the door and rush inside. Every face turns my way—all but two. Henry and Grayson, who are currently waltzing around the floor.

Grayson leads with a proud kind of dignity, his chin high, his shoulders square. Henry's blushing, and it's clear he's trying not to laugh, but his feet are right on the beat.

They look graceful. Like they belong in the movies.

Like they belong together.

Dr. O said Grayson liked me, that Caleb and I had to stop

being together to make him comfortable, but he was wrong. Grayson might have wanted me because I was safe and familiar, but by the way he's holding onto Henry, with everyone watching, it's clear who he really belongs with.

Dr. O misjudged that one. And I went along with it because my position here depended on it.

It makes me wonder what else I've missed.

It takes a moment for me to realize the music's stopped, and everyone but Geri has begun to clap. She's stalking toward me, eyes like fire, and juts a hand my direction.

"I take it you scared off my partner," she mutters.

I am stiff as a board realizing what she intends.

"I'll lead." She grabs my hand and jerks me forward. I'm taller than her by a lot, but she doesn't seem to care. It's not like I know how to lead the waltz, anyway.

My mind is still reeling as the music starts. She smiles, and through her gritted teeth, says, "Step on my feet and you're dead."

I look down, trying to keep focused on the present. On this class. On Geri's small, cold hand in mine, and the way she keeps pinching my waist when I step out of time.

Not on Margot, or Caleb, or if there's any truth behind their warning about Dr. O.

Grayson watches me, his gaze like burning coals, and when the dance ends, pitiful applause fills the room.

I'm out the door before Belk awards the winners the platinum pig. I don't have to stick around to see who won.

BACK IN MY room, I run an online search for Myra Fenrir.

If I'd looked into her after I'd started at The Loft, I would have known something was suspicious. Everyone has some kind of on-line footprint—everyone but the students at Vale Hall. Even Susan

Griffin has the *Pop Store* article about the hit-and-run accident and her supposed affair with Matthew Sterling, and her death was covered up by politicians.

But Myra Fenrir is a ghost. She has no listed number. No address. No social media pages or links to a school. Nada.

Margot Patel isn't any better. When she was kicked out, Dr. O had her erased. Wiped off the internet. I don't know if she had a Social Security number, or if she was able to get back into high school. If she had family, or anyone to take her in. When she left Vale Hall, she lost everything.

Her home and friends. A scholarship to college. Her identity.

If I were her, I'd be pissed. Maybe pissed enough to start a rumor that the director was a murderer. Maybe so mad she'd con the student who took her place and try to out her in front of a US senator and his armed bodyguards.

But part of me can't dismiss that she might actually know something.

I need to find her. I can try to sneak out to the campaign office and ambush her, but there's a good chance she knows Caleb's talked to me. If I'm not coming back, she might not be, either.

Which means I need to get her phone number.

And the only person I know who has it is Caleb.

Taking a deep breath, I put on my big girl pants and march down the stairs. I listen at Dr. O's office, but the light is out beneath the door, and no voices come from within. Caleb's not in the kitchen, or the family room, so I head down to the pit.

He's not there. The lights are off, and the room is eerily quiet. I'm leaving when I hear the compression of the couch and a muffled giggle.

Great. I've interrupted make-out time.

"Sorry," I say. "Paz, is that you? I'm looking for Caleb."

Another giggle.

"Joel?" I sigh. "Never mind."

"Caleb isn't here," calls a male voice dropped low to imitate Joel's. "Try back later."

"Wow." I flip on the lights. "Serious . . ."

A strawberry-blond head disappears behind the back of the couch. A moment later there's a thump, and Henry goes rolling across the floor. Grayson snorts a laugh as Henry snags a controller off the carpet and stares up at the blank television.

On the end table beside the couch sits Petal the Platinum Pig.

"Oh." I blink. *"Oh."*

Grayson stands and stretches. His shirt is crooked. His hair is messed up. It's now abundantly clear that Grayson and Henry are doing a lot more than dancing together.

I turn. I shouldn't interrupt this.

I shouldn't be stung by it, either, but I am.

"Want to join in?" Grayson asks. "This couch is definitely big enough."

I think of what Charlotte said about threesomes and choke.

When I turn back, Grayson's grin is sharp.

"Henry, can I talk to you a second?" I say.

Rising, Henry makes his way toward me, combing his hair with his fingers. His smile is shy and sheepish, and when he walks by, Grayson pokes him in the side and his cheeks turn as pink as his throat.

"Have you seen Caleb?" I ask.

Henry shakes his head. "Isn't he still on leave? I sent him a million messages, but he hasn't responded."

Henry must not have seen us talking outside PE.

"No." I lean closer as Grayson peers our way. "You okay?"

"Mm-hm."

"This is all good?"

Henry glances back and gives Grayson a little wave.

"This is all *incredible*," Henry whispers. There's going to be no convincing him to take a step back. Henry's been falling for Grayson since before Grayson stood up to Luke on Family Day.

Which reminds me.

"I saw your stepdad on the news."

Henry begins to pick invisible pieces of lint off his shirt.

"Oh yeah? What'd he do?"

"Seriously?" I cover his hand with mine and whisper, "Did Dr. O put you up to it?"

"No." His hand drops, taking mine with it. "Maybe."

It doesn't sit right. This is Henry, and maybe he's completed assignments for Dr. O like the rest of us, but none of them were this personal.

"It's not a big deal," says Henry. "I don't care."

"Definitely not rude, what's happening right now," calls Grayson.

I glare at him over Henry's shoulder. He seems to take this as an invitation to join us.

"Remember, he's here for a reason," I tell Henry quietly, quickly. I sound a lot like Caleb.

Henry winces, like I've hurt him. "We're all here for a reason."

"That sounds very Zen." Grayson slings an arm over Henry's shoulders. "Done talking about me yet?"

"For now," I say.

"She's kidding," says Henry.

Grayson grabs Henry in a headlock and messes up his hair.

"Let go of him."

I jump at the voice behind me. Caleb stands in the threshold of the basement, the lines around his eyes pinched, his mouth drawn in a flat line. I've never heard that grate in his voice, and it makes the fine hair on the back of my neck stand up.

Slowly, Grayson releases Henry.

"Caleb?" Henry's waiting for a response, but Caleb doesn't look at him.

He's staring at Grayson.

"We got a problem?" asks Grayson. He's got a dangerous look in his eye. The kind someone gets before they toss a match on gasoline.

"There you are." I jolt back into action. I'm not sure what Caleb's up to now, but I know the way the sky feels when a storm is coming, and right now a hurricane is on the way.

I go to Caleb, but a hand snags the back of my shirt and pulls me out of the way.

"Hey!" I shove Grayson back automatically, but am bumped aside by Caleb charging into us. He pushes Grayson hard in the chest, knocking him back two steps.

"Finally." Grayson chuckles.

"Okay," says Henry. "Okay. We all need to take a few deep, cleansing breaths, and—"

"Stay away from them," says Caleb. I try to step between him and Grayson, but Caleb's glare stays glued over my shoulder.

Grayson holds his hands wide.

"Where am I supposed to go?"

"I don't care," says Caleb. His chest rises and falls in hard strokes. His jaw flexes as his teeth press together.

"Clearly we've had a misunderstanding," says Henry with a weak laugh.

"I don't think so," says Grayson, without looking over. "It's all pretty clear, actually. Caleb here rules the school, doesn't he? And then I come in, and I take his girl, and his best friend . . ."

Caleb reaches around me, but Grayson dodges him.

"And that makes Caleb feel sad, doesn't it?" Grayson taunts. "Come on, man. We're evolved. Use feeling words."

"Shut up," I snap at Grayson. "Caleb, come on. We're leaving."

"I know what you did," says Caleb.

Fear coils inside me, ready to spring. It doesn't matter what Caleb is talking about; my mind goes to one place: Susan Griffin.

It doesn't matter how many times I tell Caleb it was an accident; he's not going to believe me.

"Oh." Grayson straightens. He looks repentant. "You do." He hooks a hand around his neck. "Well I'm glad it's out in the open, then. It's been rough keeping it a secret. I didn't know you two had a thing. She forgot to mention it, I guess."

My stomach bottoms out. For the first time since he entered the room, Caleb's gaze flicks to mine, but I can't look at him.

"Grayson, shut *up*."

Humiliation burns me to ash. I try to push Caleb toward the door. He doesn't move.

"For the record, she started it," says Grayson. "I think the whole lying thing really set her off."

Caleb flinches.

"Who started what?" asks Henry.

Grayson reaches in my direction. "Brynn, help me out here."

I can't look at any of them. "Grayson, stop."

"I thought . . ." Henry doesn't finish.

"Nothing happened," I say.

"She's right," says Grayson. "We just kissed. A lot. Of course, if I'd known where it was heading, I would have been more prepared . . ."

Faster than I can stop him, Caleb is past me. He rams into Grayson's chest, throwing them both to the ground. A curse, then the sound of ripping fabric fills my ears. I scramble toward them to break it up, but they roll and knock me to my knees. I'm thrown forward, braced on my hands. Henry is yelling for them to stop.

Grayson elbows Caleb in the side, eliciting a grunt. Caleb kicks and connects with the end table. The lamp tips off the edge and thumps onto the carpet. Then Caleb is on top, knees pinning down Grayson's arms. His glasses are somewhere beneath them. He hits Grayson once, then twice. Blood spurts from Grayson's nose, painting Caleb's fist.

"Caleb!" I throw myself into him just as Grayson kicks up. Someone's knee connects with my gut, shoving all the air out of my windpipe. I'm thrown into the table, the side of my head smacking against the wooden leg.

Pain ricochets across my skull. White dots explode like fireworks across my vision. Everything goes quiet, and as I gasp for breath, my body grows too heavy to hold up.

"Brynn?"

Caleb.

"Brynn? Get away from her! Brynn?"

Caleb's face is swimming in front of mine. His hands are on my jaw. He's shaking.

"You hit her, you fucking lunatic!" Grayson's voice is too loud.

"Brynn?" Caleb keeps saying my name. I open my jaw, trying to quiet the sudden hissing in my ears, but the pain is so sharp it steals my breath.

"Ow," I manage.

I blink, and Henry's there, and then Charlotte. I don't remember Charlotte being here. Joel's face is just beyond. They're all talking at the same time. They're all looking at me like I'm dying. Then Charlotte's pushing Grayson, and Henry's between them, and Sam's there, too, knocking Grayson into the wall.

"Stop." My voice is a whisper in a windstorm.

Caleb pulls back as if I burned him. "I'm sorry. I'm so sorry."

"Clear out."

All of the faces fall away but Caleb's, and then Moore is beside him, his brows flat.

"Everybody upstairs," he says. A pause, and then, "*Now.* Grayson and Caleb, wait for me outside the director's office."

"I'm not . . . I didn't . . ." Caleb's missing his glasses, I think vaguely. He looks younger without them. Scared.

"Get your ass upstairs," Moore orders.

And then Caleb's gone, and it's just Moore and me. He asks a bunch of questions about what hurts, and what the date is, and if I know the director's name. I sit up and bump into the end table again. The lamp is still spilled over the floor in front of me. The bulb has broken like an eggshell. Beside it, Petal looks back at me with her platinum eyes, and it occurs to me she might be bad luck.

"I don't have a concussion," I say.

Moore stands and pulls me up. The room tilts for a second, but I bear down until it passes.

"What happened?" he asks.

"Disagreement over who had the next game of *Road Racers.*"

He sighs, and over the throbbing in my head comes a pinch of regret. Moore gave me a driving lesson. He's from my neighborhood. I don't like lying to him.

But fighting's against the rules. Moore told me that my first day here. And I'm not snitching.

"Go with concussion," he says. "I know you wouldn't make up something that stupid otherwise."

Prodding the side of my head, I follow him up the stairs, Caleb's words pounding between my temples.

I know what you did.

He could've been talking about Susan, or me kissing Grayson, or something else entirely. The truth is, I have no idea what Caleb's thinking anymore.

CHAPTER 31

Twenty minutes later, I'm back in Dr. O's office. My head is pounding like a hammer on an anvil, and I have a goose egg the size of a small island on the right side of my head that Tylenol can't touch.

"Are you all right?" Dr. O, brow scrunched in worry, leads me to the cushy seat in front of the fireplace—in front of the stones hiding his safe.

"I'm fine," I say.

He sits on the love seat, where he sat the night he told me he'd assigned Geri to plant drugs on me and that he knew that Caleb and I were involved with the Wolves of Hellsgate.

I perch on the edge of the chair, unable to relax.

"Mr. Moore says you're declining medical care."

"I don't need to go to the hospital." I smile. It hurts. But if I take the trip to urgent care, this goes from a few apes beating their chests to a security incident. Moore's already filled out a report on my condition. We need to keep this as low-key as possible.

"Head injuries should be taken seriously," he says.

The police report said she had head injuries not caused by the accident. I blink, trying to quiet the cannon fire booming in my ears.

"I have an iron skull."

"Hm." Dr. O is unconvinced. "Your classmates will be punished, of course."

"Grayson's not a classmate," I say.

Dr. O's fingers weave over his bent knees. "So he started this?"

Great. "I just meant that he's not enrolled here like the rest of us."

Dr. O is quiet, waiting for me to go on.

"Unless . . . is he going here now?" There's no end to this con in sight. Matthew Sterling's not being charged with covering up a murder, which means Grayson's not testifying anytime soon.

Dr. O could keep him here indefinitely while he blackmails the senator. Which means more of tonight's fun, I'm sure.

We just kissed. A lot.

If Caleb didn't break Grayson's nose, I will.

"For the moment."

Excellent.

My mind flashes to Henry—to the look on his face when Grayson told Caleb we'd kissed. This job has turned me into a human wrecking ball, and Henry's feelings have become collateral damage.

"Grayson's become a problem, hasn't he?" The director's head tips forward. "I'm sorry you had to bear the brunt of it. I knew taking him in would have its challenges. I never anticipated it would become physical."

"It's fine."

"I have a student with a possible concussion."

"It's just a bump." I sound like my mom after Pete's lost his temper, and it makes my head hurt worse.

"I have another picking fights who's never shown a sign of violence."

"Who said Caleb started it?"

Dr. O shakes his head. "So it *was* Grayson."

"I didn't say that."

"And neither did Caleb. Grayson, however, was quite clear on his innocence."

I'm sure he was. Grayson may act comfortable—especially with Henry—but he's in survival mode, and he'll protect himself first.

I glance toward the stones where I know the safe is hidden, thinking of Susan Griffin's phone. I doubt he's given up on that, but he's tenacious, if a little naïve. He'll have a backup plan.

"I need to let one of them go." Dr. O's exhale contains both relief and regret. "We have a fragile balance here. It's my fault that's been upset." He glances up at the portrait of his sister, tension knotting his brows. "I can't send Grayson away before he testifies, not with his father's men hunting for him. After all he's been through . . . it's not safe."

My stomach gives a hard twist.

If he's not sending Grayson away, he's cutting Caleb.

"Hold on," I say. "You can't take Caleb out of the program." His family needs this. His dad's feeding tube was just infected. He has pneumonia. He could be dying right now.

Dr. O presses his fingers to his temples. "I don't know what else to do. His behavior's been erratic. He's fighting, and disappearing for hours at a time."

Because he's seeing Margot.

"I wish he would talk to me," Dr. O continues. "I'm surprised he hasn't confided in you."

He can't be surprised—he broke us up. Even if everything else got in the way, Dr. O made it clear our assignments come first.

Our assignments that involve digging around for missing interns, and planting money on our stepdads, and hiding pregnancies so we don't face the streets.

My pulse is running too fast. Dr. O's acting concerned, but it feels wrong. He wants Grayson to stay here until he testifies, but we both know that won't happen anytime soon—not while Dr. O can blackmail the senator to change his votes. He needs Grayson, but Caleb . . .

Caleb finished his assignment with the mayor's daughter. The Wolves nearly killed him because she found out what he did. Dr. O knew, and he kept security just out of reach when Caleb was attacked.

The director doesn't need Caleb. At least, not as much as he needs Grayson.

My gaze flicks from my clenched hands on my lap to Dr. O's peering gaze.

He's hurt people.

He's out of control.

People are dying.

I try to push Caleb's voice from my head, but it's too insistent.

"You know I care about my students," says Dr. O, leaning forward, the way I have with Grayson when I'm trying to set him at ease. "And their families."

My breath comes out in a huff.

His meaning is clear: he's talking about Mom, about her job with Wednesday.

About what he's done for me and what I stand to lose if I don't play ball.

"So you know I don't take these decisions lightly." He rubs a hand over his chin. "Maybe it was wrong of me to ask you to see what Caleb's been up to, but if I don't know what he's doing, I can't keep him here."

Sweat dews on my hairline. He's putting this on me. Caleb's fate, or Grayson's. I press my teeth together, trying to quiet the throbbing in my brain, to *think.*

Grayson's safe as long as he's useful to Dr. O.

Caleb may be off the deep end, but he needs Vale Hall. His family needs it. I can't let them sink just because Margot's twisted his head up with lies and made-up reports . . .

Margot. That's my play. I glance to Susan's picture, to her fragile build and her pressed lips, hoping this is the right call.

"Caleb's helping me," I say. "He thinks he found a police report from your sister's accident."

Maybe it doesn't exist, but right now it's all I've got.

Dr. O goes still, his face grave. "Why didn't you mention this before?"

"I haven't seen it yet," I say. "Matthew Sterling buried it with all the other evidence."

Dr. O's gaze flicks to Susan, then back to me. "What does this report say?"

I've never witnessed Dr. O's rage before—I didn't know he had it in him—but I can feel it now, just beneath the surface.

"Something about head injuries before the accident. I don't know the details."

"Because you haven't seen it."

"That's right." Panic slides an icy finger between my shoulder blades.

"Where did Caleb get this? I need to see it."

I can't tell him that.

"Some old contacts from his last assignment," I say, forcing myself to hold his gaze. I need to tell Caleb this so he can figure out his story. "He had to do some digging, that's why he's been gone so much. We didn't want to say anything until we knew for sure it was real."

"I see."

"He's loyal to Vale Hall," I say.

Loyal. The word hangs between us, setting my teeth on edge.

"And I doubted him." Dr. O rises slowly, clearly rattled by this new information. "Thank you for telling me. You're dismissed. Mr. Moore will take you to the clinic for an evaluation. I'll feel more confident once a doctor takes a look at your head."

His tone leaves no room for argument.

"What are you going to do?" I ask.

Dr. O stares into the dark hearth. "What I always do. I'm going to take care of my students."

CHAPTER 32

D r. O has connections. A physician is already waiting for us at the urgent care. After a battery of questions, my eyes are examined, my head is prodded, and I'm taken for an X-ray and a CAT scan to make sure my brain isn't bleeding.

Big surprise: it's not.

Caleb still hasn't responded to my text warning him about the police report by the time we get home. It's after ten, and the main floor is quiet, so I bypass the girls' hall and make straight for the boys' wing. Two hours have passed since Grayson and Caleb fought, and for all I know they've finished the job in my absence.

I'm still furious at both of them. Caleb for attacking Grayson. Grayson for taunting Caleb. I'm even mad at me for covering for Caleb after the way he's been acting. I tell myself he'd do the same for me, for my mom, but I don't know anymore.

I keep thinking about what Dr. O said—that he's taking care of his students. But he's conning us, and we've played right into his hands. A classic pigeon drop, performed by the master.

Establish rapport. Check.

Entice your mark with a taste of something they want, enough to make them greedy for more. Check.

Convince them that what they're doing, they do for the big payout—for college, for the perks of Vale Hall—when really they do it for you. Check.

Remind them they're screwed if they don't follow through.

Double, triple, quadruple check.

Only the last step remains: take the money—our secrets—and run.

But he'll only do that if we don't comply. The only way to win this game is to do exactly as he says. And it's worth it. For college. For Vale Hall. For Mom.

I've been telling myself this since I left his office. My mantra. *It's worth it. It's worth it.*

There's a commotion coming from the boys' hall as I reach the turn in the stairs. A thump, and the framed picture against the wall shakes. Voices clash together. Adrenaline spikes my system, and I run the rest of the way up.

It's Grayson and Caleb again. I know it.

As I reach the landing, my sight is blocked by the crowd, all facing the other way. Belk is shouting for them to calm down, to get back to their rooms. Sam's voice rises above the rest.

"Get off," he yells. "This is on you!"

I rush toward them, shoving Joel aside.

"What are you doing?" Belk's fingers slide off my shirt as I barrel past, into the heart of the crowd.

He's saying something else, but I barely hear him, because before me, standing outside his room, is Caleb.

I scan for a fight, still ready for anything. But apart from Sam pointing a finger at Grayson on the opposite side of Caleb, no one appears to be violent.

I don't understand what's going on. Everyone is staring at me, their gazes filled with anticipation. The heat in the hall seems to rise ten degrees.

Caleb's lip is split. There's a red welt beneath his left eye. He's holding a cardboard box with only a few things inside. I see the corner of a picture frame on top. I know the photo—it's of his family before his dad got hurt.

He's wearing a royal blue sweatshirt I haven't seen before. There's no raven, and the fabric's faded at the stress points, ripped around the collar.

And I get it then.

The breath burns as I suck it in. My gaze aligns with Caleb's. His expression is one I've never seen before, and it takes another beat to register what that look means.

Disappointment.

He is disappointed *with me*.

I'm going to take care of my students. That's what Dr. O said. He felt bad for doubting Caleb. He thanked me for telling him about the report.

I can't hold Caleb's stare any longer. My eyes fall to the box. The only possessions he has.

"This is a mistake." My voice is a trembling whisper. "This wasn't supposed to happen."

Your fault, a voice whispers from dark corners of my mind. But it can't be. I told Dr. O that Caleb was helping me. I hid the truth about Margot. I protected him.

"You did this?" Henry is suddenly beside me. His hand is on my arm. I can't look at him. I can't look away from the box in Caleb's arms.

"I . . ." I swallow. This doesn't make sense. Caleb should be staying. If anything, he should be with Dr. O explaining what he knows about the police report, or at least making up the details. "I told him you were loyal. I told him about the report—"

Caleb flinches, and I know then that I made the wrong decision.

I'd thought that report would save him, but it condemned him somehow.

Caleb starts to walk forward, to push past.

"Wait," I say.

He doesn't wait.

"No." Henry's between us, facing Caleb. "No. *No*. This is a mistake—Brynn said. She can fix it."

"Come on, Caleb," says Belk.

I am trapped underwater, my movements slow and clumsy. The conversation with Dr. O is playing out in fast-forward through my mind. I don't understand where it went wrong.

But it did, and now Caleb is getting kicked out.

"I'll talk to him," says Henry. "You stay here, and I'm going to go talk to him."

"Henry, go to your room," says Belk.

"No." Henry's shaking his head so fast his hair whips into his eyes. "Caleb's not leaving."

"You're damn right he isn't leaving," growls Sam. "If anyone's going, it's this asshole." He points to Grayson again.

"It's not his fault!" shouts Henry.

"He rammed me into those pillars downstairs because I was in his way. That raven statue nearly took my head off!"

Grayson's gaze finds mine, his expression cold. He takes a step back, away from Sam. His shoulders drop.

There are more people behind me. I don't have to look to sense them standing there. Probably the girls have heard and come to see what's going on.

"I've got to go," says Caleb quietly.

Henry's crying now. He keeps shaking his head. Caleb tries to walk past, but he puts himself in the way.

"Come on, Henry," says Caleb.

More head shaking.

"Get into your rooms, all of you!" shouts Belk.

"What the hell is going on?" asks Charlotte, behind me.

In a burst, Henry grabs Caleb's box and wrestles it free from his grip. Caleb must not have seen this coming, because he doesn't put up much of a fight. As soon as Henry's got it in his hands, he seems confused what to do. He drops it on the floor, and something within makes a sound of breaking glass.

Belk snags Henry's arm, but Henry shakes free. I feel what's coming a second before it happens, and so does Caleb, because just as Henry wheels back to punch the security guard, Caleb steps in and blocks him.

And then Caleb and his best friend are hugging, in the middle of the hall, in front of everyone, and the sound ripped from Henry's throat makes me want to die.

Tears are streaming from my eyes. I have to fix this. I have to do something.

But I can't move. If I do, Belk will take him away. Caleb will disappear, just like Margot. My feet stay grounded on the spot, forcing me to witness this. To become a wall Caleb can't move past.

This is my fault. I don't know how, but it is.

"I know what happens," Henry's saying. "You go away, and I'll never see you again."

"It's okay," Caleb says. "It's okay, Henry."

"You can't go."

"It's okay."

"I can't be here without you."

"It's okay."

"It's not. It's *not*."

Caleb's eyes meet mine over Henry's shoulder.

I'm sorry, I want to say. *This wasn't supposed to happen.*

The disappointment is gone, and all that's left is a hollow sadness, and my own guilty reflection in the frames of his glasses.

"Sam," says Caleb, as somber as a man heading to his own funeral.

And then Sam's pulling Henry back. For a moment, he's tucked into the crook of Sam's arm, then Henry breaks free and shoves into his room. The door slams behind him.

Caleb picks up his box.

Stop.

He stands.

I'll fix this.

With a nod to Sam, he walks past me. I reach for him, but there's some kind of field around him, blocking my touch.

"I'm sorry about your head," he mutters without looking up.

He follows Belk down the hall.

I should chase after them. I should chuck that box out the window. A hundred *shoulds* fill my mind, too slippery to grasp.

"What did you tell the director?"

Geri's talking, but I can't find the voice to answer.

"Come on. She wouldn't do that. It was Grayson." Sam practically spits the name.

It was me.

"Not this time, pal," Grayson says. "He didn't ask me anything. He just said I had to stay in my room until further notice."

It was me. Caleb's gone because I didn't do enough, or maybe because I did too much.

I press the heels of my hands to my temples. It doesn't make sense. Dr. O should be glad to find more information about his sister. He should be relieved that Caleb wasn't sneaking around behind his back—that he knows of.

That report should have saved him.

"Brynn?" Charlotte's standing in front of me, her brows warped in concern. "Brynn, what happened?"

"She got Caleb kicked out, just like he did Margot." Geri's voice is thin as a razor. "I guess that's the circle of life."

I flinch at the words.

"Get out of here, Geri," says Sam, but he sounds less certain.

They think I'm a snitch.

That I betrayed Caleb.

It doesn't even matter that he betrayed me first. Or that Margot screwed with his head to bring down the program. Or that he might have endangered us all by meeting with her.

They believe I broke the trust.

"Brynn?" Charlotte's arms are crossed over her chest, setting a shield between us. "That's not true, right?"

Hurrying around her, I shove past Geri and the others and run down the stairs. I don't know what I plan to do—stand in front of Belk's car, or yell at Dr. O. Something. From outside comes the sound of gravel crunching beneath tires. I race toward the front door, but the car is already halfway down the driveway. I'll never catch them.

"Brynn."

I spin to see Dr. O standing in the threshold of his office, pulling on a coat. He looks like a fighter who just made it through nine rounds.

Like *he's* the one who's just been turned out.

"What'd you do?" I demand. The others are on the spiral staircase now. Sam. Charlotte. All of them but Henry and Grayson.

"Why don't you come into my office. We'll talk."

I'm not going into that office again.

"I told you he was loyal."

"Brynn—"

"You said you'd take care of him!"

Dr. O shrugs into his coat and steps toward me. I back away.

"I said I'd take care of my students. I have to protect all of you, and if he's going on rogue assignments at your orders, it becomes a security issue . . ."

"I said he was helping! There is no *security issue*."

"Brynn, please calm down."

I can't listen to him. Every time he opens his mouth, lies come out. I look to the stairs, but Dr. O's already said what the others need to hear, and they're gazing at me in horror. Sam's hand is covering his mouth. Geri's nose is scrunched in disgust. Paz and Alice are whispering and scowling my way.

I think of all of us girls crowded together to take a picture before Charlotte's party.

They hate me now.

Charlotte hates me.

You never realize how much you love someone until they give up on you.

It doesn't matter. What matters is Caleb just got kicked out of school. He'll have to go home, tell his mother what happened. This will hurt her. Hurt his brothers.

Hurt his father.

His father.

Will his dad lose his medical care over this? That care is why Caleb is here, why he stayed. Why he took a beating from the Wolves this past summer, and came back even after Margot told him Dr. O was dangerous.

Dr. O is dangerous. Maybe not like Margot thinks, but in his own, twisted way.

I need to get out of here.

I need to find Mom and tell her the truth about Wednesday Pharmaceuticals and the house.

I need to go to Caleb's family and tell them I'm sorry, and I'll help them. I don't know what I'm going to do, but I'll figure out something.

With Dr. O calling my name, I run down the hall, past the classrooms to the garage. Inside, I grab a key ring off the hook under a handwritten note that says *Jeep.* Moore taught me enough to get out of here. I can figure the rest out on my own.

But as I turn the car on, I realize something's wrong. The shifter looks different. It's not an automatic, it's a manual. I need a different car.

The driver's side door opens, and I yelp in surprise. Moore is standing beside me. He reaches over me for the ignition and takes out the keys.

"You don't have your license," he says.

I break.

My tears feel like shards of glass, my lungs like a vacuum. I can't breathe.

I have ruined someone's life.

Not just anyone's, Caleb's.

It doesn't matter if it wasn't deliberate, or if he chose Margot over me, or if he punched Grayson in the basement.

With a few words, I have taken everything from him.

"It should have been me," I say. "If Dr. O thinks I asked Caleb for help—that I'm the one that caused the security issue—why am I still here? I haven't gotten anything from Grayson. I barely found anything on Jimmy Balder—"

"Because you weren't supposed to," Moore mutters.

He's trying to be nice—we both know anything that Sterling did to Jimmy would have been covered up—but I don't want kindness. I want Caleb and his family to be okay.

I don't realize I've stood until I'm leaning into Moore, feeling the gentle scrape of his wool sweater against my wet cheek. His arms are wrapped around me. I am a tornado encased in his steel grip.

"That's enough," he says after a minute, firmly enough to make me realize how stupid I'm being.

I gasp and shudder, and then wipe my eyes with the back of my sleeve.

He leans down, so that we're on the same level. His dark eyes pull steadiness out of my chaos.

"You're Brynn Hilder from Devon Park," he says. "You don't do this."

The last sob hiccups away.

My back straightens.

My breath is cool in my throat.

"Soldier up. You got a problem, figure out a way to fix it."

I lift my chin.

"Good," he says.

We go inside.

CHAPTER 33

Just before midnight, my phone buzzes with a text message. I reach for it on my nightstand, blinking at the bright light of the screen as my eyes adjust from the darkness. I've been alone in my room since Moore and I came back inside. It wasn't hard with everyone avoiding me.

I'm still dressed; I even have my shoes on. It feels best to be ready for anything.

Sorry! Here you go.

Ben's name pops up beside the words, along with three dots indicating another message is coming.

Since leaving the garage, Moore's words have been on repeat in my head.

You're Brynn Hilder from Devon Park.

I'm calm now. Refocused. Since I've come to Vale Hall I've wanted to shed the girl I was and become something better, something more. But this place is no better. It is a snake's den.

I thought leaving my old life meant leaving the old me, but now I see that every scrape and bruise was practice for this. I was made in the southside. I was molded by midnight sirens and muggy summers and canned vegetable casseroles. By teachers who were too busy breaking up fights to give me a minute. By harsh words, and harsh hands, and a mom who worked minimum wage to keep a roof over my head.

By everyone who thought I wasn't good enough.

I am Brynn Hilder from Devon Park.

I will not forget who I am again.

The second message—the one I requested an hour ago—pops up on my screen. It's a picture of three college guys in tuxes, laughing. Ben, Emmett, and Jimmy Balder. I'd forgotten I'd asked Ben to send it. That was the night that Mark tried to pull me into his car—the night Caleb showed up and had my back, even though he was only there because he'd followed me.

The night he saw Margot.

Moore said earlier that I wasn't supposed to find anything on Jimmy. But I did find something. I found Mark Stitz, who claimed to have seen the senator and Susan before Jimmy disappeared. He'd been clear that Sterling was telling Jimmy to run, but that hadn't made sense, just like it didn't make sense that Mark, director of interns, would have been left as a loose end when one of his employees disappeared.

At the very least, Sterling would have made sure he knew not to talk.

I expand the picture, focusing on Jimmy's face—his eyes pinched in laughter, his mouth open. He's grabbing Ben's shoulder, like what they're talking about is so funny he can't even hold himself up.

I think of his parents, wondering what happened to him—if he really did run away, or if he's dead.

I think of the devastation on Caleb's mom's face when he tells her what's happened.

Dr. O isn't just playing chess, he's playing God—saving people, crushing people. Trying to clean up the city through deceit and blackmail.

He probably doesn't even care about Jimmy's disappearance.

He probably never cared about Caleb, either.

My eyes move from Jimmy to Ben, who's cleaned up in this picture for the event. No beard, no raggedy hair. Emmett looks nice, too, as do the two people behind them. The woman in the yellow gown, and the man walking by in his too-tight tuxedo.

I sit up so fast my head swims.

I recognize this man—his smooth features and slick black hair. His arms, so thick they barely fit in the sleeves of his suit jacket. His head is turned slightly to look at the guys—at Jimmy.

In a flash, I'm out of bed and sprinting toward the door. Gripping the phone in my hand, I race down the hall, stopping at Geri's room. It takes serious control not to knock hard enough to wake the other girls, but I manage, and when I hear a rustling inside, I turn the handle.

"What the . . ." Geri's at her desk, and at the sight of me she stands so fast her chair flips on its side. Her laptop is open to a screen with pencil-thin triangles and math equations.

"Is this your dad?"

I shove the phone her way, heart thumping in my chest. I knew I recognized him at Family Day. I'd seen this photo at Risa's the night before.

"Listen, Traitor Tammy, I don't know what—"

"Just look at it."

With a dramatic sigh, she squints at the screen. Recognition cuts a scowl into her flawless skin.

"Yeah. So?"

"Why was he at an art gallery for a political fund-raiser for Grayson's dad?"

"How should I know?" Her gaze darts to the side. "In case you haven't noticed, I live here. In this room you've so rudely trespassed into. I don't keep track of where my dad goes."

"Please," I beg her. "One of these guys disappeared the night this was taken. If your dad knew him, he might be able to help me."

Her lips curve in a thin smile. "Why would he help you?"

My arm holding the phone lowers. "Well for starters, you could ask him."

"And why would I do that? You just got one of us kicked out. For all I know, I'm next on your list."

Someday, I'm going to strangle Geri. No one will be surprised. The world will breathe a collective sigh of relief. They might even give me a medal.

"You don't know anything about it," I growl.

"You're right. And I don't want to." She walks toward her vanity, smoothing down her hair in the mirror's reflection. "It's fitting anyway. He got my best friend kicked out. It was only a matter of time before karma came back to bite him."

Margot. My muscles ratchet tighter. Before I came, Margot and Geri were tight, that's what Charlotte said. Geri, like the rest of them, believed that Caleb was angry that Margot had broken up with him and ratted her out to Dr. O. The truth was that Dr. O forced Caleb's hand. The director threatened to take away his father's care if Caleb didn't say what she'd told her mark about the program.

Caleb protected his family, but Margot was let go.

"I didn't want this to happen," I say.

"I'm sure Caleb didn't, either."

"Stop." The force of my voice makes her jump. "Stop pretending you're above all this. That you can't get cut just as easily as the rest of us."

She faces me. "You really haven't learned anything, have you? The only way to get out of here is to be above *all this.*" She holds her hands out to the sides, encompassing her room, this entire school, maybe. I don't know what she's talking about. More Geri propaganda.

"Poor Brynn," she muses. "You lost the boys, you lost the girls. Lose your assignment and you can follow Caleb right out the door."

I flinch at his name.

"You don't want to help me, fine. Maybe Dr. O knows what your dad was doing there."

"Leave it alone."

At the warning in her tone, I stop.

"Why?"

Slowly, she walks around me to close the door, then leans against it, hands on the knob behind her. I glance down at her sweatshirt, which bears the words *BITE ME* in bold black letters.

"Leave my dad out of whatever plot you and Dr. O have to bring down the Sterlings."

Hold on a second.

"So he does know the senator."

Her lips seal. She's blocking the door as if she might try to stop me from leaving.

"Does he know those guys?" I pull out the phone again, scrolling to the picture. "Him. Right here." I point to Jimmy. "His name is Jimmy Balder. Has your dad ever mentioned him?"

"Put that away."

I don't.

"I could have you out of here by morning," she says, but her face has lost some color, and her voice wobbles the slightest bit.

"You don't have anything on me."

"I'd find something."

I want to hit her. I want to drag her to the floor and pummel her, the way Caleb did Grayson.

You got a problem, figure out a way to fix it.

"I'm not your enemy," I tell her.

"We are all enemies," she says quietly. "That's how this works."

She's right. We collect secrets. We share lies. When we're threatened, we do what we have to—we save ourselves.

She's alone, and she's got a secret—I can see it threatening to tear out of her. If I'm going to get something from her, I need to give something first.

"Dr. O's got my mom on the hook," I say quietly. "Somehow he convinced her to sell her house and move into an apartment he found for her. She's working for him now."

She sighs, resignation dropping her shoulders. "So he finally got you."

I nod.

"My dad has a record," she says. "If I do what I'm told, he doesn't go to prison."

This takes a moment to sink in. I never pinned Geri as the daughter of a felon. I wonder what white-collar crime he's done that Dr. O's got the dirt on.

"What does your dad do?"

"He fixes things."

"What kinds of things?"

"The kinds of things you don't talk about."

Some pretty ugly scenarios run through my mind.

"Bank accounts?" I ask. "Ballot counts for Sterling's election?"

Her head tilts. "Have you seen my father? Does he look like he spends a lot of time in front of a computer?"

No, he doesn't. He's got arms like tree trunks but doesn't look like he spends a lot of time in a gym.

"Is he a hit man or something?"

"You watch too many movies."

But she doesn't disagree.

This takes another moment to process.

I've heard of fixers. Pete used to call Eddie, his bouncer, a fixer. When someone stole from Pete, or set up shop selling pills in the same turf, Eddie took care of it.

Never did I imagine Geri would come from that kind of life.

"Does your dad work for Sterling?" The senator could have hired him to make Jimmy disappear. I'm still not sure why Sterling would warn him to get out of town beforehand, like Mark said, though.

It seems impossible that the answer to my missing person assignment could have been right down the hall this entire time.

Geri shakes her head. "He doesn't share those kinds of details."

My stomach sinks, and from the flex of her jaw, I suspect she feels the same cold dread.

She places a hand on her throat, as if trying to stop the words. "Grayson's trouble. When I was assigned to him, my dad told me to sabotage it. Get away from him, even if it meant losing my spot here."

A dozen more questions form in my mind at this confession. Geri told her father about her assignment. He knows what we really do at Vale Hall.

"Why is Grayson trouble?"

She shakes her head. "He didn't say. But I believe him. When someone in my dad's profession points out danger, you steer clear. Caleb doesn't get much, but he got that."

A piece locks in place.

"That's why you and Caleb were all over each other. Not because he was rebounding. So Grayson could focus on me without competition."

Like Dr. O wanted.

"It wasn't a hardship for Caleb, believe me," she says, annoyed. "But regardless, his plan to keep you safe backfired, didn't it? Caleb's gone, and Grayson's moved on to something you certainly can't provide."

It makes me feel a million times worse to imagine Caleb, behind the scenes, helping me succeed in my mission.

"It's awful when they go," she adds, and I know she's thinking of Margot. We may have nothing else in common, but we have both lost someone to Vale Hall, and right now, that feels like a lot.

I'm trying to process everything she's said, but it's like I'm chasing a bus that's already left the station.

Her father, a "fixer," has told her Grayson's dangerous.

Caleb believed Grayson was dangerous.

The only person telling me he's not is Dr. O, and I already know how much I can trust him.

My barometer can't be that far off. I know who is safe and who isn't. I've survived this long being able to make those kinds of split-second judgements.

But I never saw Margot coming.

I look down at the picture on the phone, still in my hand.

"Do you think your dad could have done something to Jimmy Balder?"

She inhales a quaking breath.

"My mom left when I was four. It's been Dad and me as long as I can remember. He does what he has to for the two of us." She steps closer, away from the door. Her hands are like claws, her chin low with a kind of fierceness I can't help but respect.

"He's all I have," she continues. "You can't tell Dr. O my dad has anything to do with Jimmy. If he decides Dad's a liability, if he hurts Dad in any way, I will burn you to the ground."

She doesn't want to hurt me, though. I'm almost surprised to hear the regret in her tone.

Later, in my room, I stare up into the black, trying to figure out this puzzle. There are too many pieces, and I don't know where to start.

The art gallery fund-raiser with Jimmy and Geri's dad. Susan and Matthew Sterling firing Jimmy and telling him to get out of town. Jimmy disappearing.

Susan speeding away from the senator, followed by Grayson. Possible head injuries not caused by the accident. Grayson calling his father on Susan's phone. Matthew crying when Grayson told him what happened.

I'm missing something. It's right at the tips of my fingers, but I can't quite grasp it.

As I finally drift to sleep, I'm haunted by Susan's screams, and the betrayal in Caleb's eyes, but above all else, by the familiarity in Geri's voice when she used Jimmy's name.

CHAPTER 34

By dawn, I'm ready to confront Margot.

She slipped past my defenses. She messed with Caleb's head to get back at Dr. O. I knew from the beginning she was hiding something, but I let that slip because I thought she might actually be my friend.

She's nothing more than a con. And I can't figure out what her endgame is.

She told Caleb Dr. O was dangerous, maybe to get him back for getting her kicked out. But she also led him to some police report indicating that Susan Griffin had injuries before her accident. Why would she have given him that information? Susan wasn't Caleb's assignment, nor was she Margot's.

Which brings me to the bigger question: what did Margot want from me? She asked about my schooling, but never directly about Caleb or Dr. O. If she was trying to out me to the senator, why go to the trouble of building rapport with me first?

And then there's Geri, whose father was in a picture with Jimmy Balder the last night he was seen. Geri, who was best friends with Margot.

It doesn't seem like such a stretch that Geri would be leaking information to Margot. Maybe their connection is why Jimmy's name slid so easily off Geri's tongue. Margot could have told Geri I was at The Loft looking into him.

It won't be easy getting back there. I can't ask Moore to break the rules after the driving lesson incident, and Dr. O doesn't want me leaving campus after my run-in with the detectives.

I need a cover to get out.

For the first time since I got to Vale Hall, I'm overwhelmed with nerves knocking on Charlotte's door. With everything that happened last night with Caleb, I know the thin ice I've been skating on since her birthday has broken through, and this may be a bust.

"Come in," she calls. Maybe it's my own unsteadiness, but her voice seems tense.

I push open the door and find her picking through the items in her purse.

"Hey," I say.

"Hey."

"Going somewhere?"

Her lips smush to the side. She's not wearing makeup today, and it makes her look young, breakable.

"Meeting an assignment at the movies," she says.

She doesn't move. She won't even look at me.

"Which girl?" I remember my hand's still on the doorknob, and quickly pull it off. "The financial consultant's daughter?" Her dad's skimming a percentage off his clients and using it to fund his daughter's new BMW.

Charlotte doesn't answer, and her silence slices me with truth.

"It's Tuesday," I realize.

She made an appointment with the clinic for today. She must have told security that she's out on assignment as her cover.

I can't believe I forgot.

"It's Tuesday," she says.

"Want some company?"

Her breath comes out in a rush.

"Okay."

In silence, we head toward the car, Margot pushed to the back of my mind.

I leave my phone in my room and shut the door so Moore and Belk will assume I'm upstairs studying and won't think to track me. No one sees us as we head into the garage and she grabs the keys to the Jeep.

She's starting the car when the back door opens and Sam slips in.

"We going somewhere?" he asks.

He's wearing the same NYU shirt he was when I first met him at the train yard for my recruitment rally, and his newsboy cap is pulled low over his eyes.

"Girls only," says Charlotte stiffly.

He still doesn't know. It's her choice to tell him, but I hurt for him all the same.

"Sorry, Sam," I say.

"Nope," he says, and fastens his seat belt. "Strange stuff's going on around here—I know you wouldn't turn over Caleb unless it was. So let me off when you get wherever you're going, but for the drive, I want an explanation why one of my best friends was kicked out of school last night."

"Great," mutters Charlotte. Her eyes flick to the clock on the dashboard, and I can hear her sharp intake of breath. Her appointment must be sometime soon. "You're leaving when I park," she says coldly.

"No problem," he answers.

We pull out of the garage, but no one speaks until the front gate has closed behind us. To my relief, there are no detectives camped outside the gates.

"All right." Sam crosses his arms and leans back in his seat. "I'm listening."

I can think of ten reasons why spilling any of these secrets is a bad idea, starting with Dr. O finding out, and ending with Sterling's detectives hunting us all down and killing us in our sleep, but in the end, I'm tired of hiding from my friends. I'm sick of Dr. O driving a wedge between us.

"I've been working in a restaurant where Matthew Sterling's staff meets," I start, and the rest falls out of me from there. Mark. Caleb following me to Risa's. Myra Fenrir, aka Margot. The senator and his detectives cornering me on the stairs. My mom's new job with Wednesday, and the mysterious police report I used to try to save Caleb from the streets.

By the end, Charlotte's lost somewhere on the east side, having taken one wrong turn after another, and Sam's holding his hands in front of his mouth as if praying.

"Why didn't you tell me any of this?" Charlotte finally asks.

"I don't know," I answer. "I thought I couldn't, I guess."

She's quiet, and Sam's quiet, and for once, my mind isn't racing to build another lie or figuring out a way out of one. I'm free of Dr. O's chokehold.

I've even managed to kill the tension between Sam and Charlotte.

"That's a lot," says Sam as we pass a sign for a belowground SCTA station. "But I get it. Caleb . . . I think he'd get it, too."

I don't know about that.

Charlotte's still quiet as we pull over in front of a brick office building. My stomach clenches in anxiety for her.

Sam reaches over the seat and grabs my shoulder. He doesn't say anything, just squeezes, which is enough to make it hard to swallow. I pat his hand awkwardly.

"I'm going to find Caleb and fix this," I promise him. "I don't know how, but I will."

Sam's head falls forward. "He's already offline. It's like someone pressed a kill switch and *poof.* No more Caleb Matsuki. No Ryan Ikeda or any of his other alter egos. I couldn't find a single mention or picture."

He's already been erased, the way Margot was erased when she was kicked out.

Maybe it's stupid, but I hope Moore wasn't the one to do it.

"He must have gone home," I say. "Do you have his mom's number?"

"No number," says Sam, releasing my shoulder. "No address. Didn't really have a reason to get it when the guy slept in the room next door."

"Margot might know how to reach him." It hurts to say the words out loud, but Caleb trusted her, and might still.

If I can't find her, I know where Caleb's dad is.

At least where he has been. If his care's been cut off, I don't know where he'd go.

It doesn't matter. I'll find him. I'll get his mom's address, even if that means breaking into Caleb's personal files in Dr. O's safe to do it.

Charlotte still hasn't spoken, and it occurs to me that she's waiting for Sam to leave and may be too nervous to ask.

I turn around and hitch a thumb toward the window. "There's a train station two blocks back. You can call Moore when you get—"

"No." Charlotte shifts in the front seat. "No," she says a little quieter. In the backseat Sam is frozen, one hand on the door handle. He's not looking at Charlotte, he's looking out the window, but in the side mirror I can see his reflection, and I'm pretty sure he's holding his breath.

"Brynn, you think you can ride the train back?" she asks. "I'll get you at the station in a couple hours. Sam and I need to talk."

Sam's hand falls into his lap. I'm scared and nervous for Charlotte, and so proud I think I might burst. It's easy to think handling everything by yourself is safer, and smarter, and less messy than pulling in other people. But sometimes the collateral damage is greater when you face your demons alone.

I reach for her hand and thread her fingers through mine. She nods and blows out a tense breath, and I go.

I walk half a block down, then slip into the doorway of a bakery to watch the car, just in case things don't go well. If she needs me, I'll be here.

Sam leaves the backseat and sits in the front. Through the back window I can see him take off his hat.

Neither of them move for a long time. Then he reaches for her and they're hugging. The minutes pass and they don't move. They hold on to each other like a tornado is threatening to tear them apart.

Whatever happens next, they'll figure it out together.

Like Caleb and I should have.

Swallowing my regret, I lift my chin and jog to the train that will take me closest to the Macintosh Building.

I CAN'T GO into the club. If Sterling's detectives haven't tracked me around town already, they're surely keeping tabs on my place of work. I linger inside a coffee shop across the street, hoping Margot comes in before her shift to get one of those fancy drinks she's always stashing in her locker.

An hour passes, and I've power-slurped my way through two hot chocolates by the time she finally shows, accompanied by Ben.

Our eyes meet across the cart of stirring sticks and creamers, and her smile flattens.

She knows I know about Caleb. She knows I've finally figured out who she is.

I'm out of my chair immediately, but I don't carve a direct path toward her. I make my way around the line, so that I can block off the exit in case she decides to bolt. She doesn't, though; she keeps right on talking to Ben as if my discovery is nothing out of the usual.

I want to kick something. I want to spill steaming hot coffee all over her nice wool coat.

"Oh good," says Ben when he sees me. "I've got twenty-six coffees to order. I'll buy you a puppy if you help me carry them to the office."

He looks like he's already had a little too much caffeine. He's twitchy, which makes Margot look overly calm.

"A puppy?" says Margot. "He only offered me his eternal gratitude."

"Guess he likes me better." I stare at her.

She stares back.

"The barista is going to love us," she says.

"I can't believe we're even here today," Ben adds.

I may be standing face-to-face with the slickest con artist in the city, but at Ben's grim tone, my stomach sinks.

"Why?" I ask. "Did something else happen?"

"You haven't heard?" He looks to Margot, shocked. "Mark's in the hospital. Someone jumped him last night after we got out. He's at First Presbyterian now."

"What?"

"He could've died," says Ben. "I heard he broke his arm and six ribs. If there hadn't been a witness, who knows what would've happened."

"A witness?" I'm frantically trying to absorb this new information. "They know who did this?"

"Apparently it was a big guy."

"How big?"

"I don't know," says Ben. "Scary looking is what I heard. Probably one of our voters, pissed about the health care thing."

Or Geri's father, sent by Sterling to tie up his loose ends around Jimmy's disappearance. I think of the man's arms, barely fitting in the suit jacket in that picture from the fund-raiser. *A fixer,* Geri called him.

I try to shake the image from my head, but it sticks.

"It was late," says Ben. "I didn't leave until after one. In case you missed it, my fearless leader jumped ship again."

I glance to Margot, who is watching me silently.

"Oh yeah?" I ask quietly.

"Yeah," says Ben, irritated now. "Matt reverted his stance on gun control. You know, I picked this campaign because he stood up to the big arms sellers. Now he's just as greasy as the rest of them." He looks down at his list of drinks, scribbled on a scrap of paper.

Dr. O's gotten to Sterling again. Last night he said he needed to keep Grayson at Vale Hall for his safety, but I knew the truth. On the run, Grayson's a liability. If his dad's detectives got to him before Dr. O, Grayson could change his story. Say the phone wasn't Susan's. Blow up the director's blackmail plans.

A new fury burns inside me.

"You know what?" Ben says. "Screw it. This is crazy. I'm done with this guy."

With a sound of disgust, he steps out of line and shoves the list of drinks into the trash. Giving only a half wave, he leaves the coffee shop.

With Ben gone, my focus sharpens to the point of a knife. My hands fist at my sides. The clank and hiss of the steamer falls below the cannon boom of my heart. I'm facing Margot, who stalked me, who actually had me convinced she was someone else.

"Want to sit down?" she asks.

I hold out a hand, and she leads the way to small, quiet table in the back.

Only after she sits do I.

"He told you," she says.

Even thinking Caleb's name rubs salt in the wound of my betrayal. I wish I could shoot back that I'd figured it out myself, but I can't. "He did."

"I told him not to."

"Why?"

"Full honesty?"

"Sounds like a solid plan," I say.

"I thought I might be able to recruit you."

"Recruit me for what? Your poli-sci club at Sikawa State?" I think of how passionate she was about that professor who sang about foreign trade. I'll give her this: she did her research.

She smiles, but it's not Myra's smile. This smile is harsh, and deceiving.

I smile back, because this, I understand. This makes sense to me.

"What do you want?" I ask.

She sighs, and then reaches into her purse. For a second, I think she's going to pull a knife. It wouldn't shock me at this point.

"Kind of tense, aren't you?" she says.

"It's been a wild couple of days."

She pulls out a piece of paper, folded lengthwise, and sets it on the table in front of her.

"It's awful, isn't it? Realizing you're not the puppet master, you're the puppet? Believe me, I've been there."

"Are we having a heart-to-heart?"

A line creases her brow. "We could, you know. You probably won't believe me when I say this, but I like you, Brynn. In some parallel dimension, we could've been friends."

I'm trying to keep cool, but I'm boiling, bubbles of rage popping, breaking through my composure.

She's a liar, and a con.

She is the backside of the mirror.

She is me.

Her fingers tap on the folded white paper as she leans back in her chair.

"I see why he's in love with you," she says, and my chin jerks up.

"*Caleb.* You balance him out. You run hot, he runs cool. You act, he deliberates. But you always get to the same place, don't you?"

I stare at the paper, unable to meet her gaze. I don't want to hear this. She doesn't get to talk to me about Caleb when she cheated on him with her mark, when she's been meeting him behind my back.

But my heart aches all the same.

"He needs someone solid, who doesn't bend under pressure. He admires that kind of strength." A voice behind us cracks in laughter, and we both glance that way. "I couldn't give him that. At least, not then. Things have changed since my Vale Hall days."

"Don't talk to me about Caleb."

She smirks. "Isn't that why we're having this little chat? What did he tell you?"

Not enough.

I hold her gaze. "That I should leave school because it wasn't safe."

She shakes her head. "Oh Caleb. What did he tell you about before? About me and him?"

I shift in my chair.

"You must know he told the director I was breaking the rules." I nod.

"And you know I was kicked out because of that."

I can see Caleb holding his box of personal items. So few things to take with him. Does she know he's gone now, too?

"What do you want, Margot?"

She smiles. "I want to help you."

"Somehow I doubt that."

She tucks her hair behind her ear. "Caleb told me about the senator's son."

My teeth press together.

"You need to watch yourself around Grayson Sterling," she says.

"Thanks for the tip."

"He lied about Susan Griffin's death being an accident."

I stiffen at the name, wondering how much Caleb has told her. Thinking again of the police report he mentioned, and why she would have given him that information.

"Oh yeah?"

"She'd been attacked before." Margot inhales slowly. "She met the senator outside a restaurant opening he was attending summer before last. She'd been beat up pretty badly and was looking for help. Matthew offered to drive her home, but she was too paranoid that the man that did it would find out and kill her."

"How do you know all that?"

"Jimmy told me."

I go still. "Jimmy Balder."

She's a liar. I can't believe her.

But there is no hitch or rush in her words, and her gaze holds steady.

"That's right," she says.

"How do you know Jimmy Balder? He interned for Sterling before you started at The Loft."

Her brows arch. "Caleb really didn't tell you?"

I wait.

And then, slowly, like staring at the sun through a moving cloud, the truth begins to glow, a white orb, growing brighter with each passing breath.

Margot's position at The Loft. Her reaction at Risa's, when Ben showed her the picture from the fund-raiser. Her curiosity about my mission to find my missing "friend."

Jimmy Balder was Margot's assignment.

The boy she fell in love with. The boy she cheated on Caleb with. Her mark, given to her by Dr. O.

"You were with Jimmy," I say.

She nods. "He was Dr. O's first shot at pinning Matthew Sterling. He'd just taken up an internship in the campaign office. I . . . I set myself up to meet him at a coffee shop by the river."

He was going on and on about how the building had been used in something like fifteen movies—you could always tell because of the gargoyles hanging off the sides. She'd spilled her coffee on him.

"The one by the Rosalind Hotel."

"See? I didn't lie about everything."

That story was true, only I thought it was about Caleb, not about Jimmy.

"What happened to him?" I ask.

Her lips curl. "Dr. O happened."

CHAPTER 35

You know what happens to us if we get kicked out?" Margot asks.

I nod. Behind her, the baristas shout orders to each other across the hissing copper steamer.

"Dr. O took my life. I didn't have a school record. I didn't have a bank account. I couldn't get a job or reapply at school. I stayed in a youth shelter for months before I found a place to land."

Her tone has turned angry, and I don't blame her. But she knew the risks in her actions.

"Surprised the state didn't pick you up," I say.

"Are you listening? I'm a ghost. I don't even have a name on record anymore. You know where they send kids without family?" She gives a bitter laugh. "I did the group home thing after my mom died—that's the rat hole Dr. O pulled me out of. Perhaps you've noticed he leans toward students with a similar background."

I have. At first, I thought it was because he was looking to help the kids who didn't have much, but now it's clear that there's another reason we were chosen. Family Day may keep the more diligent parents from asking questions, but on the whole, we're on our own, and have been a long time.

"I wasn't the only one he erased," she says. "Dr. O had to cover his tracks, and he knew I'd told Jimmy about Vale Hall. So he got rid of Jimmy."

He's hurt people.

He's out of control.

People are dying.

"How?" I ask.

"He hired someone to kill him."

I want to laugh her off. Tell her I'm done with her wild lies. But she holds my gaze, steady and certain.

"It was after a fund-raiser," she continues. "The one at the art gallery—Ben showed us a picture from that night at Risa's, remember?"

The picture with Geri's dad in the background, that had Margot pale as death at the restaurant when Ben showed us.

"I remember."

"After Jimmy left the fund-raiser, Matthew Sterling and the artist at the event cornered him."

"Susan Griffin." This lines up with Mark's story and seems to lower the temperature of the room a full ten degrees.

"Right. They told him someone wanted him dead, and he needed to get out of town immediately. They offered to help, but he said no. He said he needed to find me first." She swallows a shaky breath, glancing over her shoulder. "He knew from what I'd told him that Dr. O might be coming for me, too."

It's possible, but Dr. O burned Margot. I can't forget that. This still might be some desperate attempt to get back at the director that ruined her life.

"Okay," I say. "So then Dr. O, what? Pulled out a machete and chopped him up?"

"Please. He sent someone to do his dirty work." She shakes her head. "Someone I knew. That I trusted. A friend's father."

I go still.

"Geri's dad."

Margot nods. "I was waiting for Jimmy at his dorm. Maurice showed up there, said Geri had told him I was in trouble. That we should both come with him." She closes her eyes, reliving a horror I can feel stretching across the table. "It was pretty clear by the time we crossed the state line that Geri hadn't sent him."

"What happened?"

"Maurice had a gun. He said it wasn't personal, that Geri always said good things about me. Then, I don't know, he had a change of heart, I guess. He threw me out of the car and told me never to come back to Sikawa City. That was the last I saw of either of them."

In a blink, I'm in the car with Grayson as he speeds down the road toward the site of Susan's accident. When I open my eyes, I'm back with Margot.

"Maybe he let Jimmy go, too?"

She shoves back in her chair. "If he did, Jimmy would have found me."

I shiver at the certainty in her voice.

"It doesn't make sense," I say. "Why would Dr. O send me to look into Jimmy's disappearance if he knew what I'd find?"

"Because it's a perfect way to make sure he's buried the evidence. You didn't know Jimmy or me. You're a fresh pair of eyes. If you couldn't find anything, it means he did a good job."

My heel begins to tap as I remember Moore telling me in the garage that I wasn't supposed to find anything. I'd thought he meant that was because Sterling had covered it up, but maybe he'd been talking about Dr. O.

"And if I did find something?" I ask.

"He knows he can control you," she says. "He can, can't he?"

I think of Mom's new apartment, her job with Wednesday Pharmaceuticals. I think of Mark Stitz, now lying in a hospital bed. Is that because I told Dr. O that he'd seen the senator talking to Jimmy before his disappearance? The day Belk picked me up, he'd been scoping Mark as he walked by the hot dog stand. *Just need to get an idea of who's involved.*

If word about Jimmy's disappearance got out, and the senator was blamed and went to jail, Dr. O wouldn't be able to control him anymore.

I need to slow down. These are theories. She's yet to give me any proof.

I hide my trembling hands beneath the table. "It could have been Sterling that hired Geri's dad."

"It wasn't." She absently peels back the corners of the paper beneath her fingers. "Why do you think I took this job? I had to be absolutely sure Sterling wasn't involved. I knew he'd talked to Jimmy before Maurice picked us up. I thought if I got close to the staff, someone would know if the senator had knowledge of what had happened, but it turns out he's being jerked around like the rest of us."

I thought she was trying to out me to Sterling, but maybe she was just looking for clues about Jimmy, too.

"Susan knew her brother was dangerous," says Margot. "When I called her—"

"Hold on," I say. "You knew Susan?"

Margot's cheek indents. "She used to come by the house and have dinner with us. She gave me her number in case I ever needed a reference." Margot's sigh is bitter. "Once upon a time, I was trying to get into art school."

"What did you say?"

"That I'd left Vale Hall. That I was afraid for Jimmy. I asked her for help. I figured of all people, she would know what to do."

"Why?"

"Because she'd witnessed her brother's anger firsthand."

"Nice try," I say, an image of the director staring at his sister's painting filling my mind. "Dr. O adored Susan. He was a wreck when she died."

Margot snorts. "Is that what he told you?"

My heel hammers against the floor as I recall Matthew Sterling's changed votes. It wouldn't be the first time Dr. O's lied to me.

She passes the paper she took out of her purse earlier my way. "Caleb said you'd need proof."

Before I look at it, I size her up, trying to gauge if this might be another lie. She only laughs, a quiet, jaded sound, and crosses her arms over her chest.

I open the fold, reading the printed words at the top of the copy.

ORDER OF RESTRAINT.

Scanning through the handwritten words, I find Susan Griffin's name under *Applicant.* Below it reads, *Temporary order of protection against bodily harm, stalking, or threats by stepbrother, David Odin.*

I read the names again, just to be sure.

It could be a fake.

Something tells me it's not.

I place it carefully back on the lacquered table.

"Where did you get this?" Everything inside me is shaking. I know about restraining orders. I tried to get Mom to file one against Pete.

"I have my methods." She leans closer, points to a section that outlines *two head contusions from physical attack.*

Head injuries prior to the accident.

This is Caleb's police report.

He was right.

I didn't listen. I thought he was being swayed by Margot, who was trying to bring down the program out of spite. I'm not solid, like she said. I bent under the pressure of Dr. O.

I've been living under the roof of another abuser.

Dr. O must have known what this report entailed as soon as I brought it up. He got rid of Caleb because I said he'd seen it. Dr. O needed to hide the truth before anyone else found out that he'd beaten up his own sister.

"The director's hated the senator from the beginning," says

Margot. "Ever since Sterling came into office, he's been voting on bills that have taken money out of Dr. O's pocket. Susan believed in his cause, though, and when she started supporting him, Dr. O got mad. He attacked her, and when she tried to protect herself, he paid off a cop to have the restraining order disappear."

I am still, piece after piece settling into place.

Jimmy must have seen Susan after this happened—at the restaurant opening when she came to Sterling for help.

"Dr. O gets rid of people who get in his way," she says. "Me. Jimmy. Susan. Matthew Sterling."

Again, I think of Mark Stitz lying in a hospital bed at First Presbyterian. Did Geri's dad have something to do with that? Did I cause Mark to get hurt?

Have I done the same to Caleb?

"You asked what I wanted." The con is back; there is fire in Margot's eyes and ice on her tongue. "I want Dr. O to pay for Jimmy, and Susan, and everyone else he's hurt. I want to destroy him, the way he's destroyed me. I need someone on the inside to do that, and Caleb won't, not while you and the others are in danger."

I can't leave. That's what he said when I asked why he wouldn't come with me. I'd thought it was Margot, twisting up his head. That she was trying to punish him, or punish me. At the very least, I thought that he was protecting his father's care.

But he was protecting me.

Bile churns in my stomach. I need to find Caleb. I need to make sure Dr. O doesn't hurt him the way he did Jimmy. I think of Maiko, Jonathan, Christopher. Caleb's father. I need to get to them, *now.*

"He's gone," I say, ready to stand. Ready to run. "Dr. O sent him away last night."

From the distance comes the blare of sirens. Another joins it. There must be a wreck nearby.

Fear brightens Margot's gaze. "Where did he go?"

"I don't know. I thought you might."

She scrambles to grab the phone in her coat pocket and scrolls through the screen. "He hasn't called. He probably doesn't even have a phone. I didn't."

I don't have my phone, either—I left it at school, in my room, in case security tried to track where I was going today.

The sirens are getting louder. Louder. A headache pounds at the base of my skull.

"Does he know where you live? Would he go there?"

She shakes her head.

The sirens are screaming now. People are looking out the front windows into the street. As we watch, a blue police car comes to a screeching halt in front of the Macintosh Building. A second follows just behind, stopping right in front of the entrance.

Then a white van, the side painted *Channel 7 News.*

Margot and I look at each other, then jump up. There are many offices in that building, but a lot of bad seems to originate from Sterling's. She stuffs the restraining order back into her purse, and together we shove out the door, just in time to see another cruiser and news van—this one for *Pop Store*—show up.

"What's going on?" Margot says.

"There!" I point to Emmett and Ben, who've just emerged on the sidewalk beside the hot dog truck. Ben's hands are clasped over his head. Emmett's pointing at someone just inside. Out of the news vans jump reporters and men with cameras. Traffic is already stopped by the flood of pedestrians into the street.

We rush toward the other interns as the cops pull a man out of the building in handcuffs. He's wearing a blue button-down shirt and is surrounded by police. I recognize Lewis to his right, holding a coat high enough to cover the man's face.

But it doesn't matter. We all know who he is.

Matthew Sterling is being arrested.

"No comment!" Lewis is shouting at the reporters shoving their microphones through the gaps between the police.

"What's going on?" I ask when we reach Ben and Emmett.

"They think he killed someone," says Emmett.

"What?" asks Margot.

Ben's shaking his head. "I went inside to quit, and these cops nearly broke down the door trying to get to him. All I heard is they found some phone at his house with a dead woman's prints on it."

The sirens fade beneath the screaming in my head.

I look to Margot.

She stares back, and it's clear that whatever lies brought us together must be shoved aside. We're on the same team now.

Dr. O has planted Susan's phone at Matthew Sterling's house, and now the senator's taking the fall. The blackmail over changing positions on bills is over, and soon Grayson will be called to testify against his father.

He's in danger, and if anything Margot's said has been true, so is everyone else in that house.

I need to warn them.

I need to get back to Vale Hall before someone else gets hurt.

CHAPTER 36

"Geri?" I shout into the phone as I race across the platform to catch the next train. Ben won't be happy to find his cell missing from his pocket, but as I left mine at home, I didn't have much of a choice. I slipped it right out of his coat pocket as he and Emmett went to talk to the cops. It's a good thing he hasn't changed his passcode since the night I unlocked his phone at Risa's.

"Yes. *Yes.* Why are you yelling?"

"You need to call your dad. Tell him to stay away from Caleb."

Silence.

"Geri?"

"What are you talking about?" she says in a hushed tone.

"Dr. O hired him to get rid of Margot and Jimmy Balder. He might be coming after Caleb next."

"No," she says. "He wouldn't do that. You don't know what—"

I sprint toward the closing glass doors, slipping in at the last moment. The man I ram into hits the standing pole with a grunt and backs out of my way.

"I just saw Margot," I say. "She told me everything."

"You . . ."

"*Geri.*" I don't have time for this. Bands are squeezing around my chest, and the dread is thickening in my belly. "Your dad let Margot go, but Jimmy's gone, and Caleb's next. Dr. O cleans up his messes, you understand?"

Her sharp curse fills my ear.

"You have to hurry," I say.

Over the line comes the sound of a closing door and a rustle of fabric.

"Margot's okay?"

"She's okay."

"I didn't know," she says. "I swear."

"Call your dad," I tell her, groaning as the train makes its first stop. "Tell him you're close with Caleb. That dance on Family Day—tell him it was real. He saved Margot because he knew she meant something to you."

"How do you know he's doing this?"

I don't. It's just a hunch because he went after Margot and Jimmy. For all I know, Dr. O could have sent someone else after Caleb.

Caleb's smart. He knew what happened to Margot. He'll be ready for anything.

Please be ready for anything.

The train picks up new passengers and speeds on again.

"I'll call him," she says, panic lacing through her voice. "You're coming home?"

"Yes."

She hangs up.

The next stop peels back another layer of my already raw patience. I call Charlotte for a pickup, but she doesn't answer. I try Henry's phone, but it goes straight to voicemail. I can't remember Sam's number—it was erased when the phones were cleared, and I never reprogrammed it. Caleb's is already disconnected.

Where is Caleb?

Why did Dr. O plant that phone on Matthew Sterling now?

Geri's dad. Mark Stitz. Jimmy Balder. I think of Margot, driven out of town beside her boyfriend, convinced she was about to die only to be dumped on the side of the road and told to skip town.

I think of Grayson, running Susan Griffin off the road.

I think of Henry, and Sam, and Charlotte.

I have to warn them, but I have to be careful. If Dr. O knows, we'll all be in trouble.

Someone on the inside, Margot said. That's what she needs to take down Dr. O—to *destroy* him, the way he destroyed her.

I can't be that person. I need to get out before I end up disappearing. I need to get my friends out before it's too late.

But if we leave, there's no stopping Dr. O from erasing us anyway. Henry can't go home. Sam's mom is in prison. Charlotte can't stay in a youth shelter pregnant.

I don't know what to do.

At the last stop on the blue line, I run for the exit, hoping that Charlotte and Sam will miraculously be waiting in the Jeep outside. But as I scan the cars parked on the curb, it's only a black sedan I see.

And leaning against the car is Belk.

His open coat hangs down to his knees, showcasing his round torso. His black hair is tucked back in a blunt ponytail. His voice presses through from my memories: *Is that the intern supervisor? Just need to get an idea of who's involved.*

Mark is in a hospital now because of what I told Dr. O. Belk was just verifying which domino was the next to fall.

It's too late to run, he's already seen me. Even if I try, it will do me no good. I'll be hunted, and my friends won't know they're living in the house of a monster.

I wish Moore were here.

I wish Charlotte and Sam were here.

But mostly, I wish for Caleb.

"Get in," Belk says as I approach. The dead look in his eyes slows my steps.

"What are you doing here?"

"Get in," he says again.

I do.

Like before, when he picked me up at the campaign office, I sit in the backseat, chauffeured by my security officer. The leather upholstery creaks under my denim-clad thighs. I keep my thumb poised on the seat belt buckle.

He doesn't speak until we exit the lot.

"Dr. O's looking for you."

Playing dumb feels like the smartest option. "Why didn't he call me?"

"Your phone's at school," he says. "You didn't tell anyone you were leaving today."

Belk's fine when he's teaching class, but alone, he has a definite creeper vibe. Though Moore might be rigid, and not always friendly, I've never felt unsafe with him.

Not like I do now.

The train station isn't far from Vale Hall. The spaces are already stretching between the houses, giving way to giant properties nestled in the woods.

"I left a message for Moore," I say. "Charlotte said she'd pick me up after her assignment."

"And yet, here I am," says Belk.

Dr. O, or maybe Belk, must have called Charlotte looking for me and told her to come home. She would have told them I needed a ride from the station.

We're at the gate, and Belk types a code into the freestanding metal box. With a squeal, the iron bars open, and a new fear shivers down my spine.

"Where'd you take Caleb last night?" I ask.

He doesn't answer.

We roll down the drive, the gate closing with a screech behind us.

"What's Dr. O want?" I ask.

More silent treatment.

"Am I in trouble for forgetting my phone?"

Not a word.

My anxiety grows, chilling my blood. He stops in front of the house and I leave the car, stomach doing somersaults as I climb the steps to the front door. Placing my hand on the bronze handle, I'm swamped with memories of my first time here. The disbelief that this was really happening. The hope that I would be accepted.

Now there is only fear.

I will be brave. For Charlotte, and Sam, and Henry, and the others.

I am Brynn Hilder from Devon Park.

Dr. O's office is just inside the front door, on the right opposite the spiral staircase. His door is open, but I don't go inside, because there's a girl standing at the edge of the kitchen beside Moore. She's got a ragged backpack over her shoulder, and a slouch to her shoulders. Her hair is dyed black, though her roots are white blond, and when she turns, I see dark eyeliner, red lipstick, and a nose ring.

I've seen her before.

Moore is already walking toward me, the girl following a few steps behind. She's taking in the art on the walls with wide eyes, like I once did.

"I thought we discussed the phone issue." Moore heads me off, jaw clenched. I do recall a discussion, shortly after I traded phones with Caleb and Grayson took me on a joyride to the site of Susan's accident. I may have made some promises about being reachable at all times.

I lean around him, pointing to the girl.

"I know you," I say. "You work at that restaurant in Uptown. Risa's." She picked Mark's pocket, then miraculously found his wallet again as we were leaving. *Goth Girl.*

"Not anymore I don't," she says, all defiance and grit.

I recognize her tone. It used to be mine.

In a snap, I realize why she's here.

"This is June," says Moore. "Our newest student."

Heat blossoms on my cheeks. I don't want there to be a new student. She doesn't understand the risks, or what's at stake. But I can't tell her, because I don't know this girl. I have no idea if I can trust her, or if she'll take everything I say straight back to Dr. O.

Above, on the landing, there's a creak in the steps, and when I look up, Henry is coming down the stairs. His presence is a punch to the gut; his eyes are puffy, his hair a mess. At the sight of me, he shoves his hands in his pockets and glares at the floor.

I think he means to talk to me—maybe he can tell me something about this girl—but he shoves past, nearly knocking me over on the way by. I stare at his back in shock as he retreats to the kitchen.

"Wow," says June. "Friendly group." His attitude seems to please her.

I tear my eyes away from Henry, ignoring the wash of guilt in his wake. "I didn't know we were getting a new student."

"June will be a wonderful addition to the program." Dr. O's voice behind me makes me jump. "I've heard only positive things about her."

I spin toward the director, and though his voice is pleasant, his hard stare is filled with blame. He's angry at me, maybe because I left without telling anyone. Maybe because I challenged him last night about Caleb's dismissal.

It doesn't matter. He hit his sister. He expelled Caleb. The gratitude I once felt in his presence is gone.

I hate him.

But I don't show it. I lock it inside, because I have a job: protect my friends. Do what I didn't let Caleb do.

"From who?" As soon as the words are out of my mouth, I wish I could suck them back in. I look again at Goth Girl—June—and swallow acid down my throat.

Caleb recruited her.

He followed her to Risa's, where she worked. He reported back to Dr. O if she would be a good fit for the program.

"You're from Sycamore Township," I say, voice faltering.

"That's right," she answers, as if she expects a fight on this.

I want to scream.

I want to tear these expensive paintings off the wall and chuck them across the room.

The new recruit wasn't an alibi Dr. O. fabricated. She was Caleb's actual assignment.

I didn't believe him.

I didn't listen about the police report, or Dr. O being dangerous. I didn't believe him, even when he gave me his trust.

"I'd say a welcome is in order," says Dr. O.

"Welcome," I whisper to June.

She shrugs her bag higher on her shoulder. "Can I get some food or what?"

With a look that screams warning, Moore leads her back toward the kitchen.

"Brynn," says Dr. O.

He's already retreated to his office, and I follow, ready for anything as he shuts the door behind me.

"Where were you today?" His smooth exterior has been shed. Now he's pure anger encased in a designer suit. Is he that upset about my absence, or has something else gone wrong? I need the answer to that question so I can respond the right way, but this new version of him has me rattled.

He attacked his own sister.

She filed a restraining order against him.

"Did you do it?" His words press through the cage of his teeth. "Did you take that phone and hide it in the senator's house?"

The warning ringing in my ears goes silent. I search his face for tells, for some sign of a game, but all I sense is anger.

He thinks I took Susan's phone—that I planted it on the senator.

Which means he didn't do it.

Grayson found a way into that safe.

He protected himself the only way he knew how—by sending his father to jail in his stead. He's playing the odds that his dad won't admit what really happened—that his son ran Susan off the road—for fear of being charged with the cover-up of her death.

"Answer me!" Dr. O bellows.

I jump, mind flashing to the restraining order Margot showed me. I pull my sleeve over my hand, hiding her number, written in pen on my wrist.

Frantically, I try to think of an answer he might buy. I can't tell him I went with Charlotte to serve as a wingman on her assignment, because Charlotte's already been intercepted—Belk was sent to pick me up instead. If I say I went back to The Loft, I'll be disobeying a direct order, and endangering the program.

He'll never buy I was picking up something for school, or seeing Mom—I'm sure he's keeping tabs on her now that she works for Wednesday.

I have one shot, and I pray it's good enough to buy me time.

"I didn't touch that phone. I was in the city looking for Caleb."

His shoulders draw back. His chin lifts. He's a cobra, ready to strike.

I am Brynn Hilder from Devon Park. I'm not afraid.

"Why would you do that?"

I force my feet to stay planted.

I paint an angry expression on my face, and match his fury.

"Because you kicked him out," I say. "And I want to make sure he's all right."

His shoulders drop. "Did you find him?"

This is a risk. He kicked Caleb out because he knew what was on the police report I told him Caleb had found—that Susan's head injuries were caused by his hands. If he thinks I've found Caleb and I know the truth about that restraining order, I'm as good as done here.

"No."

As long as he thinks I'm upset about Caleb, he won't dig into my true whereabouts. I hope.

"Where did you look?"

"Everywhere," I say. "Shelters. Restaurants. Places we used to go. Everywhere. He's MIA."

Dr. O's gaze presses through me like I'm made of glass, but I don't falter.

"You had nothing to do with Matthew Sterling's arrest," he says.

"*No.*"

He sizes me up for another long moment, then places one hand on the doorknob. "If I find out you're lying, the way you did when you told me you couldn't stop Grayson from leaving you at the crash site, you're done here."

He knows I let Grayson go. Has he known the whole time, or did someone tell him after I blurted it out the night the detectives came?

Dr. O opens the door, but before I walk out, he sags, regret infusing every muscle.

"Caleb is a bright, resourceful boy," he says. "He's going to be all right."

It's not much proof Dr. O hasn't sent the dogs after him, but it's all I have.

CHAPTER 37

Five minutes later, I'm up in in my room getting my books for the class Moore insists I attend, when I hear the crinkle of paper against my right hip. Pulling up the hem of my shirt, I find a note sticking out of my pocket and carefully draw it out.

Roof. Tonight.

My heart trips at the thought of Caleb, somehow here, waiting for me, but I know that can't be right.

Caleb's gone, and it's my job to find him.

This is Henry's handwriting.

When he came down the stairs, he bumped into me, hard enough to throw me off balance. I've done the same on the train when I've snagged someone's wallet, only this is the reverse. Henry didn't take anything. He planted something.

The next classes pass like hours in a torture tank. Shrew drones on about the betrayal of Othello. Grayson is still in his room. Henry won't talk to anyone.

And Belk is lurking, always.

The only comfort I have is Sam, who, without making a big deal about it, finds a way to touch Charlotte at every opportunity. His foot beside hers. The back of his knuckles against her thigh. The brush of his hand when he passes her a book.

Knowing they're okay is enough to get me through dinner.

As soon as the hall quiets, I turn on some music and sneak

toward the supply closet. Up the ladder I climb, taking care to mind the squeal when I pull up the rungs. Racing through the dark, I find the attic window, pausing to remember the times I hurried to meet Caleb here.

I should have trusted him.

I'll find him, and make it right.

Henry is waiting for me at the concrete ledge in front of the spire, exactly where Caleb used to sit. He's chewing his thumbnail, the shirt beneath his sporty jacket wrinkled. I rush toward him, unsure if he's going to talk or throw me over the ledge.

"Henry, I'm sorry," I say, before he can start. "I didn't mean for this to happen, but there's something you need to know . . ."

"I did something bad."

It's then I see the panic in his red-rimmed eyes and the tremble in his jaw. It spurs a chemical reaction inside me, and in an instant, I'm ready to defend us against whatever might come.

"What?" I glance again to his shirt, thinking of yesterday, in the pit, when I walked in on him and Grayson.

"I thought he liked me."

I don't like where this is heading.

"Grayson?"

Henry nods. "He said he liked me. He *kissed* me. He said he wanted this to be over, and I just wanted to help him, you know?"

Dread is sinking in my gut like a stone in a still lake.

"What did you do?"

Henry heaves out a breath, his fists balled in the pockets of his jacket.

"He gave me the security code to his house."

My thumbs dig into my temples.

"I just wanted to help." He tilts forward like he might throw up. "I took that cell phone he wanted out of Dr. O's safe—I got it that day he gave me the money to frame Luke for embezzling, when he and Sam knocked down the raven statue outside the office."

I remember the anger in Sam's eyes and Grayson's quick retreat. It was staged. Grayson created a diversion so Henry could rob the safe.

"Grayson said I should put it in his dad's office, in this locked cabinet above his desk."

In a blink, I'm back in our classroom, the night they were talking about *Othello*. When I showed up, Grayson sent Henry away—I'd thought he was just being Grayson, but Henry said he had something to do in town.

He'd almost forgotten his bag. Did it already have Susan's phone inside it?

"Okay." I need to focus. *Think.* "It'll be okay."

I can still see the police arresting Matthew Sterling outside the campaign office. The press screaming questions as he was shoved into the back of a cop car.

Grayson's afraid of him, so this can't be all bad. Dr. O may be a threat, but that doesn't mean Matthew Sterling isn't.

"It's not okay." Henry's voice hitches. "When I was at Grayson's house, I found this in a folder in his dad's cabinet."

Henry pulls a picture out of his pocket, creased down the center. He hands it to me with quaking hands.

I unfold it.

It's a casual photo, taken at some fancy dinner. There's a chandelier in the upper corner. A red tablecloth beneath a gold candelabra. Front and center, Dr. O is smiling at the camera, the buttons on his tuxedo jacket stretched as he rests his arm around the shoulders of a boy, no more than fifteen.

Grayson Sterling.

My stomach drops.

"What is that?" Henry asks. "What are they doing together? I didn't think they knew each other."

I didn't, either.

"Brynn, they're clearly friends."

I can't look away from Grayson's smiling face. From Dr. O's hand, curled around Grayson's shoulder. *Your director,* Grayson called him, as if they'd never met. The first day he showed up after Belk found him in Nashville, Grayson was petrified Dr. O worked for his dad and was going to turn him in.

I bought it all.

But this picture tells a different story.

Grayson and Dr. O know each other.

Henry suddenly jerks back, gripping my arm with the force of a snakebite. To my left, someone is coming around the corner beside the pipes. A boy. Broad shoulders. My height. Dark hair.

"I must have missed the invite," Grayson says. His lips curl in a cocky smirk as Henry pulls me another step back.

"Who are you?" Henry asks.

"I think we're past that, aren't we, Henry?"

"What is this?" I flash the picture at Grayson, already striding toward us. He squints a little, and then blows out a breath.

"Holiday benefit, I think? Probably some charity thing. You go to enough of those, they all start to blend together."

Adrenaline surges through my veins as Grayson steps closer.

"Stop there," I tell him.

"Or what?"

Dangerous, Caleb whispers in the back of my mind. *Troubled,* Matthew Sterling said. Margot knew he couldn't be trusted. Geri's dad, a hitman, told her to stay away from him.

I thought I knew Grayson better than they did. I thought I saw something they didn't.

But Grayson and Dr. O are in this—whatever *this* is—together.

Beside me, Henry is braced for a fight—frightened but ready. Automatically, I scan Grayson's hands for a weapon.

"I trusted you," says Henry.

Grayson wags a finger at us. "You know better than to trust anyone, Henry. Isn't that the first rule of this place?"

"I got that phone for you." Henry's voice cracks. "You told me you needed it to clear your name. You said your dad was going to have you killed if he didn't go to jail."

Grayson rolls his shoulders back, looking past us, into the dark.

"I may have exaggerated."

"He's innocent?" Henry makes a sound like he's dying. "I just framed an innocent man."

I think of Matthew Sterling, sick and exhausted, on the stairs of the Macintosh Building, begging for information on his son. *He's a troubled kid. He left his medicine. He's missed appointments with his therapist. He needs help.*

The senator never threatened Grayson. He probably covered up Susan's accident to protect his son, not himself, and sent those detectives to find Grayson, not hurt him.

He tried to save Jimmy, too, and failed.

"Don't beat yourself up," Grayson says. "I've done far worse for that old man."

I shiver. *Far worse.*

Someone is dead because of him, Caleb whispers.

"You killed Susan," I whisper. "You drove her off the road on purpose."

Grayson's gaze finds mine, and for an instant, I see a flash of regret, gone as quickly as it comes.

"Why would you do that?" I ask.

"I guess we'll never know," he says.

I believed him. He had me convinced that it was an accident. That he never meant to hurt her. But now all I can think of is Geri's dad, getting rid of Jimmy Balder, and I wonder if Grayson isn't doing the same thing for Dr. O—cleaning up his messes.

"They had to get her out of the way," Henry says, thumbs digging into his temples. "That's why he wanted me to plant the phone on his dad, to get him out of the way."

"For what?" I ask. "What are you and Dr. O doing?"

"Cleaning up the city," Grayson says with a smirk. "Sometimes you have to do bad things to get rid of bad people."

"You are the bad people!" Henry shouts.

Grayson flinches, and for a moment, the sharp edges of his ego are stripped away, leaving a glimpse of the scared kid who drove me to Susan's crash site three months ago.

"That depends on which version of the story you read," Grayson tells him.

My brows lift. He killed Susan, and now he's saying she deserved it? I never met her, but everything I've heard points to her being on the good side. Now that I know what I do about Grayson and Dr. O, I'm pretty sure Matthew Sterling is on the good side, too.

I have to quiet the roaring in my head. *Think.* But none of this makes sense. Why did Dr. O tell me to befriend Grayson and make him comfortable if Grayson was already reporting everything to Dr. O in their little meetings in his office?

Does he suspect Grayson isn't telling him everything, the way he suspected Caleb wasn't?

"You told me you were hiding in Nashville." I can't even fathom all the lies he's told. "If you and Dr. O were such pals, why wouldn't you come here instead of running away?"

"Those men my father sent weren't kidding around," he says. "I did have to hide. David put me up in a hotel there."

David. The familiarity of Dr. O's first name makes my stomach turn.

"Why would you take Susan's phone from Dr. O? He needs it to blackmail your father."

"Well now he can't." Grayson's jaw clenches and then suddenly relaxes. A tell—his anger always gives him away.

He clears his throat and looks to Henry. "I guess this means we're over, pal. Let's not make it awkward, okay? I plan on sticking around for a while."

Henry stares at him as if they've never met before. I'm sick on his behalf. Grayson was set on getting that phone from the beginning, and when I didn't help him, he moved on to someone who could.

But something's off with this equation. Grayson wouldn't have needed to get the phone if Dr. O had planned on using it against the senator all along. Dr. O was genuinely upset about Sterling's arrest—he thought I had had something to do with it.

Grayson and the director may know each other, but they're not on the same page, and judging by the blades in Grayson's voice when I mentioned his dad, something tells me that's the pressure point.

Is it possible Grayson's being blackmailed, just like I am with Mom, and Geri and Caleb are with their dads?

What would make someone go that bad? Kill another person, then send his own father to prison for the crime?

"What's he got on you?" I whisper.

Grayson's gaze shoots to mine, and I see fear. Cold, steel fear. I've hit the nerve.

Grayson's being blackmailed, but how and why I don't know. Whatever the case, he's willing to take lethal measures.

"Grayson."

From the attic window comes a voice I never thought I'd be so happy to hear. Moore is framed in the attic window, looking like he might Hulk his way through the brick and glass rather than climb through the open space.

"Brynn, Henry. Everyone inside."

My gaze flicks to Grayson and back to Moore. None of us move.

"Now," Moore barks.

Grayson saunters over first, crawling through the window. I'm next, and finally Henry. By the time he's inside, Grayson has already disappeared through the twists and turns of the attic.

As Moore closes the window, the dark becomes a living thing, crawling over my skin, blinding my eyes. I don't know what I expect to happen—Grayson isn't going to jump out of the shadows and murder us, but he did kill Susan and lie about knowing Dr. O.

And trick Henry into planting evidence on his father.

I don't know who he is, but he is capable of more than I ever imagined.

"Get to your rooms," says Moore.

"I can't," says Henry.

"You have to," Moore tells him.

I need to tell him. I trust Moore, and he might be able to help us.

"Grayson and Dr. O—"

Moore's hand covers my mouth before I can finish.

"I know," he says clearly. He turns to Henry. "But that is not something we're going to discuss."

"What are we going to do?" Henry whispers.

"You're going to go back to your rooms, and get some rest. And in the morning, you're going to put big, grateful smiles on your faces. You'll go to class, and do your homework, and keep your heads down every day until graduation, understand?"

"But . . ." Henry starts.

"Do you understand?" Moore's tone is coated with ice and promise. His intention is clear: we are not getting out of here unless we play the game. Even if that means doing things we don't want to. Even if that means living with Grayson Sterling.

We can't leave.

If we do, we will be unwritten. Erased. Maybe even hunted, like Jimmy and Margot.

"I understand," says Henry, more somber than I've ever heard him. He laces his fingers with mine, a cold, firm reminder that neither of us is alone.

I nod.

Moore lowers his hand.

We all go to the supply closet exit—easier than shimmying through the crawl space that leads to the boys' wing. My skin feels raw. My bones, too soft. But I force my chin up and grit my teeth.

Because I'm Brynn Hilder, from Devon Park.

And I'm done playing by someone else's rules.

Before we part ways, Moore tells us if he finds us on the roof again, he's writing us up.

Then he tells us to lock our doors before we go to sleep.

CHAPTER 38

2 Months Later

I sit on the top step of an outdoor staircase, the iron grating digging into my hamstrings as a bitter November breeze scrapes my face and the back of my neck. Huddling into my coat, I pull my knit hat lower over my ears and hug the large envelope against my chest.

I've been waiting over an hour.

I'd wait ten more if I had to.

The heels of my Chucks drum against the metal as I take yet another look around the parking lot below. A few cars fill the lot, none of them as fancy as the blue Jeep in the back. A few people are smoking near the road. From below comes the tinny sound of piped-in music, and laughter.

A clang on the metal, and then the heavy steps of someone coming up. I jump to my feet, heart in my throat.

Please, I think. Just *please*.

I see him before he sees me. His head is down, his black hair shaggier than I've ever seen it. Despite the cold, he's not wearing a coat. Just a black-and-white-striped button-down shirt over a long-sleeved thermal. There's a red stain on the right side, below the name badge, and his jeans are worn at the crease points.

He's wearing the same shoes I am, and this gives me some small measure of hope.

I blow out a hard breath at the sight of him, and at the sound, his chin jerks up.

I found you.

Caleb stops, the wind ruffling his hair. His eyes find mine through the same black frames he left in, and his lips part the slightest bit. Heat rises in his cheeks. From the wind. Maybe from me.

I grip the envelope tighter. I'm not going to crumble. But my heart feels like I'm in the middle of a hundred-yard sprint, and there's not enough air in the whole west side to fill my lungs.

His head tips forward, and absently, he rubs the back of his neck. Then he looks up again, as if unsure I'm really here.

It's me, I want to say. *I'm sorry. I'm here. I found you. I'm going to fix this.*

I haven't seen him in eight weeks, since the night he left Vale Hall, and since then, this moment has played out a hundred different ways. In some versions he hugs me and says I'm forgiven. In others, he passes by like I'm no more than a stranger on the street.

I need to say something.

Anything.

Anytime.

"Hi," I say.

Good one.

He continues up the steps, slower, heavier now, and pulls a key ring from his pocket. Giving me room, he passes without looking up and opens the door behind me.

My throat burns. The envelope crinkles in my grip.

He goes inside, and I catch a glimpse of a small table, a hot plate, and a stack of noodle packs. He's out of sight, somewhere behind the door.

"Are you coming in?" he calls.

I exhale in a whoosh and rush inside, then carefully, I close the door behind me. I hope that's okay. I don't know how to act around him right now. Everything I want to say seems wrong.

I don't know if I should take off my hat or my coat. Maybe that looks like I'm making myself too comfortable.

He's standing in front of a coiled heater, and with a clang and a cough, it begins to hum. While he warms his hands in front of it, I take a look around the small room. There's not much to it. Half seems to be dedicated storage for the bowling alley downstairs; the other half is occupied by a deflated air mattress with a rumpled sleeping bag on top. On the windowsill is the framed picture of his family. The glass is cracked, a lightning bolt splitting him from his parents and brothers.

It is a far fall from a room with a piano, a laptop, and a queen-sized bed with throw pillows.

"How'd you find me?" His voice is low, his dark brows furrowed with uncertainty.

I read people for a job, but at this moment, I have no idea how to set him at ease.

I try a smile. "I've got a few tricks up my sleeve."

He waits.

"I, um . . ." I look for a place to sit. There's not one. "I found your mom's address."

He rocks forward, panic thinning his lips.

I hold up a hand. "Don't worry, I didn't tell her. I didn't even talk to her." I intended to when I first learned where she lived, but it became immediately clear that Caleb hadn't come home. As she carried on with her routine, she didn't seem particularly concerned that one of her sons was missing, which made me realize he didn't tell her he'd been kicked out.

Since then, I've been checking in from a distance as often as I can.

"I followed Jonathan to the care home," I say. "I overheard the office manager telling him it was no problem changing the billing address on his care to this place." I glance toward the storage area. "Ragtime Bowling."

Since I learned the name, I've researched this place as well as I could. I know they're the only bowling joint on the west side. I know the owner, John, is a recovering addict, and takes in employees with criminal records, no questions asked. I know he has a room to rent above the bowling alley that a guy named Price had before he went back to prison. A phone call and a few innocent questions lent that much.

How Caleb is covering his dad's care working here I have no idea. He can't make more than minimum wage.

The thunder of bowling balls striking pins roars through the air vents. A never-ending crash from 10:00 a.m. to 2:00 a.m.

"Jonathan said he didn't know anything about a new billing address," I say. "I think you're in the clear."

Caleb gives a single nod.

A tense silence settles between us. "I'm sorry. About Grayson. About school. You were right about everything."

He doesn't look at me.

The past eight weeks have been a balancing act—playing like everything is fine while Grayson struts around the property. He hasn't told Dr. O that we know they're working together from what I can tell—Dr. O hasn't said a word about it to me or any of the other students. But if Grayson's keeping secrets from his friend the director, I don't know why. Maybe they are trying to cut corruption out of the city in their own corrupt way, but he's got his own game going, otherwise that phone never would have found its way into his father's safe.

Whatever he's up to, I intend to find out.

"Why are you here, Brynn?" My name sounds too stiff on Caleb's lips.

I want to tell him that I've been looking for him every day. That I've made a dozen excuses to leave Vale Hall and search the city. But what does that matter when I'm the reason why he's gone?

I step closer. He breathes in slowly, chest lifting.

Everything about him breaks me.

"I should have trusted you." I take off my hat, wringing it out in my hands. "Everything got all twisted up. I didn't know who to believe. I didn't even listen to myself."

His fingers tap against his thigh.

"But you should have trusted me, too," I say. "I didn't know who Margot was when I was working with her, and I only brought up that police report because I thought it would convince Dr. O that you were dedicated to the school. I didn't know what was in it."

He sighs. "I know."

I blow out a tight breath, but my voice is still rough when I ask, "Then why didn't you try to contact me?"

A long beat passes before he answers.

"You know why."

Because it was too dangerous. Because he couldn't put his family more at risk.

"When I told Dr. O about Margot, I almost got her killed," he says quietly. "I promised never to put the people I care about at risk again." He holds my gaze, and my eyes burn with tears. "Especially you."

My chest hurts. *Everything* hurts. But I blink until the tears are gone.

"Margot's looking for you, too," I say. "She wants to help."

His brows arch. "You talked to her?"

Twenty times or more. She wants a girl on the inside to bring down Dr. O? She's got one.

"I have."

I hand him the large envelope. Our fingertips brush as he takes it, sparking heat up my arm.

"What's this?"

"Open it."

He unhooks the brass clasp and pulls out a slim Vale Hall

notebook. His fingers slide over the raven emblem, the ink stains that were always present on his fingertips faded.

"Look inside," I say.

He opens the cover while I perch on the balls of my feet.

Inside is a file folder. He looks up at me before opening it.

I move beside him, not too close, as he pulls back the cover, revealing a shot of his face, younger, but no less troubled than right now. His glasses are different, his clothes a little baggy. He's standing outside a boat on the river—an architecture cruise where he worked before he was recruited.

On the top of the typed page opposite his picture is his name. Caleb D. Matsuki. Other information follows. His birthday. His parents' names. His school records. His Social Security number. Behind it are pages on his academic performance—his transcripts and health forms. A thin envelope pokes out from the back, and he pulls it free.

"Henry intercepted that before Ms. Maddox got it," I say.

He opens the letter from the testing site, and I hold my breath as he scans through the numbers.

Caleb Matsuki. Combined SAT score: 1490.

"Holy cow," I say. "You're a genius." But I already knew that. I got a 1110, which Shrew tells me is adequate at best. I'm set to retake them in two weeks.

He swallows a breath, and then another, as if he can't quite get enough oxygen.

"Where'd you get all this?"

"The safe in Dr. O's office." The director changed the combination and the location of the safe, but unfortunately for him, he lives in a house of sneaks and con artists.

"This was a bad idea," he says. "If he finds out you did it . . ."

I smile. Still Caleb. Still worried what will happen to everyone else, even when they stab him in the back.

Something shifts inside me, locking in place. Caleb has lost everything, but he is still fighting. He's still there for his family, still worried about my safety. Still cautious. He may be at a low point, but he is not backing down.

It reminds me of something Margot said—she could see why he loved me. I may run hot and he may run cool, but I balance him.

I can still do that.

Because the things that make him Caleb—his cool head and thoughtful intentions, his unwavering dedication to his family, his consistency and focus on everything he does—are things I've been searching for my whole life.

Not a college degree or a fancy high school. A home and a family.

Not a ton of friends or expensive clothes, but the kind of people who stick, no matter what.

"I can go back to school with this," he says.

"You can."

"Brynn . . ." The way he looks at me, with genuine hope, makes me stand two inches taller.

I interrupt whatever thanks he thinks he owes.

"You're going to finish school and go to college. And I'm going to figure out a way to help your dad. We're going to get out of this mess, I promise."

Cheeks heating, I reach into my back pocket and run my fingers along the edge of a note card I'm not brave enough to pull out.

He looks down again at the file, then frowns at the one behind it. I move a little closer.

"What is this?" he asks again as he opens the page to the copied report. A pretty girl in a sweatshirt is pictured on the left. The right side has the same demographic information from Caleb's chart. "Renee Gibson. Who is she?"

"She was like you and Margot, I think," I say. "Kicked out. Erased, before you started."

He turns to the next file, finding a guy with a buzzed head and a hard glare. *Rafael Fuentes.* There's another file behind it, and another behind that. Six students I could find no record of online. I have memorized everything I can about them.

"I'm going to find them," I say.

He looks up at me again. "How?"

"I don't know. But when I do, I'm going after Dr. O."

He holds my gaze, but doesn't warn me to back off. He knows I know what's at risk.

"*Vincit omnia veritas,*" he says. *Truth conquers all.* Then, "I'll help."

My smile is bright enough to light the whole city.

"I was hoping you'd say that."

Again, our gazes match, but this time my stomach does a slow roll, and my pulse skips. I can't look away from the tiny square of light reflected in his glasses, and his dark lashes beneath, and the determined line of his mouth.

"You tried to stay at Vale Hall to protect us. *Me,*" I add with a shaky breath. "You pretended to be with Geri to keep Grayson from getting upset. I thought when you said later, it meant you didn't care, but—"

"I never stopped," he says.

My lungs feel too full. My heart pounds too hard.

"Me neither," I tell him.

His shoulders lower, the guarded look in his eyes drawing back to reveal a tentative question I never thought he'd ask again.

The answer is still yes.

The knock at the door makes us both jump. He quickly shuts the file and shoves it into the envelope.

"I'm sorry for this," I say, threading my hands behind me. My cheeks are still stained from his confession, and from the hope kindled inside me.

He tucks the envelope beneath his sleeping bag. "For what?"

The knock comes again. He rises slowly.

Warily, he goes to the door, looking at me one more time before turning the handle. He probably thinks I've called Moore or Dr. O to come get him. Maybe told his mom where he's hiding out.

That's okay. I'm going to earn back his trust.

The door caves inward as he opens it, and Henry barrels in, two full paper bags hoisted in his arms. He drops them at Caleb's feet and pulls him into a hug so tight, Caleb wheezes.

"Did you miss me?" Henry asks.

"I can't breathe," Caleb manages. But there's a smile on his face when Henry pulls back.

"Okay, okay, we get it, now move over, the pregnant girl is freezing out here."

Caleb chokes, wide eyes finding Charlotte, who is shoving past Henry into the apartment. Her wild hair's braided back today, and she's proudly wearing the shirt I made for her birthday. *GINGER PRINCESS*, it says in puff-painted letters.

It's one of the few things that always makes me smile.

"Hi." She pulls him into a hug. "Before you ask, it's not Henry's."

"Ha," he says. Then looks to Sam, carrying another two bags, full to the brim.

"Mine," Sam says, then grins wider than I've seen him do in months. He and Caleb shake hands and do the half-hug thing.

"A lot has happened since I've been gone," Caleb said.

"So much," Henry says. "I had my first and last kiss ever."

"Technically that was before he left," I say.

Sam closes the door behind him. "Henry's sworn off boys forever."

"Been there," says Charlotte, who has crossed the small room and is picking through a cardboard box of marquee letters.

"It's cozy here," says Henry with a smile. If anyone else said it, it would be condescending, but Henry always says what he means. He takes off his coat and hangs it over the heater.

"Brought you some food," says Sam, crouching down beside the bags he brought in. "Ms. Maddox's enchiladas. Sandwich stuff. Henry saved you half a cake."

"I ate the other half," says Charlotte, without apology.

"Apples," Sam goes on, sorting through the bags. "Carrots. Some other healthy stuff. And fried chicken."

"I don't have a fridge," Caleb says.

Sam glances around, his face betraying nothing. "We better eat it now, then." He sits on the floor and starts unpacking.

"I brought you some books and laundry detergent," says Charlotte. "It's in the car. Oh, and Brynn thought you'd need a prepaid phone and charger, so we got that, too."

"I brought clothes," says Henry. "I went shopping for you. We now have the exact same wardrobe."

"Nice," says Caleb. I can tell he's getting overwhelmed, and I'm scared I've blown it by bringing everyone over. "Does anyone know you're here?"

"Field trip at the history museum," says Charlotte. "Joel's holding our phones."

It's a reminder that we're here on limited time. That we won't all eat dinner later, or play *Road Racers* in the pit. We won't pass each other in pajamas, and shout good night down the hall, or wake and laugh at each other's pillow-marked faces or bedhead.

This moment is temporary.

We fall quiet. Caleb notices the stain on his shirt and tries to rub it out.

I stand beside him, willing away his self-consciousness, feeling the uncertainty of all his sleepless nights alone.

I'm here, I want to tell him. *Even if we leave, we're coming back.*

Taking a deep breath, I reach into my pocket and pull out a

green note card. I look at it a second, nerves fizzing in my chest, then give it to him.

I've written one word on it. *Trust.*

He gave me his and I let him down. But now he has mine, and I'm going to prove I'm worth every bit of his respect.

Slowly his hands drop, but he doesn't let go of the card.

He holds it so tightly the corners crinkle, and it reminds me of the cards he gave me, now worn at the edges from every night I've read them and fallen asleep with them under my pillow.

"Thank you," he says to everyone.

"There's no need for thanks, brother," says Sam.

Even with the crash from the bowling alley beneath our feet, a sense of peace slides over us. I am finally home. This is my family, and it doesn't matter where we are, as long as we're together.

We sit cross-legged on the floor, and as we eat sandwich meat and cold fried chicken, we catch up on the last two months. The daily ins and outs. The status on Joel and Paz, and Shrew's latest torturous assignments. Petal's been returned to Geri since Henry can't stand looking at her, and the new student, June, is already at odds with Moore.

Henry and I tell Caleb about Grayson's role with Susan, and the senator's arrest. Charlotte informs us she's going to keep the baby, and Sam holds her hand and says he's squirreling away money and working on fake IDs. When Henry puffs out his cheeks like a squirrel, we all laugh.

Then we pass around the cake and a single fork, and plan how we're going to burn Dr. O's empire to ashes.

ACKNOWLEDGMENTS

With Ragnarok upon us, there's a few thank-yous I need to get out before, you know, the world ends and stuff.

Thank you, reader, for continuing with Brynn and her fellow con artists on this twisted, Valhalla-myth-inspired adventure. I've loved this story from start to finish, and I hope you've enjoyed the ride.

As always, I'm grateful to the people who have made my books, and this one especially, possible. My agent, Joanna. My editor, Mel. Saraciea, Elizabeth, Lucille, Eileen, Peter, and of course, Kathleen—there would be no Vale Hall without their diligent, passionate work at Tor Teen.

To my writing friends, and my jazzerfriends, and everyone in between. To my family, my husband, my beautiful boy (who I really hope doesn't read this until his sense of right and wrong is more firmly cemented and even then doesn't judge me)—thank you. I love you. I couldn't do this without you.

Now brace yourselves. Things get really wild in book three.